Praise for
By Her Own Design

"*By Her Own Design*'s powerful voice and dedicated research bring an unsung heroine into the well-deserved spotlight. Fierce and fashionable Ann Lowe, long erased from history as the unnamed 'colored dressmaker' behind Jackie Kennedy's famous wedding dress, claws her way here from a Jim Crow Alabama childhood to a storied career as dress designer for the social elite."

—Kate Quinn, *New York Times* bestselling author of *The Diamond Eye*

"I could feel the love with which Piper Huguley crafted this tale about the life of Ann Cole Lowe, yet another 'hidden figure' in American history. Huguley expertly morphs each one of Lowe's heartbreaks into triumph and hope."

—Kaia Alderson, author of *Sisters in Arms*

"Piper Huguley's *By Her Own Design* is a sumptuous quilt with lyrical lace and detailed thread work that make an iconic life feel authentic and heartwarming. . . . Readers will love getting to know Ann Lowe and the story behind the designs."

—Vanessa Riley, bestselling author of *Island Queen*

"The facts of Ann Lowe's life are remarkable, but Huguley has taken us a step further, harnessing the art of fiction to invoke the emotions of her experiences and bring Ann Lowe to life."

—Elizabeth Way, associate curator, the Museum at FIT, and editor of *Black Designers in American Fashion*

P9-CRK-958

"From the first words of *By Her Own Design*, Ann Lowe's vibrant, determined voice positively leaps off the page. In Huguley's talented hands, Lowe's remarkable story surges out of the shadows, practically demanding to be told and shared and celebrated."

—Greer Macallister, bestselling author of
The Magician's Lie and *The Arctic Fury*

"As intricate and impressive as one of Ann Lowe's designs, Piper Huguley's *By Her Own Design* isn't just the story of a dress, or even a life. It's a whirlwind trip through an America in flux. This is biographical fiction at its very best!"

—Lauren Willig, *New York Times*
bestselling author of *Band of Sisters*

"*By Her Own Design* is a vivid, powerful, and ultimately hopeful novel about 'hidden figure' Ann Cole Lowe and her fight to create and deliver Jacqueline Kennedy's wedding dress—as well as her life-long battle for love, family, and legacy."

—Susan Elia MacNeal, *New York Times*
bestselling author of the Maggie Hope series
and *Mother Daughter Traitor Spy*

"For too many years fashion designer Ann Lowe's work has gone uncredited, but Piper Huguley's utterly compelling novel celebrates her incredible designs and work in a gripping story as intricately detailed as one of Lowe's gowns. Huguley is masterful in bringing Lowe's voice to life through her struggles and her triumphs."

—Julia Kelly, internationally bestselling author of
The Last Dance of the Debutante

By Her Own Design

A NOVEL OF ANN LOWE, FASHION DESIGNER TO THE SOCIAL REGISTER

Piper Huguley

WILLIAM MORROW
An Imprint of HarperCollins*Publishers*

P.S.™ is a trademark of HarperCollins Publishers.

BY HER OWN DESIGN. Copyright © 2022 by Piper Huguley. All rights reserved. Printed in the United States of America. No part of this book may be used or reproduced in any manner whatsoever without written permission except in the case of brief quotations embodied in critical articles and reviews. For information, address HarperCollins Publishers, 195 Broadway, New York, NY 10007.

HarperCollins books may be purchased for educational, business, or sales promotional use. For information, please email the Special Markets Department at SPsales@harpercollins.com.

FIRST EDITION

Designed by Diahann Sturge

Wedding dress photo throughout © Bachrach/Getty Images

Library of Congress Cataloging-in-Publication Data has been applied for.

ISBN 978-0-06-305974-0

22 23 24 25 26 LSC 10 9 8 7 6 5 4 3 2 1

For Margaret E. Powell (1975–2019)

"She must be her own model as well as the artist attending, creating, learning from, realizing the model, which is to say, herself. . . . Discovery of them—most of them out of print, abandoned, discredited, maligned, nearly lost—came about, as many things of value do, almost by accident."
—In Search of Our Mothers' Gardens *by Alice Walker*

Your amazing scholarship on Ann Lowe helped me in so many ways. I wish we had met. This story is an offering to spread the word about this amazing woman. I hope and pray my work will touch the heart of another textile scholar so that your dream of a comprehensive biography and exhibit of Ann Lowe's work might be realized one day.

Prologue

February 24, 1981

The shadow of the last night I will ever know falls across my face as my Ruthy comes into my bedroom and turns on Walter Cronkite to watch him read the *CBS Evening News*. "Mother, Prince Charles is finally getting married."

"High time," I say. A slight shard of pain enters my weakened heart. "Been waiting on him to marry for years."

"Yes. She's nineteen and a lady."

"Nineteen? That's a child, not a lady." My heart quickens for her. Marriage is not for children.

I should know better than anyone.

Ruthy settles next to me on the bed and slips her soft hand into mine as we listen to good old Mr. Cronkite read out the news. He is telling all of the United States about a young slip of a girl named Diana Spencer who is going to marry the future king of England.

When I hear Lady Diana's voice come across the television,

pitched up high with her aristocratic British bearing ringing through her words, I know she is a lady.

Just like my Jacqueline Bouvier Kennedy.

"She's wearing blue. I mean, a peacock-blue suit with a white blouse with peacock-blue birds on it underneath and a bow tied and knotted off to the side at her neck." Ruthy spoke into my ear, close, so I could see the young bride in my mind. "She's tall, very tall, 'cause she's eyeballing him, with lots of blond hair feather cut around her face. Her eyes are blue too. She got on flat shoes and white hosiery. And he . . ."

I wave my scrawny hand, and it never ceases to surprise me that I have the slow, impatient hand of an eighty-two-year-old woman. 'Cause it was these hands that created the most photo-graphed wedding gown in the world. "No need to describe him. I know what he looks like. Been waiting all these years for him to get a wife."

The interview ends and Mr. Cronkite goes on to talk about something else happening in the world. I ease back on my stacked pillows. "Somewhere in this world, someone's life's go-ing to change."

"What do you mean, Mother?"

"Whoever gets to do the dress." I warm up on this chilly Feb-ruary death night to my favorite subject, bringing my hands together again. "I met Mr. Hartnell when I was in Paris, you know. Did the wedding gown of the Queen of England and her sister too. But he's gone. So someone new will do it. Someone new is going to set a standard for wedding dresses, like Mr. Hart-nell did. Somebody's going to take the wedding gown fashion into the 1980s from the horrible wedding dress decade the 1970s was."

"Mother, don't say that."

"It's true. The 1970s was a bad time for designing wedding gowns. Couples not wanting to get married. The ones that did didn't want nice wedding dresses. They wanted to get married in dirt fields in bare feet rather than in a nice church. Then, Mr. Hartnell closed his business. Helen Rose too. She was my only competition, but then she started making clothes for the common folk and you know I would not make dresses for just any Mary or Betty Sue."

Ruthy, my dear daughter, laughs at me. "Not you, Mama. You have no equal. What gowns did Helen Rose do?"

"She did Grace Kelly's and Elizabeth Taylor's dresses."

Now Ruthy laughs even harder. "Elizabeth Taylor had a lot of wedding dresses. Which one?"

"The very first one, and the one in the *Father of the Bride* movie." I hear Ruthy exhale hard. I don't have to explain any more. Isn't a body on earth who doesn't know those three dresses. Plus mine.

I am not done, though. "But the 1970s—whew. Bad time. Even Princess Anne went and bought one off the rack. A real-life princess! She might have had one made and lifted up the whole industry. But no. Finally, someone new is going to bring the whole wedding dress industry out of the doldrums. And when they do, they'll use lots of fabric again. Just like I like. I see it just like I would if my left eye were back and the other one was clear to match."

But I won't see it. I'll be dead. And gone.

"You did Jackie Onassis."

"Don't call her that." I don't mean to have my voice get sharp, but I can't help it.

"Why not?"

"She married that rich little Greek out of protection. Not love. Woman's got to do that sometimes, but we don't have to call attention to that. Her mama had to do it. I had to do it. Why do you think I'm not Mrs. West?"

"I don't know, Mama."

"A name, it matters. What I put on my label mattered. To Kitty Kelley, I just might be a pair of hands or the family seamstress like she said in that book, but I have a name." I lift up off my pillows and Ruthy moves over me, settles a hand on my shoulder, and pushes me back.

"I didn't mean to get you all riled, Mother. I'm sorry."

I pat her hand to show her I forgive her. "When I married your daddy, I told him I wasn't taking it, because I couldn't have any children from my body for him. That probably got us started down the wrong path."

"Maybe." Her voice dips down a bit.

"My own name. Each name got just one syllable to fit right on my labels: Ann Cole Lowe."

It would look nice on my tombstone.

Ruthy sits down on the bed next to me and I lean into the reassuring weight of her. Her voice rings out with pride. "Mrs. Kennedy's dress is right up there with all of those beautiful wedding dresses of the 1950s. Everyone says so."

"That's right." I squeeze her soft hand. "Cause the 1950s, now, that was a wedding gown time. And just like everything else, it's going to come back. Whoever Diana chooses will bring it all back."

"You think so?" Ruthy squeezes my hand back and stands up. The commercial break is on. Time for a hot drink to warm my chilled bones.

I know it. Just like I know I won't be here to see it. Any of it. Another stabbing shard of regret, remorse, and sorrow pierces my poor weakened heart, sewing its path of destruction.

"I'll get you some Sanka. I'll be right back."

Ruthy goes out of the room, and now I can let the emotion show on my face. The face I can't see anymore. Jealousy. Hatred. Animosity. Anger. They all come into me and the power those mean emotions hold over me exhausts me more.

Someone is going to get a chance. A new chance that I didn't get. God won't let me have another chance again. It's too late.

Some would call me foolish for regretting living eighty-two years of life, a long life and a lot of years for a Black woman.

But I do. 'Cause I wanted the chance to design a show-stopping, front-page wedding dress again. Just one more time.

To let Mrs. Kennedy know.

I could get it right.

Part I

The Question

New York City, New York, September 6, 1953

By the end of my life I was stone blind 'cause I used up all of my eyesight creating beautiful gowns for the richest women in the *Social Register*. However, on this one day, the Sunday before Labor Day in the Year of Our Lord 1953, God laid his healing hands on my failing eyes so I could see a sharp cut on a water pipe in the ceiling of my dress shop. Cut wide open, maybe with a hatchet, that pipe spilled gallons of foul-smelling water onto the floor of the shop I had worked twenty years to open. The eggshell carpet, as well as the olive-green gilt chairs my clients sat on, got stained a sickening shit brown. When the landlord poked at them, the chairs squished and bubbled suds at the edges of the seats.

I might have been able to take that in, but that wasn't the worst. No, the most horrible part was that the pipe had opened up over top of the most important dress commission of my life. The most important dress of the twentieth century. The dress belonged to one Jacqueline Bouvier, who was due to marry John F. Kennedy in just six days' time. The rosettes on the ball gown skirt, my usual flower touch, seized up streaks of brown and the off-the-shoulder bodice sagged completely off the shoulders of the headless mannequin. The rest of the dress, saturated with yellow instead of ivory white, made sad-sounding drips of wastewater that plopped to my white carpet in a discordant symphony.

Is it possible for anyone, even for a piddly birdlike little Black woman like me from small-town Clayton, Alabama, to have a lower moment?

The Almighty himself put the thought in my mind: the water pipe that dumped all of that stink into my shop didn't burst all by itself. Only now I cast my poor eyesight down to my trusty step stool, turned topsy-turvy behind the mannequin in someone's haste to leave my life in a mess.

Sallie, my older sister, said the words that trailed across my mind like a dress seam: "Who hate you enough to do this, Annie?"

Sallie loved me so well, she couldn't see it. But even if I had my poor eyesight days, I saw it. I knew of a handful of people who had enough red-hot, demon hate for me in their blood that they would relish to see me fall.

Little did I know when some child rushed up into our apartment in Harlem early this Sunday morning, telling me to come to my shop quick, this would start a turning point of my life. We couldn't afford to live over the shop so me and Sallie lived in Harlem, where the rest of the Black people in 1953 New York City lived. I couldn't understand or begin to process what this child was saying to me. My shop? Water? Flooded?

But it was my knees that turned to water when I understood what he meant and thank God Sallie was there to hold me up. The men in my life came and went with regularity, but Sallie was my rock. She was the one who closed the door. "We got to get dressed. We'll go down on the subway and see what he's talking 'bout. Come on now."

She guided me into my bedroom and eased me out of my robe. She helped me on with my stockings and the heavy shoes that fixed my skinny bird legs to the ground so I could walk. She lowered the uniform of my severe black dress on my person. No one could be a lady without the perfect black dress and I had designed and worn mine just for me. She selected my silver rose brooch, one of the many flower brooches that I owned, fixed my cloche hat on my sparse hair, and guided me to the door. It wouldn't do for folks to see that I was almost bald these days.

The whole way there, she simply held me up, murmuring I don't know what in my ear, telling me it was going to be all right. People on the train must have thought we were a pair of Boston brides or something, but I was beyond caring. Sallie had always been the one of us who was solid, in frame, body, and spirit. I was a hummingbird, always flying from flower to flower, gathering nectar, and not minding anything about anyone.

When we got to the shop and entered the back door to my workroom, what a sight greeted my eyes. The beautiful, fluffy confection of a gown that I had designed exclusively for Jacqueline Bouvier sagged, saturated with putrid water. Nine of the ten bridesmaid dresses that had been lovely clouds of deep pink accented with claret-colored sashes were also ruined. Thank God that the matron and maid of honor dresses were out with other seamstresses who were finishing them or they would have been ruined as well.

The landlord and several other people kept pumping the nasty water out from the shop. My weak little eyes saw only the dresses. "We're supposed to take them up to Rhode Island for fittings on Thursday. What can we possibly do?"

Sallie shook her head. When I turned to look at her sunny face, it was more like a moon, more dark than her usual light, casting no hopeful sunbeams down on me. "Annie, this here is a right mess."

And for my rock to give me no hope meant that I had plenty of water cascading down my face to add to what they pumped out into the street. "Two thousand dollars and eight weeks of hard, hard work all gone. Ruined."

I turned to the landlord. "What could have happened?"

A large white man in middle age, he turned a red face to me. He knew who this commission was for. "I don't know, Miss Ann. Miss Sallie." Only his gracious Southern upbringing in calling us Miss saved him from appearing an entire fool. Why didn't he have answers? "I wish I could say."

I fell to my knees, letting the words in my head out. "How can this be happening to me?"

No one sought to prop me back up on my bird legs this time. That's 'cause Sallie and even the white man were crying too. I covered my face with my hands in shame.

This moment, this catastrophe, represented the ruination of my life. And I just knew it wasn't only cut open pipes responsible.

My mind flashed onto the wide, beautiful face of the young woman who was expected to slip into that dress in less than a week's time. I had been sewing for Jacqueline since she was a young girl. She came into my shop and I made the very dress for her that saw her crowned debutante of the year in 1947. When it was time for her to marry in 1952, she asked for a dress like that debutante dress—the one that reflected the shiniest moment in her young life. I was about to put needle to cloth when I received a terse note from her mother, Mrs. Auchincloss, calling off that wedding. I put it all away, but then rejoiced when she entered my shop in June 1953, saying that she was engaged again, this time to the most promising young senator in the United States, John Kennedy.

Of course, I knew that's what she was coming in to tell me, 'cause from the moment I saw her lovely face, lowering down in her shy way, glowing with innocence, I knew she was in love. Yes, this was the man for her. That other man, the earlier one, the previous engagement, was not her love. This handsome young senator who was always in the papers would take her places for sure.

I raised my face out of my hands. The previous dress. I still had the material. I had kept it up high on a shelf. I had never used it.

"Where are you going, Annie?"

"I got to find something. It got to be here somewhere."

Whenever I got upset, I reverted back to my old Alabama way of speaking. Tough times made me forget I was supposed to speak like the rich white women that I sewed for. My heavy shoes squished the wet carpet. I saw the cupboard ahead of me, but I needed to reach up to it, a problem for a tiny soul such as me. I used my step stool, but I still needed to clamber up the drawers and counters, where I stood on a high plane and opened it. I breathed out in disbelief. It was there. The fabric for what was to have been Jacqueline's very first wedding dress—it was still there. It was white, but time had dimmed the color of the length of cloth over the past year, when no daylight had lit upon it.

God was good. Let there be no doubt.

Sallie came and stood behind me, spotting me as she always did. "What is it?"

"The stuff for her first wedding. I hid it away after she

sent me the note that she was breaking up with that man. It's just ivory enough for her."

Sallie breathed out. "Thank the Almighty."

"Yes indeed. Getting the pink will be hard, and the claret for the sashes."

"So what are you going to do?"

Something lit in my soul.

"We're going to start all over again."

Sallie's daddy was a white man, so when she got scared, her face got as white as a piece of paper. My daddy, Jack Lowe, was Black as coffee, so the same thing did not happen to me.

"How can we do that? Can't we call the Ambassador?"

I stood, bolstered by my perch on the counter and looking around at the mess that was my shop. "No. We cannot call the Ambassador. He gone think a Black woman cannot handle this commission. Besides, I've had my fill of talking to him. No, we gone take care of this. Catch me."

I fell down into my sister's broad arms with no doubt whatsoever that she would catch me.

She helped me to stand as I spoke. "St. Mark's is just getting out. Let's go on to the church. We can get help there in addition to our regular crew. It's gone be the week of the holiday." Some sun broke through into my voice. I could see flowers again, just as they appeared on my little patch of ground in Alabama, or the ones I used to make at Mama's feet as she sewed.

"What that mean?"

My dear Sallie, as wonderful a fitter as she was, didn't see out of things. That's what she had me for.

"All the white people will be coming back from the beach

this week to their homes and their children will start up school. That means the church ladies might be able to spare some time to help us. Even if it's just for a few hours, it's better than nothing. We can get help from the ladies at the church in addition to our crew. And"—I put my hands on my narrow hips—"it can't be here. We can ask the pastor to use the church basement to cut until the shop is dried out."

Sallie put a hand over the *O* that was her mouth. "We better get moving, then. To the church."

Now I knew how to move. It may have been that some evil person opened water on my dresses, but still, there was a chance I could make this right and I had to take it, certainly without telling Mrs. Auchincloss or Ambassador Kennedy, one of the most powerful white men in the United States or maybe even the world, that some horrible problem had messed up Jacqueline's wedding dress.

No question but that God would help me to see my plan through.

Just as he always had. Even from the Alabama days.

Chapter One

$\mathcal{M}$y grandma, Georgia Cole, told me the key to surviving as a Black person in the world is to get you some good white people. She told it to my mother, Janie, and she told it to me. She said, get right in there with them. Get up under that right butt cheek if you have to. So we did. That's how we Cole women have survived for so long.

Clayton, Alabama, even though it is the county seat, is a piece of spit on the map of the state. It's nothing and the General's women, as they called us, weren't looking to get wiped away. Ever since I was born, two years before the start of the new century, I kept hearing about my grandparents, Georgia and General Cole, and how they outsmarted Grandma's owners so that they spit in the eye of the law and lived free in the deepest part of the deep South.

To survive in Clayton, Alabama, we were what some call good Negroes. But we were the ones living and they weren't. For instance, in order to marry Grandma in the eyes of the Lord and the law, General Cole went to my grandmother's owner and offered him twice what she was worth. The master took his money but made him promise one thing. Old General Cole, a man of his word, promised not to move away so the mistress of the plantation might still benefit from Georgia's talented needle in creating beautiful dresses just for her.

They shook on it and agreed. So Georgia got to be free; my mammy, Janie, was born free; and everyone was happy. To protect her, Georgia taught her only daughter how to sew. My mother was working hard by the time she was eight years old. She was just a child, but she had to work them little fingers to baste together the big pieces of dresses with wide stitches so that her mother could send them through the sewing machine. Georgia and Janie. They made a great team for about ten years. Then, somehow, my mama got with child, and Georgia cast her out from her house. For about two weeks. Then she brought her back and took care of her when Sallie was born.

"Then, when she came bigged up with you, I said nothing. I had a feeling you was going to be something special, Bird." Grandma Georgia called me Bird, 'cause she said I was like a hummingbird, flitting around from flower to flower.

I wouldn't hurt Sallie's feelings for anything in the world, so we never discussed how I was Grandma Georgia's favorite. I always got a little extra by her, like how when I was five she let me scrape out a little plot of ground and plant flowers on it.

My mother protested. "We can't eat flowers."

"They's pretty to look at," Georgia told her. "It's good to have something pretty to look at. Bird is a right good gardener, so when she get her white people, they might have her doing that work."

"I'm not gone work outside," I said, shocking them both. "I'm gone draw dresses and make ladies look like flowers. Just like you do."

There was a moment of silence, then mother and daughter laughed together. I recall standing there watching them hold each other up, laughing at my naive viewpoint.

I kept on. "I'm gone wear a pretty dress to a ball too."

That's when they stopped laughing.

The look on my mother's face got serious. "Bird, balls are for white people. It's our job to help them get pretty to go to the balls, we aren't the ones who go to the balls."

My grandma waved her hands. "Don't be telling her all of that now. She'll learn it quick enough. She don't understand anyway."

But I did understand. Something deep inside me twisted up. I ran outside to see that some of my flowers had died off. They had that August look, like they were too full up to live. That was wrong. Why did flowers and a little girl's dream of wearing a fancy ball dress have to die? That's when I got The Idea.

My mother and grandmother were both at their machines, like always, and their feet pressed up and down on the treadles as they pushed through lengths of beautiful silk taffeta material, sewing peacock-blue dresses as well as bright jewel tones of ruby and green.

All around their swollen feet, cracked with white lines on the soles, lay snips of cloth. Back in those times, one of the ways you would keep a girl quiet was to have her work on quilt blocks. A young girl would work up several quilt blocks, so that she would have quilts ready for her hope chest and be ready for when she would get married. So it was my job to gather these scraps and make some determination to see what was fit for keeping for my quilts and what wasn't.

I had just started to work on my own quilt blocks, but I still cut off small pieces of pretty fabric that didn't get used. What if I took some of those waste scrap pieces and made flowers from them?

I cut some of these pieces and made petals. I put them together and made a silk Shasta daisy.

When I showed it to Grandma, she oohed and aahed. "What you gone do with it, Bird?"

Then the flower wilted a bit. "I don't know. Look at it."

"It's mighty pretty, honey."

I lowered it from her face and saw my mother watching me. I didn't even bother to show it to her. I knew what she would say about something that had no purpose. At least a quilt could keep you warm. She smiled at me a bit but kept sewing. I put the flower into a box and returned to my quilt blocks, so that when I got the right number of quilts I could get married and be grown like them.

The whole thing about getting married confused me. My mother had no husband. Georgia had the General, who slept in the corner in a chair all day, drooling and spitting snuff into an old tin can. Why would I want such a thing as a husband? If I were going to make dresses that turned women into flowers, wouldn't that be enough to keep me busy?

There were days that I longed to ask that question, but my mother and grandmother were always sewing. Sallie, my sister, did better at fitting when the time came, so she didn't sew like they did. I tried not to remember the flower that I made, but I couldn't help it. Whenever I cut and pieced up a new quilt block, I made a different flower out of scraps. When it was my mother's birthday, I made a whole bouquet of silk roses for her. The surprised look on her face was what I aimed for, but the look went away. "These is mighty pretty, honey. You got your quilts working?"

"I do, Mama."

"Good. I didn't want you to be wasting all of this on me."

"It's not a waste, Mama."

"Thank you, honey." She stopped sewing for a minute, then did a rare thing. She grabbed me, holding me to her as if I were an egg, so as not to crush my little bird bones.

"You'll have them forever," I pointed out.

"I guess that's a good thing."

"'Cause real flowers die."

Word got around about my flowers, and I started selling them for folks to pretty up their houses, hats, and dresses. The money did impress Mama and she put it aside for me in a little tin bank that she nailed to the floor. When I asked her why it was nailed to the floor, she said, "So you only get it when you are desperate. It'll take a certain kind of strength for you to pull it up off the floor. I pray you ain't never that kind of desperate, but you a little Negro girl. It's gonna come. One day."

I sure didn't like the sound of that, but I kept on playing with my fabric flowers, making my quilts and selling some of both to people who liked the look of the stuff that I made. I decided to make myself my first dress to wear to church and I got some of my money before it went into the tin can to buy the goods at the store. I chose red with black polka dots. Grandma Georgia sure didn't like the looks of that fabric draped upon my skinny behind. One day, I was cooking our dinner of beans and cornbread, and when they thought I wasn't listening, she complained to my mama above the racket of the sewing machines.

"Janie, how you raising this one here? She don't have no sense. No colored woman needs to be wearing any kind of red on her. Make her look like a harlot."

"She's only ten, Mama."

"That's old enough." Grandma's frown worked up in her voice. "She look like a scrawny bird."

My mama loved me, but she was only telling the truth. I sure did look like that. My fingers gripped just a little harder on the handle of the wooden spoon I used to stir the beans.

"Some likes them like that."

Some who? I loosened my grip, pausing in my eavesdropping to think. Who likes what what way?

"We here for her. We have her."

The tuts resounded in Grandma's voice a little louder 'cause she had more gums than teeth. "Lord, the fox got many an evil plan to get into the henhouse. The General ain't as spry as he used to be and can't look out for his womenfolk."

"We her family. We love her and we'll protect her."

"Just like that high yaller boy what's sniffing around our Sal?" Grandma's voice got real high then.

I nodded my head in agreement with Grandma. Now I understood. Sal was sure going down the wayward road and my heart thumped real slow in sadness at the thought of that awful boy and my Sallie. To be sure, she never took to sewing like the three of us. Me, Mama, and Grandma were the three sides of a triangle—all mitered together like a corner. Sallie's talent was to make the dress seem like a second skin to the woman. So, even though you couldn't see the results of Sal's art, it was all in the way she helped make the dresses smooth to the body. I sure was going to ask her to help me with my red-and-black dress, soon as she could get her eyes away from that boy-man she kept eyeballing.

"I can't nail the girls to the floor like a tin can bank, Mama."

"That's true enough. As soon as you could, you went off with . . ." That's when the sewing machines went really fast to cover up my grandma's words. Eavesdropping could be so frustrating at times. How was I going to learn anything around here? I tapped the spoon on the side of the pan to get all the mushed pinto beans off it.

They were finally getting to something interesting and fascinating, and they clammed right up. It wasn't fair.

They must have known I was listening to them talk all along.

Sure enough, the next month Sal came home one morning, talking to Mama in our front room. Mama rose up and cried, holding on to my sister—a lot harder than she would hold me—like she was the coins in that tin bank.

Sal had this look on her face like she thought Mama had lost her mind. "It's gone be fine. We's getting married. I'm not going to be like you without a husband."

Mama let Sal go and fixed her mouth firm, her tears drying up. "Well, just know that if you in need, there's not much I can do to help, but I do what I can for you and the baby. Not him. He's married to you and he isn't none of mine."

Sal had on her best navy-blue dress and hat, like she was going to church. But it was Friday. The only other thing I noticed about her was that her breasts, usually huge, were even bigger and sloshed back and forth like liquid under the tight navy-blue fabric. Her fitting skills were great but the dress fitted her like a mistake.

She stepped to me, reaching for me, and hugged me more firmly than Mama did. "Come on here, Bird. I'm going off to get married. I won't be living with you anymore."

"You only sixteen, Sal. Why you got to go off now?"

She held me and kissed the top of my forehead, the place where I was always worrying away my hair. "I'm going to have a little niece or nephew for you. I'll come back and bring the baby to visit, but I won't be living here."

"This ain't fair."

I ran off from her and passed my mama in her bedroom. Darned if she didn't have some kind of thick, black bar in her hand, using it to pry up Sallie's tin can bank from the floor. Her eyes were red, wild, and open. She sure did have a desperate strength at the thought of her girl going off into the world with some wayward kind of boy-man. Mama's face looked so ferocious and so fierce, I made a promise to myself right then and there.

I would never, ever give her cause to look like that.

Chapter Two

Sal's leave-taking of us was proof that there was nothing more impatient to get grown than a girl whose woman time come on her. Mama kept saying that to me, over and over again after Sal left us. I knew nothing of a woman time, and I didn't want to know. I didn't know a word of what she said. I was just doing my usual thing, making flowers to sell. Except now, a few years later, Mama started putting them on the dresses that she sewed for the white ladies. Then someone saw my flowers and insisted that my mother sew a little bunch of violets at her waist. This was right before the United States jumped into what we called the Great War. Women were long and narrow in their shapes and they wore those awful hobble skirts. Grandma would say, "The one thing they do is keep a woman's knees together, so it can't be a fashion that's all bad." Grandma and Mama would laugh and laugh about that for some reason.

Mama fixed the needle in her mouth to thread it and sew on the purple violets I had made at either side of the party dress she was finishing. I stood there watching her.

"I make that old cut-up cloth bloom," I said, my voice large in the big front room where we all sewed in the daylight.

"Pride goeth before a fall," Mama said.

"How your quilt blocks coming, Bird?" Grandma's face reminded me of a browned, dried apple, all folded in on itself. Her eyes landed on me, kind as ever, and I just knew, as I always did, that there was a soft place in her heart for me. Always. I liked to lean on her and pinch her elbows sometimes, but Mama would frown because we should have been working, working, working.

"Right fine, Grandma."

"Janie, we all got something special. Let Annie have her time."

"Negro women need to learn something useful. Them pretties make money but ain't useful." Mama's stiches, always swift and sure, attached those unuseful violets at the hip of the dress. I might have pointed that out, but I didn't want to get smacked into the New Jerusalem.

"They useful to her. Let her play. When her woman time come, she be impatient enough to get away from us and get grown up."

"Ain't that the truth," Mama said. "When the blood time come, change happens in a girl like a dynamite 'bout to go off in her."

I stopped fashioning a Shasta daisy and noticed the look on my mama's face. My mama was beautiful. Isn't everyone's mama beautiful? But that day, the creases in her face seemed to cut deeper. Her eyes gouged in deeper, and the cracks in the corners of her mouth made red, angry slashes. She kept licking her lips to moisten them, instead of using something like Vaseline to keep them soft. Why didn't she ever stop sewing?

Grandma shook her head. "Let her enjoy this time. Woman time will come soon enough to her."

She was right. The woman time came to me and you would have thought someone touched a lit match to my loins.

WELL, SOMEONE DID. His name was Andrew Lee Cone, and he was nearly three times as old as I was. Looking back at my life, I shake my head in wonder at his interest. Is there anything less interesting than a twelve-year-old girl-child who doesn't know what she's about? But then, you couldn't tell me nothing.

He told me his name was Lee. His first words to me, along with his first appraising look at my newly swollen breasts and behind, was that he knew my daddy.

My daddy, whomever he was, was the next to last mystery in my life. My sister, Sallie, the busy mother of three children in four years, had a different daddy and you could surely tell that because of her creamy, nearly ivory-colored complexion next to my deep copper-brown tone. People marveled that we were even related, let alone had the same mama. She knew who her daddy was, a white man who sent her things from time to time. I asked Mama who my daddy was, and she would shake her head, purse her chapped up lips, and say nothing.

He must have been a trial to her. Just like I was.

So when this tall, string bean of a man come side-winding down the road, whistling between the gap in his teeth asking after my mama, I marveled that he could be looking at me, me in any sort of way other than as a kind uncle. But he was. I could tell 'cause something in my breast buds *zinged* and *zapped* like the sound of the treadle of my mama's sewing machine.

"How do?" old Lee said. "Name's Lee Cone, looking for Jack Lowe."

The red at the corners of my mother's mouth became more pronounced, and her tongue flicked out to lick a drop of red blood away. "He ain't here. Ain't been here for some years."

"This here his girl?"

My mama's eyes narrowed at this Lee person. "How you know?"

"'Cause his face is stamped upon her face, woman. Look at her."

It was sure enough true. I knew it. I looked like no one in my house. They all looked like each other and here was me, a whole other thing.

"What you want with him? He owe you money?"

"Naw, we served together on a chain gang. Told me he lived in this part of Alabama. I was coming through and I thought I would say hi."

"A chain gang?" The words came out of my mouth before I could stop them. I was mending, some of the most boring sewing a body could do. Someone could mend, make something last longer, but I resolved that when my time came to sit at the machine, I would *not* repair old things. I would create new things.

"Yes, Miss Jack."

"Why? What did you do?"

Lee laughed and spread out his hands that showed strong, long, capable-looking fingers. His hands were more like paws, big, awesome things at the end of his arms.

I shivered.

What if they were wrapped around me?

I don't know where that thought came from. Or why, or how. Some part of me wanted to go back inside to get my flower basket to hold on my lap, so it would hide me from his intense gaze. Still, something about this man—his smile, his teeth (which he had a full set of, a rare sight in Eastern Alabama), his throat with the bobbing Adam's apple, the jaunty way his open shirt collar showed curly hairs peeping out at the top, and his long slender fingers—made me smile. All of that liked to make me forget about my flower art.

"Colored man ain't got to do nothing, Miss Jack. We get picked on. You look strong enough and look like you could threaten

him, any white man can *say* you did something and there you
are. On the chain gang."

"Bird," my mama said in a voice I had never heard from her
before. "Take some money from the stove top and go bring your
sister some Vaseline."

Sal and her husband, Jerry, lived in a ramshackle brown house
down the road. She had three boys so far and everything at her
house was topsy-turvy and crusted over with snot or shit. I didn't
want to go.

"Mama, I—"

"Go, I said."

I dragged my feet out to the stove top, where we kept coin
money for small things, to get the money as I was told and then
went on down the road, pace all slow and draggy, with Mr. Lee
waving after me, wondering why my mama spoke to me like
that. Was there something Mr. Lee knew that she didn't want
me to know? Something about my daddy?

As I suspected, Sallie was out in the fields, helping her sorry
husband and trying to watch her boys all at the same time. When
she saw me coming, she left the fields and met me on the porch of
her house, where a sure enough scrub tub waited full of stinky,
dirty diapers. So by the time I reached her porch she was going at
it, cleaning boy pee and shit out of diapers and drawers.

I sighed. Loud enough to wake the General from his per-
petual, never-ending slumber. Another reason I didn't like to go
over there that much—because I knew I would get pulled into
work. I loved my nephews. They were mighty cute, and I loved
to play games and stuff with them, but now that I was twelve, I
felt that I should be doing something besides messing around in
the mud with them. I wanted to go with Mama to measure the
white ladies for their gowns but she said I wasn't ready.

"What you doing here?" my sister asked as she accepted the Vaseline gratefully. Her hands dripped from the lye soap she used to scrub the dirty diapers of her boys. She slipped the tin in her pocket. The money prospects of her family were always small 'cause Jerry was a sorry, sorry man-boy. Like Mama said, she helped when she could and Vaseline was always useful. Keeping her boys greased up helped to protect them from all kinds of harm, so Sal used a lot of it.

"Some man came and she told me to leave. Said he knew my daddy."

"He did?" A puzzle came over Sal's light features.

"Yes. They had been on a chain gang together."

Sal nodded. "Yeah, that's true."

"Well, why ain't you ever told me?"

Scrubbing on, Sallie said as calm as the moon, "Mama said I should not be telling you about him. What was the man's name?"

How come everyone knew about my life excepting for me? A little tendril of feeling curled around in my hands and I clenched them to make it go away. "He said his name was Andrew Lee Cone. Told us to call him Lee."

"Yeah, that sounds familiar." Sallie lifted her hands from the wringer and gestured to me like I was supposed to get in there with her. I wanted to, to see if it would loosen her tongue any. So there I was, helping her do her washing, even though the harsh soap water would end up chapping my hands and I would be the one in need of Vaseline.

"Your daddy was a kind soul. I remember him saying I was his pretty little hoot owl. He was black, black as night, though. You lucky to come out as light as you have when he looked like living coal walking around. Was this Lee man kinda redbone?"

"He was."

"Yeah. Sometimes he come over for a piece of pie too. Hung out with Daddy Jack a lot."

"You even knew his name? You never said it to me. Couldn't a girl know her own daddy's name?"

"I'm telling you what Mama told me to say."

My hands reddened by the minute, more from the way I was feeling left out than from the lye soap. "Why does it have to be so secret?"

"Well, he was a special kind of man. And I think he hurt Mama's heart something fierce. He got sent off to the state prison once again and he died there, up the road in Montgomery, right after you were born."

"That's mighty sad." I lifted my hands out of the water and shook them off, leaving plops of suds on her porch.

Sallie's tone showed she was less than pleased with me at how sloppy I was, but she kept on. "It was. And that's the truth. He loved you something fierce, Ann. He thought you were special, and you are. Look at how you made them flowers into something all the white girls round here got to have. Been making yourself nice clothes for the past few years. I've heard more than one person comment on that smart winter suit you made yourself for church."

I tried to remember my mama's words about pride, but I still flushed red with the rare praise. I was fast earning my way to becoming my mother's assistant whenever it was time to go to a white lady's house to take measurements and do fittings. Maybe soon, I would be more her right hand than my grandmother.

Sallie brought her own hands out of the lye water, wiping them with more care on her house dress. "Look. See me? I got in with Jerry and I'm trapped here for the next twenty years. Don't do that. You talked about going up north when we were girls.

Going to see things. Maybe getting to go to one of them schools for Negroes. Keep saving your coins in that bank. Something like that could happen for you. Something better than Clayton."

My stomach got a warm feeling whenever someone said something nice about me and it happened now. Again. "Okay, Sal, I understand."

She patted my hand. Her hand felt like an old leather strap. It made me sad, and I excused myself and ran home.

My mother was there on the porch by herself. The worried look had disappeared from her face, and she had taken up my basket of mending. "How's Sal and the boys?" she said. She never asked about Jerry.

"Fine. She was doing the wash while the boys wrestled in a big ball on the ground, like always."

"Good."

"She told me what she could about my daddy."

That stopped her from working on the mending. Still, I didn't care.

I balled up my skirt in my fist, scared to get smacked, but meeting Lee Cone that day made me brave like I never was before. "You shoulda told me these things, Mama."

Mama stood up. "You found out what you needed to know, you nosy thing."

"Not from you. What was he like?"

She stuck the needle in the cloth, putting down that boring old mending for me to pick up and finish. That made me mad and more willing to face wherever punishment awaited me.

Moving more swiftly than I had ever seen in my life, she eased her body past me to the door. Her clean smell of fresh wash and a faint air of Vaseline tickled my nose. "I'm going to check the beans. Dinner be on soon."

The front door slammed shut as she went back into the house and I went back to the chair like I knew I better. My hand dipped down into the mending basket once more, taking up an old stocking that had seen better days and I thought about those long fingers of Mr. Lee's.

What would they feel like trailing down my spine?

I pulled the needle out and got down to mending, feeling something new beckoning to me.

Chapter Three

Grandma Georgia had been a slave back in the old times of trouble, as she called them. Then, General Cole came and bought her so she could sew on her own free time for the white people. He couldn't sit around all day and watch her sew, so they lined him up to oversee other Black men. That skill came in really handy in the time of the chain gangs after the slave times.

Everyone knew what chain gangs were. Man after man would be linked together to go somewhere to clean up white people's yards—or to pick vegetables or fruit on their big farms. The gangs were cheap labor and readily available for hire and the General knew how to get a lot of work out of them. I always thought you had to do something bad to get on one. Now I wasn't so sure, but I definitely wanted to get to know Lee better and find out about him and my daddy.

It wasn't easy for Lee to get to me. I stayed at home much of the day since I didn't go to school anymore. Only places I went was Sallie's and maybe the store sometimes. So a week later, when my mama told me to go to the store for some groceries, I sure wasn't expecting old Mr. Lee to pop up on my walk there. After all, he said he was passing through town, not hanging around.

But there he was, kinda like the big bad wolf of that fairy tale. I wasn't wearing a cloak of red, but I did have on my red-and-black polka-dot dress, which I kept adding length to with extra fabric by making ruffles. Lately, though, the dress had gotten a bit tight around my hips, 'cause my shape was changing in all kinds of interesting ways. So I kept altering the dress to fit my new body. Back then, going to the store, especially the white people's store, required that you look very nice and presentable, so that they treated you well as you requested groceries and they decided if you had enough money or connections to deserve that food.

"How do, Miss Jack?"

"My name is Ann." A feeling of loss tugged at me when he called me by my daddy's name. I didn't know Jack Lowe and when he called me that, he reminded me I resembled a ghost man.

"Oh. Excuse me. Miss Ann," he said, kinda laughing.

"I shouldn't be talking with you. I have an errand." I put on my best white lady voice. Maybe he would be intimidated and go on away from me.

"An errand?"

"Yes." I tried not to look at him in his fine-cut suit. How did someone who had just come off the chain gang manage to look so well in a light-brown summer broadcloth with a stark white collar and a smooth red tie? "I mean, you grown up. Don't you have a job to do somewhere?"

Now he really laughed, showing off all of his pretty teeth for my benefit. "Let's just say I'm on vacation."

"Well then, you may go have your vacation someplace else."

"Don't you need some help?"

I thought about all of the cans and parcels I would have to carry back with my small arms. I knew help would be nice, but I usually managed alone. After all, Negroes weren't allowed to have delivery, so I never got more than I could carry. Anyway, it was just us three ladies to cook for, now that General Cole had gone to meet his Maker, and we didn't eat much. We couldn't afford to.

"I'll be fine."

"Listen at you sounding all grown up."

That man knew there was nothing better that he coulda said than I sounded grown up. He must have taken all week to think out how he could get me, like a spider in a web.

I paid him no mind as I walked along, but everything in my young body heightened at the sound of his deep man voice talking to me, and only me, like I was grown. I wanted to be grown so I could sew with Mama and Grandma Georgia.

The insides of the top of my homemade dress rubbed up against my torso, reminding me that I had flesh. Sinful flesh. Flesh that betrayed me mightily by popping in goosey bumps all over me. The bottom part of my dress, the part I kept adding and adding length to as I grew, swirled and swished around my ankles, cooling them in the hot summer sun. I knew that the growing long length of my dress hid a major disappointment of my body: my skinny legs, which made me look more like an awkward bird and less like a curvy woman.

Lee got all serious. "I didn't mean you no harm, Miss Ann. Just making conversation with a pretty lady on a fine day."

"You . . . you think I'm pretty?"

I didn't hear that too often about my looks. Lots of folk thought Sal was pretty because of her light, pale skin, but no one ever called me pretty.

"Yes, I do."

"Thank you." I lowered my eyes off him. But it was mighty hard. In that handsome suit, he put the sun itself to shame.

"You're welcome."

Then I remembered the chain gang. "Who'd you steal that suit off of?"

"Is that why you think I was on the chain gang?"

"Yes," I pushed my chin out and looked straight ahead, anywhere but at him. "I don't care what you say. You did something wrong."

"Well, miss, shows you are wrong. I didn't steal this suit. I made it."

That stopped me.

"You . . . you made that?"

"Yes, ma'am. I'm a tailor. One of the finest men's tailors in the South. I make suits for men. That's how come when I saw you sewing on that pile of mending, I got interested. You a fine seamstress yourself."

"Well, thank you. I made this here dress."

"You're quite welcome. And of course you did. You put that sash at your hip to make it look like you more filled out there. Smart. Shows you got an appreciation for line. Like an artist."

Me? An artist? With clothes. Yes, I guess he was right. I was an artist and this dress was an evolving work of art I wore. "You know about clothes?"

"Yes, ma'am. Men's clothes. But I sure can appreciate what God did for women in women's clothes."

His words poured right into my young ears like liquid honey. Here was someone else who knew about lines and saw the things that I saw. Called me an artist. Said I looked filled out, even though I wasn't. Buttered me up like a hot biscuit.

"And I like those roses you sewed at the edges there. Very nice."

"I like making them. I think women come alive like flowers when they have the right dress on."

"You sure are right. Just like you. Where did you get your pattern from?"

"The store, but I made some changes to suit me better since I'm so, well, skinny."

"There's nothing wrong with that. You still growing. The meat on your bones will come one day. You'll see. But you do a fine job in the meantime. And I bet you can make even more money if you go into the store and ask them if they can sell some of your dresses instead of them flowers that you make for the white girls."

"How did you know that?"

"By watching. And listening. I watch and listen to everything about you, Miss Ann." He put his hands in his pockets and smiled. This time, he looked less like the big bad wolf and more like a regular man. I liked that look better.

"No man ever watched me before, less it was the General and he's gone now."

"Well, trust me, girl. Your daddy, if he was here, would be watching you. He'd be proud too. He'd say, 'Look at my pretty daughter what made the dress pattern better for herself.' Shows you are smart too. Yes, he would be proud."

I gripped my basket and kept on walking. We were almost at the store. All too soon, we arrived.

He kicked a polished shoe in the red dirt a bit. "I'll wait out here while you do your shopping. If you need help, I'll be out here. All right?"

He sat himself on a chair and crossed his long legs. He looked very elegant sitting there, and my breath caught a little at the sight of him with his wavy, good hair slicked down to his head in his beautiful suit that was so well made. The suit, light brown in color, emphasized his hips and narrow waist. His shoes were not new but well polished with not a scuff on them, even though we had walked down a dusty county road together.

The white people who came into the store seemed to pay him respect, nodding and speaking to him as they entered. I went in as they did and assumed the waiting position until all of the white people had been waited on, just as my mother taught me.

Once the last white person left the store, Mr. Gaines saw me. "Hey there, Annie. How you doing? You here to get your flower money or shop?"

"Both, sir. Here is a list of our needs." I handed him the piece of paper that I had written down our food needs on. Back then, the grocer would go from shelf to shelf shopping for you, selling you what you wanted from behind the counter. The only problem with that system was that he would make substitutions based on what he *thought* you deserved rather than what you asked for. My mother had a specific list, but we knew better than to request the choicest steak or a chicken. We would be lucky indeed to receive any of what we asked for, but it depended on which grocer saw you, what your bill was, and all of that.

My gaze went to the candy barrels, trying to decide between two kinds of penny candy. I liked Good & Plenty, but the candy drops would last longer and I could get more for my penny. Mama permitted me to have that penny out of the bank money, and whenever she sent me to get the groceries, I contemplated my choices carefully. Mr. Gaines didn't like it if I mixed too many kinds together, so I always kept my choices down to two even though I sometimes wanted more. It was better to get what lasted longest. I opened my mouth to let him know I would take half lemon and half sassafras candy drops when a shadow fell next to me, charging the air.

Lee.

He had slipped inside the store and stood next to me, watching Mr. Gaines gather our groceries on the counter. He spoke to the grocer in a loud, friendly tone that startled me a bit. It never would have occurred to me to talk to him in that way. "Good day, sir. I wonder if you have any fresh chickens for this order you putting together."

Mr. Gaines stopped. "I didn't see that here on Janie's list. No, I got some fine chicken livers that will make a nice meal for her."

"I meant a nice fresh chicken, sir. Not the livers."

Mr. Gaines shook his blond head. "Well now, even with Annie's flower money, I don't think they can afford that this week."

Lee reached into his pocket and pulled out a big roll of money. "There's no need to worry about that. I'm sure you can help these ladies have some chicken this week."

Mr. Gaines's little face lit up at that money like he had swallowed up the sun. And the Son they called Jesus. He practically ran out back to wring a chicken's neck to get it ready for me to take home.

Now, all of a sudden, old Lee didn't look so old anymore to me. "Thank you, Mr. Cone. I appreciate that. We don't get chicken that much."

"You going to eat well tonight, little one. What piece of fried chicken you like the best?"

"I like the leg. Will you join us?"

"Naw, sugar. I want you ladies to eat that chicken and enjoy it on your own."

My basket was packed and ready to go. I pointed to the lemon and sassafras drops. Mr. Gaines filled a paper cone with my candy choices, twisted it, and laid it on top of the basket. Lee pointed to some other candy and he put the cone into his pocket.

I didn't even pay any mind to what he got, because the thought filled my head that I was going to have chicken for dinner, all because Lee Cone wanted me to have some.

I took up my basket, but Lee carried it as well as two more bags of groceries and not a speck of sweat got on him. As we walked, and I sucked on my lemon drops, we talked all about the lines of things as I saw them, and in that time, no longer than the hour it took to walk home, he broadened my world tenfold. Right before we turned the bend in the road to go to my house, Lee stopped, putting down the load.

"I'm not going with you to the house. Wouldn't be right. You can tote your load from here?"

"Oh yes. Thank you, Mr. Cone."

He put the basket next to me, along with the two bags, and fixed his eyes on me, the same way I had looked at the candy barrels, deciding what I liked best. His gaze took in all of me at once, from the top of my head with my braids pinned to my head in a neat crown, to the tips of my heavy black work shoes that kept me anchored to the ground. My mother wouldn't let me have anything better because she knew I would get good shoes dirty.

"Sugar, you need to call me Lee."

I swallowed a big gulp of nerves that had risen up in me. "Thank you, Mr. Lee."

He moved closer to me with his breath warming my face. My skin—my skin prickled like a thousand needles had pierced my soul. It wasn't an unpleasant feeling, but it was just a feeling that made me aware that I was alive in a way that I hadn't been before. "It's Lee, honey. Just Lee. Just for you."

"Lee." The little word seemed big.

He laid not one finger on me but handed me the basket with his long fingers slightly brushing mine as he handed it off to me.

Smiling in my face, he said, "Go on home now, Miss Ann. I'll see you tomorrow."

"That's fine." I took the basket, turned from him, and went down the road. Somehow, later, I still was not sure how I made it home with all of that stuff. When my mother opened the basket and saw the chicken, she squealed.

Mama unpacked the basket, marveling at the goods. "Since when did Gaines get so generous with Negroes? You musta made some good flower money." She lifted another candy cone from the basket and opened it. "You bought chocolate babies? You made some real good money." That must have been the kind of candy Lee got. Chocolate babies were a real luxury. She plucked one up and ate it, chomping on the chocolate candy, as she took the chicken to the sink for cleaning.

That's what she believed. I told her no different then, not when I ate my fried chicken legs that night, or the chicken salad, or the chicken stew, or the chicken soup we ate all week.

She knew nothing until I left home on Lee's arm, as Mrs. Cone, just two months later.

Chapter Four

*E*very other week for two months, when it was time to get the groceries, Lee would meet me and walk me home, always sending me home with some little extravagance that we would not have been able to afford on our own. My mother didn't question it because I had been selling my flowers all along, and she just thought I was contributing to the household food stores. Everything was fine for a few weeks until one afternoon when I was doing some finishing work on a ball gown for a lady; my mother came through the door with tears streaming down her face.

I had never seen my mother cry, and I stood up right away and ran into the corner, knowing that whatever she was crying about had something to do with me.

"Ann Cole Lowe. Why did you have me going down to the town square to hear about how Lee Cone been walking you back and forth home?"

"We didn't do nothing, Mama."

"I told you to stay away from him and here I come to find out he's grocery shopping with you. What about that?"

"Sometimes the stuff is too heavy and he help me carry it."

"You shouldn't have that much food. We don't have that kind of money."

"Well, maybe we should. Maybe I'm hungry."

My mother slammed her basket down. "Yeah, you hungry all right. Little girl, I'm only gone tell you once more. Stay away from that man."

"Why?"

"'Cause I said so. He's no good. I don't want you to come near him."

I sat down and took up the sewing again. She snatched it from me. "Get away. I'll finish it up."

She knew it would hurt my heart to be deprived of the chance of helping her create beauty on the dresses. She rarely, if ever, allowed me to sew on the beautiful ball gowns she made. She insisted those creations were only for the grown-up ladies to work on. I had quilt block after quilt block, but nothing to show for sewing on the beautiful gowns and evening dresses.

I started with my own tears. "Mama, I'm sorry. Please. I won't see him no more."

I could see the salt traces of tears on her face and it felt like a knife inside me, twisting round and round. Mama worked so hard. Too hard. She looked like she was seventy, not the fifty years old she really was. "I don't want you to ruin your life. He won't do nothing but ruin you. You not like me and Mama. You got something special, and he just a wolf, wanting to come in and steal that away from you. Please."

She turned from me and slammed her hand on our eating table. "Dear Jesus. I would lock you away, but I know there ain't nobody more determined to do what she want to do than a woman."

"I'm not a woman," I cried out. "I'm still your little girl."

She sniffed. "Naw, I done seen the signs in you. It's coming. I sniff you and know it's coming." Standing over me, she sniffed again. And another time. "You smell different. He can smell it too. That's why he's staying around the corner, lingering, hovering just like a stench."

I didn't know anything of what she was talking about, but I didn't want her to be sad. I reached up and hugged her neck. "Please, don't be sad. It's all the same."

She embraced me back. "I pray to God in heaven you right, Annie. Please. Be careful."

And knowing that, she didn't send me to get groceries and I didn't offer to go. I still had thoughts of old Lee waiting for me down the road. But what I really wanted was to sew with her and Grandma Georgia.

The next day, the day came I had always been waiting for. After a breakfast of red-eye gravy and biscuits, I washed the dishes and my mother held up the coffee pot. "Would you like coffee, Annie?"

Would I like coffee? She had never offered it to me before. "Yes." I nodded, sober as the General. "I would."

She pulled a tin cup off the shelf and poured me a warm cup of coffee. Holding it out to me, she said, "I'm going to see the state senator's wife this morning and I need you to come with me. Grandma's got the misery in her knees and I need help with the fitting. I'm going to bring you. Gotta lay down some ground rules, though."

I sipped at my coffee and she sat across from me at our little table, sipping on her own cup. I had waited for this day for too long to not listen to what she had to say.

"We know you an excellent seamstress, but what you don't know is how to behave around these white ladies. I haven't taken you before because you don't know how to be and you have a hard head. I need to tell you."

"I'm listening."

She put her coffee cup down and her eyes were intent on me. "Don't speak until they speak to you. Mostly, she's going to be speaking to me. So you need to mind that and mind me. Don't look them in the eye. Keep your eyes cast down. Like this."

Mama lowered her head and lifted her lashes at me. "Do it."

I followed her movement.

"Good. Now, go clean yourself as if you are going to church. Scrub your neck. Put on your second best, your navy-blue sailor suit."

"It's too babyish, Mama."

Her lowered posture became alive all of a sudden and I caught my breath. "When I tell you these things, it's for your own safety. We don't wear no red in white people's houses. Put on the navy blue like I told you."

I took another swig of the warm, bitter coffee and scurried away to do her biding. It made no sense to me to be as clean as if I were going to church but to wear my second best. I did it anyway.

When I was finished, I presented myself to her and she inspected me, like a panel of judges were coming to give me a prize. I guessed I rated a blue ribbon but she made me go back and comb my hair into two braids and crisscross pinned them to my head. She sighed as if she would only give me a yellow ribbon. "You'll do, I guess. Ain't got no time for the hot comb right now."

I flinched out of habit. I'm glad she didn't. The hot searing pain from the hot comb was not something I wanted to endure. It was usually only done for special occasions or church. If going to the white ladies' houses merited the hot comb, maybe I didn't want to go. I could just stay at home and sew.

Mama strutted out in the road but whenever a white vehicle or person came in the opposite direction, she lowered her eyes and posture, blending in with the Alabama flora and fauna in her dove-gray matronly dress. Well, even if my sailor suit made me look like a baby, I was glad that at least the white trim made me more visible.

"Morning!" I shouted out, waving to every passerby. When she tugged on my arm, I quieted, lowering my posture like her, having to endure her commentary about how she wished we could turn around and go back home.

"Miss Katie is the wife of our state senator here. She's a very stylish lady, and nice, but you need to behave like I told you. We cannot test her goodness to us."

I nodded and noticed, as we came over the hill, a large white house loomed over the horizon. The land looked like something in a picture book and was beautiful, of course. As we came closer, I could see landscapers working on the green, green lawn. My mother nodded to all of the Negro workers and they nodded back to her. I waved and a flicker of a smile crossed their faces. Then they got right back to work. Thank goodness the bad old times had ended. How did they live without a crick in their necks from bending so low?

We had to walk all the way around to the back of the house. My mother knocked at the door and a stern-looking Negro lady opened the door. "You here to see Miss Katie?"

"Good morning, Mary. Yes."

"Come on in. Where's Georgia?"

"She not feeling well so I'm training up my daughter. This here is Annie."

Mary fixed me with a stern look. "Lord is she thin. You been feeding her?"

My mother sighed a little. "She got a tendency to be thin like that. She eats."

"Not enough. Miss Katie don't like the look of starving people." Mary pulled out a chair at a table in the corner of her hot, bustling kitchen, the likes of which I had never seen. Everything gleamed, shiny and bright. "Y'all sit down here and I'll cut you some cornbread and clabber."

I sat down, rubbing my hands together, but my mother shook her head. "Eat your food so we can get to the job at hand. I won't call her until you've eaten."

Bowls of the cornbread and clabber mush were presented to us and I took up my spoon and ate as if we hadn't had any breakfast.

"Lord, look at her, Janie. You was right. She does eat."

Mama paused, taking a bit longer with her victuals. "That's one of those things about Annie that must come from the other side. It's not how my family is."

I gave some thought to the generous figures of my mother, grandmother, and sister and knew that was one other reason why I stuck out from them. Mary laughed, her face relaxing to look more friendly, and gestured to us to come with her.

We followed her through the house. The floors were carpeted in deep, lush, cabbage rose embroidered patterns. Beautiful china knickknacks rested on gleaming, polished wooden tables, and multiple overstuffed davenports were carefully placed against walls. The house resembled a palace inside and I had to keep from letting my jaw hang too low or else I would start drooling. We stopped before a panel of large white doors and Mary knocked gently.

"Janie's here for your fitting, ma'am."

A delicate voice sounded in the distance: "Let her come on in."

She slid the doors open and on a green stuffed davenport sat a large white lady, dressed in a pink wrapper, nibbling on toast slathered with preserves. The preserves were orange and shiny, and their sugary goodness had a spicy scent that reached out and tickled my nose. How grand it must be to live in such a way.

One day I would live that way.

I had no idea where that thought came from, but the moment I thought it, I knew it would be true.

"Good morning, Janie. Who do we have here?"

My mother's face lowered. "Ma'am. My mama isn't well and I've brought my daughter Annie to help with your fitting today."

Miss Katie frowned. "I hope she's all right. Your mama is a legend in these parts."

"Yes, ma'am. She'll be fine. She just needs a little rest and we training this one in our ways."

"Yes. Well."

"Morning!" I dropped a curtsy and my voice seemed to echo in the large room.

The woman stood and I could see her regarding me. I dropped my face toward the carpet too late. She knew I had looked at her. "Well. Where do you want me?"

My mother moved to a space in front of the fireplace. She opened her workbasket and handed me the pieces of the yellow dress she had been working on.

"Hand me the pins as I tell you, Annie," my mother hissed, low and under her breath.

"Fine, Mama." I watched as the wrapper dropped from the lady and saw her large pink body, dressed in a fine white silk chemise and silky drawers that had small ugly roses edged onto them. I wasn't impressed with the embroidery.

I held the basket and handed things to my mother as she whispered to me for them. My mother and the lady were talking about the dress as being for someone's wedding, the lady's daughter. "I wish she had gone to you for her wedding dress, Janie. I told her, but she picked someone from Montgomery."

A look of pain crossed my mother's face and I felt a twinge of resentment against this obviously foolish girl who had picked someone else to design her wedding dress. My mother and grandmother were the best. "Yes, ma'am. Daughters don't always do as we tell them, ma'am."

"Isn't that the truth? She'll be lovely, of course, but she wanted the latest style from Paris, she said. Not the look of a country seamstress."

We knew the looks from Paris! I wanted to say. Mama and Grandma made sure to stay current on all of the latest styles from the magazines that came to us. I saw my mother on her hands and knees, up and down, down and up, pinning and folding and making the dress fit the woman. I followed her, being her right arm, holding the box of pins, but as I did, I looked at the woman's face.

I will never be able to explain what happened then, but I could see into that woman's heart and soul. She showed us that she was an important woman, a woman of wealth and means, a woman in charge of herself and the community. But what I saw in her heart was fear. She was afraid that people wouldn't believe that she was the mother of a fresh, beautiful daughter. She didn't think she would look as well as the mother of the groom. That's why she called my mama a country seamstress.

My gaze went back to my mother, who was only fifty-two years old, but looked so much older than that, trying to please this woman, a seeming impossible task, but she didn't know what I knew. Even if it would get me into trouble, I had to help her.

I stepped in front of the woman as my mother pinned in the back.

"Annie, what you doing?"

I picked up a length of yellow cloth that was going to be a drape in the back and held it up to the woman's wobbling flesh. I approached her, not in deference or as if I were in fear, but firmly, boldly showing her I knew what I was talking about.

"Mama, if you pin a sash here, just right here"—I held up the cloth in a diagonal way so she could see—"it would help to narrow the waist and create a better shape for her."

The lady gave an uncomfortable laugh, but my mother got up off her knees and came around the front to see what I was talking about or to cuff me—I didn't know which one.

Stepping back behind me, she didn't cuff me, so that was good.

"Whatever is the child talking of, Janie?"

"Annie talking about something she likes to do. She likes sashes and such."

"They draw they eye down. So you can't see . . ."

"Yes, I see, Annie." My mother's hand raised up as if she were going to cuff me. I got ready to duck. The lady looked down at herself.

"Do you think it would help me, Janie?"

"Why yes, ma'am. I do. I'll add it."

I stepped back, picking up my pin box, ready to stand to be of help again.

"Thank you, Janie. Thank you, dear. I need all the help I can get. There are few things more stressful than planning a daughter's wedding."

"Don't I know it," my mother muttered under her breath, resuming her fitting.

I thought back to Sallie and her quickie wedding to Jerry, which seemed to have very little to do with what she was talking about. I had gone from knowing to not knowing in a flash.

The grown-up world had eluded me, once again.

Chapter Five

Idid not get a smack upside the head for disobeying my mother. Instead, she ignored me the entire way home. When we got to my grandmother's house down the road, my mother shooed me away. "Go on home and start dinner. Got to see Grandma for a few."

Now I knew full well she would talk with my grandmother about what had happened. I wanted to know what she thought. By the time I was twelve, I knew I would learn nothing unless I eavesdropped. Besides, I knew I would be able to run and beat my mother to the house because of the chilblains on her feet that kept her walking so slow.

The door on my grandmother's house slammed as I stood under her open bedroom window, prime listening space, to hear what they said. They spent entirely too much time talking about Grandma's general health, which was improving, but Grandma listed an entire catalogue of her complaints, which then made my mother go and remedy them with a cup of root tea. The dirt smell of the tea reached my nose and threatened to make me sneeze when they finally got to the good part.

The part about me.

My mother laughed. It was a sound I didn't hear from her too much. "That Annie got entirely too much of your spirit, Mama. What am I going to do with her?"

The sound of a long, slow slurp came from my grandma. "Pray, daughter. I was a right handful."

My mother told her all about the visit. Even though I could not see her smooth brown face with the three white chin hairs, I knew she approved. "Annie is a special child indeed."

"She know it too. Especially after that lady and then when that Lee came sniffing round. Got her smelling herself now for sure."

"She need some of that country remedy to calm her. Lord knows I needed some of that myself when I met the General. I was more than ready to give myself to him at fourteen. Course, he wanted to buy my freedom, so I would have laid down with Satan himself to escape bondage."

"I doubt that, Mama."

"Well, don't doubt that she thinking about him. In that way too, Janie. Keep an eye on her." Another slurp.

"I can't have her thinking she got the upper hand in this."

"Let her have a bit of free rein. Tell her about Jack."

Now my ears were really fine-tuned, but it was getting close to the time when I needed to get home to put the beans on so they would be soft enough to eat for dinner.

"She don't need to know nothing about him."

"Janie. That's her daddy. You know your daddy. Let her know about Jack."

"Every time you say his name, it's like a dagger to my heart."

"We all live and learn, honey. That's life."

"Yeah, well, she look too much like him, just like that fool Lee pointed out."

I hadn't looked at myself in a while, but I knew she was right.

"Look like her daddy and act like me. The worst possible combination, Janie."

My mama sighed. "If I didn't love you both, with all my heart, my life would be so easy."

"Well, you do. I mean did. And you need to act like you love Annie, lest you lose her."

That was enough. I took myself out to the road and stomped the mud off my shoes and then ran my skinny behind home to get the beans started. I didn't have a moment to myself during the next few days to think about what they had said. My mother put me to work sewing on the yellow dress, and in two days' time my grandmother returned to my mother's house to help finish it, since she felt better.

That morning, all three of us were together, sewing as equals for the first time, and something in me felt better, grown up and more mature.

June came around and it was close to my half birthday time. That's when my mother indulged me, I guess thinking that Lee had gone on his merry way, and let me go to Gaines's for some fruit for my half-birthday pie. When I came around the bend, there he was waiting for me.

I couldn't believe it. It had been weeks since my mother punished me, and he was still here. I couldn't help myself. I was so glad to see him, I ran into his arms. Picking me up, he embraced me and I felt the full length of his body pressed hard against mine.

Joy at seeing him surged all through me and he squeezed me tight in return. I had never had anyone, not any man, hug me in such a way before. It was as if I could feel every single muscle of his body, taut and pulled, match every single muscle in my body. He picked me up and I startled, feeling something else press into my belly. I wanted to leap back, but my ever-present curiosity got me. What was that? My mind was a mess of questions as I returned to the firm ground from his embrace. "I never thought I would see you again" was all I could say.

"How could you think that? I wanted to give you a present."

"That's good 'cause it's my half birthday." I fingered my light-yellow dress. It wasn't as fancy as my red with black polka dots dress, but I had made it over from an old dress of mama's to suit me.

"Well, see? I was right on time, then." He showed me all of his teeth.

"What about your job?"

"I'm always working, but I came here to make sure that you got a half-birthday present from me." He reached into a pocket inside of his jacket and pulled out a small box. He opened it and there was a small locket made of gold. Or what looked like gold. I didn't know it was fool's gold, however. All I saw was a pretty gold locket with my short name spelled out on the front.

It made me feel like the prettiest, most special girl in the world. I couldn't say anything. No one had ever given me such a thing before. He took the locket out and, not even asking for permission, put it around my neck. It was such a vain thing. I would never be able to convince my mother that I bought it for myself. I just kept fingering the gold heart part in my hand. "Thank you," I breathed.

"Is that all you've got to say?" Lee leaned down into my face with his own.

I only just turned twelve and a half. I'll never know how I knew what he wanted, but I knew. It was the same like I knew that when buds opened they would be flowers or that it was a hummingbird's job to collect nectar from flowers. It was like nature happening. So I parted my lips to his and he took them, right there on Old Post Road, right there in the middle of the day.

I was not at all disgusted by his tongue exploring my mouth. I was doing my own exploring with mine, darting, probing, tasting him. He tasted like everything forbidden to me, like everything I ever wanted. Tobacco, smoke, and bay rum all mixed together to make Lee Cone this intoxicating mixture of a man.

He had me by my waist and pulled me to him, tight and then tighter. When we broke apart, I was literally speechless.

"I knew you would be as sweet as sugar. That's why I called you that."

"Oh, Lee."

"You see? It's your half birthday, but you're my present. I got something else for you."

It all seemed to be too much. He pulled another box out and opened it. Inside was a thin gold band. "It's a wedding ring, sugar." Just in case I didn't recognize one, which I didn't. "Let's go get married."

"Married?"

"Yes, for your half birthday. It'll be an easy day for us to remember and every year, we'll celebrate it big—just for you."

I liked the sound of that, but the face of my mother rose in my mind and even though it was hard to remember the words she had told me about Lee Cone, I could never forget those tears on her dark face, or the stark white traces they left behind.

But, right here and now, a turning in my life seemed to be happening. The turn pressed upon me and seemed to be bigger than anything, even the prospect of working on pretty ball gowns. The unknown beckoned to me and I had to run after it.

"Okay, I'll go home and pack."

"Oh no. If you go home, your mama will lock you up and never let you out again. No, Ann, if you want to get married, we can go now. I'll rent a hack and we can go be married before the sun goes down. Say yes."

He pressed into me and the word came up from my lips. "Yes."

Then he grabbed my hand and took me off into a whirlwind that was not of my choosing. In less than two hours, I was Mrs. Cone and in his bed at a boardinghouse on the edge of Montgomery with my clothes off, a grown man laboring over me, sewing all of his secrets into me with the biggest, sharpest needle I had ever felt. I cried out when he pierced me, feeling such sorrow in that moment at how my mother would receive this news. But it was too late, all too late to do anything about it. In that moment, he bonded me to him. I was Ann Cone now. Mrs. Lee Cone. All his, just as he kept whispering over and over into my ear.

The transformation to me felt like I had been a short ugly caterpillar, and now I was someone's wife and a beautiful butterfly. When he shuddered against me, I was spread out and open, with all of my skinny arms and legs about him. I had no secrets anymore. He knew them all.

When it was all over, I got dressed and we went to a diner to eat our wedding supper. I had ice cream, which made it a special day indeed since the only time anyone got ice cream was on Independence Day, the birthday of the country. It was ice cream for me, because it was my half birthday and my wedding day, all rolled into one.

It was after nightfall when Lee and I rode up in a rented hack in front of my mama's house to have me go inside and get my things. To my surprise, everything was already on the front porch packed in a battered suitcase I didn't even know I had. Perched on top of the suitcase was my tin can bank. Confused, I stepped inside the house. The entire inside was dark like a tomb, and a strange scent rose up. My mother's sewing machine sat silent. She should have been working on another order, but the only thing in here was the ghost of her; she was gone.

She had known it was my half birthday. Every year, there would have been fruit pie for dinner, usually with peach or berry just for me. This year, there was nothing. The oven was cold and the house was still and quiet.

I went back out to the porch and saw a piece of paper wedged in between the tin can and the suitcase. I pulled it out and unfolded it. There, in her cramped handwriting, I read the words that broke my heart. "If you love something, you gotta let it be. I knew the moment I turned my back on you, you would run off with that no-good Lee Cone. They say you run off to lie down with him. If it true, you are no daughter of mine no more. Take your things and go on with him. I don't want to see you never no more in life."

The last bit of Ann Lowe that was in me died in that moment. I was Ann Cone. Married on my half birthday to half of a man.

Only I didn't know that yet.

What a birthday present for me.

Chapter Six

I've had two marriages.

That's enough.

It's clear that I'm no good at it. With my first one, I was a baby. The second one, well, that comes later.

Don't ask me which man I had more love for, either. It's hard work to love a Black man when the outside world is steadily kicking him in his tender parts just for being a Black man. And when they is kicking him down, so he's bent over, he's at eye level with you, so guess who he wants to kick when he's feeling bad.

Right.

But I was twelve and didn't have no daddy, so I knew none of that. The only marriage I had seen was my grandmother and the General's. By the time I come around, the General was an old man, bent over and drooling in a rocking chair for most of the day. "Gen'l," my grandma would call out to him and tell him something that she had to do for that day.

He never responded.

She didn't care.

She would lovingly fix him up, dress him, and put him in the chair every day. Some days when I would stay over, I would see her caring for him. She dressed him in a pair of pants and a linsey-woolsey shirt, bent him up, sit him on her lap, and then, standing up with him directly in front of her, walked him out to the front room. Every day. She would sit him down and fix some thin grits to spoon into his mouth. The Gen'l could eat good and he would eat everything she fed him. And she took care of everything that came out the other end of him.

Once, when I was seven, I asked her why she loved him like he was a big rag doll. Normally, I might have got a smack for that, but this day, Grandma must have been feeling generous. "This man. The one you see in front of you and me, used to be able to cut and stack four cords of wood in a day. This man, right here. He saved up his money and . . ."

She put the grits bowl down in her lap 'cause it was empty. The Gen'l had eaten them all.

"He had the nerve, the sheer nerve to go to Mr. Tompkins and talk to him about me."

My eyes got to be buttonhole slits.

"Mr. Tompkins was my owner. He owned me just like I own this chair and this table."

I didn't understand. How could that be? My face scrunched up even more, my forehead in waves.

She made me face her. "Used to be, when I was young, white people owned us. We were their property. Chairs, tables, pigs, people. Same thing. You be hearing it called slavery."

I nodded. Now I understood.

She shook her head. "I hate they got that word in you. That's their word. Not ours. Don't be having it in your mouth." She spat, right there into the grits bowl.

"They may have owned our bodies, but never our minds. That why we say bad days. Old times. The before. Never that other word."

I shook my head, still wondering what this all had to do with the Gen'l, who had fallen back to sleep and was making little *whoosh whoosh* noises out of his hairy nose.

"He talk to Mr. Tompkins. Offer him solid gold money for me. Mrs. Tompkins said no. My sewing was too good to let me go, even for gold money. But Mr. Tompkins wanted the Gen'l's coins as well as his wife's sweetness. They come to an understanding 'bout me. We could stay and work for them for wages but be free. Even gave us some acres in the woods to build us a cabin on, far away enough from them, but still close enough so we could work for them."

That still sounded like slavery to me. I mean, bad times.

"Gen'l took me and we got married and had our house and your mama and her brothers. We stayed there working for them folk until they died, first Mr. Tompkins, then his missus. Only until they was both in the burying ground did we ever get it in our heads to leave.

"That's why you got to get you some good white folks. They are worth their weight in that gold. I had a nice life for a long time 'cause of them."

I gestured to my old grandfather. "What about the Gen'l?"

"Oh yes. Wouldn't have happened if he didn't give up them gold coins for me. Buy my freedom."

"But wasn't he your master then?"

She looked off away from me, for the first time. Into the distance. For a long time.

Then she handed me the grits bowl, with her big wad of spit in it. I wanted to shrink back my hand a bit but I knew I better take it or I might get a thrashing.

"Go on to the sink and clean this bowl and remember that a woman will always have a master. Always. We ain't never get to be free. Difference between the bad times and now is that we gets to choose. We can say who we want our master to be."

I took that bowl to the sink and scrubbed it till it shone, like I knew how to do. My little head couldn't hold all of what she said. 'Cause if some man offers gold for you to a master, didn't he purchase you? Did you even get to choose? Seemed like then you had two masters instead of one.

Once the sewing got started, I made a peach-colored rose and went to the Gen'l and held it up to his shirt collar. I couldn't tell, but maybe he smiled a little bit. I pinned it to him, a custom I kept up until the day he died. When he did, I made him a lovely pink peony for his final rest.

The next time I heard about marriage was when Sallie ran off with that stupid boy down the road and started having all of them boys, one right after the other. Couldn't hardly remember no time when she wasn't bigged up or throwing up getting ready to be bigged up.

"Why can't you stop some of that?" I asked her one time when I was nine.

"Some of what?"

"You got three boys. Do you need more?"

The bags under Sallie's light eyes were dark and heavy from no sleep and probably poor nutrition from her body wracked from childbearing.

"Ain't like there's nothing to do about it. When you get close up on your husband in marriage, and he starts to feeling on your body, well, there ain't nothing like that in the world." Some other light in her face made her look even whiter than normal.

I made a face.

"That's what causes a baby?"

"Something like that."

"Well, you can have that. I want no parts of it."

And I didn't. Until three years later when Lee Cone come down the road and those zip-zapping feelings stirred up in my body when he looked at me. That's when I understood where the babies came from. I had no choice but to do whatever I had to do to get close enough to him to have those good feelings wash over my body.

That to me was marriage.

Then.

Did Grandma and the General have them feelings for each other? Must have. They had Mama and her four brothers. Sallie had Jerry. And Sallie had her boys.

There's Lee Cone looking at me. Would I have boys too?

Two mornings after Lee Cone had split me in two from our marriage, he told me to get dressed for breakfast and then we needed to hit the road to get to the other side of the capital. "Come on, gal, we got to make tracks today. Got orders to fulfill."

I didn't know what he was talking about, but now I noticed he had a new heavy, deep tone in his voice to me. Like a man voice, something I had never heard before. Not even from the General.

What had happened to the sweet words?

What had happened to the light touch?

Holding on to my hand?

Telling me my dress was pretty?

Telling me I'm nice and little?

"Can we go back to my mama's?" I crunched down on my last piece of toast.

Lee's face always had that one eyebrow, like a fuzzy caterpillar done laid on his face and died. It started wiggling up and down. "Did you see what your mama said? She act like I'm not good enough for you."

I waved my hand around. "She didn't mean that. Not at all. She did the same kind of thing when Sallie married. She was all upset for a while and then had them in for a nice chicken dinner with lots of gravy and fresh biscuits with honey in the comb."

"Well, I ain't as stupid as Sallie's husband. Someone tell me they don't want nothing to do with me and my wife, then I believe them. Simple as that. Come on. Time is wasting."

I drank the last of my glass of milk, pulled up my stockings under my dress, and followed him out of the diner.

He took out two nickels for us to get on the Montgomery trolley car across the city and then when that car got to the end of the line, we had to walk, it seemed like miles, to a house that looked a lot like my grandmother's cabin. I thought maybe for a second we had gone back to Clayton and my heart leaped up in my chest, but that wasn't the case. Unfortunately.

Lee opened up the door. There were piles upon piles of dark cloth everywhere, blocking out the light. "This here is home. Sorry there is so much piled up, but you need to get in here and make some kind of order out of it."

"Me?"

I walked on in across the threshold myself, which looking back on it, was a sure sign of trouble, but I was just a baby. Too young to know anything.

"That's what I said, Annie. This is my home and my shop. You need to make some kind of order out of it. Got some customers coming later to get measured for suits. Once you get us a meal together, we'll eat and get back to work."

"Meal? Work? I don't know how to cook."

He turned to face me, staring at me dead in my face. "You seemed smart back in Clayton and now you going dumb on me? That's what I said."

"I didn't think I was going to be working today. What about our honeymoon?" Sallie and her fool husband had a whole weekend off. That's probably why the baby came a few months after that.

Lee Cone towered over me, his hot breath just yesterday so pleasant on me in the little hotel room on the other side of town, now felt like a dragon's, nearly like to scorch my skin. "One thing you ain't going to do, gal, is start asking for a whole lot. I'm the boss around here. I'm telling you what to do. When I tell you to do something, I don't want to hear no more words. I want to hear the sounds of you getting it done. Understood?"

I stepped to the side, out of range of his hot breath. I nodded. I didn't want my husband to be all mad at me and we just got married.

I did the best I could. I fried some pork chops. They were a bit burned up, but Lee ate them. I sliced some potatoes and fried them. He ate them too even though they were more crunchy than cooked.

Then a few men came to the door and Lee swept out his hands and welcomed them into the front room of our home. I got to work measuring, cutting, pinning, sewing suits.

Dull, dark, boring, exact suits.

I thought back to what Grandma had said and then I knew.

Just like her, I had traded one master for another.

That was my marriage and I was stuck in it.

For life.

Chapter Seven

I was a little girl, playing house for real.

Course I was never the kind of little girl that wanted to do that other house-playing stuff. I was fine just sewing the pretty cloth roses I made out of my mama and grandma's scraps. That's all I ever wanted to do. To make the real pretty dresses. I remembered how that nice, rich white lady was so happy when I showed her the way to look better just by moving a panel over. How everyone looked at me, in surprise, and with respect.

Sometimes, when I was in the middle of cooking his dinner, or ironing his clothes, or cleaning the parlor, or laying up under him, I thought about that look, and wondered how I could ever get those looks of respect back in my direction again.

'Cause here I was, understanding now that I was brought in here to be his . . . well . . . the bad word.

Thinking about that look of white lady respect gave me something to hold on to in the dark times. Like when my mother hunted me down the next month and called out to me from the street. "Annie! Get on out here to me! It's time for you to come on home."

My head lifted up. I was in the middle of pinning a suit on a white gentleman. Pinning was some of the most boring stuff

I ever had to do. I can't imagine that when I was talking about lines that *this* was what Lee Cone was thinking about. It didn't have nothing to do with what I was thinking about. Not at all.

The gentleman narrowed his eyes and looked around. "What's that going on out there? Isn't there something you can do to stop that gal from caterwauling? It's enough I got to come here to your place, Lee."

Lee stopped his chalking up of a lapel. I saw his head shake a little. He looked me square in the face with his small eyes underneath his eyebrow and his expression said, *Don't you move. Not one inch.*

I stayed still. I knew better. I had a new master now.

"Mr. George, it will be all right. I'ma stop that right now, suh, yes, suh." In a second he transformed into a servile lump, all to please his customer, and it was awful to watch him bend over, avert his eyes, and slink out of the front door. A slave.

"Hurry up, gal. I got things to do."

"Yes, sir." I kept my voice low and soft, but not like I was ready to apply my lips to his flabby pink behind.

Lee stepped back inside to finish the job. "We going to have a shop soon and then you won't have to come here no more."

The man shifted his bulk around, making it harder for me to do my boring job. "I certainly hope so. Ain't no use in someone like me coming down here to where you people live unless I was getting me a good time gal and I'm a Christian man."

Lee went back outside again, his head down.

"Yes, sir." I kept on pinning his pant leg. Wasn't no use in saying that. If he was so Christian how did he know where the good time girls in Montgomery could be found?

I finished and helped him out of the pinned suit, showing him where he could change back into his own clothes so he could get on about his business. I laid the suit carefully on the appointed chair and then went to the door after Lee.

I was too short to see over his shoulder so I peered outside under his armpit.

My mama was out there, clutching up her gray skirt into her fists, wrinkling the fabric.

The gesture tore at me. Did she miss me? Was she sorry?

I smoothed down my dress. I'd made over a flour sack dress into a housedress and matching apron for wearing when I was working on the suits. I turned around to untie the apron and to put it on a hook but when I went out to the street level and looked around, she wasn't there.

I walked down the street a bit. "Mama?"

No answer.

I walked back to the house and was about to step up onto the gray porch when I saw something out of the corner of my eye by the water pump. Lee had my Mama up against the wall of the cabin. His face was so close to hers and a wagging finger of distrust curled around in my stomach. He had his arm up over her head, propping himself up and pointing his finger in her face.

My mama turned her face away in the other direction. When she turned to look back at him there were tears streaming down her dark face.

What were they saying?

Why were they whispering?

Why couldn't I hear?

Why were they so close?

I was only twelve but I knew then that he must have done with my mama what he had done to me nearly every night since I got to be Mrs. Lee Cone. It was just the way their bodies were at ease with each other. Like when you made a corner and turned it inside out, and it was a perfect right angle. That's what it was. They was at right angles with each other.

My husband and my mama?

When?

How?

Why?

The thought of them all tangled up together like we had been disturbed me so that I couldn't do or say nothing. Mr. George came stomping out of the house, saying when he would come back for his next fitting, but I heard nothing. He might as well have been talking to the tulips in our front yard. The ones I put out there to remind me of home.

I went back in the house and sat down in a chair. I tried to put the chair at the approximate place where they were propped up against the house, but not a few minutes later, I heard Lee doing his shuffling act to Mr. George down the road and he came back to the house, door slamming, him swaggering, thumbs through his belt.

He wiped his mouth with his hand.

"Where . . . where is my mama?"

"I sent her way. Told her you was mine now and she didn't need to be bringing herself round here no more."

I pointed to where Mr. George's pants were and he went to gather them up and said, "When's dinner going to be ready?"

"Dinner?"

"Yes, dinner."

"I-I." My words stuck in my throat, not wanting to give voice to what I saw but I knew I had to. "I saw you and my mama."

He stopped and turned to me, still sitting in the chair. "And what?"

He came and towered over me. I didn't like his voice, all growly like I had stirred up a sleeping dog.

"What you trying to say, Annie?"

"You . . . you . . . you look like you . . .'"

"Like I what?"

"Like you liking my mama." Somehow, I got the words out, although I kept them real soft and slow like I was speaking to Mr. George.

And then, he did the most unexpected thing. He laughed. Laughed out loud laughed. Laughed all deep in his gut laughed and pulled his shirt off over his head. "You something. You jealous of your mama?"

Everything he said had me all mixed up, like the wrong fabrics come together in a dress and make someone look ugly instead of pretty. Him and my mama? Like they was a couple? Was he my daddy? Or my husband? Then all of a sudden, everything I had done, everything I was, seemed—wrong. My mama was supposed to be here. Of course. He had wanted her. She would have been the one who could have made these suits right. She probably might have liked it too.

What would Lee want with me? I didn't know how to sew like her. I didn't know how to keep house like her. I didn't know how to cook or clean or love my man like she did. What was I doing here?

I stood up. "You . . . you must have wanted her here. 'Stead of me."

He stopped laughing and turned to me, as if he was surprised to hear me say that.

He came and stood over me again, smelling of his bergamot and stinking of the sweat of the day. "Of course I did. I been wanting your mama since your daddy told me all about her and how she could sew like a dream. I knew that if she could come and help me get my shop, I could be the best men's suit maker in all of the capital. She was the best women's dressmaker in Alabama and we could set up shop right here and be successful."

Something in my belly crawled into the corner of my soul, curled up, and died.

Now it all made sense. He had wanted my mama all along. He couldn't get her for some reason, so he settled for me. And I went, just like a puppy dog.

Where was my mama now? She was probably heartbroke. She tried to tell me about him. She knew about him because he had tried to get her before, and he had failed. So he got me instead.

I wasn't supposed to be here.

"I'm going home. I need to catch up to her."

He blocked the doorway. "What you say, gal?"

"I said I ain't supposed to be in here with you. I'm leaving."

His hand, his big hand that looked like a shadow, fell across my small face and the blow made it feel as if my cheek would turn inside out. "You ain't going nowhere but to fix up them chops. Get to it."

"Please, Mr. Lee, I mean Lee. Let me go. Let me go home."

He brought the fingers of his hand together into a fist and brought it close to my face. "You don't get to frying those chops, I'ma smack you into next week."

The acrid smell of pork fat singeing tickled my nose. I went to the wood stove and poked at the chops that sizzled and danced in the pan. I turned them over. I could barely see what I was doing—I was crying 'cause the ache of hurting my mama like to cut me into two. Every nerve in my body cried out to her like I was a little baby again.

"Shut up and stop that sniffling. You nothing but a little gal trying to get into grown folks' business."

"I could go and we could switch places and she could be here instead of me like you want." My voice, filled up with salt and sorrow, sounded like I was talking underwater.

Now I knew I was talking nonsense. If I left, wasn't neither one of us coming back here. I knew that my mama had come back for me and I didn't want her to leave empty-handed.

He laughed again, but this time, it sounded real mean. He came behind me and put his hands on me and brought them around me, moving the pan off the burner. His voice, low and hot, came into my ear. "I got who I want. Right here."

"Didn't look that way to me when you had my mama up against this house."

"Leave it alone." His hands wandered all over me, and he ran his hands down my sides, lifting up my housedress.

"What? What?" I must have sounded like a fool but I didn't know what he was doing.

He pushed me down, my face real close to the stove. It wasn't as hot as it was when the chops was cooking on there, but I was forced to look at them, the white pork fat congealing at the edges. I could hear him unbuckling his belt and pushing his pants aside, pushing himself into me, his strong hand pressing my back down, keeping me in place so I couldn't move.

Soon he was done ramming himself into me and he pulled out, leaving his stickiness dripping down my leg. I heard him zip himself up, move to the table, and sit himself down.

"Now feed me my dinner, gal, and hush up."

I did my best to rearrange myself, with the inside of my body quaking, and put the chops on a tin plate. He reached over and ate both of them, licking his fingers in loud smacks. One of the chops was supposed to be for me, but I let him have it.

I knew if I ate one of them, I would be ill.

I've never eaten another pork chop to this day.

Chapter Eight

*E*verything I wanted when I was with my mother, to sew on pretty dresses and to make ladies look like flowers to catch husbands, had died inside of me and curled up in the corner, hardened over like a hobnail.

My days became a circle of the same thing over and over again. Wake up, make breakfast, welcome customers to fit them into their suits, make lunch, clean, fit more customers, make dinner, clean, fit more customers, and then go to bed. If I got lucky, Lee went out at night and I got some time to myself where I would sit in the galvanized tub and soak to a satisfying shriveled-up prune. When I looked at my pruny fingers, I think I was trying to cleanse myself back to the Annie I was before Lee Cone came along.

Only, he might come back home drunk, stinking of liquor and cheap women, and force himself into me. Sometimes I would pretend I was asleep, but he wouldn't care. He would just turn me over and use me like he used his handkerchief.

That was my life now and across that summer, my life became a gray monotonous haze. I missed the sewing I had done with my mother and grandmother. How we were like a triangle of life, the talk, supporting one another, loving one another. Why was

I in such a hurry to leave that warm room filled with so many colors, fabrics, and textures?

I couldn't think of that often, though, I couldn't think of my mama here trying to get me to come home or of Lee's hands on her in the same way he had his hands on me. I didn't want her to suffer what I was suffering because she was my mama. I just thought it was for me to take it so that she didn't have to.

One hot August morning, when I thought I would scream from having to handle hot wool cloth for more white men who didn't clean their underdrawers, there came a loud knocking on the door that dislodged me and Lee from sleep. He had his arm over me, so that I didn't have any chance to escape or get up. I was so small, you see, it didn't take much to keep me pinned down, like I was a pretty butterfly on a board, all stretched out.

"Open this door. Right now."

The raspy voice of my grandmother came in through the open window and I sat up. Lee sat up, his eyes crusted over with nastiness. "What you want? Go on. I got customers coming soon."

"Oh no you don't. I has seen to that, Lee Cone. You got no appointments today. Now unlock this here door."

Lee opened his mouth to say something smart back to her, but I said, "You better go and see what she want. Grandma Georgia knows lots of white folk."

He sat straight up and ran a hand over his burly head. His heavy arm came off me and I breathed my first free breath of the day.

He put on his pants, buckling them up, and one of his unwashed linen shirts and went to the door. I could hear them from the bed. I didn't dare get up and go out to see her, no matter how much I wanted to. My heart lifted. Maybe she was here to get me, like the General came to get her.

"What you want, old woman?"

"You better show me some respect, Lee Cone. You don't want the back side of this hand here." My grandmother came striding in and sat on the davenport in the living room. "Annie? Get out here and see me, girl."

I slid out of the bed, unbelieving that my own grandmother was in the parlor. Why wasn't she at home? Why was she here? Was my mama okay?

I put on a robe, something that I had made from a length of discarded linen, and wrapped up in it went to her in my bare feet. "Ma'am?"

And there she was. My grandma Georgia, her hair braided up on her head, dressed in her second best, with her shoes tied on her feet.

Lee stood next to me and stared at her, scratching at his privacy.

"Is this how you welcome your grandmother, Annie?"

"Would you like something to eat, ma'am?" I was afraid to touch her. Lee might not like it and I was afraid I was dreaming and would wake up back in my gray world.

"It's seven o'clock in the morning, girl. Of course I would."

"You ain't here to be eating off our table." Lee grabbed my arm. "Not after you talking about you cancelled my appointments."

"You fool. I said that so you would let me in here."

"Well, we got to get our day started. We don't have time for company."

Grandma Georgia leveled a look at him. "I want some words with my granddaughter."

"She my wife."

"And my granddaughter."

They stood there looking at each other. Seemed like for a long time. Day ticking away.

"Fine."

"Without you here." Grandma Georgia reached into her bosom and brought some money out. Enough so that Lee Cone's eyes got wide at it. She peeled off some bills. "Go and get Annie and me some breakfast. Be quick about it."

My own eyes got wide at seeing Lee transformed into my grandmother's errand boy. He took the bills, looking at me like he dared me to defy him, and slipped out of the house.

I let out a breath I didn't know I was holding in when I saw him slip down to the corner store where Mrs. Lakey sold odds and ends and made biscuit breakfast sandwiches of streak o' lean or ham ends to sell to folks at the trolley stop. They could eat as they went to work at white folks' houses on the other side of the city.

It was only when I looked down at her that I saw my grandmother's face, crinkled up, all of her seventy-two years of age showing. I ran to her, sliding on my knees to hug her, just to prove to myself that she was here and really real. She slid her hand over my head, kissing my forehead. "I want to come home. I want to come home" was all I could say, over and over.

She patted my back over and over, like I was a small child again, and I was.

I finally pulled back from her. Her face and my face were shining with tears and she pulled out an embroidered handkerchief that I had made for her with my signature flowers in the corner and wiped our faces, our tears mingling together. I got off my knees and hugged myself up against her. "This is a mighty pretty robe, Annie. You getting better."

"I don't do nothing but sew on men's clothes all day. It's so boring and dull."

She held my two hands together and even I could feel how

cold they were in August. "It's teaching you something. How are you, child?"

"I wish I could come home." Pulled back from her, I realized how silly I sounded when she had me in her arms.

"I wish you could too."

"How's Mama?"

"She's mighty sad. She missing you too. I tried to tell her not to do you like that, but she was so mad at him."

"Him?"

"Why yes, child. She loves you."

I put my face in my hands and cried anew. "I thought she was mad at me."

"No. You just a child. How were you to know who this man was?" She looked all around her. "Now listen. It won't be long till he comes back and I got some things to say."

I listened. She opened her reticule and slipped me a little packet. "You need to drink this tea every morning. Boil you some water and drink it. It's so his seed don't take root in you."

"What you mean, Grandma?"

"You don't want a baby in you now. You're just too young. Trust me in this.

"I'll make sure to come every so often and bring you some. Hide it away from him, though. Some men don't like to know that we have ways of keeping their seed from causing us harm."

I put the packet in the pocket of my robe.

"I hope he's not hitting you. If he hits you, you need to come on away from him. I've seen many a woman get killed from a man like that."

I shook my head and lied. "No, he doesn't do that."

"He see you too valuable. Look, we can bring you the times we need embroidery done. Tell him you want fabric to make your flowers, Annie. Don't stop doing that. Every married woman needs some pin money."

"Fabric?" I spread my arms. "Out of whole cloth?"

It seemed as if anything I did wouldn't be worth whole cloth.

"Of course, child. I'll bring you scraps, 'long with the tea. You keep on making them."

I nodded. That's what was missing from this house. I took heart at the thought of making my surroundings bloom again. She patted my hands. "Just do as he says and keep drinking this tea. It's gone to work out. I have a feeling."

"A feeling?"

"You won't be here that long. I don't want to start no kind of war with him taking you on up out of here. He's got rights to you, honey. Nothing can be done about that. You a married woman for sure. But you keep making them suits and make flowers in your spare time for your pin money. Keep God in your life and heart and wait. The opportunity to get your own future will come."

She squeezed my hands as Lee came into the house, bearing a greasy bag. She stood. "I got to get back. We have our own commissions to fulfill. And if we need you, Annie, you'll come on home for our big orders, understand?"

"Yes, ma'am," I answered her.

Lee put the bag on my table. "She's my wife. She ain't going nowhere, old woman."

Grandma Georgia eyed him again, making him small again. "If you lay a hand on my granddaughter, I know all kinds of ways to get your manroot to shrivel up and fall off. Understand me?"

She turned and winked at me. Then, with slow precision, she walked out of our house, down the steps, and out into the street. I was tempted to turn my head and watch her go, but hot tears slid down my face at the sound of her slow footfalls dying away and leaving me.

Lee opened the bag and laid out three streak o' lean sandwiches made with three big cathead biscuits. I stood up and went to the stove to put a pan of water on. "I got you a sandwich. Get to eating so we can get ready for customers." He paused. "What did she tell you?"

"She said you need to let me make my flowers again for my own money."

"You going to make them out of suit scraps?" he scoffed.

I turned. "No. She'll bring me some of their scraps sometimes."

"Well as long as I don't have to come out of pocket with it."

"And she said my mama isn't mad at me."

He had nothing to say to that. I didn't think he would. Once the pan of water was hot, I pulled the little packet from my pocket and poured out a small spoonful, like Grandma Georgia said, and made my tea. It was nasty, but it helped to wash down the thick biscuit sandwich.

I had a purpose. Something to plan for. My own freedom.

Chapter Nine

*W*ithin a matter of weeks, Mama and Grandma moved to Montgomery, a few streets over. My grandmother said Sallie would be fine back in Clayton with her husband and all of the aunts and uncles surrounding them. Their concern, it seemed, had to do with me.

But then my concern had to do with my mama. How would I meet her? I should have known that she would make a way to see me.

We started going to church together, so I would have Sundays to see her. Lee would usually be too drunk to get up to go. That first Sunday when I was able to sit in Rodman Street Church between her and my grandma was like a balm to my soul. I could face the week when I was with them, and they buoyed up my soul.

With their skills, my mother and grandmother had no problem getting new clients in the capital city. One of the clients they got was the new First Lady–to-be of Alabama, Miss Lizzie O'Neal.

Since I was stuck at home with my husband, the best I could do was to hear them talking on Sundays about what they were sewing for her. We would go to church and worship the Lord, and then they would take me home with them to have lunch. I would go home in time to make dinner for my own husband, just about the time he would be waking up from his drunkenness. It was all I could expect.

However, in January my mother and grandmother had some very good news for me one Sunday. "We're sewing gowns for the inauguration ball for the first lady of Alabama and her girls. We gone need your help."

I made a bit of a face and then I smoothed it out. Emmet O'Neal was the new governor of Alabama. I heard Lee talking about how bad things would happen if O'Neal got in. Lee swung around saying, "He just like his daddy, can't stand the Negro man."

Of course, like any other Lee thing, this was just talk since Negro men didn't vote in Alabama, so it didn't matter at all if Emmet O'Neal was for Negroes or not. There wasn't a thing Lee could do about it.

"He won't let me."

"Let me handle this." My grandmother drew herself up and I let it go up to the Lord.

"Please, God, let me get those pretty dresses back into my hands again." I was so tired of seeing black, and brown, and dark blue, and gray, gray, gray. My mother held my hand during the praying, 'cause she knew what I was praying about and for.

When it was time for me to go home, we all went to my house together. I carried a pan—that's what we called leftovers back in those days—of fried chicken, biscuits, gravy, pole beans, and a piece of dried-apple-and-raisin pie.

Lee was a little surprised to see the three of us, all lined up and giving him stern looks for appearing in his undershirt and pants. "I ain't invite none of you here. This here is me and Annie's house."

My grandmother folded her hands under her heaving bosom,

a trait she did not pass down to me. "Ain't you ashamed, Andrew Lee Cone? I am your elder. Where's your respect?"

He drew himself up like he had some raising. "Sorry, ma'am."

He couldn't say anything about my mama, since they were the same age. I thought my mama would be ashamed of looking at him, but not this time. She kept her arm about me and looked dead at him, as if he had messed on her clean floor.

She spoke out in a loud voice. I think she did so to show him she wasn't afraid of him. "We got a commission. A very important one. We gone need Annie here."

He held up a hand and slid down on the davenport. "I need my wife here at home with me. I'm in charge up in here. You"—he pointed a finger to us—"you women don't have nothing to say about it. This ain't no place for suff-suff-suff . . ."

Suffering? That might have been appropriate, but we knew he was trying to say *suffragettes.* Didn't none of that have anything to do with us anyway, 'cause we were Black women, so none of us bothered to help him, in his drunken state, get the word ironed out.

Mama pulled me closer to her. "We going to sew for the first lady of Alabama on her inauguration ball gown. And for her family."

He sat up. "O'Neal's wife?"

I piped up now with boldness drawn from my mama. "Yes. And their daughters."

He looked at the two of them with some new respect. "They ain't just some regular white folks. Well." He sat up even further. "What about the governor?"

I stared at him with those young cow eyes of mine, blinking. "Huh?"

"Your *husband*"—my mother spit the word out—"wants to

know if us sewing for the first lady might mean a door might open for him to tailor for the governor."

I looked back at her, and then at him. "You said he was no good for Negroes. Why you want to sew for him?"

Grandma Georgia's lips pursed up, but she pried them open. "'Cause such a connection means something important, child. That we are important. Well now. Maybe. We have to get to work on this commission first and then we'll see."

He waved a hand. "Go on. Take her."

My mother squeezed my shoulders. "Get your grip and come on."

I stepped forward with the pan of food. "Here is your pan, Lee." I set it down in front of him, shaking with joy that I could go with my mother and grandmother.

"Get home as soon as you can, you hear?" He grabbed my wrist like I was the apple-and-raisin pie.

"I will."

"I'll be waiting here for you. I hope I don't fall behind in my orders due to this."

My mother looked all around her with that same snooty look on her face. "I'm sure you won't."

I ran to our bedroom and threw a few of my housedresses into a bag and came on back out.

I bent down, shy to kiss my husband in front of my mother. He grabbed on me, cupping me by my behind. "Don't stay too long, Annie. You come on *home*." He emphasized *home* with his voice like my mother had said *husband*.

"I will." I kissed him on the cheek and moved over to my family. My mother put my coat on me and we all took the trolley to their house a few streets away.

Mama and Grandma had moved to Montgomery into the house where my uncles Strat and Gen'l Junior lived. My uncles provided the entertainment while we sewed into the night on the beautiful aqua-blue fabric, and they played on the banjo and sang songs that we requested until they had to go to bed so they could get up for work the next day. "Mrs. O'Neal wanted flowers upraised on this skirt. Couldn't think of no one better to do it but you."

"But, Mama, you ain't never let me work on the dresses for real."

My mother's eyes grew shiny and wet. I sidled up to her, and the corner under her arm was so warm. "I'm real sorry about that. I just . . . I didn't realize that you was growing up so fast. I mean, you my youngest. I was going to get everything right with you. I made all of them mistakes with Sallie and she ran on off. Then here you come. Like a little bonus out of the blue."

She clutched the fabric a little bit and let it go. I bent my head to my work. Making them flowers required real close looking, snipping, and lifting up of the petals to get it right. I threaded the needle with a quickness and laid the cloth on my lap, making them petals rise, pointing to the sky and trying my best to get them to lift up like the Lord above had.

"Where did I come from, Mama? Was it out of the blue?" I think it was because I was Mrs. Cone that I got the courage to speak my mind.

She breathed out a little.

"Step away, Janie. Don't need no salt on that material."

She did as Grandma Georgia directed her. My mother stepped into their kitchen and poured herself a little hot water into her mug. She liked to drink it that way. Least, that's what she told me. "Jack Lowe," she said, inhaling. "That's your daddy."

"He got people in Georgia, but I don't know them. Somewhere south, down in Valdosta. I don't know. But he came through Clayton, he was a worker for the General. He had pretty teeth and a good, strong voice. He could sing the birds right out the trees."

"Lawd yes," Grandma chimed in, bending to her seam.

Mama laughed a little bit. "I always hoped maybe you got some of that, but you're more like me."

"I guess he was dark too." I flipped my thumb up to create another blue petal.

"Yes. With smooth shiny skin. He was a beautiful man. I don't know what he might have gotten up to with your husband, though."

"I always wonder. You think he knew Daddy?"

"He mighta lied about that." Grandma nodded. "I wouldn't put it past old Andy Lee."

"Why you keep calling him out on his whole Christian name, Mama?" my mother said.

"'Cause he's deceptive. I call folks by the name their mama said when they looked down on 'em. So he's Andrew to me. Just like I called you Janie and you called her Annie."

"Ann, Mama." My mother turned to me again, sipping on her water. "He say that's the name of a sister of his who died when she was real young. His favorite sister, went off while they were having a church picnic and drowned in the river."

"That's a sad story."

"Yes it is. But he loved her something fierce and I wanted him to love you the same way, so I agreed to call you that. I would have done anything he wanted as long as it would bind him to me."

"But it didn't work." I moved the fabric clockwise to get to the next set of petals that needed to be hemmed.

"No. He started that singing I suppose and got some other women to pay him some mind."

My grandmother's lips fixed as she kept hemming the edges of the rose-colored gown she was working on.

"He got shot." My mother put her hands around the cup. "Some say he was with someone else's wife. If he had a stayed at home with his, he would still be here."

I closed my eyes. *Oh, Daddy. I wish you'da loved me enough to stay at home.* Didn't any man believe in staying at home? What was so wrong at home that they was always wanting to go out?

I opened my eyes and saw my mother looking down into her mug, lost in thought. "I'm so sorry, Mama."

I whipped the edges of my hemming around faster. She put her mug down and came over and smoothed my hair. "You happy, Annie? Are you happy with him?"

"I'm doing my best, Mama."

"If he ever, I mean ever, makes you unhappy, you come on home to me. You hear me, girl? You come on back home."

I nodded.

"Step away, Annie. No salt on that fabric."

I did what Grandma said. Stepped away so I could wash my hands and wrap my arms around my mother, one more time, in love and in forgiveness.

For everything.

Part II
The Answer

September 6, 1953

The train barely moved fast enough for me, until we were back at 138th and Edgecombe at St. Mark's United Methodist Church. We slipped into the side door, and we could hear Reverend Walter asking for prayer. We came in just as he was getting ready to convert the heathen. Just the right moment.

Our church was packed, but that didn't stop me. I rushed up to the front, falling on bended knee in front of the pastor. He looked a little surprised at me kneeling at his feet. Sallie rushed over and laid hands on me, maybe to save me from embarrassment, but I needed this and was willing to do what I must to get it.

"Miss Ann, we pray for your strength and salvation in the Lord."

"Thank you, Reverend, I need all of his mercy and strength that I can get."

"Something heavy laying on your heart?"

That was my moment.

I stood and faced him, something that the women of the church rarely did, since women in the church were supposed to keep their heads covered and bowed low. "Satan made himself real in my life. I need the presence of the Lord's help."

He reached for me and embraced me. My head came to about the middle of his chest, and I could inhale the scent

of the bergamot he used. The scent reminded me of Lee
Cone in that moment and I had to stop myself from pushing
him away from me until he fell down.

"Oh Lord, help our sister Ann out of her time of need."

The crowd in the church murmured. I gently pushed
him back and turned toward the congregation. "A water
pipe burst in my store. It ruined the wedding dress and nine
bridesmaid dresses for the wedding this coming Saturday.
What am I going to do?" I opened my arms and flung them
out in front of me.

The murmur grew louder. The noise of the crowd rose
and swelled. Alarm, panic, fear broke out. "You only sew
for the best folks, Miss Ann," someone shouted out.

"What wedding is this?" asked another.

"The wedding of Senator John Kennedy and his bride,
Jacqueline Bouvier."

Now an uproar ensued and nerves fluttered round in my
hummingbird belly. At least twenty ladies, from what I could
see, stepped stockinged legs and high-heeled shoes out into
the aisle. My goodness, everyone knew that you didn't step
out in the aisle when church had not been dismissed, but
these women of God didn't seem to care. Summer church
hats of all colors—pink, baby blue, light dove gray, mint
green, red, peach, butter yellow—aligned themselves in front
of me. I could see Sallie out the corner of my eye, and even
that she had tears streaming down her pale cheeks.

I stood up straight, strengthened by this infusion of
God's help. "Pastor, I'ma need the recreation hall today and
tomorrow until my shop gets dried out."

He laid his hand on my shoulder, coming close enough
to remind me of Lee Cone again. Could Lee have done

this? Could he have wanted to hurt me so bad? Could he have lain in wait for nearly forty years, just to pop up in my life at this moment to get revenge on me? I swallowed the harsh, bitter taste of the green bile that rose up in my throat, remembering my poor shop.

He might have.

I pushed the thought from my mind, focusing my dim sight on the pastor once more. He spoke to me in a reassuring way. "It's yours, Miss Ann. Long as you wield your wonder with that magic needle of yours, it's yours. We'll do all we can to help you to pull off this commission."

"I'm appreciating that. Thank you."

I turned to address the women who had lined up with me. Only Sallie would help me with the actual wedding dress. I separated the nine women into three teams of three each. They would work on the bridesmaid dresses, which were cut very simply and could be put together fairly quickly. I had my time back in Tampa when I could sew one of these dresses in a day myself, so I knew that if these women helped me, I could finish the bridesmaid dresses. It was Jackie's dress that consumed my mind, Jackie's dress that was my main worry.

Several men stepped forward to help and I knew that they would help me clear out my shop so that I could get back in there as soon as possible. Some of them reassured me that I might be able to get to the sewing machines within two days.

I could fix it all. I would fix it all.

'Cause no one, absolutely no one, told Ambassador Joseph Kennedy no.

It would not start with me.

Chapter Ten

*A*ll successful artists must have a patron. And one thing that my mother and grandmother taught me from the beginning was to be on the lookout for a successful patron. Patrons aren't just about money, which is one reason why I was never rolling in the greenback bills. It's the pride in being exclusive, in being a secret name that gets passed around, in building a certain clientele. That's the best way.

So my husband didn't want me to sew for no one but him, but once Miss Lizzie laid her eyes on those roses, she demanded to know from my mother who had made them. A small Negro boy was sent to my house to come and fetch me to the hotel where the governor and his lady were staying so that they could bring me forth.

The little boy kept playing with his hat. "Said to fetch you right way, ma'am."

I usually knew all of the boys on this side of town, but this boy was new to me.

Lee pulled up his suspenders. "We just don't do whatever you say, young man. My wife is my wife and she stay here."

The boy stood up straight. "But Miss Lizzie is calling for her to come to the hotel." He turned to me, addressing me: "Your mama there too."

I turned to Lee. "I have to go." I went to my husband and laid my head on his shoulder. "Please, Lee."

"What if you in trouble?" My husband inspected the strange boy. I know he saw the holes in his overalls and bare feet as a problem.

"I'm not. I think it's a good thing. Please."

Honestly, I think he was jealous that I was getting called to the hotel and not him. "Maybe your husband need to go with you."

The boy met his inspecting gaze, looking Lee over without any bit of respect. "Miss Lizzie say her. Suh."

Lee threw down his tape. That was my cue. I turned to the boy. "I'll come with you as soon as I change out of this housedress."

Back in those days, you didn't wear your skirts down unless you were a grown lady. But I was a married lady so I made sure that I had sewn myself a long-skirted walking suit, from some of the dark-blue wool that was a castoff of my husband's supplies. I put on my suit and added a big, broad, navy straw hat that I had dressed with a cluster of my flowers, white roses, off to the side, and stepped forward.

"I'm ready." I picked up my reticule.

The boy laughed.

I drew back in alarm. "What are you laughing at?"

"You look like you are dressed up in your mammy's clothes."

"You need to help me up onto the wagon if I'm to get in." My skirt was too narrow for me to step up on my own.

He scoffed but put his cupped hands low. I stepped into them with my white work boot and he flipped me into the wagon back, knocking my hat askew.

I adjusted myself as best as I could as I was unceremoniously driven through the streets of Montgomery toward the Lanvin Hotel, where the soon-to-be first couple were staying before they moved into the brand-new governor's mansion just north of the capital building.

He helped me out and I was able to disembark without too much trouble. My mother waited in the back of the lobby by the servants' stairs. My narrow skirt made the going hard, but I hobbled up the five flights to the top floor, where Miss Lizzie O'Neal waited on us.

The large room buzzed with lots of activity.

I went in and stood next to my mother and we waited off to the side, I suppose for some kind of opportunity for Miss Lizzie to have a moment for us.

She told me to sit in a small chair by the entrance. I sat.

The room was not her bedroom, because there was no bed, but there were large overstuffed davenports and chaise couches. There were paintings on the walls of all kinds of art, portraits and landscapes, but sitting on tables all around were sculptures depicting young women like me, with curly hair and larger features.

I pointed. "Mama, who is that?"

"Hush, Annie. I don't know."

Mrs. O'Neal was surrounded by an assortment of women who were writing things down on paper and holding out tapes against her. A whole tray of delectable pastries was in front of her, but all I could focus on was the thin waspish woman dressed in a silken robe who was directing it all. I stared at her. Who was she?

Her eyes swept over me in a way that was about inspecting me, not engaging me.

"Take off your hat," my mother whispered and I reached up to pull out my hatpin and take off my big hat, then settled it in my lap, where it probably made my face harder to see.

"You here, Janie?" the woman called. My mother stepped forward.

"Ma'am?"

"This your daughter?"

"Yes." She gestured to me more wildly than usual to get up and come stand next to her.

"My daughter, Annie, Mrs. O'Neal."

She turned toward me and I saw a woman who was around Grandma Georgia's age, but her wrinkled face made her seem ten years older than my grandma. I could see she carried a lot of worry on her face, which made me wonder how Mr. Emmet treated her. A man's treatment of his wife always showed up in his wife's face, telling me what kind of dress was necessary: a dress to recapture or to keep his attention. This was a recapture job.

Her hair, brown but graying, was piled up on her head in a pompadour and her eyes were ocean blue.

"Why my goodness, Janie. She's just a child."

"Annie is young, ma'am, but my mother and I taught her everything she knows. And even more."

The woman eyed me up and down. "Well, I should say so. She is well versed in sewing French style. Tell me, Annie, how do you know of the latest French fashion?"

Mama and Grandma kept all of the magazines that showed off the latest fashions. Ever since I left home and married Lee, I had fallen behind in my study, but once I was able to go over to my mother's house again, I was an eager student of their contents. "I read all the magazines and books I can to stay current. I can look at a dress and make my own patterns and . . ."

Her plucked eyebrows raised up on her forehead. "You? Make your own patterns?"

"Yes, ma'am."

She folded her hands and looked at me. "Were you looking at my sculptures?"

"Yes, ma'am."

"Do you like them, Annie?"

"I do. They're lovely."

"Thank you. They are copies made by an artist of your people. Do you know Edmonia Lewis?"

I tried the multisyllabic name on my tongue, but it got all twisted. "No, ma'am."

"I picked those sculptures because they represent Alabama's rich Indian history. We must have it represented here." She pointed. "That one is Hiawatha, an Indian princess. The other is Hagar. Do you know Hagar?"

"We're Christians, ma'am. We know our Bible." My mother interrupted, moving closer to me.

"I see." But she peered at me more closely. "You like that one better?"

"Yes, ma'am. She look like me."

Mrs. O'Neal laughed and I looked up at my mother. What was wrong with that? Mama wore the face she wore for white people, blank of emotion, feeling, and thought. She would not look any other way until we left this woman.

"Well now. Indeed." She eyed me up and down and then looked away. "Thank you, Janie. You may go."

We backed away from her and out of the door.

"Why did she want to see me? I didn't even get to tell her about how Lee could help her husband look better."

My mother grabbed me by my arm as I hobbled along beside her. "You better not be bringing Lee up. Stop worrying about him and worry about you. Get your hat on so we can take the streetcar."

Once downstairs, she practically ran out into the busy Montgomery street, past the old Market Square, where bad word people were sold in the bad times. "Just 'cause you married to him, you still going to listen to me."

It was if she had the strength of Jacob, Gabriel, and Goliath all at once. I had never seen her move so fast. "You going too fast, mama."

"We got to get this streetcar. You done nearly put me off of my time, girl. It's valuable."

I knew what she meant. Lee was always talking about time was money. The streetcar was just appearing in view. We paid our fare, went to the back, and sat down.

We were both breathing hard. Mama took out a hanky with her fancy edging stitched all around and mopped her forehead under her small hat. "You need to learn how to deal with white folks better."

"I know that." Her words ruffled me up a bit. She grabbed my wrist.

"No. I mean, you can't just bring up Lee like that. They don't like the feeling that you are trying to get something from them. It's about building a relationship. You may not see the payoff right away, but you will in the long run. You want to get someone to take care of you. But you have to lay it in there gentle."

She grabbed my hand and held it, something she had never done. "You have to take care of yourself. He didn't want you to sew on your stuff but on his stuff because he's jealous of what you can do. What you do . . ." She mopped her forehead again. "What you do is special. Even more than me and Mama."

I shook my head, suddenly afraid to hear these words from her, afraid to talk to her this way. "No."

"Yes. It's special and you have to use it specially. I let you meet Miss Lizzie because you going to do something special in the world and it's important for you to know a lady like that."

I waved my hand. I didn't want to hear any more. "I understand."

"You got to save it for yourself. Don't throw it away on Lee and his stupid suits. He's always going to look out for himself. You got to look out for you, Annie. Promise me."

"I promise." My words came quick, anything to get her to stop talking like this.

"And keep drinking that tea. You too young for a baby."

"Don't want no baby."

"Good." She let go of my hand, since her stop was coming up soon.

"I'll see you in church on Sunday."

And like a ghost, she slipped away from my side, getting off the streetcar, which barely slowed down for her.

I waved to her for as long as I could, looking at her there in the street in her stylish beige walking suit and small brown hat, proud that my mother looked so good.

When I turned from her, to anticipate my own stop, I could barely wait to get home. My hands itched for my needle. It had been too long since I had sewn for me, sewn for what was in my heart and mind. Lee was just going to have to deal with it.

Sewing was my way of seeing the world, of feeling the world. I had to get back to it. I wasn't going to let him smother that expression out of me.

When I crossed the threshold, there Lee was with his old iron on the stove, pressing seams. "Well? What did the governor say?"

"I didn't see the governor. Only saw Miss Lizzie."

"What did she say?"

I reflected back on the kind blue eyes. "She liked my roses." I touched the little cluster of roses on my hat.

"And you told her?"

"Told her what?" I took off my hat and jacket, tying on a work apron.

"Told her your husband sews men's suits and how fine I could make the governor look."

"I wish you had been there. I wasn't even in there that long."

I walked into the kitchen to peel potatoes. My sewing spirit danced inside of me. I couldn't wait to get the needle in my hand, but the potatoes came first. "Can't go in like that. I made a connection with her. Next time, I can tell her about your suits."

Lee put the iron down and came into the kitchen. "We make money off of selling suits."

I grasped the handle of my knife a little harder. "Yes, we do."

"So you have to talk about them. All the time. Wherever you go." He stood over me. I ignored him, focusing on the potatoes, peeling on them with my little knife.

"I do. Didn't some of the church men come to get suits?"

"I mean the governor. I need me some more white men clients like that."

I put the knife down. "They gone come. You got to be patient."

He grabbed my arm. "You better be doing what I say, Annie."

"You need to let me go, Lee. I won't be able to do no sewing if you holding my arm too tight."

I breathed out.

So did he.

And he let me go.

"All right. But I've got my eye on you."

I turned to face him, his breath hot on my face. "I'm counting on that."

He grabbed my cheek, hard like, and kissed my lips real quick, swatted me on my flat bottom extra hard. Like he was beating my behind. "Hurry up. I'm hungry."

Oh, I would hurry. But not 'cause of his hunger.

I would hurry for me.

Because of my hunger.

Chapter Eleven

I passed three years in peace like that. I kept drinking that tea, sewing with my mother and grandmother, and maintaining a home and keeping my husband happy. No, he never made contact with the governor to get his suits done, because the governor once chided his wife for her relying on Negro seamstresses for her wardrobe. Well, that's not actually what he said, but a much more harsh word that isn't fit for my mouth and my mind. And, as Grandma Georgia always said, it's a word not uttered by quality white folk.

When he said it, right in front of us during a fitting session, Miss Lizzie seemed embarrassed but what could she say? The three of us kept our heads low and when the governor left, Miss Lizzie fanned herself.

"My husband has old ideas. I pray you won't hold it against him."

"No, ma'am," my mother said.

"No, ma'am," Grandma Georgia said.

I was pressing a seam and didn't realize that my agreement was necessary. When I turned around, all three of them were looking at me, their eyes wide open. My mouth opened. "Yes, ma'am?"

Nervous laughter came from my mother and grandmother, laughs I had never heard from them before. "She's young, Miss Lizzie. She wasn't paying any attention."

Miss Lizzie laughed too, but it was forced. "I know. I well recall when my girls were her age. Their minds were always elsewhere. Usually on young men."

She turned to me. "Do you have your young man you think about?"

"I'm married, ma'am. To Lee Cone, a tailor. Been his wife for nearly four years now." Bless me, this was when I thought I might be able to get a mention of my husband in to her.

She stepped out of the nearly finished dress my mother held. "Oh my. Honestly? A child bride. Such a backward kind of thing."

I opened my mouth, but my mother beat me to the punch. "You having girls, ma'am, you know that they don't always listen."

She laughed and went behind the partition to dress herself after her fitting. "Oh yes, I do know that."

Once she went behind the partition, my mama gestured to me to leave the room. Wildly. I didn't know what was wrong with her at first, 'cause Grandma Georgia said, "Well, ma'am. We'll be seeing you next time."

"Yes indeed. Thank you so much. Georgia. Janie. And . . ."

"Name's Annie, ma'am," I piped up and my mother practically pushed me.

"Oh yes. Thank you, Annie."

We collected ourselves into our little triangle out in the hall.

This time, Grandma Georgia grabbed my arm. "Girl, that's it. You don't need to be coming with us anymore. You too much of a risk."

I had grown taller than her but I was aware of her frail nature and I followed her like one of David's lambs. "Yes, ma'am."

When we went out to the streetcar, it seemed like they both were taking a longer time to step up onto the back, where Negroes could get on. It usually was higher back there and harder to get on.

"Hurry up, aunties," the conductor yelled out to the both of them and I helped them as best as I could. Finally we all were on and I paid our fare so that my mother and grandmother could sit. When I made my way to the back to sit near them, they were deep in conversation about something and clearly didn't want to include me.

I couldn't act as if I wasn't shaken up by the way they both had showed their frailty just now. I knew that my mother had me when she was older, so she was in her mid-fifties and Grandma Georgia was much older than that. Why did they have to keep working? I should have been able to take care of them both. I closed my eyes at the frustration of it all.

Once again, they still saw me as a little child instead of a woman and . . . *What if I had a child?* Maybe then they would see me as older and not just a child. I had been drinking that nasty tea for four years and maybe . . .

My mind spun around so much with the idea that I nearly didn't look up when it was their turn to get off the streetcar.

That night, Lee was surprised by my level of enthusiasm for him, since he was much happier about doing that act than I was. I was such a little fool, but sure enough, by the time winter came around, I knew that his seed had taken root inside of me and I was with child.

I couldn't keep anything down. My already thin body grew even more thin.

My grandmother was as good as her word. They had stopped taking me to the governor's mansion, but they still needed me to do some finishing work on the dresses and, of course, I made an endless supply of flowers, especially roses, my specialty. Sunday was my one day when I met with them in person and they took me home with them to feed me the good food they made and not the bad food I made for me and Lee. So I couldn't stay hidden. Anything pop out on me would show right away.

One Sunday, Grandma Georgia inspected me, peering at me close. "You been drinking your tea?"

"Ma'am?" I put the white people mask look on my face.

She stepped back and let her old red eyes sweep over me one more time. "'Less I miss my guess, you is carrying, about two months. So I asked you if you still drinking the tea."

I could never hide anything from her. "I-I—"

She shook her head. "Sometimes you build up a tolerance. We bought you some time with it. You still small in the hips, though. You gone need watching."

Then she called out, making me jump, "Janie! Look like Annie gone have a baby."

My mother came in from the kitchen and looked at me, just like her mama had looked at me. "You about right, Mama." She sighed. "You still so young. I pray it'll be okay."

"It will be, Mama. Don't worry. I can be a good mother to my baby."

She reached over and gave me a hug, something she didn't do very often. I reveled in the sweet scent of her floral talcum powder as she held me close. She pulled me back and looked at me. Tears ran down her face. "Once you have a child, your life is not your own anymore. Do you know what I'm talking about, Annie?"

"Yes, Mama." Her words scared me, but I wasn't going to let her know that. It was too late.

"Oh, Annie. Nothing for you needs to change. You can still be successful. You can still do what you been doing. Designing."

"Janie, what you telling that girl?"

"I told Annie a long time ago, she got a talent. We been doing some alterations on Miss Lizzie's clothes—it's because of what Annie can do. Now that she got a little one coming, she can't give up on her dream." She held me out from her. "You should go to New York someday."

"New York?" Grandma hooted.

"Yes, Mama. Maybe even Paris. Why should she just stay down here in Alabama, where the governor calls us names?"

"Now listen, Janie, he pays good money."

"Yes. I know. But we pay a price that's not of my liking."

My grandmother turned away. "We better start making you everything that you need. Babies require a lot. Does Lee know?"

No, he didn't. He just assumed that my time for having babies was not going to come since I hadn't had any. He knew nothing about the tea. So when I told him, he seemed half pleased and a bit scared too. I could tell.

"Well. Okay, then. I hope it's a boy" was all he said.

"Why?"

"I need someone to apprentice my tailor business too. Especially since you wouldn't stick to it."

"It's just not the kind of sewing I like." I tried to pat his shoulder but he moved away from me. Whenever he did that, it made me feel so alone in the world. That's why I was also glad to be having a baby. I needed some company for the times that I was lonely.

The time my baby grew in my body went by so fast. I kept up with my activities and we sewed all through a busy Easter, summer, and bridal season. My baby was due in the hottest time in

Alabama, in August. Every time my grandmother looked at me from June on, she would shake her head. "You ain't gone make it to August."

My mother would just pat my hand "It's gone be fine. We'll be there for you when you need us." I could see the shadow of worry in her eyes and I wondered what she was thinking. She only had me and Sallie, years apart, but Grandma Georgia had many children. I knew that I would be well taken care of in their hands.

And one hot July day, just after the fourth of July, which was not treated like a holiday in the first Confederate capital of the South, but rather as a day of mourning, I heard a pop and water gushed down my legs near the pile of suits I was ironing.

"The suits," Lee shrieked as if something had set him on fire and I jumped back from the cloth so as not to soil it. The gushing water went on the hand-braided rug I stood on instead. My first thought went to how I would have to wash that rug out. It would probably be less labor if I made another one instead. Then, my mind shifted to the task at hand.

My baby.

"I have to get Grandma and Mama."

Lee sighed, like I was a problem. "You go on into the bedroom. I'll get them. Make yourself comfortable." He pulled on his shoes and his summer jacket and left me there.

In the living room.

By myself, standing on a soaked rug and a pile of water.

I fetched some dishcloths and cleaned up the floor. I soaked the rug in some lye soap and then cleaned myself and put on a fresh nightgown and got into our bed, which I lined with brown paper bags and old newspapers and covered it all with soft, old linens. By the time I did all of that, my mother and grandmother were there and the pains were more intense.

I labored all day. I kept asking Grandma and Mama, "When the baby gone come?"

Mama shook her head. "You got narrow hips. Your little body's fighting. Trying to make a way for that baby to come into the world."

She turned and she and Grandma talked away from me. I didn't like it.

"Somebody got to get dinner for Lee." I didn't know what I was saying anymore, but I knew it was late in the day and Lee would raise up a fuss about his meal.

Grandma peered down at me. "The only thought in your head needs to be getting this baby here and keeping yourself alive."

"I'm not gone die, am I?"

"Not if I can help it, Annie. Pray that's not on the Lord's mind."

The pain twisted my thin body back and forth, to and fro. I fought that pain like Jacob wrestling the angel and it sure felt as if that baby would mess with my hips in the same way.

I pushed my son out of my body just before dawn on July 6, 1914. My boy was a small skinny baby full of wrinkles like an old man. He was long though, and I hoped that meant he wouldn't be short. I laughed to see him and his little wise face. He looked as old as the General. Who was the parent in this relationship?

When they put him on me, he rooted around and found my small breasts and they started crying with milk that was just for him. He had my heart in that instant.

My grandmother looked down at us with tears in her eyes. "Annie. You enjoy him. He gone be the only one you ever gone have."

My hands cradled the little body lying on my chest. "What you mean?"

"This birthing." My mother sat down next to me. "It worked on your insides. Ripped them up some. You won't be having no more. You were too small. Not really ready for a baby." She patted him. "So he's precious."

The feelings that rose up in me were a mix of utter joy at this small, sweet-smelling child on me and a whole lot of tears—for what? A future that meant that I wasn't going to be like Sallie? What was there to be sad about? I didn't understand or know, but I cried anyway.

"So what you going to name this precious one, Annie?"

"I'm calling him Arthur Lee." *A Connecticut Yankee in King Arthur's Court* was one of my favorite stories and I wanted Lee to know that his son would carry on his name.

My mother nodded. "A good, strong name for a good, strong boy."

I turned him over in my hands and held him out to her. "I wanted you to see my boy, Mama."

"I see him, honey. I see him."

She bent down to kiss him on his sweet, smooth head and put a blanket on him, swaddling him tight like he was the little Baby Jesus in a Christmas play. I blew out a breath.

My child, my only child, knew my mother. I could feel the satisfaction wash over me like a wave of fabric fresh off the bolt.

I didn't know that by the time the day of mourning rolled around again in the next year, God would take a firework to my life, blowing it all apart.

Chapter Twelve

I was only fifteen, but Arthur's arrival changed my world. My boy rounded my previously stick-thin figure and shaped my heart. His cries never bothered me. I understood that was his way of speaking to me, 'cause he was so young. So fashioning a special sling to keep him close to my heart, I carried him with me, humming "Steal Away" to him as I cleaned, cooked, sewed with my husband, and helped my mother and grandmother with their society lady sewing.

"I'm gone have to hate to admit it, but that is the best-behaved boy I have ever seen," my grandmother claimed after an October Sunday of me helping them. At three months old, his face was rounding and he looked like a little cherub as he peeked out of his sling with his wise eyes.

"That boy is an old man," my mother said proudly. "He been here before."

"Yes, indeed. He look like he about to take charge for sure."

Their comments made me laugh but Arthur made me sublimely happy.

The exception was Lee.

Lee did not like the baby. He acted like a baby himself because he was jealous that he no longer had sway or hold over my body anymore. Everything he wanted was all turned over to Arthur. Whenever I would have to get up in the night to see to him, he would scowl and say, "That boy is always hungry."

"He's a baby, Lee. He can't help it."

"He knows. He knows just what he's doing."

I would bring him in so that I could feed him. Maybe Lee would see how cute he was and what a good baby he was. Instead, Lee seemed to hate that the baby took nourishment from my body. I thought it was a miracle.

He would say, curling his lip up, "Like a cow or something. Disgusting."

"You used to like to suck and lick on them too."

"That's different."

"I don't see how."

"Stuff wasn't coming out of them."

I watched Arthur's cheeks puff in and out with his effort to nurse. He was so smart. And we had a secret language, like whenever he was done feeding, he would lean his little head back and smack his lips in delight, like he was a chef. It made me laugh every time.

I made sure not to leave Arthur in Lee's care. My son was constantly with me, like a little friend I had always wanted, but never had. Even when one night my uncle General Jr. came to my house. I ran to the door, wrapped up in my robe.

"Mama don't feel good. Strat done gone for the doctor," he told me.

Lee came up behind me. "What is it now?"

"Grandma needs a doctor. I need to go over there." First thing, after I put on a shirtwaist, a skirt, and my boots, that I grabbed was my baby. Arthur lay there in his little cradle, like he was expecting me to come for him, his black eyes shining bright. He would have reached his little arms up to me if he could have. He settled right down in his little sling and went to sleep.

I got in the wagon with my uncle and we went to my grandmother's house. When we got there, Mama was there trying to get her to speak, but it looked like all of the speech had left my grandmother. Her mouth was sloped down, but her eyes were expressive, like she wanted to talk but she couldn't.

"I found her like this," Mama explained, breathing hard. "I don't know what happened."

That's when the doctor arrived. Sometimes, in those days, having the doctor come wasn't always a good thing. But because of the connections Mama and Grandma had with Montgomery society, the doctor was the husband of one of their clients. White doctors weren't always fond of treating Black customers, because they were afraid they wouldn't get paid, but with us, that wasn't a problem.

He stood up after examining Grandma in the chair she sat in. "Seems like Georgia has had a paralyzation of the mind. That's a stroke, Janie. There's not much more you can do but to make her comfortable."

"Will she get better?"

"In time. But not in the short run. I've seen some good things happen, but it takes a lot of work and patience." He turned away from us and walked to the door.

Uncle Strat picked Grandma Georgia up as if she were Arthur and carried her into her bedroom. Mama's face crumbled. "What we going to do?"

"It'll be okay, Mama. I'm going to help you. I'm here." I held her hand and she touched Arthur's little head.

"You're a blessing for sure, Annie. Thank God for you."

All the sewing happened at their house. The more I thought about how hard it was for them to get on the streetcar, the anger rushed like a river to my fingertips until it burst out of my mouth one day when Mama was taking care of Grandma, bathing her body parts as tenderly as I did for Arthur.

"Why can't we have a shop?" I said to Mama. "The ladies could come to us and we could take care of them there instead of us running all over town to them."

"A shop takes money. Money we don't have."

"We can get some money. Make more dresses." Visions of dresses danced through my mind.

"Hush. We Negro. Negro women don't have shops."

I opened my mouth, but closed it to think on Mama's words. Was that the real reason? That wasn't right. I didn't want to upset Mama, though. "I'll go out with Arthur and get the measurements from the ladies."

"It's getting to be time to sew for the New Year's ball and the Christmas parties and the like. It's our busiest time."

"I'll help."

"What will Lee have to say?"

Arthur yawned against me. "He won't have anything to say about it."

"Are you sure?"

Having Arthur had made me see what a child Lee was. He could be managed.

I didn't like the way my mother's face was all crinkled up with worry. I wanted to reach up and smooth her cares away. "I'm sure. Please, Mama. Don't worry."

But she did. Every time I went over there, she was working on Grandma, trying to get her to talk, trying to get her to eat. Her senses had left her. She looked a lot like the General when he was ill. I was over there a lot of days, and I would put Arthur on the bed next to Grandma, since that would be one thing that would get her to look animated or to try to stretch out her crooked right hand that had stiffened up.

Mama took to making dinner for us, so I could take a pan of food to Lee at the end of the day if I was doing work for them. He would sit and eat it. Then I would give Arthur his bath and put him down for bed, while I would do finishing work for Lee on some of his suits.

He never expressed his gratitude at how hard I was working, but instead would only grunt if I asked him a question or asked him if he were still hungry.

I paid it no mind. Mama needed my help and for the first time, I was a grown-up woman. I was Arthur's mother, Georgia's granddaughter, Janie's daughter, and Lee's wife—all wrapped up in the same little person. It was a lot.

Just when I thought it couldn't get to be any more, the worst happened.

I was sewing over at Grandma's house one day, and Mama was cooking when she collapsed. The stew she was making spilled over on the stove. The uncles were at work and Grandma was sleeping in the other room and Arthur was down for a nap. Oh, what I would give to be a little girl back in Clayton again.

I shook Mama, over and over again. I called her name, and her eyes looked like they rolled back in her head. "Mama. Mama. Mama."

She didn't answer me. I ran out of the house onto the porch. "Won't someone please help? Someone please help me!" I kept screaming. "I need help! Please."

An older woman who lived down the street, a nodding acquaintance who was passing by on her way home, saw my misery, told me she was a nurse, and came inside with me.

She saw Mama there on the floor and grabbed at the cross she wore around her neck. "Lord Jesus."

She kneeled down next to her. She felt on my Mama, felt for her pulse. "Fetch me the looking glass, child."

I knew what she wanted it for, but something in my knees resisted her direction.

"Go on, honey. Go get it."

I got it from the bureau, as Grandma snored, her twisted mouth open and drooling, just like Arthur.

When I brought it in, the woman had closed my mother's eyes. She held the mirror in front of her nose.

Nothing.

"She gone, child."

"She can't be. I mean, that cannot be. Grandma just had a seizing of the mind a few weeks ago."

The lady clasped my hands. "How old are you?"

"Fifteen," I whispered, and saying the number out loud made me realize how young I was for all of this to be happening to me.

"Bless you. I know she had sons but . . . is there someone who . . . who can dress the body?"

My eyes went to her kind face, full of woes, but she had stopped to help me in my time of need. "There's no one. Only me."

She bent down and placed her hand over mine. "I'll help you."

The lady called for a little boy to go and get Uncle Strat and Uncle General Junior from the livery where they worked a few streets over. There was no point in calling for Lee, who would be too much of a burden.

When the lady left, I sat holding mama's hand. She was warm, but so still, not moving at all. When the uncles came they looked down at her, stunned that their older sister had died before their mama did.

We filled the tin washtub with water and soap, undressed her, and covered her with a sheet, and Uncle Strat helped us put her into the tub. Not one word was spoken between us as we washed Mama's tired body. I chose her best church outfit—her brown serge walking suit with white edging. Nothing less would do for her. But I made sure to pull some of the best red silk scraps from my scrap bag to make into a pretty rose corsage to put on the lapel. I washed and styled her hair in a crown of braids around her head. Covering her with a quilt, the uncles lifted Mama up onto our prepared table so the lady and I could lay her out. She looked like a queen.

Once the lady left with Uncle Strat to walk her home, I talked to Mama fast, feeling like this was the very last time I would get to speak to her. Alone. "You rest now, Mama. Rest. I'm going to take care of everything. You believed in my talent, and I'm going to get that shop. They can't stop me from having my own space for women to come, have tea, relax, see dresses, and feel at home. I'm going to have it. You'll see. Just for you and Grandma."

Uncle Strat came back and all of a sudden, there seemed to be so much to do, but as we sat up talking in the kitchen we all agreed on the looming main task.

"All them dresses Janie had on order got to be done," Uncle Strat said.

"The dresses for the Christmas balls and the New Year's balls," I intoned.

"Yes," Uncle Gen'l said. "We gone need that money to bury her."

We would need some pretty white silk to make my mother's

shroud. The kind we used to make dresses for white ladies' ball gowns and wedding dresses.

"How are we going to get the funeral arrangements taken care of?" So much was on my shoulders, and I sighed.

Fortunately, the church women came in the morning, as if they were a crowd of small birds, and took everything from me. They set up a schedule to take shifts to see to Grandma, they cooked breakfast, they even cared for Arthur. They shooed me off so that I could do what I had to do.

Finish the dresses.

Go to the governor's mansion to see the first lady to tell her about my circumstances.

They didn't want to let me in, but then I drew myself up as tall as my small frame would take me and I insisted.

Miss Lizzie sat at a small writing desk, working on some papers. She lifted her head and fixed her blue eyes on me. "Please make this brief, girl. I have appointments this morning." I lowered my head and made myself small as my mother taught me.

"Miss Lizzie, my mama, Janie, has gone on to her reward."

Grasping her neck, she took her pearls into her fingers, playing with them. "Well, my goodness. Didn't Auntie Georgia die too?"

A chill ran through me. "No, Miss Lizzie. But she is ill, very ill and not herself."

She put her pen down. "Well, land sakes. Didn't Mr. Emmet tell me about trusting Negro seamstresses? What will be done about my New Year's dress? I'm to be the Snow Queen."

The woman's face was all screwed up at her loss, with no caring of mine. That's when a small voice inside of me made me stand up, like I had before, and face her.

"There will be no disruption in service, ma'am. I'll finish the order."

"You? But they said you didn't know what you needed to know yet. I mean—Annie, isn't it? You're the child bride. How old are you?"

That's when it hit me. It was December 12. My sixteenth birthday. "I'm sixteen this very day, ma'am. And my name is Mrs. Cone. I will finish the order."

I took some more information down from her, and left her, still astonished at my insistence in being called Mrs. Cone. At my age. In that voice. Not a country voice, but a voice like a lady's. Like my mother taught me.

Because that's who I was.

I delivered the dresses on December 18, December 21, December 24, and December 26 for Christmas and New Year's with time to spare for Miss Lizzie to be Snow Queen.

So when the new year struck on to 1915, I made the promise to myself.

I would get that shop one day.

For all of us.

Chapter Thirteen

Even though Lee didn't like it, I had to move into Grandma Georgia's house to take care of her. Uncle Strat and Uncle General couldn't take care of themselves let alone Grandma. I was the only one left, with my Arthur playing at my feet, who could take care of them and keep the business afloat. I honestly think that Lee hoped that I would work from home so that the ladies would come and get suits from him for their husbands.

When the Alabama society ladies saw what I did with Miss Lizzie's dresses and they heard of my plight, they were willing to come to where I was so I could fit them there instead of going out. I rearranged the parlor of the house like a dress shop and conducted my business there. This, of course, made Lee angry because our house was smaller and didn't have the same capacity.

I would sit Grandma in a chair so that she could make her helpless gestures and grunts as I advised the customers. Some of the women were sorry to see Grandma Georgia that way, but her sense of style was still strong, so most didn't mind. They didn't mind Arthur either. There are few things that white ladies love more than a Black child or that other word, *pickaninny,* that they used. I would block my heart and mind from hearing them when they chucked him under his chin, because they would give him a few pennies that I put in his piggy bank.

He was such a pleasant baby, he would go to anyone in the shop, his uncles, even Grandma. Her mind and lips were weak, but she could still hold him and help to feed him. The only one he didn't care for was Lee. The way he would screech and scream whenever Lee would toss him too high made me nervous.

Once Arthur spit up on him and I thought Lee was going to hit him.

I would never let that happen.

I ran over and snatched Arthur from his father to clean him up.

"What he do that for?" Lee whined.

"'Cause you stirring up his stomach so when you do that. He don't like it."

Arthur calmed down once I wiped his face and put a clean dress on him. Some of the women even admired the layette dresses I made for him and commissioned them from me as well. I was happy to oblige. Back then, all children, both boys and girls, wore dresses and they were easy to make and I could charge a nice amount for them, especially if I embroidered them.

Just after Easter in 1916, I came back to the house one morning and saw Uncle Strat with tears streaming down his face. He didn't have to say anything. Grandma had died in the night.

Finally. I didn't have to keep up the balancing act anymore. She was at rest with her General and her beloved daughter and friend once more.

When I told Lee what had happened, I wanted to collapse into some comforting arms. I wanted someone to hold me up and reassure me that my world would stop shifting, stop changing, stop churning. I wanted love.

I got none of that. Instead, he said, "Well, then, we'll go on home."

I set Arthur down. He was almost two. He toddled right to his toy box, as if he knew that he needed to occupy himself for a bit. He really was the best child. It saddened me that I could never have another, but I was at peace because I would probably never have another child as well behaved as he was.

"We home," I informed him.

Lee shook his head. "Naw. Your Miss Lizzie ain't first lady anymore, and business is starting to thin out due to the war. Time to go home to Dothan. I need to be around my folks."

This was the first time I had ever heard him mention that he had folks. I repeated the word, like a parrot.

"Yes. My people live there. There are some rich families who like to vacation up in those parts by the lake. So we'll go there for my suit business."

"And what about these ladies here? My mother and grand-mother's clients?"

"They dead. Those ladies will find someone else. You're my wife." He pointed his long finger at me, in my face. "No more sewing. 'Less you helping me. It's time you start acting like you my wife and do as I say."

I snapped my lips shut for the moment and went to get dinner ready. Lee had a point. My uncles had been courting a pair of sisters. They would probably marry and would be able to sustain the house themselves. But still, it saddened me that this meant Lee planned to keep me doing his will rather than my own de-sires. I didn't want to sew on no more hot, dull men's clothes. The ham got burned and Lee was mad but so was I.

In very short order we moved from Montgomery northward to Dothan. His father was deceased, but his mother, Nanette Cone, still lived there, working as a maid and housekeeper for the white people who vacationed in Dothan.

I wasn't used to someone with the broad forward manner of Mama Cone, but I instantly recognized that she was a good woman with a large heart. She meant no harm, even if the first words out of her upon meeting me were: "She still has breast milk on her breath, Lee."

I drew myself up in my walking suit. I was eighteen now, but because I was petite, some people still thought me a child and mistook me for Arthur's big sister.

Lee didn't say anything but just went for the food his mother laid out for our homecoming. He picked up a fried chicken leg and crunched into it. He was probably glad to have some real food—I still was not a good cook. His mother slapped his hand and I nearly giggled. She gave me a side glance and a smile. "Did I tell you to start eating? Your aunts and uncles and cousins are coming too."

"We hungry after getting off of the train." He picked up the leg that had bounced out of his hand and retreated to a far corner where his mother couldn't get him.

Arthur reached his arms out to Mama Cone and she took him up, cooing. "What a sweet good boy. He's the spit of your daddy."

"He's the one with breast milk on his breath. She spoil him," Lee mumbled between gulps of chicken. The thought of a crispy chicken leg made my own mouth water.

"Why don't you go on to the other room to freshen up, honey? You look right pretty in your suit."

"Thank you, ma'am."

Arthur took to her immediately, a realization that made me happy and sad all at once. I tried to reassure myself that this was different. This woman was his grandmother, and how wonderful was that? Especially now that his other grandmother was with the Lord. I went where she directed me, into a huge dark room with a big bed. I took off my hat and put it on a trunk lid. I had to swing my leg up high to be able to sit on the bed.

When I did, I rolled to the middle and the big bed enveloped me. I giggled, but the feathers surrounded me as if I were on a cloud and I laid back into the embrace of this strange and fantastic bed and slept as if I were Arthur.

I didn't realize how much I had been pushing myself over the past few years and I needed that rest so much. When I opened my eyes again, it was clearly later in the day. I sat up, wondering if Arthur needed me. When I yanked open the door, he was in the middle of a circle of ladies with large bosoms who were plying him with bits of cake and shreds of chicken.

The room was full of women, but I could hear the loud voice of Lee boasting outdoors, with a choir of loud, happy, male voices, who probably had some hooch, from the sound of it. My husband was not someone to keep away from good hooch, if offered.

Mama Cone smiled at me and welcomed me into the room full of, as I found out, her three sisters, Lee's aunts, and a few neighbor ladies. Everyone marveled over my shirtwaist and clothes and I was happy to be part of a circle of women again. I missed my mother and grandmother, but this circumstance with these Cone women was like a homecoming.

Lee and the men built up a cabin for us and we moved in. I was a bit upset to have to go back to cabin living after my house in Montgomery for so long, but I made the best of it. Lee got some male clients and created light summer suits for them, so we were busy for a while. Then, one day, when I wasn't as busy helping, I decided to go into town to pick up some things, including more fabric, so that I could make the cabin look more appealing and less dark. I chose a new walking outfit I had made of a light tan muslin for the summer; the cut of the jacket was a bit long to help me look more mature.

Dothan was as small a town as Clayton, so I knew small-town customs, even if I had spent the past few years in big-city Montgomery. At least Dothan had a department store, unlike Clayton, but I knew how to behave. Even if I had arrived first, if a white person wanted help, I had to wait until the clerk was finished with them before it was my turn. Since on this day six white ladies were lined up, I kept to the back, looking through the latest pattern books. I thought I might as well get some ideas while I waited.

A lady who wasn't waiting but was walking through the fabric department spoke. "Your suit is beautiful, my dear." I looked around. Was she addressing me? That was another thing in those days—it was bad form to speak to a white person out of turn, so I brought my hand to my chest to make sure.

"Yes, dear. I'm speaking to you." The woman was older and wore a rather old-fashioned day dress made of a lavenderish dove-gray lace. The color and the cut of the dress made her sag, as if gravity had fingers on her. I longed to do something, to be of help.

But Lee wouldn't have let me.

I kept my gaze low and nodded. "Yes, ma'am. Thank you."

"Who made such a suit?"

This was yet another problem. I didn't want her to think I was bragging or that I looked better than she did. Which I did. The feelings of white ladies could be very tender and easily hurt.

"A dressmaker, ma'am."

The woman rummaged in her reticule, pulling out a card. "Please. I would appreciate it if you could let the dressmaker know about me. I'm Mrs. D. C. Lee. Josephine. I'm in dire need of a seamstress."

"You are?" I said, taking the card in my fingers.

"I have five daughters. My twin girls are getting married later this year and they need wedding dresses, trousseaux, the whole works. Your suit is very well made. The quality is amazing." She had a kind face, but I could tell that having all of those daughters who needed clothes was a worry on her. The worry caused her to overlook her own needs, given what she was wearing.

I dared to look up from the card and right into her eyes. That was not the way to behave and I knew it. "You can tell that just by what I'm wearing?"

Mrs. Lee nodded. "I've been to Paris, my dear—before the war, of course. I know the latest fashion. That suit that you're wearing is the perfect reflection of the latest thing. You stand out, here in little Dothan." The woman laughed a bit, but I bit the inside of my cheek, keeping silent. It didn't do good for a Black woman to stand out too much. I should have worn something else. I should have kept to my usual dark suit or one of my flour-sack dresses.

"Please. If you could let the dressmaker know. We are vacationing here and visiting with family. We're going back to Tampa soon." She leaned in to me, whispering, "My husband was a citrus magnate, so I pay very well." She drew the reticule back on to her arm.

"Oh. I'll let her know." I kept my voice like Miss Lizzie's: low and even.

She had soft wrinkles around her merry blue eyes. That's how I knew those girls were driving her crazy. "Please do. Thank you, my dear."

I watched Mrs. Lee walk out of the door of the store. Why didn't I tell her I had made my suit? Why was I so shy? I looked down at the calling card that had her name inscribed on it in broad, swirling, fancy letters. She had twin daughters who both needed trousseaux and wedding gowns? So much sewing! So many dresses!

But I didn't have a machine and Lee wanted me to go back to the old way, the way I helped him before Mama and Grandma went to Jesus.

When the clerk called on me with disgust in her voice, I turned away. I didn't like the way she spoke to me, so in that moment I left the store, walking as fast as my little legs could carry me.

I needed to catch up to Mrs. Lee.

Chapter Fourteen

I didn't catch up with the lady. Likely she had a car waiting for her outside to step into that drove her away.

Dothan had not been the gold mine that Lee predicted it would be for him. The connections that he had did not pan out and he was doing far less tailoring. Instead of working, he was living off our savings, channeling it into alcohol and hanging out with his cousins, who were not good influences for him.

This opportunity to work for Mrs. Lee could be an answer for us. Twin girls who needed wedding dresses and trousseaux? Now that sounded like a gold mine.

When I got home, Mama Nanette was playing a game with Arthur, who was all giggles. Still, he lifted his arms up to me saying that sweet word I loved to hear from him, "Mama." I bent down to give him a hug. No doubt who his second favorite person was in the world.

"You look tired, daughter. You need a nap."

"No, Mama Nan. I'm fine. I just . . . well, something happened while I was out."

"Everything all right?" She settled herself into the davenport. I sat next to her as Arthur went back to his building blocks.

"When I was at the store, a lady came up and gave me her calling card. She wanted to know who made my suit."

Mama Nan smiled. "You see there! What did you tell her?"

I shook my head. "I couldn't say. I thought, I mean . . . sometimes they think you are showing off and I didn't want to say."

She nodded, understanding.

"So she gave me a card and told me to give it to the seamstress."

"She did right." She clapped her hands.

"Said she has twin girls getting married and they need wedding dresses and whole trousseaux."

"Oh my. Lots of opportunity there."

"But she lives in Tampa. And Lee doesn't want me to sew." I lowered my head in shame.

Mama Nanette moved to me. "Honey. Lee is my child. My only son." She covered my hand with hers. "I guess that's why he knows he has my heart. But you his wife. And you have to do what you can to lift up your family. That's what I had to do with his daddy."

"You did?"

"Yes. I didn't want to. I loved him. But I had five children. He wasn't helping me take care of them, so I had to take care of them by going to work." She shook her head. "I was surprised when Lee came back here. He told me everything, talking about all the fine ladies you sewed for. All that business down there in Montgomery—even sewing for Miss Lizzie O'Neal. But I guess this is more of what *he* wanted, 'stead of you?"

Now I was the one doing the nodding. "Well." She patted my hands, released them, and reached out for Arthur. "I don't have much of the means to help you. Still working for myself. So you know what you got to do. If you want to leave Arthur here, I'll take care of him for you." Arthur came right to her.

I lifted my head, my eyes filling up with tears at the thought. "Oh no. I could never. I mean, I couldn't."

She held my son just a little closer to her. "I knew you would say that. So, I'll take care of him while you go on and talk to Lee."

I turned to the door, dragging my feet. I kept my head up. Why should I be sorry? I had a good opportunity in front of me. There was nothing to be ashamed of.

She patted Arthur's little behind to still him. "I hope he say the right thing."

"Me too." I smoothed Arthur's little arm and kissed it. "I'll be back."

I trudged the few houses down the dirt road to where our cabin was, thinking all the while of what Mama Nan had said. Why did we leave Montgomery? I had given up all of that good, well-paying business, business that my mother and grandmother had built up for me over years, to other seamstresses there. Why did Lee want to leave all of that behind for here? Yes, Mama Nan was wonderful, now that I had no mother, but she seemed just as mystified as I did. Did we need to be here at all?

Opening the door to my house, I went inside, where I had left the dishes in the tin sink. The house was empty. Maybe Lee was working somewhere. I hoped so. I cleaned up the cabin as best as I could and fingered the card. When Lee came in, he was feeling no pain, as they say. All of our savings, money I had helped to build up with finishing my mother's sewing orders, was flowing down his throat in a river of hooch. I swallowed hard and stood up.

"Where's the boy at?"

"He's with your mother." My voice was low but strong.

"Good." He ran a hand around my waist, cupping my bottom. "I'm in the mood for some loving from my wife."

I pulled from him. "Well, I came home to talk to you. A white lady needs a seamstress and I wanted to ask you if I could go."

"Go? Gal, what you talking about?"

"She lives in Tampa. She was up here on vacation."

"Why does she want you? Little skinny thing?" He smacked my behind and went to his bottle. He poured off another shot in a tin cup.

"She saw my suit and asked me who made it."

He laughed, swilling the drink down. "Ain't that something. You just minding your own business and someone come and ask you about your suit. No one asks me about mine."

"That's 'cause you aren't wearing them out in public. If you cleaned yourself up some . . ." That was all I got out. My breath whooshed from me as he swept me up and pinned me to the hard wood wall with his body.

"That's enough out of you. You don't tell me what to do. Ever. Understood?"

"Why you make us move up here? I had business that was making good money and you made me give it up."

"I already told you. No more sewing. No. More. You only sew for me."

He pressed the full length of himself against me. His hard pressing on me hurt in my middle and I twisted myself from side to side trying to get away from how heavy he was on me and his humid, rancid, fetid, alcoholly breath. "You're supposed to be caring for me in this house while I work. That's how it goes. Nobody wants you to sew."

"That's not true. The first lady—"

He pushed my skirt up, setting it to ripping, and I focused my thought in my mind about how to make the repair. If it were on the seam, that would be easy, but I thought it wasn't, so I could fix the rip and cover it by embroidering some grape vines and leaves on it, as a reminder to myself of how I now had an opportunity. A chance to create my own vineyard. My own shop. My own life.

"Yeah, I know. She always wanted you. And yet, you never, ever let her know what I could do for her husband. It was like you wanted me to fail."

"That's not true, Lee. Mama said—"

"Hush. Your mama dead, thank God. I was tired of her telling you what to do. You supposed to listen to me. Do what I say. You my wife. Mine."

How come had he so many hands? All of him, every part of him, was bent on doing me harm. How could I get away from this?

First Kings, chapter 21, verse 6

I will not give thee my vineyard.

I will not give thee my vineyard.

If I went to Tampa. I wouldn't have to put up with this anymore.

If I went to Tampa, I could live with Arthur and not have to worry about how Lee talks to him.

If I went to Tampa, I could sew on all the pretty dresses I wanted to.

If I went to Tampa, I could make my own patterns, create new ways to dress.

If I went to Tampa, I would be like that woman who made Miss Lizzie's Indian statue.

If I went to Tampa, I could be an artist.

That moment, when my drunk husband had me pressed against the wall of this horrible dirt floor cabin he dragged me back to, that was when I knew my destiny. I understood what my mother was trying to tell me on the streetcar those years ago before she died.

I'm an artist.

I had seen paintings and sculpture only in the pretty houses where we went to make dresses for women in new clothes. Those Indian statues at the new governor's mansion, when Miss Lizzie told me about Edmonia Lewis.

It never occurred to me until now that that's what I was trying to do, as my mind went away from my body in that terrible moment when my husband pushed himself into me.

An artist who creates, who designs, who makes.

I left my limp body in that moment, so my mind, my own mind, took me to Florida.

How? I would have to take the train, but Lee had all of the money. I didn't even have that much flower pin money. I needed to go to Mrs. Lee's and see if I could get money from her to help me. I didn't want to have to do it, but she said she needed a dressmaker, a seamstress, a designer, an artist, someone to help her. That someone was me.

Lee shuddered up against me and stepped away from me to zip himself up. My mind came back to my body and I slumped down the hard wooden wall, feeling pain in my arms where his thrusting inside of me had rubbed my upper arms raw. They stung through the sleeves of my shirtwaist. I took it off and saw bloodstains on my sleeves.

I got up and went to the tin sink. I stood there in my slip, trying to get the water as cold as I could to soak the blood out. I took off my skirt, saw the rip, just where I had imagined it would be, and went to repair it.

Lee had staggered to the bed and was snoring, apparently worn out from his use of me.

So was I.

I sat in my sewing corner, blocking out the wet, sloppy sounds of Lee sleeping his drunk off, making that vine trail over the rip, and thinking through a favorite hymn that was popular now.

> *I come to the garden alone,*
> *While the dew is still on the roses,*
> *And the voice I hear falling on my ear,*
> *The Son of God discloses*
> *And He walks with me, and He talks with me,*
> *And He tells me I am His own,*
> *And the joy we share as we tarry there,*
> *None other has ever known!*

My singing voice was poor but humming and thinking through those words helped me. I worked on my physical wounds with some Mercurochrome and cloth bandages. The Mercurochrome burned like a series of pinpricks on my arms, but my happy heart healed as I packed a small grip with a few pieces of my and Arthur's things that I knew I would need. I could make more. Once I had put on my shirtwaist, I turned, surveying the one-room cabin, taking in the mean existence I had lived for a few weeks.

I would never, ever come back here and I would never again live in a cabin with a dirt floor. That was over.

I looked at old Lee, snoring and slobbering on the bed like an old hound dog. For the first time since Grandma Georgia told me my insides were all torn up, something burbled up my spine like a pressed-open seam. I couldn't have any more of Lee's babies. There was no need to fear anything. I had been with Lee for six years, a lot of my life, but I was free of him now. I could start a new life for me and my son.

I could do it.

I just had to leave him.

With that thought, I turned and walked out of the door. Mama Nanette would let him know what I had to do. It would be best coming from her, not me. I went to the livery down the street, got our horse, and rode it to Mrs. Lee's house.

Of course, it was a lovely castle-looking place on the water. I went to the side of the house, where the help would go in, tied up the horse, and knocked. A kind-faced Negro woman came to the door. I handed her the card and she let me sit in the kitchen while she went to tell Mrs. Lee I had arrived.

Mrs. Lee came to the kitchen, her hands clasped. I stood to meet her. "Oh, hello there. Did you have more information for me about the seamstress?"

"Yes, ma'am. It's me. I'm the seamstress."

Her face changed looks from surprise to shock. My heart sank down into my shoes. She didn't believe me. I tried to explain. "I didn't know what to say when you asked me. No one ever asked me that before."

She still said nothing and I saw my chance slipping away from me, like silk, right out of my hands.

I spoke up. "I've sewed for all kinds of ladies, including the first lady of Alabama, Miss Lizzie O'Neal. If you want me to come, I'll come, but I don't have any money to get there."

She held up a hand, but the look on her face didn't seem convinced that I was telling her the truth. "Oh no, we would pay for your travel, of course."

Is there still a problem? My heartbeat skipped stitches down my spine. I prayed inside of my mind. *Please, please, please.*

"I can go now. I'm going to bring my son, he's almost two, if that's okay."

"Oh my, yes. We have a room at the house for you to live. You mean you can get started right away?"

"Yes, ma'am."

The anxious look on her face disappeared. She clasped her hands. "Thank God. A prayer answered. You sit here. Philomena will give you some cake and tea while I can get the money."

She left and I sat down, relieved. I thought she was going to tell me she didn't want a Negro seamstress.

Philomena's sweet pound cake and hot tea filled my belly and when I was done, Mrs. Lee came to me with a bill and a letter. "This letter is for you to give the girls at the house. I'll send a telegram too. Here's twenty dollars. You should be able to get on the train and get a ride to the house with this. Cary operates a hack at the station. Tell him my name and he will take you to the house."

I was not someone who cried, but tears filled my eyes. "Thank you so much for this chance, Mrs. Lee. I'm so grateful."

Once I got back to Mama Nanette, her face sagged down when I told her I was taking Arthur, but she still brightened when I told her my plan and reassured me she would break the news to Lee. "God bless you, honey."

Within the hour, I had picked up my baby from his grandmother and was on a train, headed south, to my new home of Tampa, Florida.

Chapter Fifteen

For the first time in such a long time, I felt a godly hand in my artistic endeavor. I mean, this woman, a lovely widow, Mrs. Dempsey Cowan Lee, saw fit to press the money in my hand and let me settle my affairs to come to Tampa. Much, much later, when we were friends, I learned that she had known and understood the look in my eyes that day that I knocked on her door.

Fear.

God's grace had stirred her heart to action to help me. God's grace had allowed me to find the white people who would be good to me. Just like Grandma Georgia said, God's grace would let me be taken care of from that point on.

Not every white woman would have wanted to help me in my hour of need. She might have shut the door, she might have said go on to your kind, she might have said don't you have anything you can sell to get money to go. She might have made me prove I could sew.

But not Mrs. Lee. No. Instead she pressed that money into my hand, more money than a lot of Negroes ever saw at one time, wrote a note of introduction, and let me get as far away from Lee Cone as I could.

So I did.

The heat in Florida was on a completely different scale than it had been in Montgomery and Dothan. However, when I disembarked off the train, away from the helpful porters who had made friends with my little son and seen to our comfort the entire way south, I saw the palm trees, tasted the salt in the moist air on my tongue, and knew I was home.

Even when I saw gigantic palmetto bugs scurry about my feet while I looked around the train station for a hack to take me to Lake Thonotosassa, I never failed to be amused, instead of frightened by them. Freedom tasted like humid salty air.

I did as Mrs. Lee said and hired Mr. Cary's hack to take me to her home. And what a home it was too! A large white house set back from the water, with pillars and a huge green backyard with all kinds of glossy trees bearing large round fruits on them. Oranges! Lemons! Limes! Just ripe for the picking. The Lees had come to Florida from Alabama many years ago to make their fortune in citrus, but this was their home, not a grove. You could just walk right up and pick fruit from the trees. The groves were farther on, as far as the eye could see.

Mr. Cary dropped me at the back door, as was appropriate. I didn't know what the customs were here, but I surely did not want to get off on the wrong foot after such grace from Mrs. Lee.

A thin, older Black woman opened the door and a sweet smell of sugar drifted out to us. "Yes, chile?"

I smiled at her. So did Arthur. "Cookie." He said just as clear as day.

And as always, my son was my ambassador in the world. The furrowed brow of the woman relaxed. She laughed. "Why bless his soul. Isn't he something? He knows I'm baking."

"Yes, ma'am." I held the letter out to her from under Arthur's bottom. "I'm Mrs. Cone. This is Arthur. Mrs. Lee sent me to be the seamstress."

The woman clapped her hands. "She sent a telegram saying you was coming, but I didn't know you was going to be so . . . Come on in, child. I mean, Mrs. Cone. Bless you."

The driver of the hack was well known to the cook lady, and he brought in our things in exchange for a handful of ginger cookies.

"I'm Wilda. I'm the cook and housekeeper for Mrs. Lee and the girls. Been here for about ten years."

I put Arthur down and he ran into the kitchen. "Oh, he's fine. He can't hurt nothing in here. He wants a cookie, I'm thinking."

Arthur held his hand out and the woman put what looked like a fat ginger cookie in his hand.

"My other hand?" He held it up to her.

"Oh my." Her hand went to her chest.

"No, ma'am." I stepped forward and broke the cookie Arthur was holding in two, satisfying his request without spoiling his appetite.

She laughed. "What a cute little shaver Arthur is." She held up another cookie to give to me. "You barely look old enough to be his mama, Mrs. Cone, but you sure is a blessing. Mrs. Lee got five girls and there ain't no seamstresses round here what can keep up with their demand. You'll have plenty to do. Sit down and eat your snack and I'll show you to your room."

She poured us glasses of milk and we had our snack before she took us down the hall on the other side of the kitchen.

"She told me to get a crib in here for the baby." I didn't know what a crib was, but when she turned on a light, there was a narrow bed with a colorful piecy quilt on it and a desk against another wall, and a dresser next to it with a large washbowl and pitcher. The crib was a small gray metal bed, pushed in the corner next to the desk. The walls of the room were painted a soothing green color.

"Mrs. Lee said to make sure the crib was iron so that the bugs wouldn't bother the baby."

I didn't even know what that meant, but Mrs. Lee had been that thoughtful of my baby.

It would do. I could make my new start here.

"Thank you, Miss Wilda, for all of your help."

"You welcome."

"I'll put Arthur down for a nap and get ready to start."

Miss Wilda laughed. "The twins aren't here until tomorrow. Mrs. Lee will be here soon. Only one here is Miss Nell. She's the youngest, but she's not the one you'll be making dresses for for the wedding."

The disappointment showed on my face. I was ready to get to work, but I supposed I would have to wait.

"Rest yourself, honey. There'll be enough to do soon enough."

She left Arthur and me to unpack our things and be comfortable. We both lay down for a nap, he in the crib and me on the bed, and when we woke up, we could smell food cooking. I washed up and washed him up as well.

In the kitchen Miss Wilda had rigged up a chair with thick books on it so Arthur could sit at the table to eat and I placed him on top of the stack.

A bright-eyed little girl with a huge white bow in her bouncy brown ringlets wandered into the kitchen. She was ten or eleven years old, from what I could see. "Wilda, is it time for dinner yet?"

An older white lady came in after the girl. "Wilda, I don't know how she gets away. Nell, come along."

"She's no trouble, Mrs. Bracey. Dinner's about ready."

"Who are they?"

She pointed to us. Her eyes widened at Arthur. "A little Negro baby! He's so cute!"

Something squeezed in my stomach. The fondness of white folks for Black children was well known, but Miss Wilda had the situation firmly in hand. "You need to mind your own, Miss Nell. This is Mrs. Cone, the new seamstress, and her baby, Arthur. She got hold of him. You need to go on with Mrs. Bracey to the dining room and I'll be right out to serve you dinner."

The look on the little girl's face pulled down low to the ground, and she trudged on out of the kitchen. Even her big bow sagged.

Her disappointment was like a little cloud left in the room. "She didn't mean any harm," I said but Wilda did not reply. She passed me a plate heaped with half a broiled chicken, pole beans, potatoes and gravy, and a fat biscuit split in half and oozing with melted butter. I asked her for another, smaller plate so I could divide the food with Arthur. It was way too much just for me.

She obliged then went to serve Nell and her nanny. When she returned, she made a plate for herself, said a loud prayer over the food, and then we ate.

"Nell is a sweet girl, but she can be a handful. I'm not wanting to encourage her unruliness. She was a bit of a daddy's girl and since he died, well, she's taken advantage of the situation."

Something pinged in my heart. I knew what it was not to have a father. Anytime I had a customer who didn't have a daddy, well, we connected right away.

Once we were finished with the meal, Miss Wilda tried to serve us some peach pie, but I turned her down. Nell came skipping back into the kitchen.

"Did you show Mrs. Cone the sewing room, Wilda?"

"Now how am I going to do that when I'm in here cooking the dinner and such?"

"No, I guess not." A look of happiness dawned on her face. "I could show it to her. There would be no harm in that, now would there?"

Miss Wilda sighed. "No. You go on ahead."

I picked Arthur up from his rigged-up chair.

Miss Wilda waved her hand. "Oh, you can leave him here. I got some things for him to play with. He seems like a good baby."

He was, thank the Lord, and once I saw he was comfortable with a few toys, I followed Nell into the spacious dining room where she and Mrs. Bracey had just eaten at a long rectangle of a dining room table, out through a decorated parlor, and to the front of the house, where a long wooden staircase beckoned. "It's upstairs. Can you climb it?"

"Sure." I picked up the edge of my skirt and followed her up the long, large staircase covered in dark green carpet. I've seen some fine homes, I mean, I did sew for the first lady of Alabama in the brand-new governor's mansion, but this was money on a whole other level.

"Daddy made his fortune in the citrus. It's still supporting us," Nell said.

"Yes, I see." I smiled down on the little girl.

When we got to the top of the stairs, Nell gestured to a series of rooms, identifying them as the suites for her sisters, and then a small room at the end of the hall. "This is the sewing room."

She opened the door and pulled up a shade so that the fading light of my first day in Tampa might shine in. "Soon, we are going to have electricity and then we won't have to bother with lamplight."

I only nodded, enraptured by a room that had bolts of fabric lined up like a fortress all along the walls. The fabric was covered with muslin so it didn't get dusty or ruined by light shining on it, but it was clear bolts of all kinds of silk, satin, cotton, linen, and muslin in what looked like every shade of the rainbow were there in the room. Boxes lined up like soldiers on wooden shelves. In the corner stood forms, actual forms, to drape and measure on. A sewing machine, one of the newest models, beckoned in the corner.

"Is this okay?"

Okay? It was paradise. I could barely speak. Had this all been done for me? I asked Nell.

"There have been sewing ladies who come and sew for us for a while, but then they leave. Five girls and Mama is too much work. We never had anyone live here before."

It was an answer to my prayers, the opportunities to make all of the pretty dresses I wanted. A place where they didn't even have a man living. I touched the machine, tipped the boxes, found that they had every single kind of notion anyone would want. Buttons, pins, ribbons, edging, bolts of lace, anything.

"This is quite a sewing room," I said, managing to breathe out.

"Well, we'll keep you busy, for sure."

"Thank you, Nell. I appreciate the tour." I pointed to the blond doll she had under her arm. "What about her? Wouldn't she like a new dress?"

Nell looked at doll in surprise. "Oh, she has some clothes. I just wanted her to wear play clothes."

"I see. Well, if she ever needs anything, let me know."

The bright eyes widened. "You make dolly clothes?"

"Oh yes." I held up a hand to my mouth, whispering from the backside of it. "I've even made dresses for dolls to match what their mamas wear."

"Honestly?"

I nodded slowly. "I'll take care of it. She can get measured at the same time as you do."

"Why, I never. Thank you, Mrs. Cone. What's your Christian name?"

I bit my lip. I knew what I liked to be called, but I didn't want to start any trouble here. After all, this was still the South. "Annie."

"Thank you, Annie. We'd better go back downstairs now."

She turned to lead the way, but I lingered a bit to pull the shades back down so that no light would come in to damage the goods in the room.

Then I followed Nell back down the stairs to the kitchen and the hallway where my room was.

My dreams that night were full of design possibilities, of dresses in citrusy colors of yellow, green, and orange, all befitting the daughters of a citrus magnate.

Chapter Sixteen

Tampa, in the house full of the Lee women, was a shaft of light to me in those days—they kept me so busy, I didn't have time to wonder whether or not I had done right to leave my husband behind like that. After a few weeks, I got a letter from Lee's mother, telling me that he had already taken up with some new fourteen-year-old.

Reading those words, I seethed. He was determined to go around and kill the dreams of young girls by miring them down in marriage and motherhood. Thank God my Arthur was such a good boy. Nell came to love to play with him, and in turn Mrs. Lee, as I called her, the twin girls, her other daughters, as well as Wilda, all loved on him as if they were his other mothers.

The wedding of the twins was a few months off, but that time period when I was settling down with all of the beautiful fabrics that I wanted to create with was like heaven to me. I woke up every day to a hot breakfast waiting for me, one that I didn't have to make. I would play with Arthur for a bit before turning him over to Wilda, who doted on him. I would go upstairs and sew for the girls, have a nice hot lunch of soup, and put Arthur down for a nap before I went to do more sewing. Wilda would have a grand dinner ready for the Lees and she always made sure that I got generous portions of whatever they had. I would put Arthur down to sleep after dinner, and some nights, I would climb the stairs one more time to do some finishing work on the dresses. I had heard that Florida had its own ways with how Black people were treated, but I never saw anything but the utmost kindness and respect paid to me in Lake Thonotosassa.

The twins, who were marrying brothers, wanted everything alike—their wedding dresses, trousseaux, everything. "That way," one of them told me, "we'll always be together even when we are apart."

Their respective husbands were settling in Atlanta and Nashville, a state apart, so there was a bittersweet reason behind their requests. As I sewed on the gowns for their engagement ball, twin dresses of golden silk adorned with cascades of blooms on the hems of the capes that draped from their shoulders, they reminded me that I was not the only woman who would have to make an adjustment to a new life.

The dance, being hosted at the white stone mansion of another citrus magnate, came sooner than anyone realized and off those beautiful young women went, escorted on the arms of their handsome fiancés, look-alike brothers who were the cat's meow, as they would say.

After I watched them go, I gave Arthur his bath and put him down to sleep and lay down for an early night myself. Because our room was on the lower level of the house, where the door was, I heard the girls come in from their late night, their heeled Mary Janes clicking in the kitchen as they opened the iceboxes with their fiancés for a late-night snack. Wilda came out of her room, always ready to attend to their needs, always ready to serve. Whenever I saw her interact with the Lee daughters, she mothered those girls more than their own mother did.

Bits and pieces of their conversation drifted down the hall to me and nudged me awake. "Oh, Wilda, everyone marveled about our dresses. Annie is simply the best."

"I'm so glad."

"Yes, I'm so glad she came here," they said together as they spoke through mouths full of whatever Wilda was serving them, probably leftover lemon chess pie.

"She's our secret."

"Yes, our best-kept secret."

"She's very talented, I'll say that for her. She does beautiful work."

"We'll be in the paper tomorrow. The society columnist."

"The society columnist said that we looked like angels."

"And everyone . . ."

The other twin took up her words to finish. "Everyone cannot wait for the wedding."

"I know. It's going to be just beautiful." Wilda clapped her hands. "That's enough now. All of you. Kiss your future husbands good night. You won't have many more nights when you can be without them."

A general laugh went up at what Wilda insinuated and I turned over, curling my toes in delight. How had I been so lucky as to come here to this lovely paradise to do just what I always wanted to do? This was the first time since my mother died that I could say that I was genuinely happy.

If Lee had not insisted that we move to Dothan, I would have never run into Mrs. Lee. So Lee's desire to be spoiled by his mother turned out to be a blessing for me. I would never cease to be grateful.

Descriptions of the twin wedding dresses, as well as the blue buckskin going away outfits that the twins wore to the train, appeared not just in the Tampa papers, but in the newspapers in the future homes of the couples, in Atlanta and Nashville. That was quite a notice for me. No, my name didn't appear in the articles, but the names of the twins and their husbands were quite prominent. People would see the write-ups and wonder what was going on down in Tampa with these new-sounding fashions the twins were wearing and they might care to find out who was behind it all.

So I started a measure book. Everything that I made got noted in that book, with swatches of fabric glued in, a small sketch of the dress, and a description in my own hand. I did not want to duplicate my efforts. Every woman was unique, and every woman deserved her own unique dress. That was the goal for me.

Once Mrs. Lee asked me when I was measuring her for a day dress where my patterns were. "In my head, ma'am."

"Your head?"

"Yes." I paused as I tried to think of a way I could explain. "A woman is like a mystery. If I figure out the ways that I can make a dress she would look pretty in, and like herself, then I have solved the mystery. There are certain ways I can put panels together to make the dress look right on her. Just for her. And I have tried, I've determined not to make any dresses look the same. Except for the twins and bridesmaids in a wedding, of course. Oh, and the little dresses I make for Nell's doll." I smiled.

She came out from behind the dressing partition in the pinned-together muslin I had put on her for the day dress.

"You mean to tell me this is a one-of-a-kind original? No one else has a day dress like I'm going to have?"

"No, ma'am. I have so many ideas in my head, seems like I could never run out. Turn around, please."

"You're quite a unique individual, Annie."

"Thank you, ma'am." I was pleased with her compliments, but I had my job to do. I went right back to work.

She had that thinking look on her face again—the same look she had on her face when she was in Dothan. "It seems to me that you should go to school."

Something shrunk inside of me at the mention of the word. "School?" I had just gotten here.

"Why yes. You could go to design school."

"They have such things, ma'am?" I stopped my work and looked up at her.

"Yes, indeed. Up in New York. Or Paris."

Then I laughed. "Paris? You might as well have said the moon, Mrs. Lee."

The woman turned, craning her neck to see me. "I'm serious. You could go to Paris."

Mama had said the same words to me. A breeze blew by my cheek at her words. Mama. She was looking out for me again.

"Bless you for thinking so."

"Or New York, then. It's closer."

I finished pinning in silence and directed her to take off the muslin piece so that I might start to put the actual dress together. I felt that warmth whenever I knew my mother was with me and guided my footsteps.

Design school. I surely liked the sound of that. My mother did say that what I did was something else.

I was enjoying my time in Tampa, but oddly enough, even though I was close in age to the oldest Lee daughter, I was drawn more to both Mrs. Lee and Wilda, who in a strange way, reminded me of my dear departed mother and grandmother.

Mrs. Lee, as I worked on a dress, would be drawn to the sewing room at any time she wasn't performing some charitable function in Tampa. She liked to play with Arthur in the little crib that was rigged up for him in the sewing room while I worked. She or Wilda would take him outside sometimes so that I could work unbothered. Whenever I told her she didn't have to, she would say, "I'm getting ready to be a grandmother. Is it okay to use your sweet boy for practice?"

I had no objections. It all seemed too wonderful to be true, but it was. Leaving Lee had gotten me this far.

God had guided my steps for sure.

Chapter Seventeen

After the twins were married and had left with their husbands and extensive trousseaux, I was able to have a bit of a breather. I had told Wilda that I was interested in training some young women to work with me so that they could get into a profession. I met some of these young ladies at Wilda's church, since she had invited me to go to church with her every Sunday. One of her young nephews came out to the lake to ride us to church in a wagon behind his mule.

Wilda's niece, Paulina, was fourteen and had graduated from school. She was a perfect trainee. She reminded me a bit of myself and I found it very satisfying to show this young woman a trade—a way for her to make money—with another option beyond being a maid or cook.

My life in Tampa had settled into a sort of a pattern when I was invited to lunch at the Tampa Bay Hotel one Sunday after church by their ladies' society. I think they wanted me to join them. They had rented out a back room in the hotel for their luncheon. It was an opportunity to show myself in the community a bit more, so I went with Wilda and her family.

The Tampa Bay Hotel was quite an impressive structure, with

redbrick turrets topped in blue domes at all four corners of the hotel building, which spread across many acres of land. Wilda told me that the man who built it, Henry Plant, modeled it after a Moorish palace in faraway Africa. "That's our people," Wilda said proudly, "so they let us have our event here."

"Good afternoon, ladies," a doorman greeted us. Dressed in resplendent red with shining gold buttons, he matched the building in grandeur. This was what it was like to have access to the finer things in life. His deep voice sent a frisson of feeling to my fingers as he opened the door for us.

"Good afternoon, Caleb. Good to see you." Wilda nodded at him and shepherded us through the side door toward the back dining room where we were to have our luncheon. I adjusted my reticule and patted my hair under my hat. I couldn't help myself. I turned around and that man was smiling at me still, showing all of his pretty teeth.

"Who was that?" I asked Wilda when I sat down.

"Who was who?" Wilda seemed genuinely confused at my question.

"That man who smiled so big."

"There wasn't a man." Wilda shook her head.

"Yes there was. At the door."

"Oh, the doorman. That's Caleb West. You'll be seeing him come springtime. He comes to help out the gardeners at the house. Was he looking at you in some way?"

"He showed me all of his teeth, for sure." I laughed.

A plate of tea sandwiches circulated, and I selected three for my plate, as well as a slice of pound cake. I accepted hot tea too.

"He does that." Wilda looked me over. "You just getting out of a marriage. You trying to jump into one?"

"No indeed." I shook my head. "I've had enough of marriage to suit me for a long while."

"Good. 'Cause I know the Lees got plenty of work for you to do."

"I appreciate it." I chewed a chicken salad sandwich with small delicate bites. "Mrs. Lee even said she would talk me up among her friends."

"That's a good white woman." Wilda nodded her head. "Would give you the last dime she had."

Yes, Mrs. Lee was a good white woman. Just what my grandmother and mother told me to look for. Tampa sure was a blessing. There were times I fleetingly thought of the misery of my life with Lee, but it wasn't often.

"So pay Caleb no mind."

"He is single though, Auntie," Paulina, Wilda's young niece who was my apprentice, said. "Ain't got no wife."

"No. He got a mama. His mother is the type who isn't looking for any kind of woman to get near her son."

"Is she in the church?"

Wilda made a face. "She part of the Second Street Church."

"Who are they?"

Paulina leaned in, warming up to telling me all about it. "They left us to start their own church."

"They did?"

Wilda shook her head, sipping on her tea. "They didn't like the way the minister was preaching. Thought he was too noisy and not dignified enough. So they made their own church and hired their own minister to have quiet church, 'stead of doing as God commanded and make a joyful noise unto Him." She shook her head, breaking into her pound cake with a fork. "Too dry," she declared.

"Everyone isn't as good a cook as you are, Auntie," Paulina mused, but was not opposed to taking up her cake.

"So now, his mother?" I picked up a cucumber sandwich.

"Oh yes. She's over at Second Street running things. And I bet she would have something to say to any woman who tried to take her Caleb away."

"There's a lot to be said for a man who respects his mother." I ate a crunchy corner of pound cake. It was dry, but edible enough if you took a quick swallow of tea right after.

"The way your husband did?"

I sighed. She was right, of course. "I think Mama Nanette misses Arthur."

"She probably wants you to come and get her son off of her hands."

"Oh no. He has moved on." I paused, swallowing the crunchy cake. "To someone else."

"So what you going to do about that?" Wilda's features came together like ruching.

I blinked. "I'm not sure what you mean."

"Well, I'm not suggesting anything to get at another husband. Lord knows men are a trial and tribulation. But if you needed it, you should get a divorce."

"Are we allowed to get those?" I paid attention now. I didn't know I could do such a thing.

Wilda knew what I meant by *we*.

"If you had the money, a judge will hear your case. And dissolve your marriage."

Dissolve. I liked the sound of that. Marriage to Lee had been a big mistake. All I had wanted was to sew on the ladies' dresses, all in a hurry to grow up. I wish I had known what marriage was all about. That's why I was bringing Paulina along in the way that I was. I didn't want her or any other young women making foolish mistakes as I had.

Wilda knew, since the Lees gave me room and board, that the salary they paid me was something I had been saving. I had thoughts, as I always did, of getting a little shop together for myself, but the situation at the Lee house was so comfortable, I imagined that some of my salary savings might be spared for such a cause as divorce papers.

Freedom from Lee Cone.

The speaker cleared her throat for the presentations to start and my mind focused, not on the program, but on what I could do to be free of Lee. It seemed to be a wonder, to go back to being Annie Lowe, as I had been, and not Annie Cone.

When I left, I smiled broadly at Caleb West from under my frilled hat and he waved at me as the wagon trudged away to take us all back to the lake house on that late Sunday afternoon.

Months passed and as Paulina came to help me, I was able to work fast. I had built up a small storehouse of clothes for the Lees, so I began to sew summer daywear, suits, and evening apparel for their friends as well. The ladies all loved my efforts and, thankfully, paid me well enough so that I could start to look for a place to open a shop.

The problem was an old one, though. If I opened a shop, the only place I could open it would be in the Negro part of town, and the white ladies would never go there. I had no choice but to save my money and to pray about it.

One day, Mrs. Lee came to me with an idea. "Have you thought more about going to school, Annie?"

"Not since you mentioned it last fall, ma'am."

"Well, a few of my friends were speaking about it to me the other day. You do wonderful work here, of course, but we wonder just how much more you could do if you went to school." She pushed a folded newspaper to me. "You should ask about the particulars for this school."

I read the ad that she showed me for a school in New York— S. T. Taylor Design School. Not Paris. I was glad of that since I didn't know how to speak French.

"If you ask them about admission, costs, figure out room and board, et cetera, we might be able to stake your education."

My mouth opened. "Ma'am?"

Mrs. Lee held up a hand and shook her head. "I always wanted my girls to go to school like I did in Georgia. The twins did not go to college but got married instead. Dear Mr. Lee and I had the funds set aside for their college educations. My other daughters may opt to go, but since they, and especially Nell, won't be going for some time, I can help someone else in the meantime. I want that to be you."

"But Arthur." My heart squeezed into a small fist at the thought of my son. I couldn't imagine taking him to such a far-off place. "Who would care for him? I wouldn't want him to be with strangers."

I handed the paper back to her. I didn't want to disappoint her. "It's such a generous offer. I appreciate you thinking of me."

"I understand, Annie." She took the paper back and looked over at my precious son, sleeping in the crib. "They are only little once. But just as we did, you do have to think of the future and how you can, well, stake him in his life. He won't always be little. I know you don't want him to be a laborer or anything like that. So, you have to provide an education for him. When you have an education, you can charge more for the wonderful work that you do and help Arthur get a good start in life."

I nodded. Those things were at the back of my mind. His schooling seemed so far off, but Mrs. Lee had a point.

"I grew up one of eleven. My daddy in Georgia was a judge. I was born after the war, but my older siblings, as well as me, we were raised up with Negro mammies. And they loved us so. Like their own." She laughed a little. "Maybe more than their own. And ever since I became a mother to mine, I have felt something about that. That their children didn't get care like we did. I don't ever hear you talk about what Arthur's father has done for him."

I lowered my head. "No, ma'am."

"Then think about what you have to do for him. He's such a dear boy and you've, well, you've been such a miracle worker out here at the lake." She handed the paper back over. "Think about it."

Good white people indeed.

I did as she directed. The thought of going to school all day studying dresses had me thinking of Edmonia Lewis and her Hiawatha and Hagar sculptures. She had gone to school. If she could go off to school to learn sculpture, then why shouldn't I learn more about my dresses?

And I knew who would take Arthur in. Gladly.

So I wrote the school and I wrote Miss Nan too. And within a few weeks, I received information from the school. I wrote out all of the information on a paper and showed it to Mrs. Lee. I thought she would be horrified at what I wrote there, but after she added it all up for me, she nodded. "Yes. This is half of what it would have cost for one of the twins to go to school. We can do this."

She folded the paper. "What about Arthur?"

"I've written to his grandmother. She will take him in." I lowered my head.

"For a year," Mrs. Lee whispered.

"Yes." My eyes shined at the thought of not being with Arthur for a whole year. Would he even know me anymore?

"We'll miss you."

My eyes hurt as I looked at her so I blinked fast and hard. "Thank you, Mrs. Lee."

"We'll be fine. *You*, Annie. It is you who must take care of yourself."

School. A design school. The difference between being just a seamstress and something more. Edmonia Lewis went to school for her art and I would do the same for mine. Even if it meant a separation from the best part of me.

But Arthur would be loved by his grandmother, and he would be with his father for that time. That was more than I had.

I needed to give Arthur more than what I had.

I wanted to give Arthur more than what I had.

It was what I had lived for.

Chapter Eighteen

It was hard to believe that the Lees would be so kind as to stake my schooling. Once I received the letter from Mama Nan, who agreed to take Arthur for the year, and the acceptance from the school, Mrs. Lee sent a check with the deposit and found out, through her acquaintances, of a boardinghouse in Harlem, the Negro part of New York, where it was safe for me to stay. Once she did that, she opened an account for me at a New York bank and showed me the bank book with the school tuition, plus enough for room and board for the year in the account. Three thousand dollars.

She also handed me a train ticket that routed through Dothan, to Atlanta, to Philadelphia, and finally to New York. *Thank you* seemed to be too small a word to say.

"We know you will do well, and you'll bring back some fabulous designs for me to wear." Mrs. Lee smiled and her smile reflected all of her excitement. That woman was not shy at all in speaking of her love for clothes.

As I was getting ready to leave in April, Caleb West came to the house to help with the spring planting. Feeding the workers was such a tremendous task that Wilda needed all hands on deck to help prepare large meals for the planters to eat, picnic style, at large long tables set up in the grove. I couldn't help with the cooking, but I could dole out food.

I knew it was him when he stepped to me at the table. "How do?" he said.

"Hello, sir."

"I recall you. You were the little bit what came to my hotel a few months ago."

I nodded. Why should a man remember who I was? My blood ran hot and cold all through me.

"You want a plate, Caleb West?" Wilda's lips were pursed together as she stepped over between us.

"Yes, ma'am."

She gestured toward the table. "Get it and move on. We got a lot of workers to feed today."

I lowered my head and dished out his food. I felt it was my fault he got in trouble with the usually cordial Wilda.

Laughing all over himself, he spoke up. "Yes, ma'am, Miss Wilda."

He took the plate of sliced pork, greens, potatoes, and a wedge of chess pie perched on the side from my hand. Our fingers met and slid against each other.

Something that felt like hurt, pain, and the devil all at once tingled up my arm. What was that?

He smiled down at me, as if he knew.

I just nodded, sliding my eyes away. "When do you get to eat, little bit?"

"My name, sir, is Annie." I was tired of his nickname for me. Everyone always named me something 'cause I was small.

"I'm Caleb West, like Miss Wilda say. She doesn't like me 'cause of my mama, so I'm sure she said some bad stuff to you 'bout me." He spoke loud enough so Wilda could hear it and then he laughed and laughed.

My mouth was open partway and I made myself close it. "She's a very kind woman. She's helped me adjust while I've come here. If there is something about you that is bad, I'll trust what she says."

"Huh. Well, that's as much as you know, Miss Annie. Come eat your dinner with me and I'll tell you all about it."

I noticed that he had lingered after all of the other workers. He knew the kitchen help would only get to eat after all of the men had been served. I picked up a plate, dished a small amount on it, and followed him to one end of an empty picnic table. Then we sat down. Together. At the same time.

"Miss Wilda and my mother have been at it for years. They both good women who are just alike, so they don't like each other. You know how that is."

He picked up his fork and began to dig in.

"Excuse me. Don't you pray?"

He put his fork down. "Go ahead."

I bowed my head. "Dear Lord. Please bless us on this day. Help the citrus to flourish and grow and provide us with nourishment and sustenance for the year. Look out for all of your children here on earth no matter what our pathways happen to be. In your name. Amen."

I lifted my head and it looked to me like he hadn't bothered to bow his. Like he had just stared at me the whole time I prayed. "Thank you, Miss Annie."

"You're welcome." I picked at my plate, eating about half of the food there.

Caleb ate all of his, wiping his lips when he was finished. "I'll take that. No need of it going to waste. No wonder you so little."

He pushed my plate in front of him and ate all of my food as well.

I watched, astounded at how much food he put away.

"You sew the clothes for the Lee family?"

"And others."

"They good people. I don't need this citrus planting money, but I know they need help so I come out here. And of course for Miss Wilda's food." He waved at her, because she had brought her plate to our table, sitting close enough to hear, but far away enough to give the impression that she was not chaperoning.

But she was.

She huffed and turned back to her plate, speaking to Paulina, who was seated next to her.

Caleb smiled at me, pointing his thumb at her. "She likes how I eat her food, but she won't admit it."

"I see."

"So. Tell me all about you. You a seamstress and you living with the Lees. They've been keeping you a secret a while now."

"I've been going to First Avenue Church ever since I got here."

"Yeah. Well, you know why I don't go there. But I heard tell about you. The pretty little seamstress with a fine son. Where's he?"

"You certainly know all about me." I fought to keep my jaw closed.

"Yes, I do. His name is Arthur."

"Miss Nell is keeping him. She likes to play games with him. Her mother feels it's good practice for when she gets to be a mother."

"You're special. Talk nice and can get white people to watch your child. Yes. You something all right."

He sat up, gathered our plates, and spoke out in his deep ringing voice: "This food was nearly as good as my mother's."

He winked at me.

Wilda exploded. "Why, Caleb West, I'm sure it's just as good as hers, if not better than." I covered my mouth at his antics then stood up and we walked over to the serving tables.

He looked directly at me as he put our dishes in the basin. "Will you step out with me sometime?"

I lowered my head. "I don't know if I can oblige, Mr. West."

He looked down at me. A horn sounded in the distance. It was time for the workers to return to the grove. He didn't seem to care.

"You don't like me?" His voice softened, but the tone in it made me lift my head and look at his handsome face.

"I'm sure you're very nice. I don't know you."

"If you step out with me, you'll get to know me."

I didn't like how his soft voice had gotten to be a snake, wrapping itself around me, trying to hex me. "I'm still married, Mr. West. That's why."

"You have a husband?"

"Yes. He's in Dothan up in Alabama. My son's father. I don't think it would be a good idea for me to be seeing other men while I'm still married."

"Well he's a fool for leaving you down here all my yourself." I peered into his brown eyes. He seemed to mean what he said.

"I left him behind." I folded my hands, fingering the place where my wedding ring used to be before I came to Tampa. "I'm trying to get a divorce."

He shoved his hands into his pockets. "Gal, Negroes don't get divorces."

"Well I want one." Had Wilda been right? I hope she was.

"You even more unusual than I thought," he marveled, turning, ready to go back to work and leave me behind. As I thought he would.

"And I'll be going away to school for a little while. So, it's not really a good idea for me to start going with someone right now."

Walking away, he nodded his head.

Too bad. I liked the stinging way his touch had jolted me back to a part of myself that I didn't know existed, even with Lee.

Turning around, he came back and stood next to me, gesturing with his hand. "Maybe you'll write me when you are away?" He kept his voice lower still. "We could be pen pals."

That wouldn't hurt anything. "I would like that."

He cupped his hand around his mouth, aiming his words in the direction of Wilda, who had busied herself at the serving table so she could hear, wiping it down as we talked. "Wilda knows where I live. She'll give you the address, even though she won't want to." He said the last part real loud so Wilda was sure to hear it.

He held out his hand and I put my small one in it. Gently shaking it, he turned it over and put his moist juicy lips to the back side of it. That devil feeling came back to me and I swallowed. Hard. Maybe that would make it go away.

It didn't.

No. It lingered, throbbed, wrapped around me, tightening its hold on my heart. "It's nice to meet you, Miss Annie."

The intimate moment was over in an instant. Caleb got loud again. "Good to see you, Miss Wilda. I'll tell my mother that your pie was pretty good." I giggled.

"Get out of here, Caleb West," she shouted from behind me. "Get yourself on back to work and leave this girl alone." I turned to her and she was actually shaking her fist at him as he jogged back toward the groves.

Was the relationship she had with his mother all that was wrong with him? I respected Miss Wilda ever since I had been in

Tampa. I didn't want to hurt her feelings by asking her for Caleb West's address.

I opened my mouth to ask her more, but everything about him was swept to the side as we washed the dishes after the men returned to the grove. I resolved to put Caleb West and his strange feelings, strange smile, beautiful teeth, and large rounded arms out of my mind. God had another purpose for me and I had best put my mind to it.

One week later, I said a sad goodbye to the Lees, Wilda, and Paulina and took the train to Dothan to take Arthur to his grandmother.

One of Lee's brothers came to pick us up at the train depot. It was early in the morning and he bundled us in the back of his wagon. My trunk went on ahead to New York and I carried only a small grip with me. I didn't bring much for Arthur because I knew I would be able to give Mama Nan some money to keep him and she would see to what he needed. Just as I would if he were with me.

We were spirited to Mama Nan's and when we got there, she wrapped the both of us in a big hug. Arthur went right to her, recalling his grandmother well and although it made my heart ache a bit, I knew that I was doing right for his future.

"Is he here?"

"He's at the cabin, no doubt sleeping it off, daughter. He didn't take this news very well."

"Well I appreciate that you didn't say anything about when we were coming."

"He'll know you were here, because of Arthur."

"I hope I'll be gone before that. I'm not staying long." My skin prickled like I wore needles.

She put Arthur down at her feet and he went to the corner where she kept a toy box for any of her grandchildren who visited her.

"This is a wonderful opportunity you have landed, daughter. God's blessing is on your work. You have to do what you do."

She showed me to her small bedroom, where I freshened up while she made us both breakfast. I told her all about the gowns and dresses I had made during the months that I was in Tampa. She loved hearing all the details, as if they were from a story in the society papers.

The Atlanta train wasn't due to leave until near midnight, so we had a good long visit.

The time soon came that I had to part from my baby. The inevitable time.

"Come, Arthur. I'ma give you a bath."

"It's not Saturday." My bright boy pointedly let me know when he was due for a bath. I bit my lip to stop from laughing at him, but when I heated the water in the galvanized tub and put some soap flakes in there, he was persuaded to jump in. Like the good boy he was.

"When you wake up," I explained to him as he bedded down on the small pallet in Mama Nan's room, "I'm not going to be here."

"Where you going to be, Mama?"

"I'm going to a city. To a special school. But I'll be back for you. Soon. You will stay here with Mama Nan and Daddy will come to see you."

"He will?" His small forehead wrinkled up.

"He will."

"And you won't be back for a while?" His sweet voice made a seam into my heart, as I held on to the last words he would speak to me for a long time.

"It will go by so fast, you'll see." I couldn't resolve to send him any letters because Mama Nan couldn't read and who knew what Lee would do with a letter I sent. "I will send you something from the city. You'll know I'm thinking about you when you get it."

He seemed satisfied with that and so, to thank him, I told him as many stories as he wanted. I told them all to him, over and over and over again until his long, curly eyelashes swept down toward his sweet cheeks.

One sweep.

Another sweep.

One more sweep.

Then those beautiful lashes stayed down and my precious boy was off to dreamland. I wanted to kiss his soft cheeks just once more, but that would not help his sleep. Instead, I inhaled the sweet, sweet scent of his freshly washed hair and relished the way it sprung under my lips when I put the lightest kiss on the crown of his head.

Just before eleven I left in the back of my brother-in-law's wagon, slipping out of town without having to face Lee.

Or so I thought. Lee's brother left me on the platform to wait for the train and I was nervous the whole time. I was right to be.

The train whistle sounded in the distance and I stood up from the colored waiting room as if a firework was in me. The man who worked the train station signaled that I was getting up too soon, but I wanted to be on that train, away from Dothan, and away from Lee.

The door opened, and a gust of wind blew Lee in. He saw me and his eyes narrowed as he came forward, marching, stepping, hell-bent on destruction.

I stood next to the white man who was beginning to process the people who were there to get on the train.

"Get over here, Annie," Lee said.

"I won't."

"I told you to get over here."

The white man looked at Lee. "Do you have a ticket, boy?"

"I do not."

"Then step out of the way."

I moved closer to the white man.

"Oh, I see how it is, Annie. You have all of the opportunity in the world and you just leave me and your baby here like we are nothing to you."

I turned away from him.

The white man announced all of the train stops between Dothan and Atlanta and I gave him a gaze that said *Please process me first.*

He paid me no mind.

"You a disgrace, Annie. A disgrace. How dare you leave us?" Lee stood apart from the line, insulting me as I waited to get on the train.

"Go home, Lee. You . . . you're intoxicated. Please."

"Where did you learn a long word like that? An ignorant thing like you?" He grabbed my arm and his hold on me was like steel, death, and hate all rolled into one. The way he touched me was as if the very last thing he was going to do was to let me get on that train.

I closed my eyes and made a wish. Or it was more like a prayer. Something about David and Goliath popped into my mind. So many times I had heard the story of little David overcoming that big, strong Philistine who didn't expect to be defeated. Lee wouldn't expect to be defeated either. Not by little, teeny Annie.

I need strength, God.

"Let me go, Lee." And my arm slipped from his grasp.

I thrust my ticket at the white man and walked away. I was not afraid of Lee anymore. Not even Lee was going to stop me from being what I was.

A designer.

Chapter Nineteen

It had been many years since I had been in a classroom, given that my education stopped at the eighth grade. Even then, what I got in the way of education had been spotty. I had recognized early on that my teachers in some areas, like math, didn't know much more than I did. In that part of Alabama, teachers only needed a few years of school beyond us to be able to teach.

I think I spoke so well and wrote well enough because those were areas of strength for Grandma Georgia and Mama. Still, my application to S. T. Taylor Design School must have impressed them enough because they sent me an enthusiastic acceptance letter.

The first time I stepped foot off the train in New York City, I could sense a new and different feeling there. Montgomery and then Tampa were the biggest cities I had known. Even though they were big, there was still something of the slower Southern pace about them. New York City practically throbbed.

It was wonderful. I could see now why Mrs. Lee thought it essential for me to come here.

The boardinghouse was perfect. Only young Negro women stayed there, and we each had a small bedroom to ourselves.

It was overseen by an older widow, Mrs. Wilkerson, who kept things nice for us. The cleanliness of the place impressed me and the looks of the other young women, some there for school, some for work, showed they all were serious-minded and not just about a good time. I was invited to take a nap before dinner of thinly cut pork chops, rice, gravy, and green beans. There was a custard pie for dessert.

In the evenings, young women stayed in the parlor, at Mrs. Wilkerson's encouragement, reading Paul Laurence Dunbar and other poets aloud in excited and vibrant voices. Sometimes, they had their gentlemen friends join the readings, providing a male voice if the poem required it. This way, they could pass the time and avoid slipping off to their rooms and engaging in illicit activities. I would sit off quietly to the side and watch them, smiling at their antics as I wrote to Mrs. Lee.

I noticed there was a small hand-cranked sewing machine in a corner of the parlor and I asked Mrs. Wilkerson if it was available for use. "Why yes. It's here in case young ladies wish to make their clothes instead of buying something more expensive."

Thank God. Mrs. Lee had been generous, but now I had a way to make even more money to save for my shop. My hands always itched to be productive and if it meant helping others and gaining a clientele here in New York, that was so much the better.

Mrs. Wilkerson guided her ladies to an A.M.E. church that was down the street and we went in groups every week. That first Sunday, I found myself giving thanks to the Almighty for this opportunity and asked Him to guide my footsteps in going back to school after being away from it for such a long time.

I made sure to get up very early on Monday to make my way to the campus to enroll for classes. I ate a good breakfast—for me—of porridge and a slice of bacon. I had learned about the streetcars and trolley systems I would have to take to get to the school.

"The line for the underground railway isn't ready yet for you to take, dearie," Mrs. Wilkerson told me.

"That's okay. It sounds like a lot to do right now, and I would like to get used to the school first." I had never seen such a wonder before. One new thing at a time.

"You'll get used to it quick enough."

So it was a streetcar and then a trolley that dropped me off right in front of the school building. Today I wore my rust-colored day suit with a cream-colored shirtwaist. The things I chose for myself were always made well, but not too showy. I was not a canvas—that was the intent for those I made my creations for. I had always wondered at how Mrs. Lee was drawn to my subdued dove-gray suit, but then, she was a woman with fantastic taste and a great eye.

The design school was on the fourth floor of a small building. When I entered I could see a marble staircase on the left, but there was also an elevator.

What a remarkable thing. People were going to higher floors without having to climb the stairs! And back then, you could see the people being lifted up and away into the air as they went. How wonderful!

I watched several people get off. There was a man in front in a navy-blue double-breasted uniform who was in charge of opening and closing the crisscross gates to the elevator. The marble staircase off to the left beckoned, but who would want to walk up the stairs when such a wonderful invention existed?

A number of young women, all dressed in a rather showy way in a bright rainbow of colors and each wearing a large hat, chattered and clattered into the elevator. Everyone seemed to know each other, which made me feel smaller than I already was, but I plunged ahead.

I stepped into the front of the elevator, a plain wren in my brown suit and small hat, to be the next to travel on that wonder, but a stern look from the operator made me hesitate. "What do you want?"

"I need to get to the fourth floor to the registrar's office."

The man's eyes widened, then narrowed. "You'll have to wait until this elevator space is clear. Or take the stairs."

I stepped off the elevator crammed with the young women, all of whom stared at me in an uncomfortable silence that sounded louder than anything I'd ever heard. The operator closed the gates in my face and took them up, up, up, zooming away from me.

Well.

There was nothing for me to do but to start climbing the stairs. I took my time and eventually reached the fourth floor and easily found the registrar's office, which was now crammed full of the young women I had seen on the first floor. Everyone was filling out a registration card.

The entire room went quiet when I stepped inside. More loud silence. When I reached the registrar's desk I greeted her with a cheerful voice. "I'm Ann Lowe Cone. I'm here to register for design school."

"Excuse me." The red-haired young woman in front of me wore a nice blue serge suit trimmed in white that looked like a uniform for the school. She stood up and left the room. When she returned, practically in the next minute, a gentleman in an impeccably tailored gray pin-striped suit came with her.

"I'm S. T. Taylor," the gentleman said.

I turned toward him. "Oh. Hello, sir. It's nice to meet you. I'm looking forward to coming to your school."

"Um. Yes. Right this way." He spread his hand in a gesture to the door and I walked through, with him following me, as every eye watched us departing the registration room.

Was he coming to register me and to discuss the classes that I needed to take? That would be so helpful, but my difficulty in getting upstairs in the first place made something that I didn't want to name turn over in my stomach and I remembered the sweet porridge and salty bacon I had eaten. I swallowed the sourness, praying they didn't come up. Not now.

We passed several classrooms, large sunny rooms with slanted desks perfect for drawing. There was another room full of sewing machines, all electronic, in the latest style. This school was like a fairyland for me.

Please let me go here.

Another prayer-wish.

I don't know why that popped in my mind, but something told me that having the named gentleman of the school take me down the hall to his office was not a good thing. "Please. Have a seat, Miss . . ."

"Mrs. Cone."

His forehead wrinkled. "That name sounds familiar."

"Yes." I opened my reticule where I carried my letter. "Here."

He took the letter from my trembling fingers and opened it. "Excuse me."

He left the office and I breathed out, feeling my corset tighter than ever. I was a firm believer in how undergarments played a pivotal role in defining a woman's shape and in the way they supported the fabric of a garment. Right now, I was feeling a little constricted and I found myself gazing at the forms, fabric, and fashion books that were on his shelves to distract myself.

Soon, though, Mr. Taylor returned with my letter in hand. "Mrs. Cone, there has been a mistake."

"What mistake?"

"Your admittance. We thought . . . well, we thought that you were an older lady of some years, given this, but I think that someone of your tender years might need a more basic school."

I folded my hands. "I've been sewing since I was eight."

"Well, this isn't a sewing school." He breathed out. "It's a design school. One of my assistants is processing your refund and . . ."

"I don't want a refund. I want my schedule."

"Well, that won't be possible, Mrs. Cone."

"Why not?"

"A design school, such as this, is very expensive. Maybe too much for someone of your young years to pay for."

I reached again into my reticule and pulled out my bankbook. I flipped it open to the first page, where the numbers lined up neatly. I held it out to him, my hand no longer trembling. "Is this enough money to go here?"

Mr. Taylor looked at the bankbook and his eyes nearly bugged out of his head. "Why, I . . . why, my goodness."

"Mrs. Dempsey Cowan Lee of Tampa, Florida, said I should go to this school. She paid. Is there a problem with me coming here?"

I was afraid of the answer but I knew I had to make him say it. Heat flushed all over me. No. I hadn't come this far and this close to hear S. T. Taylor of this design school tell me no.

"Well, to be blunt, Mrs. Cone, we did not know that you were a Negro."

"Did you need to be told that in advance? Or was the money Mrs. Lee sent as a deposit not good enough?"

"Now see here." He adjusted his waistcoat.

"Yes, sir?" I folded my hands and looked at him expectantly.

"We've never had a Negro here before."

"And now you do." I gazed directly into his gray eyes.

He coughed. "I'm afraid the students will . . ."

"You are the one in charge of things here. Why can't you set it up so I can attend and it be okay with them?"

"I don't make the rules." He moved some papers on his desk.

"Your name is on the school, Mr. Taylor."

It struck me that his name was the same word as Lee's profession. I wondered at the coincidence of it all. Would Lee Cone never leave me alone?

"Yes, but . . ."

I stood up, ready to be a canvas if I had to be. "I made this day suit. I don't usually dress myself as I would a client or act as a sandwich board, but my work was good enough to catch the eye of Mrs. Lee in Tampa. She is the widow of a very wealthy citrus magnate. I made the trousseaux and wedding gowns for her twin daughters last year."

His eyes wandered over the suit and I knew he could see evidence of my craftsmanship, even though the suit was plain. "What patterns did you use?"

I turned back around to face him. "I don't use patterns, sir."

Mr. Taylor jerked back in his seat. Good.

"No patterns?"

"No, sir. I see what I need to do in my head and I make it possible."

He stood. "I apologize, Mrs. Cone. Stay here. I'll return shortly."

I sat back down, my legs trembling and weak. Why did this have to happen? Just because I was a Negro? I had been so welcome in Tampa that it hadn't even occurred to me that would be a problem here in New York. Some folks had talked about how much better things were for Negros in the great North. I never expected to run into this kind of problem here.

It would be awful to have to return to Tampa, defeated, with my tail between my legs. I would have to go back to Dothan and Lee would be there, taunting me at how I thought I was something special and how the big white world had shown me I was just a Negro and worse than that, a Negro woman.

To Lee, as he had said to me many times, a Negro woman was nothing special.

I bit my bottom lip to keep it still and thought the prayer-wish in my head.

Please let me stay here.

Please let me stay here.

Please let me stay here.

The only good thing would be that I could see Arthur's sweet face that much quicker, but then what kind of example would I be setting for him? I had to let him see, as a boy of the Negro race, that he could do something better for himself. That his mother was not just a seamstress but a designer who created or made up dresses out of her head. If I went back, he would never, ever be proud of me and then I wouldn't be able to send him to a college one day.

I would be a failure.

All because of something I couldn't help.

The door opened and I inclined my face to it, blinking hard to keep my tears at bay.

"Mrs. Cone. I believe that, well, we have a compromise. If you will agree to it," Mr. Taylor announced.

I stood. "I can stay?"

He held out a registration slip. "Miss Winters will discuss the

particulars of the arrangement with you. Thank you for coming
to S. T. Taylor Design School—and welcome."

He nodded and extended his hand toward the door and the
red-haired lady emerged from there.

"Oh. Thank you. Thank you so much, Mr. Taylor." I gripped
my reticule in my relief.

Something in his eyes didn't face me directly, I realized later,
but I was so happy that I was allowed to stay, that I didn't care.

Miss Winters, a young lady as frosty as her name, took me back
to the larger room where everyone else was signing up for their
classes. "You will take Introduction to the Principles of Design,
Fabric and Textiles, and Fitting for Ladies. All of your classes will
take place in Classroom 24."

She handed me a sheet and told me where to sign. I did as I
was bid. She retrieved a stack of textbooks and handed them to
me, smiling at me with a grin that I didn't like. It was not friendly.

"We'll see you for class at 8 A.M."

I went down the marble staircase and out the door. I had done
it! I clutched the books to myself and walked to the trolley. As
soon as I got to the boardinghouse for lunch, I ate my sandwich
and spent the rest of the day looking in delight through the textbooks at this new world of information.

When I showed up at 7:55 A.M. the next day, Miss Winters took
me to Classroom 24. I sat at one of the desks with a slanted face
and watched as everyone else went to the classroom next door,
laughing and chatting. I looked at the clock in front of the room.
8:00 A.M.

My room was empty. Next door was where everyone gathered. I was supposed to be in Classroom 25, not 24, too.

"Good morning, students," Mr. Taylor intoned. "Welcome to

Introduction to the Principles of Design." His voice floated down the hall to me.

Why was I not next door? Had Miss Winters made a mistake?

I went to her office and knocked. When she opened the door, she looked down her long nose at me as if I were offal under her boot heel.

"Excuse me. Should I not be in Classroom 25? The one next door?"

"No. This was the arrangement. Mr. Taylor has allowed you to stay, but you will take all of your classes from Classroom 24. The back door of Classroom 25 is open for you to hear."

"But I cannot see the board or the examples or . . ."

Her eyes gleamed with mischief. "That's the arrangement. Take it or leave it, Mrs. Cone. And it is too late to refund your tuition now that the term has started." That thin, cold smile pulled across her lips again.

Something in me sunk, but then I thought about having to go back to Dothan to face Lee. And I knew what I would do.

There was a cloakroom, a place where the students would keep their wraps in the winter time, between Classrooms 24 and 25. When I got back to Classroom 24, I pulled my desk to the very front of the room, just before it became the cloakroom for Classroom 25. I angled my seat so that I could hear Mr. Taylor and had a straight shot to see the board with my young eyes. It was prayer-wish time.

Please let me be successful and not waste Mrs. Lee's money.

I had no choice.

Chapter Twenty

When I was about seven, my mother had to go to a big house in Clayton to make last-minute adjustments on a fitting for a bridal gown. Grandma wasn't feeling well, so Mama took me along but I had to promise to be quiet and work on my flowers. She sewed up a little pink reticule for me so I could carry my scraps of fabric, needles, thread, and trimmings. It had drawstrings and I wore it on my wrist—like I was a grown lady. The woman getting married had a little sister who was also going to be in the wedding. When we got there, the bride said, "Oh look, here's someone to play with Susie."

The bride's mother looked at me and said, "Isn't she a sweet little pickaninny? Yes, you and Susie should go out and play."

Play? I wanted to sit with my mother, watch her work so I could fashion my fabric roses, but when I saw my mother nod at me, I went with Susie to her backyard, where she had a playhouse—a duplicate of the house where she lived.

She told me we were going to have a tea party. We went to the kitchen of the main house and the cook gave us some ginger cookies on a pretty plate. We took the pretty plate to the playhouse.

Susie had a real china teapot and poured the tea into small china cups. It was only water, but she called it tea. When she poured mine, she dunked a lump of dirt in my cup.

"What did you do that for?"

"So it will match us. Mine matches me and now yours matches you."

This seemed perfectly satisfactory to Susie, but I did not like it at all. Even I knew better than to drink water with a big dirt clod in it.

She offered me a ginger cookie, but I was afraid to take one, lest it fade into my brown hand. I sat, rigid, thinking about how my skin matched the cup with dirt in it. Susie was happy at her little tea party, but I just sat there, waiting for enough time to pass so that I could walk home with my mother and ask her questions about the bridal gown and forget all about stupid, mean Susie.

Now, at the design school, I had no distractions from people who wanted to treat me as less than. I had only my work. So that's what I did. If I had to be in the adjacent classroom, which was really the back of a cloakroom, I would make it comfortable.

Much of my time in New York City was lonely. I missed Arthur and my supportive Floridian friends. I needed to keep my days filled so that I would be less aware of how I was being treated at school and to mark off time, so every day, on my way home, I went to my new fabric haunts in the Garment District, between Thirty-First and Forty-Second Streets. I arrived back at the boardinghouse in time for dinner and the evening activities.

A lot of the buyers in the Garment District were Jewish and took to me because they knew I knew quality. They recognized instantly that I made my own clothes and spoke to me as an artisan, which lit a warm fire in my soul. When I explained that I was a student at the design school, some expressed surprise. One of the buyers even dubbed it a horrible school after I told them how I was treated.

We understood one another because the Jewish buyers also knew what it was like to be outcast in an unwelcoming world. Over time, the buyers gifted me with remnants, which I used to make my trademark flowers to sell—more money for my shop— and, when I received a big remnant of linen, a hanging curtain for the classroom cloakroom. The curtain, which I put together using the hand-cranked machine in the boardinghouse parlor, covered the wooden shelving that hung over the coats in the cloakroom. Each day, as the students were dismissed, they had to pass my little haven, which I regularly added something else decorative to. Once I had the curtain hung, I made clusters of linen flowers to gather up the cloth at intervals, like bunting.

When I had hung the first cluster, one of the students stopped at my desk.

"Who made that?" She pointed a slender finger at the mini cluster.

"I did."

I turned around and adjusted my slope desk to be ready for that day's lessons. I had also decorated the desk with an end of white velvet with gold trimmings.

"You did? Made the flowers?"

"Yes. I've been making them since I was a small child."

"Mary," the young woman called to a friend. "Look at this."

Mary came forward and saw the small clusters. Her eyes slid up and down my body, seemingly inspecting me for some reason. "Why are you putting them there?"

"Since I have to be here by the orders of Mr. Taylor, I am enhancing my surroundings in the best way that I can."

"Mr. Taylor said you had to be here?"

"Yes. This is where I have to sit for class." *Since I cannot sit in the same room with the rest of you because of my mud-colored skin.* It was on the tip of my tongue to say the same words that I wanted to say to Susie oh so long ago.

Mr. Taylor came swanning in. "Everyone, please find your seats! Everyone!"

The girls went to their desks and he stood at the back of Classroom 25, stopped by the display in the cloakroom. "Well. This is something."

Mary spoke up. "She said she made those flower clusters." Her tone implied that she didn't believe me.

I took on the fullest Miss-Lizzie-First-Lady-of-Alabama-tone when I spoke up: "I've been making them since I was a small child."

He looked at the clusters of rosebuds all around the cloakroom. "It's very fine work."

"Thank you. It's very easy. I use scraps."

"It would be just the thing for an evening gown I'm designing." Now Mary's tone came more softly.

An idea hit me. "I could show them."

Mr. Taylor opened his mouth and then gestured with his hands for me to enter Classroom 25. I stepped foot into the light, with the spring sun shining into the room.

"We have a little time around today's lesson. Everyone! This is Mrs. Cone. She says that she makes flowers out of fabric."

"I do make flowers out of fabric, Mr. Taylor." I swallowed as all of the attention of the entire room of eyes of varying shades stared at me. I was dressed in my dove gray today, muted but respectful. "I sold them for extra money as a girl, and for pin money when I was married to my husband."

He paled a little. "You are no longer married? I thought you were a widow."

The room stilled. "No, sir. He wasn't the kindest of husbands and so I took my son and started a new life."

"I see. Well, onto the flowers."

I took up a length of our practice fabric. "There are several kinds that you can make, but I decided on clusters of roses for my decorations, for back there in, Classroom 24." I cleared my throat and Mr. Taylor had the grace to redden. Good.

Twenty minutes later, everyone had made their own clusters, some much better than others, which enabled me to walk around the room, learning names and making suggestions for improvement.

"What about the others?" Mary demanded.

I spread my hands. "I know Mr. Taylor wants us to get started with class today. I would be happy to show something else at another time." I nodded to him and made my strides back to the cloakroom.

When I reached the threshold between the rooms, Mr. Taylor spoke. "Mrs. Cone, thank you for that lesson."

I turned on my heel. "You're welcome, sir."

I slid into my seat, setting my desk to the right angle so that I could see his board and hear his lesson.

That day, when we had our lunch break, several of the students made room for me to get on the elevator.

That was a start.

Over time, as Mr. Taylor taught various techniques, he would come back to the cloakroom to see my work and marvel over the extraordinary quality of what I had done. One day he taught the round flowers that I put on many a skirt of many an Alabama belle. He called it trapunto. He walked among my classmates and showed them my work, then came back to my little desk area. "This is an exquisite example, Mrs. Cone. Where did you learn your skill?"

"My mother and her mother before her. Both sewed for the finest of ladies in the South. We were the dressmakers behind the first lady of Alabama's gowns when her husband was inaugurated in 1911."

Everyone swiveled to look at me, angled from the cloakroom. "You did?"

"Yes. My grandmother's work was so fine, the people that owned her asked my grandfather to keep her around as a condition of selling her so that she could continue to sew for her missus. She put these round flowers on her dress all the time."

"Where did she learn it, then?" Mr. Taylor demanded.

"I do not know, sir, she departed this world several years ago. So did my mother. When she died, she was not finished with an order of four dresses for the first lady. I had to finish the order myself."

"You did?"

"Yes, sir."

"Well, no wonder your work is of such high quality. It seems that your mother and grandmother were some of the best possible teachers out there."

"I would like to think so, sir."

He turned from me to continue the lesson, but after that, he allowed me to come forth from the cloakroom to show other students alternate ways of creating a sewing effect if someone did not completely understand what he said.

One Friday in May, he asked me to stay after class. "I would like to arrange for you to take tests in some of the classes," he said, "so that we may more correctly establish what classes you need to take and what you don't. Your work is of such high quality that you may not need to be here for the entire length of the program. I may be able to give you some credits toward your degree. Given what you have told me about your family, it would not be right for me to keep taking your money when you know so much already."

So, I sat for the exams and by the time I had completed them, he had figured out the remainder of my courses. I would finish the certificate for the program in October, instead of next April, six months early.

I wrote to the Lees to tell them of my achievement and they were very pleased at how I had distinguished myself in New York City. Mama Nan was also very pleased to hear this news in a letter that I wrote to Lee's aunt and she resolved to keep it secret that I would be returning sooner than I thought. Lee had been to the house several times to see Arthur and make friends with him, after he had gotten up off the new teenage bride he had acquired—illegally.

When I learned of that, I made sure to write to the county clerk in Dothan and sent the money to start the procedures of divorce from Lee. But he surprised me by beating me to it. By the time the hot, humid New York summer of 1917 ended, the divorce papers came to me. I signed them and I was a free woman.

I had a few friends at the Garment markets and made arrangements through them for special bolts of material to be shipped to Florida for the Christmas ball sewing for the Lees that I would need to do. I knew the ladies in Tampa would be delighted at my selections. It would be good to return to New York every so often and seek out fabrics from my friends so that Mrs. Lee and her daughters would have the best material in the United States.

When October came, and I finished the course, there was a small graduation ceremony. Many of the students' families were there, but I was alone. In the huge crowd of families watching the graduation fashion show, there was no one to support me or to marvel over my work. I was fine with that.

However, when my models came out, many in the audience exclaimed at my designs and swarmed me once the show was over with requests to design for them. But I refused, for two reasons.

I had come to New York alone and made a success of myself with support from the Lees. It seemed only fair for me to remain exclusive to them and their friends. This was the beginning of a policy I had created in honor of my grandmother: I would sew only for the highest of society. I was not interested in sewing for anyone at a cut-rate price, for it was those in the highest society who had treated me well.

The second reason was obvious to me, but not to the other people asking me to design for them. Not once, in all of the months when I had helped the other students, showed them what to do, aided Mr. Taylor in teaching them, or agreed to show my work as an example, not once had any of them suggested that I should come out of the cloakroom into the light of the classroom.

Not once.

So, for that humiliation, I would keep my work exclusively for those who could pay for it.

Chapter Twenty-One

I could barely be still long enough to leave New York and to hold my baby in my arms again. He had gotten so big while I was away. Of course he came to me, but I could tell that I had been away from him a long time—a good chunk of his little life. His good-natured way that he showed to everyone, including me, made tears come to my eyes.

Mama Nan told me all would be well. "We need to work out some kind of way to help you. Like that he should come visit every summer. He's no trouble. I love him and his cousins love him too. He needs his family."

I agreed. "How was Lee with him?"

She turned away. "He doesn't really understand Arthur. He's not really like him."

"I see. Well, we'll be leaving in the morning."

Mama Nan treated me like a queen and marveled over my certificate and told me how proud she was of me. "It's hard enough to be a Negro woman and, my word, you have done well to get in with some good white folks so you can get a good start in life."

"That's what my grandmother would say."

Her headscarf bounced as she nodded her head. "She right.

That's the only way right now for our people. And you can make a little way in the world and lift him up." She inclined her head toward Arthur, who was eating his dinner. "Send him to a college maybe."

"That's my plan. I don't want him to have a hard time."

She patted my hand. "You've struggled enough. And I know marriage to Lee didn't make it any easier."

"Well, we aren't married any longer. So it's okay."

She looked away. "He went ahead and married that young girl. She has no more sense than the good God gave a looney bird."

A little ruffle flittered in my stomach. Not over Lee, but in thinking of another young girl who would have her childhood and innocence stolen from her. Still, I wanted to be nice to her since she might have a child who would be related to my son. I wish I could have told her about Grandma's tea.

The next morning, we left Dothan on the train without incident and by the next day, we arrived at the stop at Lake Thonotosassa, where the Lees had arranged for Caleb West to pick us up.

The early morning dawned bright and hot, even though there was a swirl of fall in the air. Caleb West smiled from the train platform, where he waited as the train pulled into the station, waving wildly at us. I wasn't sure of his reception of me, since he had written a letter to me every so often but I had made no reply. My cheeks warmed at the memory of how I had not done as I had intended.

"It is sure good to see you again, Mrs. Cone. And look, you have your boy with you."

I was a little shy to see him here. I was grimy from riding in the Jim Crow section of the train with my young son in tow. The journey made it hard to sleep, and so we were both a little off-kilter. Still, when Arthur saw Caleb, he lifted his arms to him. "Up."

"*Up?* Ain't this boy something?"

Caleb obliged him and Arthur laid his head down on Caleb's broad shoulder, making himself comfortable at once. Caleb rubbed his back as Arthur drifted to sleep. "Fine boy you have here, Mrs. Cone."

"Thank you." He carried Arthur to the wagon and laid him down in the back on top of some sacks, and my son slept on.

"Bless him. He's so tired. I'll come back for your trunk. It'll be all right."

I felt a little jealous of Arthur sleeping in the back but after Caleb helped me up onto the wagon seat next to him, a settled feeling came into me. Safety. A feeling that I was not used to. At all.

"They say you did well at that school."

"Who told you?"

"Mrs. Lee. Wilda wouldn't tell me nothing."

I laughed a little bit, and so did he, thinking of how Wilda disliked him.

His deep voice took on a serious tone. "So was it as easy up there for us as some say?"

I sobered too, and that settled, safe feeling that I had betrayed me. "It was hard. Much harder than I thought it would be. That was why I didn't write. It was hard."

As the mule plodded along the dirt road in the early morning, I told Caleb West everything that had happened to me in New York. And he listened to me. It was a good feeling to have a friend to talk to. I had made acquaintance with people in New York, but no real friends. It had been a long time since I had poured my heart out to someone not related to me. Too long.

When we pulled into the Lees' yard way, Wilda opened the door and came out, waving her arms at us. My heart beat a little harder to see her. She had gotten a little more frail in the six months that I had been away. "Praise be! You're back."

I ran into her arms, embracing her as if I were a little child. It was good to be missed by someone and I said so.

"Oh, honey, I'm not the only one who missed you! Believe me, you were missed, but we all so proud of what you did up there in New York City." She pulled me back. "I have a special breakfast ready, with all of the trimmings."

And she surely did. Fresh hot biscuits, fried fish, fried chicken, grits, scrambled eggs, bacon, and orange marmalade. It was the best food that I had eaten, but the company of Wilda and Caleb, who she reluctantly said could eat with us since he had gotten up so early to pick me up from the train, was worth it. Soon he left to go back for my trunk and Miss Wilda and I watched him depart.

Miss Wilda folded her arms. "I guess you could do worse."

"Oh, Miss Wilda. I just got back here. I'm not looking for a man."

"Honey. We all looking."

We both laughed and then I held up my hand. "Good news. It ended up that Lee divorced me. Said I ran away with another man, so they gave him the divorce."

"Fool. 'Less he's counting Arthur, who's just three. He's not another man. Sounds as if you are well shed of him."

"Well, if someone's mama cannot speak well of them . . . let's just say that Mama Nan was very supportive while she had Arthur. And he's married to someone else now."

Wilda shook her head. "Someone else's innocent child. I'll pray for her. But the Lees will be getting up soon and I know that Miss Josie will be happy to see you."

And she was.

Time passed as I settled back into my happy life of sewing dresses for the Lees and their chosen friends. Mrs. Lee's son, LaMarcus, was to be married in the spring of 1919 and his bride wanted a dress made by me. I was happy to oblige her and designed something especially for her so she could brag her design was straight from New York City. The groom had served in World War I and came home to marry his bride in his handsome uniform.

Seeing the two of them together so happy after their wedding triggered something in me. I was lonely. Caleb West had been very patient with me ever since my return from New York. And he gave me space and time. He and Arthur got along so well. It tickled me to see my son with the influence of a man in his life. Arthur was going to be five and as he got older, the more he would need a man's hand.

So, one day on our usual Sunday walk on the beach of the lake, I let Caleb hold my hand and before I went back into the house, we shared a brief kiss. It had been many years since I let a man kiss me, but when his lips reached out to me, I lifted my chin up, up, up to him. When our lips met, parts of me that I had forgotten existed thawed out from neglect and rose back to life like when Jesus was resurrected. Caleb's hand cupped my chin so gently, I wanted to cry that a man could be so tender to me.

Lee had never been tender like that.

Caleb West had seen into my soul in the kiss we shared. When I had told him the story of my humiliation in New York, I had bonded with him in a way that I had never bonded with Lee. For I was a woman now, a fully-grown woman, and could make my own choices.

Then the Spanish flu came, and I almost lost him. How was it possible that some teeny germs no one could even see could strike down a man in his prime? He had fallen down at work in front of some customers, who were disgusted that he had dared to get sick on the job.

Mrs. Lee knew what he had come to mean to me, and she let me go to him to care for him. "You can leave Arthur here. If you go into Tampa, you should stay there and take care of him and his mother, instead of going back and forth from here, which might put him in danger."

Once again, or really for the third time, the Lees had come to the rescue in my life. I didn't want to leave Arthur behind, but Paulina, who had been hired in my absence in the house, took over his care while she practiced on her sewing, along with other duties like helping her aunt Wilda in the kitchen, so I was covered.

The Wests, however, had no one else to help them. It was up to me. Caleb had nearly worn himself out taking care of his mother. She unfortunately died of the Spanish flu, so I never really came to know her.

Once she was buried, I nursed Caleb and we got closer over the months as his strength depleted. There was nothing to do but to help him be clean and change his sheets, and isolate ourselves from others until he finally came around and slowly regained his strength.

"I don't know how to even thank you, Annie. I feel so grateful that you've come into my life. I can't even . . . I mean, I'm sad that Mama died, but I feel God's blessing that you were able to help us both."

"There was no one else to do it. I didn't want to leave you all alone."

He held my hand. "What about Arthur?"

"Paulina at the Lees' is taking care of him. I had thoughts

about taking him back to Dothan to his grandmother's, where the flu isn't as bad, but the Lees really helped me out."

"I'm glad they did."

"They've been like family to me. A real blessing. How could I not pass it on?"

He squeezed my hand. "I've been thinking. Really thinking, here in this bed after this terrible flu tried to take me on away from here. I want you in my life. For good. Will you be my wife, Annie?"

His wife. Mrs. West, instead of Mrs. Cone. Caleb's instead of Lee's.

A new name for a new life.

I squeezed his hand, then looked down at our joined hands. "I think I told you I want to open a shop. A dress shop. When I do that, I'll want to live over the shop."

"That's okay with me. And Arthur should be with us. He's a fine boy. I'd be proud to make him my son, if you wouldn't mind that."

A father for Arthur. A man, a real man, not a fool like Lee, to look out for him and love him. To show him a man's way. To be with him. To do things for him that I never could.

Still, something held me back from accepting Caleb. "I just want to be sure you understand, I'm saving for this shop and to make sure Arthur gets a better start in life. I hope to send him to a Negro college one day."

"Whatever you want for him, Annie, is what I want. And maybe, down the road, we can have little ones of our own." Caleb shook his head.

Well, there was the rub. There would be no little ones of our own. I gulped. "When I had Arthur, I was so young, it tore me up inside. They said I would never have any more babies. So maybe you need to get someone else to be your wife." I let go of his hand, but he grasped me by the wrist.

I lowered my head. He tilted my chin up. "Aww, Annie. I don't care nothing about where they come from. We can adopt. I just want to be with you, honey."

I slid into his chest and he held me to him, tight, tight, tight. Tears slid down my face at the thought that in this journey for me to be respected and seen in the world as a person who designed things, I could find someone who would love me for myself and would understand. It amazed me.

It seemed to be a wonderous thing. Too wonderous to be believed.

And it was.

Chapter Twenty-Two

*W*ell, I knew folk would be shocked to learn that I was going to have a real wedding and not a visit to a courthouse, but I didn't care about what I was going to wear.

Mrs. Lee certainly was.

"Annie, you must have a gown made from some of the goods that you've sent down here to us."

In my heart and mind, I knew that the designs I saw in my head were not for me. They were God's way of speaking to me about what other women needed.

"Ma'am, I have several suits. I'm perfectly fine wearing one of them. We're going to have a picnic in the orange groves where we first came together. That's all we need. We want the folks who are dear to us to have a good time, but we don't need a fine church wedding. All of my money needs to go to my shop."

It was the beginning of 1920, and a lot of time had gone past since Caleb's illness. Arthur was shooting up like a weed and soon I would have to make his short pants to wear to school. It was so hard to believe that so much time was flying by.

One night after I came down out of the sewing room for dinner, the five of us—Wilda, Paulina, Caleb, Arthur, and me—were eating our dinner. The Lees had been served in the dining room. They were having their good time with their family and we were having ours in the kitchen. Suddenly, the doorway between the dining room and the kitchen blew open, and there appeared Mrs. Lee *and* Mr. LaMarcus, her son who was visiting.

We all wiped our mouths and stood up. It was one thing if Mrs. Lee came in. She was our boss, of course, but she was like regular folk. However, Mr. LaMarcus was like the big boss and so it was a whole other thing if he came into the kitchen.

Wilda looked toward him. She was really the only one who could look him in the eye because she was older than him and had more of the manners from the bad old times. "Sir?"

"Good evening, folks. I hate to disturb your dinner, but . . ." He looked embarrassed, a rare look for such a powerful white man. He turned to Mrs. Lee, who stepped forward. "These matters are usually in my mother's jurisdiction."

"Annie, now listen. Don't get married in the courthouse. If you don't want a church wedding, that's fine too. What about the garden? Here?"

Caleb and I looked at each other, puzzled.

"Ma'am?" Caleb said.

"If you get married here in the garden, at least you can have a nice dress for yourself. Think of how it might be a form of advertising for folks to see what you can do."

"And we will pay for it, as a wedding gift. So that you don't have to take from your shop funds." Mr. LaMarcus's face grew less red. "There, Mother. I said it. May I return to my roast now?"

She patted his shoulder. "Of course, dear."

He turned to leave and we sat back down.

"Annie. Just give it some thought. Please." She turned and went back into the dining room. When she did, we all laughed a little bit, but under our breath so she couldn't hear. The last thing we wanted to do was to cause offense to Mrs. Lee, who was such a fine employer.

"I never saw white folks carry on so about a colored wedding," Wilda declared, helping herself to half a pork chop.

Caleb shook his head. "Seems to me that the getting married is the thing, not the ceremony."

I pushed back my plate. I wasn't hungry any longer. "That's why I told her I don't care what I wear."

Paulina spoke up: "Still, she makes a good point. It is kind of an advertisement to show what you can do."

I nodded. "That's the only possible way I might be able to imagine something for myself other than my usual plain walking suits."

Paulina nodded. "Yes, and instead of a hat, I'll fix your hair and put orange blossoms in."

I shook my head. "Now you are going too far. I'm not some young virgin getting married." I certainly wasn't. Caleb and me had had all kinds of fun over the past year since he had recovered from the flu. I discovered what it was really like to have a man in your bed and to have real pleasure from the act. We might have jumped the gun a bit, but I felt cheated all of those years I was Lee's wife and had no idea he knew nothing about what he was doing.

Paulina helped herself to some more potatoes, but Wilda moved the bowl from her before she could get carried away.

"That was nice of them to offer to pay." Wilda nodded.

"It was. Although I really would rather that money go to the shop." I fretted and bowed my head to finish my dinner. Every spare cent was spoken for and making a dress that I would only wear one time seemed so wasteful.

The kind of waste that white folks could afford.

No one said anything else. They knew what my dream was. They probably all agreed. Even if I made myself a new dress that I was supposed to only wear once, I knew I could figure out what to do with it after the wedding so that it didn't go to waste.

I had sent several lengths of pure white silk, bolts of it, to Florida for wedding gowns that I might make for ladies there. Enough remained for dresses for the other Lee daughters, and even for my friend Miss Nellie whenever she got married in the future. She was a lanky, long-legged seventeen-year-old, and she certainly didn't need a wedding gown yet. When I went to the sewing room, I uncovered the silk, fretting, thinking about how to use the smallest amount of it—and then the idea occurred to me.

The end of the Great War and the coming of Spanish flu had changed a few things. I didn't have to have some grand gown. I could style myself a dress with a ragged hem and wear the orange blossoms in my hair. An uneven hem, short in the front, longer in the back, would work fine for the wedding and then I could alter the design later so the dress had a shorter hem. The shorter hem, or ragged hem, had been growing in popularity on regular dresses over the last year, due to some fabric shortages in the wake of the war. I didn't recall seeing this hem on any wedding dresses, though. If I made a ragged hem dress, I would need new shoes, but if I bought the right kind, I could get some wear out of them too.

The plan was made and the great day arrived. Sallie wasn't able to come, but Mama Nan did and stayed with us at Caleb's house. Arthur was happy to see his grandmother again, and he would stay with her while Caleb and I honeymooned at a cottage not far away.

It was a beautiful, hot April day. Paulina and Nell insisted on helping me dress. Mama Nan was also there to see my new wedding finery, a dress of my own design with long bell sleeves, a square neckline, and the ragged hem of white silk that showed the lower part of short legs in the front and made a sweeping short train in the back.

As promised, Paulina dressed my hair with oil and used a hot comb to straighten it, then wove in orange blossoms. She had taken a hairdressing course in Tampa with a woman who had gone to one of Madame C. J. Walker's beauty schools. It looked very good, much better than my usual. Paulina had been leaning more toward doing hair, away from sewing. I was a little bit disappointed with her choice but she had become such a good young friend to me, I just wanted her to be happy. Honestly, she could do both, but I would be on the lookout for another young girl to train. I hoped to hire someone soon after we returned from our honeymoon.

"You're the bee's knees, Annie," Nell whispered when I turned around, completely dressed.

Mama Nan clapped her hands together. "Caleb's going to love it."

"Thank you all. This is something else for me. I'm not used to being the center of attention." I smoothed the dress down.

There was a knock at the door and Mrs. Lee was there. "Everyone is gathered outside in the garden. I would like to have a word with the bride, please."

Paulina, Nell, and Mama Nan went outside, leaving me alone with Mrs. Lee.

I was a bit nervous. "Thank you, ma'am. For the gift of the fabric for the dress."

She nodded her head. "Leave it to you to think of something practical and beautiful all at the same time. It's so clever. Everyone who sees it will want one."

"Nell says it's the bee's knees. I didn't even know bees had knees." I liked to make her laugh at the antics of her youngest child.

However, Mrs. Lee smiled but did not laugh. "Nell would."

What did she want?

"I'm happy for you getting married, Annie. I'm going to miss having you on the grounds but I understand that you want your own home. It was so prudent of Caleb to make sure he had a home before a wife."

"Yes. That was something that mattered to him." And honestly, was made easier by his mother's death.

"When you marry, you bring your things together with your husband's. However"—she stepped closer to me—"your shop, your dream, must be something that is separate from him. You were planning on that, right?"

It was a question that had haunted me. Caleb had asked me about it. "I was thinking about that. Do you think I should?"

"Oh my, yes. It must be separate. Promise me that you will do that."

"Yes, ma'am. I promise."

"Keep your shop nest egg in your own name. Not Annie West, but Annie Cone."

I nodded my head. "I can do that."

"The shop must be something of yours, not his." She patted my hand with her own smooth hand, one that had never known a hard day's work. "Trust me in this."

"I do. Thank you for the advice."

She withdrew into the hallway and I looked in the long mirror at myself. Mrs. Lee had been the white person my grandmother told me I should look for to take care of me. I was about to marry Caleb West, yes, but I was certainly going to do as she directed me. My shop was something I had been working for since before this marriage. I certainly wouldn't stop now.

The door opened and I heard the pianoforte from the Lee parlor playing soft music. They had pushed it out toward the garden so that there would be music to accompany me down the aisle. I took in a deep breath. This was a real marriage, a grown woman's marriage. As I walked down the steps and toward my new destiny as Annie West, I took up a small bouquet of orange blossoms and mixed greens that the girls made for me. The fashion those days was to have a large armful of something, but I thought so much showiness for a second marriage was ridiculous. It was enough to have a new dress. The line had to be drawn somewhere.

As I walked down the aisle alone, I heard several women, some of the ladies from Caleb's church who had witnessed him grow up, inhale with a sharp breath. *Yes.* This dress was very effective. I was glad that I had agreed to make it and show myself off to the best advantage that I could.

Caleb greeted me in his new light summer suit of tan with mint-green accessories. He had a wide boater hat to match. He looked so handsome.

When I stepped to the decorated arbor, I put my hand in his, ready to become his wife. When the pastor mentioned the part about all my worldly goods, my fingers clasped onto my bouquet a little harder and some of the stems ran a green line onto the fabric of my dress. But I was determined to have my shop remain as my shop.

Quite a start to my new life as Mrs. West.

Chapter Twenty-Three

I mean, Caleb West had skills. He made a woman out of me and I don't mind saying so. Not at all. I still have dreams I wake up from with that tingly feeling all over myself from what he was able to do to me. And there are still times when I wonder . . . what if I had married him sooner? Maybe he would have understood me better what he did. Maybe he might have better understood my intended path in life.

After all, he always told me that those people in New York were fools and he was beyond glad that I had come home to Tampa like I had some sense. He was right, but I still had this niggling feeling that a little shop in Tampa, like the one that I opened the next year after we married, once we sold the house and moved into the space over the shop, wasn't what I was destined for.

Those folk in New York were wrong about me. To not have invited me into the room to learn was a large mistake and they were going to know it.

Someday.

Until then, I spent the next three years as Annie Cone West, sewing beautiful gowns for Floridian society by day, and as Mrs. West by night, freely writhing under, over, beside, and any which way with my husband. Of course, I was also Arthur's proud mother. One of the reasons we moved the shop space onto the verge of the colored part of Tampa was so Arthur could walk to school every morning.

I cried a bit when I sewed him his first short pants. No more dresses for him. He was growing up into a sweet boy, one who did very well at his school studies, as I knew he would. Sometimes, when I put him to bed, I wondered what he would do with his life. I had a hope that one day, maybe he would help me, but I didn't want to put that on him. He had to have his own dreams, make his own path in the world, and I would let him decide that . . . after he graduated from a good Negro college.

One afternoon, in 1924, I was getting ready to close when Mrs. Sabre, a lovely olive-skinned woman whom I had made dresses for, came to my door.

I opened it for her, ready to welcome her. "Thank you for coming. What can I help you with today?"

I allowed her to precede me into the shop. She sat down on one of the sloped velvet upholstered couches I had in the front waiting area. The couches were there for when someone had an official appointment, but since she had not made one, I gathered this was a social visit.

"Would you like a lemonade from the icebox?"

"Oh no. Annie, I came by to ask you something." I sat on a couch nearby, but not next to her. "I'm the head of the Gasparilla festivities this year."

"Isn't that wonderful? Congratulations."

"Yes." She smoothed her gloves down. "As such, I want a co-ordinated look for our royal court this year. I thought that you would be the perfect one to design that look."

I folded my hands, not sure if I was hearing her right. Gasparilla in Tampa was an annual January festivity that culminated in a parade with floats. There was a royal court of about ten couples with a pair crowned as King and Queen. I took Arthur without fail to watch the parade and to catch the treats that came off the floats as they went by. We had always enjoyed it.

The Krewe, or the club that drew the court members and those who worked on the floats, were from Tampa's highest society. I loved watching the Lees on their floats coming down the parade route. We always waved. LaMarcus Lee had been part of the court as well as one of the other daughters, Grace. I wouldn't doubt that my young friend Nell, once she reached the right age, might be on the court as well.

"This is quite an honor, Mrs. Sabre. I mean . . ." I stopped and swallowed. I hated to have to put reservations on such an offer that would be wonderful advertising for my shop, but I had to know before I got my hopes up. "Does everyone else want this?"

She tilted her head. "Why, Annie. What do you mean?"

"Ma'am, it's one thing to do dresses for the Lees and one or two others. But to have the responsibility of the whole court's look. Well, will it be okay?"

She stared at me.

I stared at her.

Was she going to make me say it?

Anytime I gave voice to it, it came into the room like a long laid-away ghost. It would haunt me—being kept in that room, separate from the others even though I knew I was the best student in the class. Having to live in Harlem with those of my kind, instead of at the boardinghouse with all of the other design school students. All of the repeated indignities.

I cleared my throat. "Will the court members be willing to come to my shop to be fit and measured?" I spread my hand out. "Here. In the colored part of Tampa."

Mrs. Sabre shook her head so vigorously, I was afraid that her Marcel wave might loosen.

"Oh my, Annie. Yes. Why, everyone knows you and knows that you do marvelous work. Of course. As a matter of fact, I wanted to arrange a meeting with you and the committee to talk over the ideas that you had. For a theme. Will next Tuesday morning work?"

"Yes. Yes, it will." I exhaled a breath.

Once she left, I put a hand to my chest. Something that I had not been expecting. Gasparilla designer.

I grabbed my sketch pad and drew a few things, but they weren't what I wanted.

Arthur came home from school. He was nine now, and I was so proud of him in his long pants. He had a bit of a look like me, but I always wondered if he didn't look more like Jack Lowe, the father I had never known. Lee would have been able to tell me that, but we hadn't spoken in years, even though Arthur went to Dothan every summer to see his grandmother.

He grabbed a snack and went to do his homework. I kept working so long, I forgot to start dinner. Lord knew I could barely boil an egg right, but I still had to try to make some kind of food to keep my child growing and to satisfy my husband. When Caleb came home from work, nothing was ready, but I had generated many sketches, none of which was quite the thing.

"I'm starving, wife."

"I know that, but look." I showed him the sketch pad and told him about what happened.

"What are they going to pay?"

I stopped. Mrs. Sabre didn't say anything about money. I guess they would talk about that on Tuesday. So that's what I told him. I realized I better get to thinking about it—what it would cost to make ten grand costumes.

"It's such an honor to be asked. How about milk and bread for dinner?"

"Annie, a man needs more than milk and bread for dinner."

I lowered my arms. He was right.

He slid his arms around me. "Look, maybe we can go down the street to the Bordell's. We can eat and bring Arthur some food home."

He danced me around. "We can do a little dancing and then come home." Lowering his lips to my neck, he kissed me there, pushing his way up my dress and up to my ear, whispering a few naughty things that were intended to titillate me.

They would have worked too. Usually.

Except I couldn't get the Gasparilla out of my mind. My desire to impress the committee meant so much, even more than going out with Caleb.

"On a weeknight?"

"Well, honey, there's no dinner and . . ." He spread his hands.

I looked at the light bread in front of me on the table. "How about a sandwich?" I didn't want to leave. I didn't want to dance. I wanted to stay at home in case the idea, the theme I needed, came to me.

Disappointment hovered in his eyes. "Okay. A sandwich. But tomorrow is Friday and I want to do Bordell's with a hot meal."

I clapped my hands and slid my arms around him. "Yes, honey. That's what we will do."

When both of my men sat down to the table that night eating cold sliced chicken sandwiches, I didn't feel that bad about it. I mean, a sandwich was a healthy meal. Just because they'd had the same for lunch, should I have felt bad? There were some people who didn't get to have much of anything for dinner, anyway. I would be sure to point that out to Arthur when I tucked him into bed.

I tried to seed the idea in my mind that night, so I would dream about it, but nothing came to me. Nothing helpful, anyway.

I made sure Caleb had a better breakfast, especially after his stomach was growling in the morning, and sent him off to work with a lingering kiss, but my fingers itched to get to my notepad to sketch out my ideas. I worked all day but I still didn't have enough designs.

When Caleb came home, he got ready for Bordell's right away. I had to change into a nice dress to go with him, even as my mind swirled around with ideas. What would work? What could I do that would make both the men and women look like royalty?

At Bordell's, Caleb went full out and got a steak. I didn't really care what I ordered. I could barely eat.

"Annie?"

"I'm sorry, honey. My mind is so full right now."

"You can't just put it to the side and spend some time with me?"

I grabbed his hand. "Of course. Tell me about your day." He did, but of course my mind slipped off again.

He didn't want to dance and neither did I. Heading for home, we walked down the street together hand in hand, feeling free because Arthur was with Paulina tonight. When we went into our bedroom, he traced his hands all over me, knowing how to undo the fastenings on my dress. It was my ragged-hem wedding gown, with the hem now even, but I had dyed it a green color to hide the stains that the stems had left on it on our wedding day.

He slid his hands all down my corset and unlaced me, murmuring sweet words and kissing me all up and down my heated body.

His attentions to me caused my mind to float, to coast, to dream, while I paid attention to the swirling feeling in my belly. Placing me on our bed, gently, he undressed himself in front of me, slowly, never taking his eyes off me.

I had learned that he liked me to do the same and I kept my gaze fixed on him as I waited for him to lay down beside me, so that we could trace our fingers over our heated skins. My green dress pooled on the floor, creating a circle like water. Like the ocean. Like waves.

I sat bolt upright, as naked as the day I was born, my fingers itching for my sketch pad, which was downstairs in my shop.

"What's wrong, honey?"

"The idea. The court. I know what the theme should be."

I stood up.

"Now?"

I went to where my robe hung and put it on. "I'll be right back. I promise. I just need to get it down now before it leaves my head."

I think he was calling my name, but I heard nothing, saw nothing, did nothing but make moves to get to that sketch pad before the idea slipped from me.

King Neptune and his wife, Salacia. The myths were some of Arthur's favorite stories to hear at bedtime. The story of how Neptune wooed Salacia filled my mind. In some ways, the story was like Caleb's and mine.

I stayed a while at my little table in the back of my store, dressed in my robe, making sketches of ten costumes, casting each court member in a role in the love story between King Neptune and his queen. By the time I was finished, the upstairs was dark.

Caleb had turned out the lights in our room and had gone to bed.

Alone.

Without me.

I wanted to apologize to him, but he was sound asleep and I knew he had to get his rest because he had to work the next day.

Still, when I realized I had been downstairs for five hours and had ruined our time together tonight, something in me twisted.

I took in a deep breath. What had compelled me to ignore my husband and son over these past few days to get this design right? Why would I do such a thing? Who was I?

When I slipped into the bed and turned over, I knew what it was—the title that had caused me to ignore all else because it fit me and described exactly what I wanted to be and who I was.

Gasparilla designer.

Those words felt as if I were home in my skin.

Finally.

Chapter Twenty-Four

*T*hat's how they would bill me, little Ann Lowe, a small woman from Clayton, Alabama.

Gasparilla designer.

Ann Lowe, Gasparilla designer.

And they let me, a Negro, do that job in 1924, 1925, and, yes, in 1926. Once one was over, I would think of the theme for the next year's event. The exposure made my business increase, but I still designed only for the most elite people in Tampa.

The city's elite came to my small shop, not minding that it was on the edge of an area where Negroes lived, and sipped the hot tea that I offered to them while we talked about what they needed. Those consults, and their money, which came from citrus and tobacco, sustained me and showed me what real respect for what I did was like.

My husband and son also were part of my business. Caleb said he got used to my craziness. He would laugh and say, "The muse came in the room!" whenever I would leap out of bed in a fit of inspiration. Arthur was old enough now to be an errand boy and he was so helpful. I kept my hopes that he might help me one day close to my heart and instead continued to put money to the side for his Negro college education, maybe to Lincoln, maybe to Howard. I was so proud of him.

When a grown-up and college-educated Nell Lee came into my shop just after Christmas 1926 with a dual commission for me, I was proud too. I never had a little girl, and always thought I would want one. Sewing Nell's doll's clothes had given me that feeling, and I was a bit sad when she grew out of that because I had no more excuse to make those miniature clothes.

But God bless her, she came in wrapped up in a sealskin muff, her arms spread wide, saying, "Annie! Are you ready for me?"

I walked over to her and we embraced. I would never think of embracing her mother, godly woman that she was, but Nell was different.

"I'm going to be the Gasparilla queen!"

"Praise be!" After years of being on the court, one of the Lees had made it to the top. "I'll make you the best dress that ever was."

"That's not all, Annie." She held out her hand, where a large square-cut emerald rested on her finger. "John proposed. I'm getting married!"

"God bless you! And you want a wedding dress." She nodded and we embraced again. What a wonderful session that was. When I went to bed that night with Caleb, I reminisced on it and told him about my feelings for Nell.

Caleb rolled over. "She's just a white woman. Same as the rest."

"But that's what I'm telling you. She's not the same as the rest. She's like a daughter to me."

He turned on his side to face me. "Honey, if you want a daughter, let's adopt. We can help one of these young girls here in the Tampa area. Show them your trade so that they don't have to work as maids and such in white men's houses."

We had talked about adopting before, especially after I told him about how having Arthur so young had tore up my insides.

"The Lees have been good to us. Why can't you see that?"

Caleb sighed. "They fine. As white folks go. I just don't want you to go overboard with all of that, that's all." He turned back over, away from me to face the wall, a clear sign that this conversation was over.

His reaction hurt my feelings some, but I did give more thought to what he said. I had trained a small staff of housewives who worked in the shop during the day for some extra money. Still, I wanted someone I could trust to join the business. I had planned for Paulina to be that person, but she loved doing hair and besides, she married and moved away. So I thought some more about what Caleb said, but focused my efforts on making my Nell look utterly stunning for the Gasparilla festivities.

Around this time I noticed that my Gasparilla designs were spreading my name to places beyond Tampa. After she returned from visiting her son's new friends in Palm Beach, Mrs. Lee told me that she had been asked about a dress while she was there.

"LaMarcus and I were so honored to be invited. It was quite an event. I mean, Annie, if you had seen the place. It was spectacular and encompassed the entire beachfront."

I put a hand to my chest. "I can't imagine such a thing."

"It was beautiful—an entire convention of orange grove owners. Imagine that this woman, Mrs. Hutton, who owns the estate, noticed my dress out of all of the other wives' dresses. And commented to me about it. I thought she was being nice."

"That was nice of her." I lowered my head and kept sketching, thrilled inside, but also proud.

"Oh wait, Annie. That isn't the end of it. The lady, Mrs. Hutton, asked me if she could see the dress."

I looked up at her. "She did?"

"Yes. Well, of course I was so shocked, but she was such a lovely hostess, I obliged her. After breakfast, I took her to my rooms and she looked at the inside of the dress."

My heart beat fast. "What did she see?"

"Well, your label of course, but she turned the dress this way and that. Looked at the seams. Complimented me on how I didn't have a single line or jiggle. I told her all about your philosophy about a woman's undergarments and the creation of a shape."

I nodded. "It's extremely important."

"Yes. And wearing a dress of yours is so comfortable that it's like wearing a glove. Mrs. Hutton made note of it all and wished me a safe journey home." She sighed. "The estate's name means 'sea to lake.' No, wait . . . it's called"—she tapped a finger to her forehead—"Mar-a-Lago. That's it. So beautiful. And what do you think of that, Annie? Wouldn't it be wonderful if such a woman like Mrs. Hutton wanted a dress from you?"

"It would but I'm just a little Tampa seamstress." Even as I said the words, I wanted to hush my tongue. I was the Gasparilla designer, three years running.

"Maybe you know Mrs. Hutton by another name. She is very wealthy. She runs the Post fortune. A most unusual woman. You know of Postum and General Foods?"

"Oh, that Post?" I recalled the brands that sat on many a household shelf, including mine.

"Yes. That's her! She's an executive and collects art. The art-work, my goodness. Mar-a-Lago was like a museum. Just beautiful."

"Well, I thank you for telling me the story, ma'am. Nell is due to come in for her fitting soon."

"And I know you've done something special for her for both

occasions. It's hard to believe that my youngest is leaving the nest. John is such a fine young man."

I nodded my agreement with her. I had certainly done the best for our Nell. I had designed her Gasparilla gown based on Aphrodite, the goddess of love, rising from the seafoam. It would be the most stunning Gasparilla queen gown ever—all for my Nell.

The same went for her wedding gown when she married Mr. John Greening later that spring. I spared nothing in the design for Nell. The ragged-hem gown was made of the best duchesse double-faced satin and featured a spectacular train that trailed from her shoulders. The shoes, white silk with pearl beaded buckles, came all the way from Paris. The veil had a headdress in the Russian-court style and the veiling was edged in orange blossoms, of course.

The wedding took place at night. I attended as an invited guest, after I made sure Nell's dress was perfect. Tears stood in my eyes as I watched her brother escort her, the queen of the Gasparilla, to meet her love at the end of the aisle. Candles were lit all around as the couple said their vows. I couldn't believe that little Nell was a married lady now.

I had done my job. The last Lee wedding seemed as if it were some kind of final chapter in my life. I told Caleb so when I returned home that night and all he said was "Good."

Well, that wasn't nice of him, even though I knew that he believed I spent too much time thinking about the Lee family. Still, Nell's wedding made me think again about his idea to adopt a girl I could train and bring into the sewing trade.

I spent the next week trying to figure out how we might search in the church for a nice young lady, maybe someone Arthur's age or younger, to be our daughter and to apprentice with me here in the shop. I looked up from my sketches one day to see

Mrs. Lee enter my shop, waving a copy of the Tampa Bay newspaper. "Look at this coverage."

There was a layout of my dresses, featuring Nell in her wedding dress at the center. "Isn't she beautiful?"

"Yes, she is, Annie. Your dress helped her to be that way."

"I had no idea they were going to do this."

"It's good for your business." She picked up the paper. "Do you know what I'm going to do? I'm going to mail this off to Mrs. Hutton."

"You are?"

"She should see it."

"If you think so." I closed my sketchbook, feeling nervous.

"I do."

There was no changing Mrs. Lee's mind when she got it into her head to do something. I was honored but the last thing I expected was to receive a letter from Mrs. Hutton saying that she wanted to schedule an appointment for a consultation when she would be visiting Tampa in a few weeks.

Arthur helped me to clean my shop and make sure every couch was well upholstered with new fresh velvet and shiny new studs. I loved how he seemed to be willing to help me with my shop. Caleb wouldn't have done it.

When the great day came, Mrs. Hutton arrived at my shop in a car, accompanied by Mrs. Lee, who seemed to be very nervous. I'm not sure why, given the circumstances, but I was surprisingly cool.

They both sat and I offered my usual choices of tea or lemonade.

I could see, in the regal way she carried her fox fur and beautiful line of clothes and her jewelry—oh how it sparkled—that Mrs. Hutton was a lover of fine things. We visited for an hour and a half, and at the end of the time, Mrs. Lee squeezed my hand in her excitement at the commission. Mrs. Hutton paid me a nice sum and I was free to go ahead and create a dress for this amazing woman—a woman who was not only someone's wife but also a businesswoman who ran a company.

The dress I created had a dove-gray sheath with a lace overlay and a ragged hem. I normally wrapped a finished dress in a white sheet and shipped it to the customer, but Mrs. Hutton had her driver pick up her dress, so instead I packaged it in tissue in a long white box.

The dress made an appearance in the society column in the New York papers and Mrs. Lee was beyond excited. "Annie. Do you know what that means? You can go to New York and be a success there. Once the elite of New York know you, you've got the highest status. Only Paris is better."

"Oh, ma'am. I don't expect to go there."

"Well, you never know, Annie." She turned to me. "Have you thought of opening a shop there?"

I swallowed, feeling a small frisson of nerves chill me. My entire dream. "We live here in Tampa, ma'am."

"Talk it over with Caleb and I'll discuss it with LaMarcus to see how we might help. We aren't Mrs. Hutton and her illustrious husband, Mr. E. F. Hutton, but you should tap into your connections up there and see if it might be possible."

Possible. Yes. With her generosity, Mrs. Lee had exposed me to possibility as well as to Mrs. Hutton, a woman who owned her own company. I could never forget my own mother, who told me to go to New York one day—something she could not imagine for herself.

Mrs. Lee left, clasping her hands in excitement. Later that night, I spoke to Caleb about the idea and emphasized the better opportunities for him in New York—and for Arthur. I was surprised to hear him saying that he was receptive to the idea. It took a couple of years, but in 1928, we moved to New York City.

Six months there had not been enough for me. I was determined to have New York see what I could do now.

Chapter Twenty-Five

$\mathcal{W}$e weren't the only Negroes contemplating a move up North, as others called it. Our church (Caleb switched to First after his mother died), lost a few families each year as they went north to Philadelphia, Washington, D.C., or New York City. The proposal by the Lees to help me open a shop made the whole idea very intriguing. Caleb had no other family, in Tampa or elsewhere, so why not leave?

Mrs. Hutton had been extremely pleased with her dress and expressed interest in future commissions. I wrote to her and told her that I was thinking of moving to New York and she replied to me—me, a little Negro woman with a dress shop in Tampa—and told me that I most certainly should. "Much of high society would love to see your work, Ann, and you would certainly do well here."

So, in 1928, after my dear Nell gave birth to her first daughter, the West family went up north. It was the right time for Arthur to go as well. He had just finished the eighth grade and Tampa was certainly not looking to educate an intelligent young Black man any further than that. Neither myself nor Caleb went to school beyond the eighth grade, but I wanted more for Arthur. There would be no Negro college without him going to high school and New York had high schools for Negro boys.

Before we moved, the Lees, in combination with some of the other society families of the area, presented me with twenty thousand dollars, more than ample payment for my last Gasparilla as designer.

"We know you will do very well, Annie," Mrs. Lee said, presenting me with the bankbook. "Go with God and let us know how you are doing."

I stepped away with the small red book in my hand, afraid to show emotion, afraid I would break down and cry at her generosity. My twelve years in Tampa had been the making of me and had shown me that I could do more, be more than a Negro seamstress, if given the chance.

The trip north was uneventful and once we reached New York, we knew where to go.

Harlem.

Harlem was the central point of Black life, culture, and progress, even more so than when I had lived there to go to the design school years before. The school didn't exist any longer, which was one balm in a potential wound, because I didn't have to feel that Mr. Taylor was still working hard to keep someone like me from becoming a designer. I was proud to say that he hadn't kept me from achieving my dream.

Now I was aiming for something even bigger with the introduction of commissions from the glamorous and famous Mrs. Hutton. Knowing her gave me entrée to the upper reaches of society. Once we had our apartment, I looked for a shop with living space over it, but one was hard to find. The 1920s was a good time for designers and lots of people had shops. I would have to wait.

From my previous time in New York, I knew that wealthy department stores didn't mind using design students or young designers to do their bespoke work. The difference was that when I was in school, they didn't expect to hire Negro women for that work. Had things changed? There was only one way to find out. I went around to several stores but had no luck. Tired, and with my courage flagging a bit, I went to Saks Fifth Avenue, a well-known department store where the wealthy shopped.

I had dressed myself a little better this time, in a light color and with a hat with veiling on it, a vanity I would not usually permit myself, and inquired at Saks about obtaining bespoke designer work. The supervisor of the shop was very familiar to me.

"Miss Winters!" I exclaimed. "I would have never expected to see you here."

Her cheeks matched her red hair, which now carried a touch of gray. "Mrs. Cone, I'm so glad to see you."

"It's Mrs. West now, thank you. I've moved back to New York and I'm looking for work." I tucked my clutch purse a little closer to me, but she waved her hand.

"Well, I know what you can do. You're hired. When can you start?"

Of course she didn't mention our previous clashes. I certainly wasn't going to. I thanked God for the connection, no matter how it had come about. I kept the money from the Saks job banked and hoped for a place of my own soon.

Caleb found a job as a doorman for an apartment building where white people lived, in Upper Manhattan. I was disappointed for him because he had wanted to do something else in New York when we left Tampa. He never said what, but I could tell when I saw his eyes that his energy lagged.

I was helpless to do anything for him because Saks kept me

very busy. The entire next year and a half, I saved and worked and worked and saved.

Then the stock market crashed in October 1929. Caleb lost his job and his spirit lagged even further. I lost some of my very good clients. However, because I was designing only for the elite—who still had money, although less of it and so I charged less—they still ordered from me. So I kept very busy, to the point where I regularly couldn't prepare dinner for my family. Caleb began to fix meals for me whenever I would get home, at nine or ten o'clock at night. I could tell that the move to New York wasn't making him very happy, but I couldn't do anything about the economy.

The downturn meant that I was able to get a shop for very little money in 1933. By living over the space, we could save some money on rent too. What mattered was green money, and I still had some of that left in spite of the hard times.

However, because the economy was the rule of the day, fashion became less interesting. The style of clothes popular now required a different skill set than mine—I designed with a free hand and had an eye for using beautiful and expensive fabrics. But I could economize and change the lines as necessary. My dresses with less fabric still looked beautiful with a little floral embellishment, and plenty of my clients still wanted that particular look.

Later on, many called this time the Great Depression, but I wasn't sad. I had enough saved by 1933 so that Arthur could attend one of my dream schools for him, Lincoln University in Pennsylvania, which was not very far away. But still, he was grown now and out of our day-to-day life by then. However, I had another reason to find joy when little Ruth Ann came into our lives.

Caleb and I, through our church, St. Mark's Episcopal, heard word of a fatherless family who had also just lost the mother to tuberculosis. The practice at the time was to send the children to an orphanage or to anyone who would adopt them. There were five children and no one wanted to take all of them. The young girl in the family, Ruth Ann, just six years old, came to live with us.

We met her after services one Sunday. She arrived at the church with a small bag. Her hair had bits of fuzz and lint in it. My hands itched to take care of her. The pastor's wife brought her to me. "This is Ruth Ann."

I reached out to her and took the small, cold hand in mine. "Isn't that something? My name is Ann too."

The child nodded. Her long bronze-colored face was so sad, my heart took to her right away.

"She looks wonderful to me, Annie," Caleb boomed.

Ruth Ann looked up at him and the hint of a smile dawned at the corners of her mouth.

"I agree." And that's how my daughter came into my life.

I enjoyed having a young girl in the house. She was such a joy. I combed and styled her hair like she was a little doll. Of course, I created dresses for her from the ends from my work, and she went to school as the best-dressed child.

Our lives coasted along so well.

Too well.

Looking back, I wondered: Did Caleb and I bring Ruth Ann into our lives to keep us together as we were falling apart? Such a heavy task for a small girl.

I really shouldn't have been surprised when, one day in 1940, I came home early from work and Caleb was in our apartment with another woman.

How bold did he have to be to carry on with someone else

when I was in the shop downstairs, working to keep us alive during these hard times?

I shut the door on them, but the skinny woman who had the gall to be with my husband in my bedroom ran out of the apartment, clutching her purse to her cheaply made, shoddy red dress.

Caleb came out, suspenders down, shirt undone. He sat down in an armchair and put his head in his hands. "Annie . . . listen, I . . ."

"I don't want to hear it. Not one word."

He lifted his head and looked at me. "Wait a minute. Are you angry?"

"What do you mean, am I angry? Of course I'm angry. I just caught you in my bed with another woman. While I'm downstairs working so hard to support us."

He slapped his meaty thigh. "So you are angry at me?"

"I'm working hard to keep this shop, to feed us, and you bring a whore into this house to sleep with."

His eyes blazed. "You take that back. She's not a whore."

Something in his look made the pit of my stomach stab with a thousand needles. "She's a whore because she came in this house to sleep with someone else's husband. That's a whore."

Caleb pointed after her. "I don't appreciate you talking about me as if I'm your possession."

"Well, you are my husband. What of it?"

He shook his head. "Annie, we haven't been anything to each other for a long time. Let's face it."

I opened my mouth, but he was right. The ravages of the time and the move to New York had taken a toll on him as well as our marriage. We had had something in Tampa. Now we did not. I sighed. "I thought coming here would help us."

"It's made it worse. I'm more dependent on you than ever

and . . ." He swallowed, balling his fists up. "That's hard for a man. To be dependent on a woman."

I clasped my sweaty hands together. "All I ever wanted was for us to work together. To have this shop together. That's all."

He shook his head. "Annie, the shop was always about you. That was your dream, not mine. I got to have my own dream."

"Well, Caleb, I've made it so that I'm here. No, I can't cook, but I'm here."

"You ain't here. Your mind is always on the shop, it's always elsewhere. Never on me. You leap out of bed, always reaching for that sketch pad. Never for me."

I wanted to deny it, but I couldn't. He was right again.

He stood. "I'll pack my things and leave."

I wanted to stop him, but the words were stuck in my throat. "What about Ruth?"

"I'll get her from school and tell her."

Ruth wasn't a child of my body, but we were so connected, I could feel how this would break her. She was a daddy's girl in a way that I never got to be. She loved Caleb, much more than I did. I never had a father, and given how she had lost both of her biological parents, I hated to deprive her of Caleb.

"What are you going to do?"

"I'll see. I don't know if I'm one for this cold weather, so I might have to go back home. I don't know, Annie."

There was nothing more to say. I stood on wobbly legs and went back down to my shop, to prepare for my next appointment, swallowing tears that refused to rise to the surface.

That was a hard time for me and Ruth, for sure. Arthur tried to come home and support us as much as possible, but he was a grown-up college graduate, which sure didn't mean that much for a Black man, as we came to learn. He was a grocery delivery boy.

But still, he was out in the world working and shouldn't have to worry about his mother. Fortunately, a letter that saved us came a few weeks after Caleb left.

My sister, Sallie. Her husband had gone on to meet his Maker. Her sons' wives thought she existed to babysit her grands, but she was done raising children and she wanted to come to New York to see me.

When Sallie's letter arrived, I felt all of God's favor come back to me. We hadn't seen each other in so many years but I felt the need for family and a blood connection in this hard time of my life right now.

I picked her up at Grand Central. I could tell that her traveling dress, although neatly pressed and of good quality, had been patched over too often. She had a pasteboard suitcase and her gray felt cloche had been turned inside and out and refelted in the worn places quite a few times.

The years had been hard on her. But then, I was someone who had been cared for and about. I was over forty years old myself, but still doing well. Sallie, at fifty, was getting to be an old lady, but still had a lot of life left in her.

When I saw her walking to me, tears pricked in my eyes and I laid my head down on her soft, bosomy breasts. Sallie had always been taller and heavier than me.

I just let it all out.

"Aww, now, Annie. I'm here now." She patted my back with the family pat, the same way I used to put Arthur to sleep when he was a tiny baby.

I tried to explain as I inhaled between crying gasps: "My husband left me for another woman, and I'm all alone."

She wrapped her arms around me. "Now, now. You ain't been alone a minute, Annie. I'm here. Who is this, now?"

Ruth had hung back, probably shocked to see me fall apart. I tried to gather myself for my child's sake. Why was I falling to pieces out here in the public eye, where potential clients could see me? My nights with no Caleb warmth next to me had hit harder than I was willing to admit.

I reached down and smoothed Ruth's pigtails. "This is my Ruth. Ruth Ann West. This here is my sister, Sallie." Having Sallie there took my speech straight back to Clayton.

"Ruth, honey. I'm your aunt Sallie. You going to show me all of New York?"

My daughter's smile lit up her sweet face. "Yes, ma'am."

She took hold of my sister's hand, and I took hold of Sallie's other hand and the three of us walked out of the train station, a new family unit, ready to start a new chapter in our lives.

Chapter Twenty-Six

Sallie's arrival in my life was the gift I had not known I needed. I was so worried that Ruth would miss her father—and she did, but Sallie was like another mother, a better mother, one who could cook. My sister took over the care of us, making sure we ate, getting Ruth off to school, and, nearly as wonderful, helping in the shop. Sallie never begrudged me the sewing talent that I had—she always supported me—but now, away from everyone else, I could see her own talent as a fitter was still with her. She had her own approach to the art of fitting a woman and her assistance in the shop brought light back to her cheeks.

"I'm having a fine time," Sallie said one day. She always sounded like a Southern belle. "I love my grands, and they can visit, but Annie, this is the first time in my life I'm doing something that I love that's for me. And I'm helping you."

"God sent you to me, Sallie, that's the sure enough truth of it."

It made me feel sober to think of how Mama and Grandma would be proud that we had found our way to one another after so much time apart. We were a gift to each other.

Caleb had found someone who was happy to be his Mrs. West and pay all of her attention to him. I was happy for him, and

Ruth went to him every summer to spend time with him and his new wife, also named Annie. Goody for him.

Instead of keeping his name, as I kept Lee's name after my divorce, once I divorced Caleb, I returned to who I was when I was born: Ann Cole Lowe. This name was my name. I would design under this name perpetually and never, ever change it again for any man.

War loomed again in far-off Europe, but this time it threatened to take Arthur, my college-graduate son, with it. I was not surprised when he told me he was signing up for the army.

His words did not surprise me, but that didn't mean I had to like them. "Come back safe, son." I pressed a hand to my heart, thinking of all the ways that I might discourage him but knowing that would be the wrong thing to do.

"I will. Also, I want to marry my sweetheart, before I go."

Another skipped heartbeat. He had been dating Cora Carter, a Negro socialite, for some time now. I had not met her yet and honestly, I had dreaded this moment for a while.

"Son, this is wonderful news." I needed to embrace this new reality of sharing Arthur with someone else. I adopted Ruth to have a daughter and now I would be welcoming another daughter.

"I'm going to bring her here soon and we'll be married before I ship off. I want her to be able to know you and Ruth as family."

Cora's people lived in Queens, as fate would have it, and they came over to our apartment one Sunday for dinner, which Sallie cooked. We all sat down after and made plans for the wedding over a sweet potato pie that wasn't too sweet because sugar was rationed.

I tried to peer at Cora to see what Arthur saw in this girl. She had smooth brown skin as her best feature, a high bust, a flat stomach, and long, long legs. She was able to look Arthur in the eye, and not many were able to do that. I would have to cut her dress length on the bias to make the fabric stretch to accommodate her. "There won't be much time to get a dress together for you, Cora, but I've been fast with them in my day."

Arthur linked his hand through Cora's. "Mother, well, we are just going to City Hall next week since I ship out in ten days."

"I can make a wedding dress in two days." I waved my hands around. "It will be just fine and—"

"Oh no, ma'am." Cora spoke in a slightly husky voice. "I could never marry in a fine dress. We have to save everything for the war effort. That wouldn't help Arthur come home to me."

He tightened his hold on her hand.

"Oh." There was an entire world in that one syllable that dropped from my lips.

"We all have to do the patriotic thing now, don't we?" said Cora's mother, a sharp-nosed woman who looked down at us the moment she stepped into our apartment. "Double V for double victory."

"Victory abroad and here at home for Negroes." Cora turned to Arthur and they rested their foreheads against each other's, doing everything short of cooing like two turtledoves.

My son would marry. And not have a dress of mine at his wedding.

"I have a suit I will wear," Cora cooed.

A little light entered my heart. I wanted, no needed, to be a part of my son's nuptials in some way. "I can make you a lovely corsage."

"Make a corsage?" Old sharp nose chimed in.

Arthur turned his attention to his future mother-in-law. "My mother makes cloth flowers. Beautiful ones."

Cora laughed a little. "Oh no, honey. I want a real one. Real flowers."

Poor Arthur looked as if he had been caught in a vice grip of his own making, so I had to relieve him.

"Oh, that's fine."

"The young people," Cora's mother said, "they are all doing everything their own way now."

They left twenty minutes later.

Cora was a lovely girl, very nice, but it was clear that we didn't think the same at all.

Everyone, everywhere, made sacrifices to show their patriotism and intention of defeating the enemy abroad, but fortunately, there were still enough people of the rich class for me to design for. I was sewing in my own shop but was also working under the label of Sonja; my name, Ann Lowe, was set in small letters underneath hers but still present. I had met Sonja at Saks and discovered that we had very similar approaches in thinking about dresses. So when she started up her own label, I agreed to come on board and create certain designs with her. Ever since the 1930s I had accepted cut-rate prices for my designs, and I was making less money selling my own dresses.

I had all kinds of rich women seeking out my dresses: women who were married into or from families like the Du Ponts, Lodges, Vanderbilts, Coopers, and the like. Still, if I suggested a price uptick, they would tsk and accuse me of not being patriotic at this difficult time.

What could I do? I didn't want to lose their business. And I loved making the dresses, even in wartime, even under someone else's name. I never wanted to give up doing what I loved, creating the art that needed to emerge in the world, just because of money. We were all doing fine, and I didn't want for a roof over my head or food to eat. I didn't need to be rich.

And so, I became society's best-kept secret. My name was passed around by word of mouth. I didn't advertise, because I did not want to appeal to just any Mary or Sue. I wanted to see descriptions of my dresses in the papers the next day and the only way that would happen would be if they were worn by the finest and most famous names in the *Social Register*.

I sewed on. And one day, I gained an important new client who would transform my life.

When she stepped into my shop, I had to stop myself from staring at her. I was stunned at her beauty. Many society matrons were attractive. After all, my clientele had the means to be able to purchase whatever they needed to make themselves attractive, but this woman was something special, almost like a model.

But people who were models did not consult with me. I had not even had my own fashion show yet, something that I wanted to do at some point.

"Hello. How may I help you?"

The woman extended a slim hand to me. "Good morning. I was referred to you by my friend, Mrs. Weathers." The name was familiar to me, of course. "I'm getting remarried and I would like to have a suit made for my wedding."

"Please step into my office, Miss. . . ."

"I'm Mrs. Bouvier, née Lee. I'm going to marry Mr. Hugh Auchincloss."

An image returned to my memory. Oh yes. Who didn't know who Mrs. Bouvier was? "Ah yes, Mrs. Bouvier, please sit. It's nice to meet you in person."

Her voice lowered. "I suspect you've seen me in the society pages."

She took a seat across from me, her head up, posture perfect, and legs crossed neatly at the ankles. Her well-made dress with seams, a floral print from last season, was pressed smooth and topped off with a string of pearls that were probably inherited.

Every inch of her was a perfect lady.

I nodded my head. A shadow of something came across her face. I could tell the memory of it was still painful for her. Everyone in society knew her story.

Mrs. Bouvier had been humiliated by Mr. Bouvier when a society photographer took a picture of what she thought was of her alone in her riding clothes, perched on a fence. However, next to her was some woman and Mr. Bouvier on the other side of her, holding the other woman's hand as if *she* were Mrs. Bouvier—all behind her back.

Such a tragedy. She had no choice but to leave him, even if she still loved him.

I put my hands on my knees. "I've been divorced myself. Twice now."

She nodded. "Marriage can be quite difficult. But I've found love once more with Mr. Auchincloss."

I gave her a look of sympathy, as I knew to do when women came into my store for designs. While Hugh Auchincloss was a very rich man, he was not nearly as attractive as Mr. Bouvier, known as Black Jack for his dark good looks. She, like many women of a certain age who did not have an occupation or large settlements of dowries upon them, needed a rich husband to protect her and to support her. And she had found one.

I couldn't blame her. She still probably carried a torch for Mr. Bouvier, which made me sad, but she had found a way out of her predicament.

"It's wonderful that you have. Life is hard for women and we have to do what we have to do. Especially if we have children. Do you have children, Mrs. Bouvier?

I knew she did, but children were an easy topic to speak about that relaxed clients. Her eyes lit up, as did most women's whenever you asked about their children. "Yes. I have two daughters, Jacqueline and Lee."

"How wonderful. How old are they?"

"Jacqueline is fourteen. Lee is ten. Girls need . . . well, they need a father figure at that age to show them . . . how a woman should be treated. Don't you think so?"

"I do." I nodded, even though my heart sank because I had failed to provide that for Ruth. My heart still ached about it, even though Ruth was older and fine now.

But Mrs. Bouvier carried a determined gleam in her eye and I knew that she felt she was doing what she needed to provide that kind of security for her daughters. I had to hold on to this shop, and she had to marry. That was the way of the world.

We had a wonderful discussion about what she felt would be appropriate for a second wedding to an enlisted man during wartime.

What she wanted would be tailored, elegant, and beautiful on her. When she came to be fitted into the dress, an ivory suit coat with a piped edge and a long skirt that just hit the floor, she brought her daughters.

The two young women who accompanied her were clearly related to her. The younger, smaller one looked more like Mrs. Bouvier and had a nervous, flighty energy. She was still in her young years, that awkward age where she might want to play with dolls but beg to be considered older in the next moment. One can tell when a young girl has been spoiled and that was her Lee. Once more, that name had intersected in my life in a major way.

The older daughter had a different look. She took after her father, Black Jack Bouvier, but his features, so handsome on a male, came across entirely different on his daughter. Taking account of the individual parts of her, you would think her eyes were too far apart, her hands too large, and her feet too big—it seemed almost as if she were going to have a growth spurt into herself, like how you could tell from its oversized features that a puppy would become a big dog. She was going to grow into something, for sure. Peering at her, someone could easily mistake her for being homely, but suddenly all of these parts of her would come together—someday, but not now—in a way that made her stunning, like her mother. That's what made her a rare beauty. It was her carriage, in the way she held herself. Regal and refined.

When Mrs. Bouvier asked questions about how she appeared in her gown, the younger girl expressed excitement.

However, the older girl, Jacqueline, as I recalled it, quietly made a point about the piping on the jacket. Her words came across in an even manner. She was not rude, but just matter of fact. "It's not even."

Her mother looked down. "Oh, Jaqueline, I don't think . . ."

I looked down. Blinked. Jacqueline was absolutely right.

I needed to get new glasses. More and more, I had days when my eyesight was cloudy as if I were trying to see through fog.

I retrieved my pin cushion, ready to pin the piping to even it out. "Thank you, Miss Bouvier."

Was it her young eyes that had pointed out the mistake? Or was it an impeccable sense of line and style from someone who was an art appreciator, someone who knew the language and feeling of art and saw edging that wasn't quite right? It could be both.

Jacqueline then spoke her well-chosen words. "It's cut so well and fits you just wonderfully, Mama. Uncle Hugh will think you are a beautiful bride."

Her voice, pitched low and throaty, and the smooth sophistication of her words impressed me.

So I said for the second time in as many minutes, "Thank you, Miss Bouvier."

She tilted her head to me in a semi nod. Oh yes. Here was someone special.

Little did I know then, on that summer afternoon in 1942, that my special relationship with Jacqueline Bouvier had begun.

Chapter Twenty-Seven

In the war days, every scrap of newly produced fabric went to uniforms for the war effort, so the best that any employed designer could do was to create uniforms. Then, if that wasn't possible, the best that could be done was to design something that looked like a uniform, because everyone wanted to be patriotic. The scarcity of the 1930s and the war right after made for bleak days for fashion design and I was forced to close the shop.

Sallie, Ruth, and I moved into an apartment with my daughter-in-law, Cora, and my first grandchild, Audrey. Not an ideal environment, but of course, since I was busy with my sketches and sewing, I didn't clash much with Cora, who was far from a fashion plate.

Now I worked exclusively for Sonja out of Saks Fifth Avenue, bringing in my clients, including Mrs. Auchincloss when she was in New York as well as other high-class clientele. Sonja, a Jewish woman, was an avid supporter of my work. While the style of the times did not inspire me, the war would end and with it this bleak streak of clothing design. I would finally be able to work on the ideas I had been sketching so they would be in the world, going to balls and parties and weddings—free from my mind.

That time came in April 1945—Germany surrendered, and we ran out into the streets in jubilation. I was happy because my son would be coming home to his family and I had a new sense of what might finally happen for my dresses once restrictions on fabric were released. I would go wild with it.

Once Arthur came home, I knew that Ruth, Sallie, and I would have to move elsewhere, so we found an apartment uptown in Harlem. The next year, 1946, Ruth, my now beautiful Ruth, was graduating from high school and that fall she would attend Lincoln just as her brother had.

I was so proud of both of my children. Caleb even brought his new Annie to Ruth's graduation celebration and we were able to be cordial. My sweet Mama Nan died that year, the sole spot of sorrow in that year during which, sometime around summer, the restrictions on fabric were eased and I sought to create a new feminine line.

Hemlines would go down, and that meant a designer would not have compromise in their use of fabric. Lots of tucks, lots of gathers required a lot of fabric, and created a look almost like a hoop skirt from Civil War times, but shorter. All the returning former soldier husbands wouldn't mind seeing their wives with small, waspish waists.

This idea was in my mind when Sonja spoke to me just after Christmas in 1946. It was a nasty day outside, and I was a bit blue because I had sent Ruth back to finish her first year at Lincoln.

"We have a special new client coming in," Sonja intoned. She was not a small woman, like I was, so her deep alto voice boomed out to me as I sat at my desk.

"Will she want sketches?"

"Yes. And your special flower touch. She's a very feminine, graceful woman."

"Who could it be?"

Sonja smiled. "It's Olivia de Havilland."

The pencil slipped from my hand. "Excuse me?"

"She needs a gown for the Academy Awards this year. She's on her way to France and has heard some wonderful things about you. She's stopping here in New York for a fitting with you."

My hand went to my chest. "Me?"

"Yes, Ann. Give her your best, will you?"

Will I? Ruth would be thrilled. We both loved Olivia de Havilland as Miss Melly in *Gone with the Wind*. Her portrayal of the ultimate Southern belle reminded me of Mrs. Lizzie O'Neal, who had been so good to us in Montgomery, and Mrs. Lee in Tampa. I had yet to see the same font of goodness and womanhood here in New York. Even my New York patroness, Mrs. Hutton, was a tough businesswoman. Olivia de Havilland would make for an amazing commission and I went right to work on a gown that would be special and just for her.

When she came to Saks, she was well-dressed in a day suit with all of the proper foundational undergarments and heels, gloves, and a small hat—a lady.

"Ann does something special with flowers," Sonja pointed out in her big voice.

"I do, ma'am." I showed her a fabric flower. "We can let them decorate the skirt of your dress, with so much fabric."

"Will it be heavy?" The delicate eyebrows came together.

"Oh no. It won't be heavy."

"It sounds like a lot of fabric in the skirt with fabric flowers." I saw her point. No woman wanted to wear a heavy dress for an entire evening.

An idea came to me. "What if they are painted on?"

Sonja's eyes turned to me. She had never seen that before.

Neither had I but I would make it work for Olivia de Havilland. She clasped her hands together. "That's marvelous, Mrs. Lowe."

I felt a little awkward hearing her say Mrs. No one called me Mrs. Lowe, especially since, technically, I was Mrs. West, even though I wasn't married to Caleb West any longer. But who would stop Olivia de Havilland? I spoke up, "It's just Miss Lowe." She nodded and we had an understanding. We had professional names, our own names, as professional women.

The neckline of the dress would be reduced to a strapless neckline, to compensate for the fabric in the skirt. It would be beautiful on her. I could hardly wait.

"Are you visiting Paris, ma'am?" Sonja asked her.

"Yes. I'll be there for the Paris fashion shows. I love them."

"They are having them again?" There was open surprise in Sonja's voice. The shows had been suspended because of the war.

"Why yes." The star pulled her gloves on. "They are starting them up again, and I cannot wait. Thank you so much for all of your help."

She would be fitted and retrieve the gown when she returned from France, on her way back to the West Coast. The Oscar ceremony she would wear the gown to was in mid-March.

"I did not know that the French shows had started up again," Sonja said to me. "What would it be to go? Have you ever been, Annie?"

I shook my head. "I've never been to Paris. I can't speak French. I wouldn't know what to do."

I could hear my mother talking about Paris in the back of my mind, her thoughts and hopes that I might go there one day. Of course, anywhere I could talk about fashion would be a godsend and Paris, well, that was the mountaintop for me. I thought no more about it, but instead, focused my efforts on writing a letter to Ruth to tell her all about the consultation visit and what a lady Olivia de Havilland was.

A few weeks later, Sonja called me into her office. "There has been a newspaper asking me about you. It's a Negro one. The *Chronicler,* I think?"

I sat in the chair nearest to her. We had a very equivalent relationship, with no sense of hierarchy to it. "I've heard of it."

"They said they would like to send you to see the fashions in the haute couture houses of Paris. They would pay for your expenses. All you would have to do is write an article a day for them."

It was far from the appropriate thing to do, but I gawped.

Sonja held up a finger. "You wouldn't be going as a designer, but rather to observe all of the fashion. It's next month."

"Yes, I remember what Miss de Havilland said."

"Well? I think you should go. It would be a good influence for you."

I pushed the excitement away from me, like feeding cloth into a sewing machine. "I cannot possibly get the paperwork done in time."

Sonja waved a hand. "Those things can be taken care of."

"I would need a room on the ship."

Her eyes rounded. "Oh, there is no ship. They want to you to fly on an airplane. You can write about that too."

I laughed. A Negro? On a plane? How would that work? "I'm not Charles Lindbergh."

"That's what they say." She handed out a paper. "You're welcome to go. I would love to see the kinds of things you would design after experiencing Paris and the fashion there."

She stood. "It's a once in a lifetime opportunity, Annie. It's your choice, but it just might be the making of you."

Once again, I was grateful to have a benefactress to see to

my growth. Of course, I would go. Sallie and Arthur were a bit nervous about my getting on an airplane, but it would take days off the travel time to Europe, which most people did back then on a ship, so the trip would be a week and a half instead of three weeks. The plane would leave from New Jersey and touch down in Paris. Sonja gave me a little book and together we practiced some French phrases. Sonja was so delighted that her Negro designer would be going to Paris.

So was I.

Chapter Twenty-Eight

I didn't go out often for lunch but it must have been fate that I went out to run some errands for my Paris trip one chilly January day. When I made my way back to Sonja's department, I cut through Saks' women's specialty evening wear department toward the design room and, out of the corner of my eye, I saw a tall, elegant figure looking through some dresses. She was familiar to me, but I couldn't say why. Something about her, the way she held her head and her hands, was striking.

Was she a model?

She couldn't have been. This woman didn't have the vanity, the assurance of a model. She certainly had the hands and feet of one, though.

Taking an armful of dresses, she headed to the dressing room and I went back to work with Sonja.

The encounter bothered me all afternoon and I wondered who the elegant young woman was until Sonja brought me an appointment slip a few days later. "Mrs. Janet Auchincloss wants to bring her daughter in for her debutante dress."

That was it. The young woman was the daughter of Mrs. Bouvier, now Mrs. Auchincloss. The one with the longer name. Jacqueline.

What was she doing shopping off the rack when I could make her whatever she needed?

It couldn't have been a question of affordability, because Mrs. Auchincloss paid all of her bills. Hugh Auchincloss was as rich as Midas. That might have been the reason she married him, many said, but I had heard they made a successful marriage. And after my forays with marriage, I was not one to say. As much as I loved my designing, to have a man care for me without having to worry about what I charged for a dress would have been a true gift. But from what I could see out in the world, that man did not exist.

Arthur had been taking care of my savings and money. Bless his heart, he was good at keeping the books and had been working as a businessman in Harlem after the war. He had never liked that I hadn't gotten the proper credit for the de Havilland dress and he reminded me of it at times.

"Miss de Havilland is a lovely woman. She introduced me to Mr. Dior," I pointed out to him.

"Mama, I don't care. You need to have your own shop. Then the Olivia de Havillands of the world will respect you."

Bless him. He was right, but I didn't want to impose on him any more. I knew his life wasn't easy. Cora was always wanting him to do something else, be something else. She and I never got along well after the wedding, even when she gave me a beautiful granddaughter, Audrey, whom I doted on with all the girl things I couldn't do for her father. I just didn't like the way Cora was with Arthur, though. But she couldn't interfere with the love Arthur had for me and what I was doing to prove that a Negro woman could be a designer. He said soon I would have enough for a shop and I would be able to leave Sonja behind. I could hardly wait.

WHEN IT WAS time to go to Paris, I was a little afraid, but I should not have been. Thank God I was not segregated on the airplane. I was brought to my own cubicle quarters, where the stewardess showed me how my seat folded down into a bed for sleeping. The flight would take sixteen hours. While we were in the air, we would be served all of our meals, as well as wine.

As I sat there sipping some kind of white wine in a long elegant glass, taking peeks at another journalist, a chic brunette across the aisle who was very pleasant and struck up a conversation with me, I marveled at it all.

What if Mama and Grandma could see me now, on this airplane, going to Paris? I remembered when I told them I was going to be at one of the big parties the journalists would publish in the papers about, but this, in some ways, was just as good or even better.

My appetite seemed to be whetted by the fact that we were up in the air, somehow Lord, but I ate all of my steak, potatoes, and green beans. I had a good sleep because I drank my wine.

When the passengers awoke, a yeasty smell tickled our noses. A horn-shaped pastry was served to us on a plate with slices of oranges.

The oranges I knew, but not the pastry. "It's a croissant," the brunette journalist told me. "Very French. Try it."

I did and its crusty warmth broke apart in my mouth, butter dotting my fingers. It tasted like heaven.

"Do the French people eat like this every day?"

The woman laughed. "They do."

"No wonder I never had any appetite in the USA."

I felt a little guilty condemning the food that my family and Wilda had made, but this bread was something altogether different and new.

Once the airplane landed, I found my accommodations and took a walk, as advised, to help me to get used to the five-hour time difference.

No one looked at me strangely because I was a Negro. People walked and looked directly at me. I did not have to look down at the ground. Arthur had told me, man of the world that he was, that this would happen.

"They don't care about our skin color there, Mama. There, we are as free to walk around as they are."

And I found his words to be true. For the most part. When I went to the fashion show, I had a hard time with my credentials. They just couldn't believe that a small Negro woman was supposed to view the fashion shows as a journalist. Only my airplane friend, who saw me trying to get in, helped me to gain entry.

That incident went into one of my articles along with my first impressions of Paris.

Still, the show that I had struggled to get into, the Dior show, had the most people attending. And when the models walked out, it was as if all of my fantasies had come to life. They all had small waists and rounded shoulders, and wore firm undergarments. Had this Dior person gone into my mind and stolen my ideas?

I didn't know if I should be excited because I had likeminded thoughts as Dior or disappointed because a male fashion designer named Dior would surely get the attention that I would not. All because of the color of his skin.

I heard someone call my name, and I saw the lovely Olivia de Havilland calling to me. Olivia de Havilland was saying my name? I went to her.

"I didn't expect to see you here, Miss Lowe."

I explained to her my luck after she had left her appointment. As I was talking, the designer himself appeared at her side and eyed me up and down, as if I were a curiosity. "Oh, Christian," Miss de Havilland said to him, "this is the woman I was telling you about. She is doing my dress for the Academy Awards. Miss Lowe, please meet Christian Dior."

He lifted my hand and kissed it.

A white man.

I nearly fainted but managed to hold on to my wide hat. "I can see what you mean. She does have a similar sense of style."

"I thought the same as I watched your show today, sir."

He noticed my plain but well-executed outfit. "Is this of your creation, Miss Lowe?" His accent was so thick I could barely understand him.

"Yes. I believe that I am not a canvas, like the lovely Miss de Havilland here, but having come to Paris, I knew that I should try to look my best."

"Turn around."

I obeyed, a rush of heat rising to the top of my head. Not being a model, I was not used to being inspected.

"Madam, you dress like a Frenchwoman."

"I assure you, Mr. Dior, I was born in Clayton, Alabama."

Olivia de Havilland's well-manicured eyebrows went up.

"Oh yes, ma'am. My grandmother sewed dresses for the real Scarlett O'Hara. I myself made clothes for the first lady of Alabama."

They both nodded. "I must be going," Mr. Dior said. "I am happy to have made your acquaintance, Miss Lowe."

"Thank you, sir."

I turned from them both and made my way back to my small hotel room, stunned at all that had happened to me in such a short time. Surely, I would now be on my way.

I kept that feeling in my heart for weeks thereafter and was so happy when, over the radio, I heard that Olivia de Havilland won the Academy Award.

That meant the dress would be in the papers. With my name on it.

I could barely sleep.

The next morning, I went to work, and Sonja came into the design room, waving the newspaper. "Look at Miss de Havilland in our dress."

"Our dress?" The words slipped from my mouth without me censoring them.

Sonja stopped, seeming to be surprised at my response. "Yes. See here."

She had five New York newspapers, all of them with Olivia de Havilland looking lovely, holding a golden trophy. All five said Sonja made the dress. The name Ann Lowe didn't appear anywhere. She picked up the papers, holding them to her, delighted. "Imagine the business we'll get."

Yes, she would get all of the business, all of the attention.

I would get nothing.

All of that was confirmed in my mind when *Life* magazine published reports from the haute couture houses, calling the Dior show "The New Look."

No. His New Look was an Old Look that I had updated for the time after the war. A time when we were again allowed fabric and rubber for corsets and bras.

This double blow served to prove one thing to me: I needed my own shop again.

ON A QUIET early February afternoon after my Paris trip, my client Mrs. Auchincloss and her daughters came in for their appointment. Mrs. Auchincloss was as lovely and elegant as ever, even though she was expecting a happy event, clearly very soon. Her clothes were cut to suit her. She looked like a grown-up lady—too many maternity clothes made women look like children. Although the post-wartime fashions now favored a small waist, something she did not presently have given her shape, she still looked as stunning as when she first stepped into my shop.

Mrs. Auchincloss stepped forward, nodding her head. "It's so good to see you again, Miss Lowe. Girls, Miss Lowe. Miss Lowe, this is Jacqueline and Lee. My daughters."

I nodded to the girls. The taller, clearly older one, was the same young woman I saw shopping off the rack back in January before while the younger, more petite in every way, still had the look of mischievousness about her that I remembered from working on her mother's wedding outfit years prior.

"What can I do for you today?"

"Jacqueline is going to debut this year and will need a suitable dress."

"I want one too," Lee interjected with look-at-me energy saturating her voice.

Mrs. Auchincloss waved her hands. "Yes, Lee. Miss Lowe will make you something suitable as well."

Oh yes. It was clear the dynamic here. The younger sister was quite used to getting what she wanted, working her cute little pout, no doubt. I knew those tricks well.

"Please, come this way and make yourselves comfortable." I pointed out the most comfortable couch in the design room.

They sat, one daughter on either side of their mother, and something in my heart tugged when I saw Jacqueline's concern for her mother. Lee looked far less engrossed in her mother, and far more embarrassed by her condition. A debutante year meant that Jacqueline would be eighteen and from what I recall, Lee was four years younger, though she acted far younger.

I brought out my sketch pad. "I've done deb dresses before but let me know if you have something special you like."

"It will be white, of course." Jacqueline kept her voice low and sure.

"How full of a skirt?"

"Not that full."

"The war is over," Lee pointed out. Ahh, a girl after my own heart.

"Everyone will have a full skirt for that reason, Lee," her sister informed her.

"I see." I drew a less full skirt. "Sleeves? Shoulders?"

"No sleeves, on the shoulders, here." She pointed to her midarm. Her mother, however, pointed to the curve of her shoulder, so I drew the sleeve there. It was always a tenuous line to walk between what mothers wanted and what daughters wanted.

"I want pink," Lee put in.

"Hold on. We need to get Jacqueline's dress down first." Mrs. Auchincloss's slim ringed hand slid just a little bit over her belly. Form was that a woman in a delicate condition didn't like to call attention to herself, but no doubt she was checking in on her baby, as a good mother should.

Lee leaned back, not at all interested in the negotiations, and picked up some magazines and started thumbing through them, muttering, "Well, I'm going to have a full skirt."

"Do you like flowers, Miss Jacqueline?"

"Oh yes, I do." I drew a few of them on the line of the bodice. "White roses here, with a tulle overlay for the skirt."

I presented her with the drawing. Mrs. Auchincloss looked at it, liking it, but Jacqueline was not pleased.

She pointed to the waist. "How about something there for balance?"

More roses maybe? I quickly drew a line of them across.

"More," she said, "almost like a low girdle."

Ahh. Now I understood. I sketched them in, and I could see what she meant. I recalled her great eye for line and style during her mother's wedding outfit fitting.

I showed her the sketch, and she said, "Yes. I like that very much."

They all did, except for Lee. I drew a sketch that I thought was suitable for her, in pink, but her mother was far more enthusiastic about it than Lee was. One thing I'd learned over the years is that when it is someone's turn to be a debutante or get married, you let her shine. It was her day. Lee would have her own day in four years.

"We'll do a fitting if that is okay." Jacqueline stood and we both went into the back, while Lee and her mother relaxed out front.

Sallie was the one who would normally do this job for me at my own shop, but now I was compelled to do it because Sonja did not have an official fitter at Saks. "I wondered, Miss Bouvier. I thought I saw you shopping in the store's evening gowns last week. Would this dress be what you really want?"

A sad look crossed her face. "Oh, please, Miss Lowe. Don't let my mother know I was here. I needed an off-the-rack gown for another occasion. Something more suitable, I mean, nothing in your league."

"Of course. I just want to make sure you have what you want. Stand still."

Her posture was perfect, just perfect.

"See . . . my father. If he were to have something for me, like a debutante party, I couldn't wear a dress like what you are making for me. I couldn't wear bespoke."

I shook my head. She wasn't the first young woman I had seen have this issue. "So he'll have a party for you as well."

Her eyes sparkled. "Oh yes. He promised. A Bouvier party. Something *très élégant*."

"I'm sure it will be." I jotted down a few notes. "But does the other dress, I mean, is it okay? For your needs?"

She turned to face me, her wide-set eyes a tad softer than they were before. "It will have to do, Miss Lowe. I would never dream of asking him for something just for another party, and it was all I could afford, I mean apart from what Mother gives me."

I bit my lip. "Bring it by here one day, if you can. I can add some special touches to it if you want."

The look in her eyes spread like a glow across her face. "You would? Oh, thank you so much. I want to look as pretty for Daddy's party as well."

"Of course. We can make it work." I nodded my head. "You can send Lee back."

She sauntered out elegantly, every bit of Miss Porter's training in her stride. When Lee came back, she wanted reassurances that she would not look like a baby, and I assured her that she would not. "It'll be lovely, Miss Lee. As lovely as you are."

I could tell that was enough to please her, for now—she looked like a kitten lapping up cream.

About a month later, my Ruthy, who liked to read the society pages, read of the birth of Mrs. Auchincloss's baby. A son. Just a bit more security in her well-made marriage. After the birth of her brother, she and Lee came to retrieve their dresses for the debutante ball.

One morning, Ruthy was again looking through the society pages and saw a picture of Jacqueline in my custom dress at an event to introduce "Master Jamie and Jacqueline."

"I thought she was going to have two deb balls." I shook my head as I sipped my coffee. Then it occurred to me: If her father couldn't afford a better dress for her, then he probably could not afford a ball.

Poor girl. Something in my heart connected with her. She had her father at least, even if it was only every so often. And the disappointment of not having the second ball must have hurt. I said a quick prayer for her.

Another day that summer, Jacqueline was announced as Deb of the Year for 1947. *Life* magazine featured a series of pictures showing a glowing young lady tossing the tulle of my dress up past the girdle of roses around her waist. I turned all of the pages in the magazine, going through all of the pictures, looking, looking, looking.

She had not mentioned my name.

It didn't matter. The deb season was over and there would be no benefit from it until 1948. Still, when Arthur came to me the next day and told me that he had found suitable shop space for me—on Lexington Avenue, in a part of New York that my clients would not be unwillling to travel to—I wondered if having my name mentioned in *Life* magazine in 1947 as the designer of Jacqueline's deb dress would have given me an extra lift in sales. I could have put those profits toward my newest endeavor.

Then I remembered that putting my name in the paper, as if I were typical, would have been vulgar. My designs were high society's best-kept secret. The dresses I made were not just for any Betty or Sue. They were for the highest society matrons. They knew who I was. They would find their way to the new Lexington store.

It was time, past time, for me to strike out on my own again. Thank God I would have my son in business with me, helping me, guiding me.

God was making all of my dreams come true.

Part III

The Dream Comes True

Chapter Twenty-Nine

*M*any don't know, but Jacqueline was engaged one time before. To another John.

She came into my shop with her mother and sister for an appointment in the hot summer of June 1952. Her face was alight.

"Jacqueline is engaged," Janet Auchincloss said as if someone had a gun to her back, not the tone that I would have expected from the society maven.

Lee jumped in so someone would look at her. "Mother doesn't like him. Honestly," she said, turning to them both, "I want my gown for Michael."

"This is a dual appointment?" I drew back a little, my fingers threading around my favorite drawing pencil. "What a blessing, Mrs. Auchincloss. Congratulations."

I wanted her to relax and to get that constipated look off her face. Lee's words did the trick. Mrs. Auchincloss waved her hand. "What kind of woman would come for an appointment when she has not had a proposal yet?"

"I've told you, Mother. We've discussed it. He's going to come to you and Uncle Hughdie next week."

Jacqueline stepped forward, her voice level when she spoke. "John is not quite in Mother's social circle. He's not in the *Register*."

Well, I had to control my face at that bit of news. "He's not?" I mean, even I was in the *Social Register* as an approved merchant. It had been one of my proudest moments to be included. The *Register* had long been my book, my bible of who I needed to know, who anyone who was anybody needed to know. There were multiple volumes of the *Register* for various cities and if someone wasn't listed, well . . . I usually was too busy to make a dress for those people. I swallowed.

"Even Miss Lowe knows that a man who isn't in the *Register* cannot possibly take care of you, Jacqueline."

"Let's all sit." As I guided my guests to the couches, I knew making them comfortable would help take the tension out of the appointment. Jacqueline sat on the one closest to me and Lee sat on another with her mother.

Jacqueline kept her dark eyes focused on me, singularly. "Our wedding will be something small. Not too large. Uncle Hughdie has agreed that we might marry at Hammersmith Farm, his home in Rhode Island." She turned to her mother. "He may not be as well-connected as some, but he's a stockbroker. Like Daddy."

"Well that's a relief." Mrs. Auchincloss's mouth formed into a seam of disapproval.

Jacqueline smiled at me. I returned her warm and gracious posture. "Something like my deb dress. Only more so."

"More so is the thing these days." I made broad strokes on the paper. "I have thoughts in mind of what my grandmother used to do for her mistress in old Alabama. Something like that."

"Don't give all the good ideas to Jackie," Lee practically screamed. "I'm getting married soon too."

Janet Auchincloss put her hand on her daughter's leg and dug in a little to keep the girl still. Lee was barely twenty. What was she in such a rush for? She wasn't in the family way.

Then it clicked.

She was in a hurry to beat her older sister, of course. I had seen this phenomenon before, but usually it wasn't so . . . obvious. I just continued with my faint outlines of a dress that I had in mind.

I showed the drawing to Jackie. "Yes. I like that very much." Twin sapphires in a vintage setting twinkled on her broad hand. Her hands weren't dainty but I could see that Jacqueline, who was a cub reporter on a newspaper in Washington, D.C., had some purpose in her life and I liked that. A woman should always have a purpose. Those who didn't were usually headed for trouble.

I nodded to Lee. "Don't you worry. I've never duplicated one of my dresses yet." I pointed to the open swatch and design book on my desk, my system for ensuring that my dresses were unique and singular. "Been designing one-of-a-kind dresses for more than thirty-five years. So when the time comes, and you have a ring on your finger, I'll create something just for you."

That quieted Lee. Her sister had a ring. She did not.

"I'll want ivory."

"Perfect. A deposit of fifty dollars will let me buy the material."

Mrs. Auchincloss made an inelegant sound as she opened her purse to bring forth her checkbook. "How much will the dress cost, overall?"

"Three hundred."

"Oh no. She's marrying a stockbroker who isn't even in the *Register*, Miss Lowe. You'll have to take away some of those skirts. You aren't Elizabeth Taylor, Jacqueline."

Jacqueline's eyes turned down in the corners.

"Michael is the love child of the Duke of Kent. He's royalty!"

Lee piped up. I smiled and nodded at Lee before turning back to Jacqueline.

Every woman should have the wedding dress she wanted. "I think I can do something similar to this in the one-hundred-seventy-five-dollar range. Of course, I'll still need the deposit to secure the fabric."

Jacqueline's eyes lighted again, and the sight gladdened my heart. Mrs. Auchincloss waved a hand. "That's fine. Send the bill to Hugh's office." She stood. "Thank you so much, Miss Lowe."

I nodded. "Gladly."

Lee opened her mouth, but her mother turned her to the door. Rightfully.

I always read the engagement notices in the paper, of course, since knowing which society women were planning to marry affected my business, and the next month, the notice about Lee's engagement appeared. I shook my head. I guess she would be in my shop soon enough.

A month later, though, just after Labor Day, Mrs. Auchincloss sent me a note telling me that Jacqueline's engagement had been ended, *Thank the heavens above,* she wrote. She also set an appointment for just before Christmastime to consult about Lee's dress, which I had expected. When I saw Lee's name connected with a Michael Canfield in the paper, I couldn't help but think about how her rushing to marry before her older sister was not a good sign. The length of fabric I had set aside for Jacqueline's dress went to the top of my cupboard. I was a bit chagrined to see Lee win out over her sister in the wedding sweepstakes. Maybe Lee sensed how I felt about the whole matter because she did not keep the appointment with me; she commissioned someone else—a cheaper designer, I found out later—to make her wedding dress, which ended up costing her more in the long run because of all of the extra frills Lee wanted.

But I knew that would happen.

THE NEXT YEAR, in June, Jacqueline was back in my shop again, her face alight in an entirely different way. I knew it was because she had met and captured America's most available young bachelor. She had tossed John Husted out of her life once she met the more exciting Senator John Kennedy. This time, she had a new man and wanted a new look.

"I want plain. Sleek, slim."

"But when you were going to marry before, you said to make it like your debutante dress. Only more so."

She waved a hand. "That dress was for another man. This one is for my fiancé."

"Less fabric?" I gestured at Mrs. Auchincloss with my pencil. I could see her lips were pursed up tight. Why? Didn't she like this senator? The handsome young man in a hurry, hurry, hurry?

"Yes," Jacqueline said.

"It's not really what . . ." I stopped. How could I say this to her? The fashion that year, 1953, didn't depend on less fabric—it was all about more, more, more. Elizabeth Taylor's dual impact on wedding dresses the year before, both the dress she wore to start her short real-life marriage and the one that would forever exist on film in *Father of the Bride,* was all the rage now. Helen Rose saw to that. A big dress like that one would put me in the headlines, just like she had been.

Jacqueline slightly lowered her voice, which meant that she

was very serious. "You should know by now, Miss Lowe. I've never been afraid of not fitting in. I . . ."

She stopped because the door to my shop had swung open and the room filled with the humid June air. There, standing in my doorway, blocking my doorway, filling my doorway, was a man.

Not Arthur. He knew how to slip in and out without causing a scene. My clients and staff were used to his comings and goings in the shop. The appointment of my son to take care of matters had been a godsend—when I saw how well he handled everything, I knew God had rewarded me well.

No. This was a white man.

A tall, big-talking white man with big ways and a big voice.

"Jack-que-line!" he practically shouted. Mrs. Auchincloss's eyes rolled back in her head so far I could see the red veiny bottoms of them. Lee giggled as she would do at any humiliation to her mother or sister, and Jacqueline's cool countenance got a little warm.

"I'm so sorry, Miss Lowe," Mrs. Auchincloss said when she had gathered herself. "I'm so, so sorry."

"I'm not sure what for, ma'am."

"That . . ." She paused. "The Ambassador has felt the need to come into your shop. I'll handle him." She turned on her heel and went over to the man, who was still in the doorway.

"Are you okay, Jacqueline?" I said her name as she preferred it, rhyming her name with *queen* to offset the harsh way the man—I mean, the Ambassador—said it.

She just nodded her head.

Lee giggled, cupping her hand around her mouth, and whispered to me, most imprudently, "Mother does not like him at all. He's a Democrat."

"That's not true, Lee," Jacqueline whispered back. She turned to me. "It's that they both like to be in charge. But they cannot both be in charge, you see?"

"I see." And I did. This happened all the time in weddings, but usually it was the mothers of the bride and groom clashing. This battle had a different texture to it.

Lee looked over her shoulder, but Jacqueline refused to do so. I couldn't blame her. The confrontation between the two had been tense, too tense. All I could see were Mrs. Auchincloss's shoulders squared in her day dress, ready to do battle.

Then the shoulders rounded again. She turned on her heel and the Ambassador took her by the arm and escorted her to where we sat.

Lee's pretty face, a mask of confusion, rearranged into a smirk as she removed herself from the couch where she sat next to her sister so that the Ambassador could get to Jacqueline. "Ahh, ladies. Lovely day, isn't it?" He leaned down to kiss Jacqueline on the cheek and she kissed him back. I could tell by the gleam in his eyes that he was one who liked ladies, not unlike his son. The thought of both made the seam in my stomach tuck in even tighter for whatever Jacqueline would go through in her life.

Jacqueline Husted would have had a calm life.

Jacqueline Kennedy's life? Tumultuous.

Was quiet little Jacqueline ready for the ride?

"It is, Mr. Kennedy." Jacqueline kept her voice breathy and light.

"I was in the neighborhood and I just wanted to see what was going on. How do you do, Mrs. . . ?"

He turned to me, offering his hand, which I took, and let me tell you, that was a *man* shaking my hand.

I withdrew my hand as quickly as I could. I needed it to make this dress.

"I'm Miss Lowe."

"Ahh yes. When I heard that Mrs. Auchincloss had a Negro dressmaker, well, I was so happy to hear that. This is just what we need in this wedding to show the population that we know well of the Negro problem in this country. To have you do the dress is one of the best things for my son." He patted Jack-que-line's knee and she smiled at him.

"I'm so glad, sir," I said, although I could see nothing of what Jacqueline's dress had to do with the Negro problem, as he called it.

He must have read my mind.

"Jack's going to be president one day, you know. So we need a dress that, well, it can't be an ordinary dress, Miss Lowe. It's got to be a tremendous kind of a dress. A gown, as it were. Fit for our queen, Jack-que-line here." He made wide gestures with his hands.

Mrs. Auchincloss leaned down, picking up the sketch pad out of my hands. "Miss Lowe here has a lovely design, reminiscent of a Southern belle. The kind of old-fashioned look that will suit, Mr. Kennedy, that tremendousness that you are thinking of."

He looked over the sketch. "This. This is exactly the kind of dress I'm talking about. But even more, more than that. A dress to capture the imagination of the Old South, not to mention their votes!" He guffawed at his cleverness. No one else did.

My hand, free of my sketch pad, seemed empty. I balled it into a fist and looked over at Jacqueline. Both of them had ganged up on her. She had no way out and her face showed it—her eyebrows were drawn together in defeat. My heart went out to her. If her father were here, if he had been able to pay, if he could have protected her, she could have had her heart's desire. He would have fought for her.

But with this, this man, this powerful man and her powerful mama aligned, she didn't have a chance.

And I had no choice but to deliver what they wanted, because it was his money that was making this all possible. This would be the five-hundred-dollar dress that Ambassador Kennedy was paying for, and ten bridesmaid gowns in pink sateen with claret velvet bows, a two-thousand-dollar commission. A once-in-a-lifetime opportunity for me to receive the credit I deserved.

I thought of this now, as my shop filled in every corner with my church family, in pairs of the best seamstresses surrounding the pink sateen dresses for the bridesmaids. Then there was me, sewing the flower bells on a panel of the skirt, making the rosette round and round, using up the lengths of fabric that had been chosen for marrying a different John.

The creation of the rosettes, which I learned in design school was called trapunto, was a foundational technique used by my mother and grandmother, so it really surprised me that my missing father should come to my mind today. I think the memory of the appearance of the Ambassador served to underline that there was a new overwhelming male presence in her life that Jacqueline was being handed off to, one for whom she had no ready response. I knew just what that was like, because Lee Cone served that function for me.

SALLIE LEANED OVER with the ruching on the bodice between her thumbs. She was the only other person in the shop who I allowed to help me work on Jacqueline's wedding gown. "A penny for your thoughts, sister."

"I hope Mr. Kennedy appreciates all of this."

"Are you going to tell him?" Her voice was low.

"Certainly not!"

"I did not think so."

"It's not for him to know. The job must be finished. There is no other consequence in this situation."

"Are you upset that he called you a Negro?"

"It's what I am."

Sallie nodded. "Still, I think it was imprudent of him to say it so often. As if it was a benefit to him in some way."

"Powerful men create stories to get what they want." I sat up straight. "I'm not surprised. Only, Jacqueline . . ."

"I'm sure." Sallie's forehead wrinkled.

I turned to Sallie. "There are few things more sad than a bride who isn't wearing the dress of her dreams."

"It'll be beautiful on her."

"I didn't say that it wouldn't be. I just hope she knows what she is getting in to. Ever since she came to the shop this summer to say she was marrying this new John, this more famous John, well . . . I've felt something about it." I shook my head. "I can't explain it. And I don't want to sew it into this dress. So I'll keep my thoughts to myself."

Sallie bent back to her task, and I sewed on, finishing my rosette.

I straightened my back. Coming up on fifty-five in December, my body was creaking and groaning in ways that I had never known before. Then, depending on the light, my eyes were certainly not as reliable as they once were, but I could do this work by feel. Sewing these gorgeous dresses was in my blood too much. My fingers would do the work that my eyes could not. I went around the shop, supervising the five pairs of women who were working on the bridesmaid dresses. I could get everything done in time for Wednesday if we kept up this pace for the next two days.

I would be so grateful for these women who volunteered to help me out of this very tough spot.

But I would not, could not pay them for their trouble. It would be a loss of thousands of dollars for me.

I could never let such a powerful man know that such a terrible thing had happened. Could you imagine? Me going to him with my hand out asking for another check?

No, I would be indebted to these sisters for the rest of my life and I would pay in silent commissions of a wedding dress for a daughter or daughter-in-law here, or a prom dress there. I would have to secretly relax my covenant of not sewing for anyone outside of the *Social Register.*

But I would meet my obligations to them. Quietly.

Because Jacqueline Bouvier would not want to wear a wedding dress that was just like what a Negro woman would wear.

That was the truth of my life and I had to face it.

She would never, ever know.

September 8, 1953

Here's where we are, the point you were wanting to hear about. Is this why you all came to help me sew so many dresses in record time?

What is Jackie Kennedy really like?

Well, I call her Jacqueline, like her mama named her.

Her mama, amazing woman that she is, told her girls to call me Miss Lowe and they did. I deserve that respect even though no one ever called my mama or grandmother by their titles in Alabama. Even Miss Lizzie O'Neal said "Janie." Or "Georgia." Or, to me, "Annie."

When my time to sew come.

I mean *came*.

I steady my sewing hands as they move to create these ruffles. Ruffles upon ruffles, upon ruffles. Fluted cloth like hills and valleys, the peaks and low places in a woman's life. That's what these are to me. That these large rosettes will be a big round happy place of life, but the real truth of a woman's life is that there are high places and low, low ones.

I stand to wash my hands again. This cloth has to stay what it is, ivory. Not candlelight. The ivory is a better shade for Jacqueline's brunette beauty. Matches that tint in her skin that she got from her daddy, Black Jack Bouvier. Because who in the *Social Register* did not know that rascal?

So. You wash your hands too.

Go ahead. Plenty of soap and water at the sink, because I keep everything clean in my shop. It's my shop, my place of pride, my space. On Lexington Avenue in New York City.

A place my mama and grandma never could have even imagined I would go.

But they saw something. And claimed it for me in their prayers, even though they had no idea what they were praying for. That's what it is to be a mama. A good mama. Like Janet Auchincloss was, even though I could tell at that bridal appointment that Jacqueline was like me back in the Lee Cone days.

And I wanted to tell her: "Don't rush it. It will come."

"Be patient."

"Wait."

So I sewed all of that into this dress when I made it first time around.

All I can feel now is despair. Despair that I have to sew so fast with you all, deprive myself of food, sleep, time—all because of a cut-off pipe in my beautiful shop.

And the ruffles flutter fast, fast, fast on this dress.

Like Jacqueline Bouvier is running, running, running to her destiny.

So, to pass the time, I'll tell you what I, society's invisible hands, know about this woman who is destined to be a first lady, like Mamie Eisenhower—if her powerful father-in-law has anything to say about it.

But you've got to keep it quiet and to yourself.

That's what a lady would do.

I'm only doing it because I owe you one.

'Cause you are helping me to mine.

Destiny.

Chapter Thirty

September 10, 1953

*W*as it possible to work any harder? Could my fingers sew any faster? I could not, would not let anyone know of this horrible catastrophe in my life. I knew I could do this. With a little help from my church sisters and my real sister, I could do it.

This time brought me back to the days in Tampa, when I had young women come to my shop in the morning wanting a gown for an affair that night. And I would be able to pull that off—an Ann Lowe original in a matter of hours!

It also was a matter of appreciating a woman's curvy form, of creating the dress-to-be to fit like her skin did to her body. Those women were confident that all they had to do was put the dress on.

That's what I said: Put the dress on.

No bra.

No girdle.

No underwear lines visible at all.

Everything had to be smooth, smooth, smooth.

Every seam covered with quality lace. Quality goods, not the kind that made you itch. When a client once told me that she didn't like lace because it was itchy, I nearly cried. What had she been wearing to think such a thing? For to me, lace was the ultimate floral recreation. Lace has its own way of talking, its own language. It was a language that I myself couldn't capture, but I could appreciate its use in the gowns I designed.

Rushing to make new dresses for Jacqueline and her bridesmaids now was the same thing as putting together a dress in a day in Tampa. At my age now it wasn't possible to sew a gown a day, but two gowns a day between teams of women was achievable.

And for Jacqueline's dress, the Montgomery Southern belle dress for which I would not stint on fabric like in the war days . . . well, that was for me to do.

It was a quarter after five A.M. on that Thursday when I finished the last stich on Jacqueline's dress. My church ladies had finished with the bridesmaid dresses the afternoon before.

Thank you, God, for getting me this far.

After fielding a second call from Mrs. Auchincloss on Wednesday because the dresses had not been delivered yet, I readied myself for the train to Rhode Island, which left in a few hours. Arthur and Sallie were traveling with me to help deliver the dresses to Hammersmith Farm.

I fell down, exhausted onto my cot in the back of my rejuvenated shop, thanks to the hard work of the men of the church. I didn't want to go home, because if anything else were to happen, I would put my body between it and any of the dresses that we had covered in plastic wrap and acid-free tissue paper. Once we made the delivery, Arthur and Sallie would return to New York while I stayed in Rhode Island to fit the dresses. I would then accompany Jacqueline to the church and stay for the reception before I returned to New York later Saturday afternoon.

When Sallie came to the shop at eight o'clock, I went home to pack my suitcase.

"You look tired, Mama," Arthur said when he came to the apartment to drive us to the train station in his car, his pride and joy. With some careful balancing, we all fit inside along with sixteen bridesmaid dress boxes and the wedding dress, of course. I breathed a sigh of relief when this crucial commission was out of the shop.

"I'm fine." I imagined Mrs. Auchincloss up at Hammersmith Farm, wondering where I was. I knew. I was on my way, praise Him.

Arthur ran a hand over his handsome wavy hair. Where did he get that good hair from? Not from me and my thin locks. Maybe Lee had something to offer after all. I loved watching Arthur fumble through it. "I feel so responsible. I'm the one who found this space for you, after all."

"Things happen, son. Let's not dwell on it. We made it. Let's get to the station."

I directed Arthur to drive and when we got to Penn Station, I willed the train to come on time, which it did. I felt the years slip from me as I watched the city fall away and the train traveled north, ever northward to Boston, and then on to Newport, Rhode Island, where a special train depot had been built. Newport was where the wealthiest had summered for many years and when we arrived at Hammersmith Farm's rolling green hills, I marveled.

"This. Is. Stunning," Arthur said in his way, so appreciative of beauty, no matter what it was. I patted his arm.

"I told you that Mrs. Auchincloss doesn't do anything by halves. She wanted a rich man, she married one." I could not keep the tone of pride out of my voice. Good for her.

"It's too bad she didn't know any other rich men to refer us to." Sallie's joking smile reached across her broad pretty face.

I shook my head. "No more for me. I'm rich in every way that matters. As hard as this week was, I've got the best with both of you supporting me, supporting my dream to make these beautiful dresses. It's all I've ever wanted. It's all I ever needed."

They both shook their heads at me, not liking it when I got a little too truthful, or too emotional, with them, but it was the gospel truth. I would not have made it here without either one of them.

We had to take two taxi cabs for ourselves and the dresses. I kept my arms on Jacqueline's gown the whole time. I would not let it out of my sight until it was in her hands.

When I climbed out of the cab, my small arms struggled with the weight of the dress, so I let Arthur carry it as we approached the vast front door.

I rang the doorbell and waited.

A tall man opened it, screwing up his face immediately at my appearance. I knew that face. It was the same kind of expression S. T. Taylor wore when I first stepped foot into his precious design school.

I did not need to see him right now. I tried not to slump over from exhaustion, but my usual costume of a tastefully appointed black dress and matching hat were clean, well ironed, and tasteful.

My thin hair had been pressed and styled in a neat chignon, and a small button hat with a black veil covered my head. I was chic and able to blend into my surroundings at a moment's notice. Black dress, black hair, Negro woman—all ready to disappear.

Except now I must stand out. And up.

"Yes?" He sounded out, his broad hand placed possessively on the door's edge.

"Hello. I'm here to deliver the dresses for the wedding." I

cleared my throat. I would say it again, to be better understood if need be. My voice was husky from lack of sleep, but I did get it out clear enough the first time.

"All deliveries are in the back." He tried to close the door, but my arm shot out to hold it open. Later, I realized I had put my precious hands in danger but I did not care.

In that moment our eyes met—his blue and hard, mine brown and hot—in a confrontation as old as time.

"This is no ordinary delivery, sir. These are the dresses for Miss Jacqueline's wedding. I am Ann Lowe, the designer. Mrs. Auchincloss is waiting for me," I informed him, borrowing some of the cold from his eyes and putting it into my voice.

"Listen here, girl. You got some nerve coming to the front door of Hammersmith Farm. When it's time to deliver something, your people go in the back." Blood rushed into his face, as it usually did whenever someone of his heritage got upset.

"Sir"—and I made sure to put an emphasis in my fully Arctic tone of voice—"if we are to deliver these dresses in the back, there will be no wedding dresses for Miss Jacqueline and her bridesmaids."

And I meant it too. I had been through too much in making the second round of dresses. I was on a knife's edge and I wouldn't mind going over it. I had faced down worse in my day. I might be going on fifty-five but I was ready to do battle with him. Arthur drew by my side with the wedding dress box, ready to smooth my path, as he so often did, with a kind word to this horrible man, when I saw Miss Lee coming down the steps.

I called out to her. "Mrs. Canfield! Your bridesmaid's dress is here."

Lee could never resist hearing about her dresses. Her pretty face was completely without expression, but as she drew closer she could see the situation. "Oh no. This is Miss Lowe. She designed the dresses, please let her through. Mother's been waiting."

When Lee pressed on the man's arm, he had no choice but to yield.

Thank you, God. But for his sake, not mine.

"Thank you, Mrs. Canfield. Where should we put them?"

I stepped through the door, past the mean butler and into the lighted foyer, like an empress. Young women came in from everywhere, and after it had been made clear that we could use some help, a small party of them marched down to the taxi cabs in excitement, looking to retrieve the boxes containing their dresses. The mean butler had no choice but to join them.

It sure lifted my heart to see those young women come to our rescue.

Arthur stepped forward with the bride's box in hand and put it on a blue and white overstuffed chair in the living room. Out of the corner of my eye, I recognized a somber Jacqueline, dressed casually in a sleeveless blouse and blue clam diggers, step forward, her eyes on the biggest white box.

I went to her, my hands folded. "It's your dress, Miss Jacqueline."

"I see, Miss Lowe. Thank you. I'm sure it's very nice."

I was about to suggest we go start the fitting, but she maneuvered around the crowd of babbling bridesmaids and toward some other room in the back. She didn't want to see her wedding dress? What bride didn't want to see her dress again?

Mrs. Auchincloss stepped up to us. "Oh, I'm so glad to see you, Miss Lowe. There's a room off the parlor for you to stay in and to have the dresses fitted. There's a full-length mirror in there for your use."

Arthur stepped forward with my overnight bag and placed it

outside the door of the room. He came back to me, and said, "Seems like you are ready to start, Mama."

He leaned down and gave me a kiss on the cheek. Sallie did the same and they went outside to the remaining taxi cab, which was waiting to take them back to the train station.

Inside the house there was lots of excitement as the bridesmaids found their dresses. Each dress box had a name on it and as the women searched for the right box, there was a cacophony of jabbering voices, arms waving, and trading of boxes. Except from Jacqueline.

"The milliner has been here with the Juliet caps. We were just waiting for the dresses," Lee told me, her sly voice full of meaning.

"Well, I'm here," I told her.

Her mother stood next to me. "It's just about time for the rehearsal dinner at the club, so there really isn't any time for the fittings now, Miss Lowe. I expect the final fittings will happen as they come back from dinner and into tomorrow."

I gestured toward the other room. "What about Jacqueline?"

Mrs. Auchincloss grasped her hands. "She's got a bad case of nerves, a very bad case. I'm at my wit's end about it. She . . . I just don't know. She's usually reserved, of course, but this . . . well."

Jacqueline remerged, a lit cigarette between her slim fingers. "Miss Lowe, you might relax while we are in rehearsal at St. Mary's. When we come back, I'm sure you'll have your hands full trying to make sure everything works out right."

She had no idea.

So, I did as she bid. While they were in rehearsal, I went to the small maid's room in the back of the house and took a nice, long nap. I awakened to the sound of a house filled with young people jabbering, smoking, pretend dancing, and making a lot of wonderful, happy noise.

I straddled the world at seeing them, so full of life and vigor, and the house staff, serious and stern, making all kinds of preparations for the reception that would also take place there. Mrs. Auchincloss was indeed at her wit's end and I could see that Arthur and Cora had done me a favor by marrying in their quiet way.

My work soon started. One at a time, Mrs. Auchincloss garnered a wayward bridesmaid to come to me and have her fitting. The Kennedy girls and Lee, of course, came quickly. When I looked up, it was two A.M. and I had less than a handful of the bridesmaids to go.

And Jacqueline.

Everything had quieted down. I went back to my small room, but I could see the shapely elegant outline of the bride, hovering outside smoking another cigarette, looking out on the rolling grassy grounds of Hammersmith Farm. The ocean sounded just beyond, and, as I knew from living in Tampa, the sound of water made for a splendid night's sleep.

Well, maybe not for a nervous bride.

I approached her. "Is everything all right, Miss Jacqueline?"

"Ahh, Miss Lowe." She drew a last puff and then snuffed out her cigarette in an ashtray on a table. "I'm just fine. I'm about to get to sleep."

Sleep? "We still need to do our final fitting."

The way she drew back made me think I had said something wrong. Then she smiled. "Of course."

"Are you sure you are well?"

Her energy that usually held her upright so well slumped a bit. "I'm just . . . well, worried about my father. He hasn't arrived yet."

"Well, he still has tomorrow. I mean today. It's Friday, isn't it?" I smiled a little at my unusual disorientation and she reflected my smile back to me. "Is he coming from the city?"

"Yes. There's a car ready to take him to his hotel. I just assumed he didn't want to come here until he had to. He wouldn't be comfortable in seeing"—she made a sweeping, elegant gesture over the grounds—"Hammersmith Farm."

I understood what she meant. All of the grandeur of Hammersmith Farm represented what Jack Bouvier failed to give Janet and their daughters. She had to marry someone else to have it. "I can assure you, Miss Jacqueline, he won't see any of it. All he'll see is you."

She bit her lip, nodding her head. A rare moment of uncertainty from the usually reserved bride.

Turning from me, she made her way through the door. "Good night, Miss Lowe. I'll see you in the morning."

I opened my mouth to try to convince her to let me start the fitting now, but I stopped myself. Bless her. At least she had a father who would come and gather her up to take her down the aisle to her new future and new husband.

I had never had that.

Chapter Thirty-One

I was up again by eight o'clock, when I heard more workmen hammering and sawing outside for the reception tomorrow. From the looks of it they were building a bandstand. One of the maids knocked on my door, offering me a plate of scrambled eggs and some fruit. I took the food gratefully. I suspected it would be a long workday.

I was right.

I fit more bridesmaid gowns during the day, but still had not gotten to see Jacqueline. The wedding party was getting ready to leave for a gathering at some club that night, so once again, I would have to wait until they returned.

Mrs. Auchincloss had told me to use the phone if I needed to, so I made a rare and precious long-distance call to the shop to check on everything. The Newport operator connected me to New York City and Arthur answered the phone.

"Everything is fine here, Mama. We miss you. Aunt Sallie is right here."

"I miss you too, son. Let Sallie know I wish she was here with me with those expert fitting hands of hers."

"Me too!" I heard faintly from her.

"The only one I have left to fit is Jacqueline."

"You haven't put her in the dress yet?" Sallie had taken over the phone from Arthur.

"No." I guess some sadness had crept into my voice because Sallie took on her mothering role of me again. She was always there for me whenever I needed her.

"What is the matter, Annie? I know you wouldn't burden Arthur with it. He's in the back of the shop."

"I don't think she likes her dress." There it was. I said it. The fear that had stalked my heart the whole time, spoken out loud. "She's avoiding me. And the fitting."

"I'm so sorry, sister."

"I mean, I knew. This dress, it's what the Ambassador wanted. What her mother wanted. Not what she wanted. So she's avoiding it."

I could hear Sallie sigh all the way to Rhode Island. I looked about me. No one was around. "Of course, there are some issues with her father, and whether he will show up in the right . . . condition."

"Oh dear. That's what it is, sister, I'm sure. How could she fail to love such a beautiful dress?"

"I don't know."

"Well, the whole thing with her father, handsome devil that he is, is on her mind. I'm sure she will come back from the gathering ready to be fit."

When I hung up the phone, I felt better. I took a seat in the hallway and waited, accompanied by a cup of hot tea that one of the cooks provided to me, so that the family would see me when they came in.

Jacqueline and her mother came in, side by side, their faces masks. "Miss Lowe, may we help you?" Mrs. Auchincloss said to me.

I stood. "I need to get our beautiful bride in her dress so I can make adjustments before tomorrow." I kept my tone light, but I could tell her usually smooth countenance was ruffled—she kept fiddling with her pearls.

"I'm ready now, Miss Lowe." Jacqueline's lovely face resembled the chief mourner at a funeral.

I gestured to the back room where the dress waited for us, and she came along with me.

I took the top off the dress box and pulled back the tissue paper to free the dress from the wrappings.

As with any other Ann Lowe creation, the undergarments were built into the dress. I puddled the dress on the floor so Jacqueline could step into it. Mrs. Auchincloss entered the room and shut the door, cooing as she saw the gown. The size of the dress left little extra space so the three of us stood pretty close together inside the maid's room. I pulled the dress up her long torso smoothly, and she put her elegant arms inside the off-the-shoulder sleeves.

"Oh, Jacqueline. You are stunning." Her mother clasped her hands together, clearly satisfied.

I adjusted the front of the dress and helped to fasten her in the back. Some liked small buttons, but instead I had made an invisible seam with hooks, so that the dress appeared to be one uninterrupted piece. The folds of the dress aided in this intention.

She grasped the skirts and shook them out.

"Thank you, Mother. Do you think Father will like it?"

Mrs. Auchincloss coughed and opened the door a crack so that she could slide out. "We need your grandmother's veil so we can see the complete picture."

I had donned my wrist pincushion with all of its pins, needles, and threads, but I stepped around Jacqueline. "I can go see if one of the upstairs maids will bring it."

"Please do, Miss Lowe."

I had no idea why Jacqueline brought up her father, but I knew when a mother and daughter needed to work something out without me in the room. I ran the errand and the maid brought forth a brown box. I opened it to take a peek. A length of beautiful Irish lace lay inside. Lee had worn the same veil at her wedding five months before with that tacky Pauline Trigère dress of hers, but now the veil had been reconfigured for Jacqueline so it formed a cap on top of her gamine hairstyle. It would be lovely.

I eagerly approached the back room, wanting to continue with my fitting and to see the dress and veil together when Jacqueline and her mother's conversation floated out to me.

"This dress looks like a lampshade." Jacqueline's distressed voice smacked me in the face and my fingertips started to sweat.

"It does not. Look at the fine work, all of these stitches."

"It's awful. I cannot wait to take it off."

"Hush, Jacqueline. You don't want anyone to hear. This dress will make the front page of every newspaper. It's just what will be needed to create a sensation. You'll start a new trend, like Elizabeth Taylor."

"Heaven forbid. Where is she? I need a cigarette."

"Be patient. And be a grown woman, for heaven's sake."

"This is supposed to be my wedding."

"You're marrying into a very powerful and rich family. You have to make compromises."

"I'm sure you would know about that."

"Yes, I've had to make compromises to ensure that you girls were well provided for."

I heard Jacqueline sigh. "Oh, now here we go. You're going to blame Father."

"I'm not blaming him. I'm just saying that I've done what was necessary to make sure you are provided for. Uncle Hughdie . . ."

"He's been a saint. A living saint."

"I don't care for your tone, Jacqueline."

"It would be better if I had a cigarette. Give me one now and I'll drop it on this dress by accident."

"And thank God that Miss Lowe's exceptional skills would repair it. My goodness, it's just a dress. You only have to wear it for one day."

Then Jacqueline said something I couldn't hear.

"Yes, you do have them. I can see them from here."

"Jack likes a woman with a larger chest. This dress presses down on what little bosom I have. I look like a boy."

"No one told you to go get that haircut."

"That's not what I mean, Mother."

"Well, it's what I mean. I don't know why you did that to yourself."

"My hair is too thick and coarse. The less that I have to deal with, the better."

"That Audrey Hepburn style isn't suitable for everyone."

"That's a low blow, Mother. You know Jack dated her."

"I don't know why you are carrying on so. You're perfectly lovely in your own right."

"I don't feel perfectly lovely. Jack might run out of St. Mary's in the other direction, right back into Audrey Hepburn's arms."

"I doubt that. Besides. Mr. Kennedy wouldn't allow it. He doesn't want his son to marry a common actress."

She gave a little laugh. That was probably the point when I should have gone in, but I had rarely heard such a critique of anything I made before. All of my worst fears had come to light. Something that I had created wasn't going to be well accepted.

I had failed.

Well, I had to go in and make the fit better. I wasn't going to give up now. Maybe then Jacqueline would see the dress in a better light and change her mind.

"Knock, knock." I said, entering the room.

They both turned to me, and I made my face as expressionless as theirs. I handed the veil box to Mrs. Auchincloss and turned to Jackie. "Let me see what I can do here."

There was a bit of a sag in the shoulders, and I could see her point about the front. If I had more cloth, I would have made more show of her bosom, but there was only so much that I could do now. The rest had been for God to complete.

Mrs. Auchincloss lifted the veil out of the box by the halo, staring at it. "Here it is." Her voice tripped along, as light and floaty as the lace. "You are the fourth Lee woman to wear this on your wedding day."

Being shorter than Jacqueline, there wasn't much I could do to help with the veil. I did make a fuss, though.

The bride nodded. "Yes. It's gorgeous, isn't it?"

She affixed it to her daughter's head and even though I was still in the middle of the fitting, I could see that the veil helped— the sight of the it transformed Jacqueline. Women wear fancy ball gowns in life every day, but it is the veil that makes a bride.

"Oh, Miss Bouvier." I couldn't help myself. She stunned. Even if she didn't see it, she would do the same to all who saw her.

"You're so beautiful, my dear daughter. My firstborn," her mother said.

Jacqueline looked into the full-length mirror and I could see tears rising in her eyes. I wished they were tears of happiness instead of misery.

Her mother took off the veil and laid it in the box again.

Once I made the pin fit, basting parts together to adjust it, I gestured to Jacqueline. "You're free once again, Miss Bouvier." I kept my voice light, but honestly, the way she had spoken about the dress made me think that's how she really saw it.

I unfastened the hooks in the back and the dress slid down to the floor. Jacqueline stepped out of it, reaching for her day dress once again. "Thank you, Miss Lowe."

"Thank you, Miss Bouvier." I took the full-skirted dress onto my lap to fix the shoulders. Jacqueline had broad shoulders and taking them in a bit would make her look slightly less square and more rounded.

Mrs. Auchincloss turned to me. "Once you are finished we'll send a maid in to bring the dress upstairs." She left the room.

I nodded and, turning the seams inside out, I lowered my head to get to work, determined to get the alterations just right.

Jacqueline continued dressing in the quiet and then went to the phone on the nightstand. "I'm sorry, Miss Lowe. I need to check one thing, if you don't mind."

"Of course not. I'm busy with this."

She picked up the phone and asked the Newport operator to connect her to the Newport Inn. "Yes, please, has Mr. John Vernou Bouvier III checked in?" There was a pause while she waited.

Sallie might have been right. The worries about her father may have caused Jacqueline to take out her frustrations on the dress. Still, it made my inner stomach shrink to think that she thought her dress ugly when I only sought to create beauty in the world. "I see. Well, maybe he checked in under Jack? Jack Bouvier?"

She waited again. A long time.

"Well, he was supposed to check in today. And here it's already 9 P.M."

The wedding was in thirteen hours. The pain I felt in my heart at her words shifted to pain for her.

"Thank you for looking."

She hung up the phone lightly in its cradle.

"Well?" I usually never intervened in the personal matters of my clients, but if this was what was bothering her, she should give voice to it, instead of putting her feelings toward a harmless, innocent wedding gown.

"My father hasn't arrived yet."

"He will, I'm sure. He wouldn't miss this day for anything."

She slipped down, sitting on my bed while I sat in the chair, hand stitching to custom fit this dress to her body.

"I want to believe that, Miss Lowe."

I smiled and nodded. "Believe it."

Then she seemed to realize that she had been vulnerable, too open with someone whom she shouldn't be, and she straightened herself again and stood up from my bed. "I'll send the maid down for the dress in the morning."

"Yes. It should hang over night."

"Good night, Miss Lowe."

"Good night, Miss Bouvier."

Maybe I shouldn't have said what I did, but I was only trying to help her.

Giving her hope was probably the most foolish thing I ever did.

Chapter Thirty-Two

No one goes to bed for a morning wedding. I knew not to. I had to attend a bride in the morning, so when I parted company with Jacqueline Friday night, I just stayed up, finishing details on her dress.

At 6:00 A.M., a maid came for the dress. She seemed overwhelmed by it, so I offered to carry the dress and she helped me. She led the way and we both went into the vast upstairs of the house, through mazes of rooms and corridors. When we arrived at Jacqueline's room, we heard raised voices through the door from where we stood in the hallway. The maid's brows scrunched together and we both waited at the door, trying to decide when it would be best to knock or go in.

Jacqueline's usually quiet voice was much louder today. "He's my father, of course I want him there."

"Jacqueline, it's not realistic," her mother said.

"I've been trying to call him all night but he won't pick up the phone."

"Then doesn't that tell you something?"

"I'll leave this house and look for him myself." The bold threat, low but firm, resonated down the hall. I looked down at the dress in my arms.

Mrs. Auchincloss's reply was muffled.

"I want him there."

Heavy footsteps came to the door and it opened, revealing Mrs. Auchincloss, a scarf tied on her head and wearing a house-coat, looking like any normal 1950s housewife instead of the glamourous woman she was.

"Mrs. Auchincloss, we brought the dress and veil."

She spread her arm toward the room where her daughter was. "Of course, this way."

Jacqueline sat in front of the vanity in her robe, undergarments, garters, and hose, powdering her nose. Her red-rimmed eyes reflected her sorrow. The maid helped me put the dress on the bed and then she fled the room after Mrs. Auchincloss.

"Thank you, Miss Lowe. I'm sorry. My mother caught me trying to call my father and we had a little . . . discussion about it."

"I see."

Jacqueline continued as if she were talking to herself. "I mean, he took Lee down the aisle and she doesn't have the same connection with him that I do. I know he'll be there for me."

I placed the dress on the bed, standing alongside her as she continued her ministrations. "If I may, Miss Bouvier."

She eyed me in the mirror, sniffling. "Yes?"

"I never knew my father. He died when I was a baby."

My words caused her to put down her makeup puff. "I'm sorry. That's awful. I couldn't imagine my life without my father. He and I . . . well, we have so much in common. I'm the one who looks like him. He just couldn't . . ."

One lone tear made its way down her beautiful angled face.

I handed her a handkerchief. "I didn't say that to make you feel sad. I see you're sad enough on a day when you should be joyful. But at least you know your daddy. You know he loves you. He's been there for you. But sometimes, and I even say this to myself about my daddy, Jack Lowe, we daughters build up our daddies to be more than what they are. And, Miss Bouvier. Jacqueline. You're twenty-four years old. You know ain't none of them perfect. Because daddies are men too."

A sniffle.

"If you're being honest, and I've known you ever since before you were a debutante, you know that your daddy is every inch a proud man. He was at Lee's wedding because he knew no one else would be there."

"We were all there, Miss Lowe."

I shook my head and folded my arms. "And your ceremony compares to Lee's how? I mean at your wedding and the reception. There will be what, eight hundred people at the wedding? Twelve hundred at the reception? Won't the entire Senate be there?"

She nodded. "That's what the Ambassador wanted. And why he said I needed a big dress so everyone could see me. You were there. In the shop"

"I was. And I know that kind of man too. I remembered the old Montgomery Southern belles my grandma Georgia sewed for and I made you that kind of dress." I think something in me was still a bit hurt at her lampshade characterization.

She turned and looked at the dress. "I must say, the bodice is so, well, reminiscent of old Austria. It reminds me of Empress Sisi."

"An empress?" I drew back a little. "My dress?"

"Yes, Miss Lowe, the folding technique you used is something right out of old Austria and its most beautiful empress, Empress Sisi."

"Well, I see I have a trip ahead of me to the New York Public

Library, Miss Bouvier. I've never heard of her as a style icon before."

She nodded, wiping at her eyes with the hanky. "You'll see."

"Well." I stepped toward the dress, which was still lying on the bed. Perhaps I had overstepped my bounds with Jacqueline, but maybe by being shocked a bit, she would see how fortunate she was.

"Has your daddy told you he loves you?" I whispered.

"Many times." She dabbed at her face.

"Keep those words in your heart. Think of his voice in your head. Carry that with you. 'Cause to be honest, that's more than some of us have had."

Jacqueline got really quiet then. A knock on the door revealed her mother, dressed in the café-au-lait-brown lace dress that I had made for her for Lee's wedding.

"Well, are you ready to get into your dress, Jacqueline?"

She looked at me. I nodded at her.

"Yes, Mother. Thank you, Miss Lowe."

She stood. I reached for the dress and puddled it on the floor, ready for her to step into. I pulled my attempt at Southern belle—or as she put it, the Empress—to give her some womanly curve up her angular frame. During my alterations, I had figured out something new for her bodice and when she adjusted it on herself, she seemed a little surprised. "This isn't what I expected. At all."

I finished hooking up the back and smoothed the seams. I always left the veil for the mothers. "Glad to keep you guessing, Miss Bouvier. If you'll excuse me, I'll get dressed myself."

"Thank you, Miss Lowe," Mrs. Auchincloss said over her shoulder to me.

I passed by a fully dressed Mrs. Canfield in her Juliet cap and pink dress. Nodding at her, I went to my room and put on a lace dove-gray tea dress, something I kept in reserve for weddings, because I didn't believe in wearing black to a wedding. I wanted the happy couple to have every chance at happiness.

I RODE IN the car behind the bridal limousine with the other invited servants to St. Mary's, which was only a few minutes away. When we approached the church, the crowd expanded and the noise, the noise of thousands of people, grew louder. I knew there would be a crowd and everything inside of me went topsy-turvy. What would people think of the dress? This kind of widespread exposure could help my shop greatly. I might become busier than ever before, might have more commissions. This dress could be the making of me.

Prayer-wish time.

Dear God, let it be so.

Money had never been a friend of mine. Given what had happened in my shop with the burst pipe, and the fact that I could not tell the Ambassador what had happened, I had lost so much on this commission. But Arthur had assured me that the exposure in *Life* magazine, which was going to report on the wedding, could help me garner even more business with the high-society crowd.

"Think of it, Mama. The entire Senate. They all have wives. They will all see your work."

I craned my head so I could see out ahead of me. Jacqueline was tall, and her head, crowned with her becoming short brown curls and the exquisite lace veil, popped up above everyone else's. I cleaned my glasses on an edge of my lace dress and put them on again. My eyesight was giving me even more difficulty these days and being short was a curse at times. I hoped to find a brilliantined head of black shining in the sun next to Jacqueline's. But the sun reflected off the balding pate of Mr. Auchincloss. As I feared.

The car I rode in was having a difficult time cutting through the crowd, but I could not wait. I opened the car door, against the objections of the driver, and with brisk steps walked to the side door of the church, where all the guests were being admitted, my invitation in my hand.

The groomsmen gave me no trouble as I entered. Given the many people and photographers that had swarmed her in the front of the church, I met Jacqueline in the back as the organ music swelled. Her eyes went to mine.

"Oh Miss Lowe. He's not here. My daddy's not here." Her quiet voice tremored in the cold stone recess of the church. Outside was a warm September day, but the darkness of the closed-in stone of St. Mary's caused the back part of the church to have a tomblike chill. Maybe short sleeves on the dress wasn't the best choice. Jacqueline wouldn't be in the back for long, though.

Mr. Auchincloss did not seem the least bit surprised to see me. He stepped back from her, as if he wished to give us some privacy.

I kept my voice low, just for her. "I know, Miss Bouvier, I know. Hold him in your heart." I gestured toward the smoothed-down tucking on the front of her dress, remembering how I made sure each strip of cloth lay down at a precise right angle to each other.

"I wish . . ." Her quiet voice broke a bit.

Time to be a bit stern.

"Wishes won't help. He's with you. Inside." I adjusted the lovely lace veiling around her face. I faced her and by the virtue of my gaze, made her face me. "You're marrying the man that you love. Think on that. Keep that next to you. And in time, maybe after you return from your honeymoon with your new husband, your daddy can be there for you. Just. Just not today."

The light of despair left her eyes. She pulled her shoulders back just the right amount so that they rounded in a flattering way. My technique to make them appear smaller had worked well. Posture mattered.

The bridesmaids lined up in pairs and began to go down the aisle.

I saw Mrs. Auchincloss out of the corner of my eye. She mouthed two words to me: "Thank you."

I nodded at her.

I walked around Jacqueline, making a last-minute check for loose threads. I went back around her the other way, adjusting her skirts one panel at a time. Someone handed her a large bouquet of pink and white. I sighed with pleasure to see the flowers. Pink and white orchids. White gardenias. Excellent choice.

I framed her face with the veil once more. "Congratulations."

Mr. Auchincloss stepped in, ready to accompany her.

She took his arm with a sure, gloved hand and together, they walked down the aisle, one step at a time.

It was too late to sit now, so I remained standing. I cleaned my glasses another time to help me see. Still, I was so small and the church was so vast. I was able to make my way to the midpoint of the church and watch from behind a pillar, getting a good look at her handsome groom with all of that thick hair that he had. Jacqueline's face lit up at the sight of him, just as I hoped it would, and I smiled.

My poor gaze took in the whole setup at the front of the church, since I hadn't yet seen it, and that's when my heart began to beat fast.

Pink gladioli.

Who in their right mind thought that pink gladioli should be at a wedding? Such bad luck!

Gladioli were the one flower I never sought to recreate, because they were funeral flowers. Certainly not a flower for a wedding.

The coldness from the stone pillar I stood next to seeped into me, causing me to remember that I'd had no breakfast and not much rest in the past week.

I was not a superstitious woman, far from it, but I had a terrible feeling that this would not be a long marriage.

Chapter Thirty-Three

When I stepped outside of my usual comfort to speak to Jacqueline in a personal way, I knew it would cost me. But I had no idea how steep the price would be.

None of the newspapers spoke my name.

Descriptions of the dress appeared in newspapers around the world.

But none mentioned my name.

Just like the Olivia de Havilland dress all over again. And the no credit in *Life* for the deb dresses for both Bouvier girls.

But worse.

Because there was no name attached at all.

It was as if the dress had made itself.

My being society's best-kept secret really worked—all too well. Maybe not getting credit for my work was just recompense for listening to the buyer of the bridal gown instead of the bride.

Arthur consistently consoled me. "We have plenty of business. Many young girls still come to you for party dresses, deb dresses. The books are balanced."

"All thanks to you, son. I don't know what I would do without you."

His handsome face dimpled. "You would still make all of the wonderous dresses that you make, Mama. You should just focus on that."

I bent over to kiss him on his forehead. "I thank God for you every day."

He was right—the mid 1950s were going very well. When Mrs. Auchincloss came into the shop one winter day in 1955 with a familiar-looking fresh-faced young girl, I leaped to my feet, so surprised I was to see her. When they came closer, I could see it was Nina Auchincloss, who had been the maid of honor at the Kennedy wedding.

"Miss Lowe. So good to see you are still in business."

"I'm getting along here and there, Mrs. Auchincloss. What can I do to help you? Is Janet ready for her debutante ball?"

She gave a tinkle-sounding laugh. "Oh my goodness, no."

"How are your girls?"

"Mrs. Canfield and Mrs. Kennedy are fine. Seemingly in a race to make me a grandmother, although . . ." She looked down and then away. "Mrs. Kennedy is having an awful time of it. It's so hard for her. She's up to her neck in fecund Kennedy women and she . . . well, she just had a miscarriage."

An ache rose in my heart. I knew what that feeling was, in those moments after I had Arthur, being told that I was infertile. I had always had a suspicion that was another reason why Caleb West had left me. Ruth wasn't enough for him. Oh, he still came to see her and was a good father to her, but he had recently been busy with the two baby boys his new Annie had given him.

"I'm so sorry to hear that, Mrs. Auchincloss."

"Thank you." She gestured to the young woman with her.

"This is my stepdaughter, Nina Auchincloss. She is the one who will debut in the summer."

I clasped my hands. "How delightful. You're growing up so well, Nina. I remember fitting you for the wedding."

"I loved the dress you made for Jacqueline. It was so lovely." Her cheeks glowed red and her eyes sparkled.

I laughed a bit at her infectious youth and enthusiasm. "I'm glad you liked it."

"Everyone gasped when she started down the aisle. I would like that for my deb dress too."

I picked up my sketch pad and a pencil. "Well, tell me what you want, Miss Nina, and I'll do my best."

It was wonderful to design her a dress full of hopes and dreams. When she was crowned Deb of the Year for 1955 and appeared in *Vogue* a few weeks later, I was astonished and amused to see my name in the magazine. Finally!

Mrs. Lee from Tampa, my lovely patron, sent me a note about the *Vogue* article along with a clipping. It was the last note I got from her—a few weeks later, her daughter Nell told me her mother had died and that she had chosen to be buried in one of the dresses that I had made for her. The tears sparked pain in my eyes as they usually did, but I didn't mind crying a few tears for that sweet benefactress of mine.

WE WERE NOW doing so well that Arthur purchased a new shop for me farther up Lexington Avenue, and we moved our operations there just in time for the holiday commissions for Christmas parties and Christmas weddings.

And there were many of them too! I had such a flood of activity in those years. More and more, I designed for the Best and my name, the best-kept secret name, was getting out and bringing in commissions from all over the country—just as Arthur had predicted it would.

In between everything else happening in 1956, I made a baby layette for Jacqueline Kennedy. I read of her happy event in the papers and saw a picture of her in the papers at the 1956 Democratic National Convention, looking happy and round. I thought it was a strange place for her to be, as large as she was, with her history. Still, Jack Kennedy was up for vice president against Estes Kefauver. Ruth, Sallie—who was living with Ruth and me in Harlem—and I watched the coverage on the television Arthur had bought for us. I didn't want the TV at first, but when *The Nat King Cole Show* debuted later that fall, I was glad we had it.

Watching the convention coverage, Sallie's usually kind face carried a stormy look as her beautiful eyes clouded over. "I hope he doesn't get it."

"Why not?"

"Estes Kefauver couldn't win last time, and he certainly won't win this time."

I shook my head and wiped my glasses, so I could see her better. "Could you imagine? Vice president? Our Jacqueline as the second lady?"

"And a new baby," Ruth put in.

"Yes, indeed."

Ruth turned to me. "Did you send the layette, Mama?"

"No, I haven't yet."

"I'll send it if you want me to."

A hand, I don't know whose, but perhaps God's hand, fate's hand, rested on my shoulder. "No. That's okay. I'll do it."

Barely a week later, Mrs. Kennedy gave birth to a stillborn girl.

I thought back on that chilly feeling I had at St. Mary's and wondered if it had played a part in my reluctance to send the layette.

I regretted not sending the layette earlier to show that I had no hard feelings toward Jacqueline. Just a few weeks later, I read an announcement for Nina Auchincloss's engagement to a young lawyer. Naturally, she would come to me to make her bridal dress as well as the bridesmaid dresses. Many young women for whom I made debutante dresses returned to me for their wedding gowns. It was just the way society worked. At least, that was how it had worked with Jacqueline.

However, more time passed, and it was already May 1957, when I saw the official engagement posted in the newspaper about an early June wedding being planned for Nina and her fiancé. That meant that Nina had opted to go elsewhere for her wedding dress. What had I done wrong?

The pain of losing a commission always hurt.

"Brings to mind Lee Bouvier. Did I ever tell you about her?"

"Only a thousand times, Mama."

"She told me that I was too expensive. Cost too much money. But for her cost was no object. There was something that she didn't like. We don't know."

"I'm sorry, Mama."

"Nina's young. She might have decided to do something different." Ruth patted my arm.

"Says here that Mrs. Kennedy was the matron of honor."

"I'm three times her age. She might think I'm too old to make her wedding gown."

"That can't be true, Mama."

"Maybe Jacqueline told her I said something to her before her wedding. Got out of line. Out of place with her."

"I remember, Mama. You told me."

"Did I? Well, I know this: If I hadn't said what I said to her about her father, she wouldn't have had the strength to walk down that aisle. She was limp, I tell you, devastated. I had to tell her, same as I'm telling you, men stay in the disappointing business."

"Yes, Mama. They also are saying that Mrs. Kennedy is in the family way again."

"Lord bless her. She seem like she been carrying every year since they married. I'ma put her on the prayer list at church this time that she makes it through."

I meant it too.

When I read that her notorious daddy died two months later, I made up my mind to send her the layette, even though it was too soon.

I enclosed a note, telling her I hoped that she had enjoyed her life with her father for as long as she could and now she could look forward to having a family of her own, and that maybe this layette set would be the thing needed to start a new life.

She sent me the requisite thank-you note for my regards and condolences, but no explanations.

I was still so happy for her that November when she finally had her baby, a healthy girl named Caroline Lee after her sister.

What a lovely thing.

That was the last happy memory I had for a long, long, time.

Chapter Thirty-Four

*W*hen Mama died, me and my uncles made an agreement not to tell Grandma Georgia, but it was as if she knew Mama's spirit wasn't on the earth anymore. She went downhill really fast. I didn't understand why. Mama wasn't her only child. She had a total of ten children, not including a son who had died as a baby. Still, I just never, ever expected that when my mama died Grandma Georgia would find it difficult, if not impossible, to live the rest of her own life.

She couldn't function anymore.

She didn't want to live anymore.

I would point toward her shelf. "There, Grandma. There's a picture of Mama." It was a smeary *carte de visite*, but it was all that we had.

Grandma Georgia shook her head. "Ja-ja-ne-ee." I knew what she was saying. She wanted her real daughter, Janie. Not any old picture.

I took the picture and turned it around to face the wall since it offended Grandma.

Even bringing Arthur in to see her wasn't enough. She would pat him and smile a half smile. The uncles didn't bring her joy either. They came in and stood around, looking at her in her helpless state, reverting to children themselves.

All she would say was, "Ja-ja-ne-ee."

Sometimes, while I was finishing up the New Year's commission for the first lady of Alabama without both my mama and my grandma, watching the needle stab in and out of the fancy dress silk, I felt stabbed too. Why wasn't I enough? What was wrong with me?

But when she was gone, I tried not to grieve too much, but instead thought that dear Grandma Georgia had gotten what she wanted—reunited in heaven with her best friend and daughter.

That was then.

This was now.

I welcomed the new year of 1958, knowing I was going to be sixty years old, an age my parents didn't get to see. I felt fortunate. The shop was doing well, my family was doing well. Ruth had found a nice man and they would wed in the spring. She told me she wanted to make her own dress and I let her, with only the occasional suggestion. I was proud of her skill. It wasn't like mine, but good enough for her to make, and more importantly wear, the dress that she wanted, an opportunity that every bride should have, even Jacqueline Kennedy.

A cloudy gray lay over everything in my life, even if a given day was sunny and bright. I could not deny that my sight was going. I went to a doctor about it and he said that I had glaucoma, a hereditary disease. I recall Grandma going through something similar. The fact that we used our eyes a lot and sewed close probably didn't help matters any.

One January morning, Sallie and I opened the shop as we always did. It was the usual cold, frosty morning of winter in New York, with lots of slush on the ground. We each wore our old lady boots, as we jokingly called them, rubbers we fit over our shoes so we could make our way from the subway down the street to the shop with dry feet.

Usually, Arthur arrived as soon as the shop door was open, but on this day he was late.

That was not like Arthur.

Just as he knew how to occupy himself when he was a baby, he knew how I felt about wasting time.

"I hope Cora wasn't picking on him again." I bustled about, trying to fix some tea on the hot plate in the back room of my shop to warm Sallie and me. My fingers needed to be nimble for the day's work on commissions for spring wedding gowns and deb dresses.

"Now, sister. They've been married for almost fifteen years. She wouldn't do that."

"I'm not so sure. She came from high ideas and always was trying to get Arthur to be high-minded with her."

"Did you enjoy dinner with them last night?"

"I did. Audrey got a young man, bless her."

Sallie laughed. "Well, that was bound to happen. How old is she now?"

"She's fourteen."

"Well, there you have it. She's plenty old enough."

I shook my head, pouring tea into a cup. "I guess so. I don't want her to be like me. Still, when and if she gets married and has kids, I'll be a great-grandma. I don't feel that old."

"Ha! I'm a great-grandma. It's wonderful knowing that you are going to go on."

Several of the seamstresses came in, reporting in for work. They poured cups of tea for themselves and got down to business.

I had an appointment to meet with a young socialite about her deb dress at ten o'clock. She had good ideas and we talked for a while. When I looked at the clock as the meeting ended, it was 10:45 A.M.

Still no Arthur.

I stood up, stretching from the stiffness that had set in during my appointment from sitting too long in one spot, and reached for the phone. Mentally preparing myself to speak to Cora, I had lifted the receiver to ask the operator to dial Arthur's number for me when out of the corner of my eye I saw Ruth came into the shop, breathless.

I didn't like seeing her there, her face twisted up like ruching. She should not have been there.

Where was Arthur?

Why wasn't HE here?

I put the receiver down. "Ruth, honey, you supposed to be at work. What you doing here?" I grasped her hands. They were ice cold. "How many times have I told you to wear your gloves? Especially now. You don't want your husband thinking he's married to a hired hand when he wants to cuddle with you in bed."

I focused on her hands through my usual filmy gray cloud, warming them so I didn't have to see her ruching face.

"Mama. Mama, listen to me."

Her voice broke open like basting. She was going to say something I did not want to hear.

About Arthur.

The picture flashed in my mind of holding his little slithery body when Mama handed him to me for the very first time. He was so small, so wriggly, I had to open my hands up and make them firm to take his body onto mine. The weight of him, the smell of him, the existence of him hooked into the center of my chest and had been there ever since.

Until this moment.

"There's been an accident. A car accident."

I felt Sallie's arms go around me.

An ocean of blood rushed to my ears. *I don't want to hear this. I don't want to hear this.*

What would I do without Arthur? How would I live without Arthur?

In that second, time slowed. Ruth had on the pink chantilly lipstick I had bought her as part of a makeup kit for Christmas. She had put it on right for once, without it feathering, 'cause she was always biting at her lips and ruining the look of her lipstick.

Her eyes, oh those merry eyes of Ruth's, were not merry now. She herself looked as if she were being ripped apart having to tell me these awful words, the terrible words that meant that my life would always be divided.

Before Arthur.

Arthur.

After Arthur.

I did not want After Arthur time. Only Arthur time.

I'll do whatever you say, God. I'll be whatever you say. If you want to take my sight and I never do another dress. Is that what you want? For me to stay in Arthur time.

My art?

My soul?

So be it.

Take it.

Take it from me.

Only.

Keep me in Arthur time.

Ruth's pink chantilly lips spoke words only in a scramble. They were all mixed up.

"The road slippery. Ice. And he was in his car off road ditch."

I gripped her cold hands harder, willing them to warm. "So they took him to the hospital? Which hospital? We have to go to him."

I turned in Sallie's arms, my mouth filled with the taste of orange pekoe tea. "You can stay here with the girls. I'll go. We can get Cora and go to him."

Sallie's gray eyes were filled with tears. For the first time in my life, I wanted to hit my older sister.

No!

This is Arthur time.

Not After Arthur time.

Stay with me, here. Stay with me here.

She had lost a son too. My nephew, Angus. One of the ones whose diapers I had to clean before Lee Cone came to pick me off my mama to marry me and make . . .

Arthur.

I grasped her arms. "Sallie. Stay with the girls and make sure they work on these dresses."

I tried to take a step forward, but my legs, they didn't work anymore.

"Mama, Mama, Mama." Ruth's voice filled my ears. She had been trying to call me. I willed myself to face my pretty daughter. The daughter I had always wanted. The daughter I designed pretty dresses for. The daughter I was helping to make her wedding dress.

Now, she was here, telling me about After Arthur time. My hands opened up, just like they did when I had to hold my only, wriggly baby.

"Stop. No." I wretched myself from Sallie's iron hold, the will in my body to stay in Arthur time giving me strength I never knew I had.

I held up my hand, looking into Ruth's face, at the tears running down her face. "We going to the hospital. Which one? Where they live? The Bronx? Get me my purse. We can pay for a cab." My words went back to the old way, the Alabama way of talking. But now, I had to hurry. Talk fast, no drawn-out speech. Time was wasting. I inched my hand up Ruth's arm, grabbing her.

"Mama." The long, drawn-out way in which my daughter said that word was the same sound as my heart ripping into two.

"The hospital name? Come on. We see Cora and Audrey and . . ."

"He gone. He's gone, Mama."

I closed my hands.

And used them to beat her. Why did I need a daughter? What had possessed me to bring someone into my life who was going to tell me Arthur was gone?

She gripped my fists and so did Sallie.

"We go to the hospital. They gone fix him."

Ruth wrapped her arms around me and Sallie, and the two of them made a sandwich of me, with me in the middle. Their doing that was the only thing that kept me up off the ground.

'Cause I could feel the ground calling me, pulling me down, weighing me down. I wanted to lie down on the cold ground because that was where Arthur would go.

An acrid, sharp stink rose to my nose. Another pipe burst?

No.

It was me.

My urine.

The liquid ran down my legs in a stream of hot wetness, soaking the rug in a widening yellow spot that later Sallie had to replace with extra carpet, 'cause all the scrubbing in the world wouldn't get it out.

Ruth put her arms around me.

Got me into my coat.

Walked me out of the store.

Got me home.

Somehow.

She ran the bath for me, as I lay down on the bed, unable to move, wanting only the ground.

Later, when my mind was mine again, I remembered how lovingly she took off my black dress, my girdle, bra, and wet hose.

Poor Ruth guided me to the tub and helped to scrub me, from the tips of my toes all the way up to my neck and face, using warm bath water to slough the tears, the never-ending tears, away.

She helped me out of the tub and wiped me down, put a fresh nightgown on me, and tucked me into my bed, where I lost all sense of time and purpose.

People came.

Audrey came.

Cora came.

Cora's mother, Mrs. Carter, came.

My minister came.

I had nothing for any of them. I had lost it all. Lost everything.

I had no function, no purpose in After Arthur time.

Chapter Thirty-Five

My dreams were tortured by Arthur asking me why I had asked him to give up his whole life for me, for my dream, for my work.

When I woke up, my face was wet with my own tears. When the despair came to me in the daytime, the oh-so-long daytime, I had no tears left. Only days of time that seemed unending, followed by hours of long, long nights where there was no more Arthur in the world.

Sallie sat next to me on the bed. She never ceased taking care of me, and once I'd woken up with the dawn, she squeezed my hand.

"Annie. You know that the funeral is tomorrow."

I sat up. "Who said?"

She reached over and grasped my other hand. "It's been a week. We can't hold him out forever, Annie. His body, his soul, got to go to the Lord."

"Sallie, I asked you. Who said?"

She avoided looking at my face. "The Carters. They planned it, 'cause, well, Cora ain't been well either. The funeral home, they had a space on Friday and, that's when it gone be."

For the first time since it happened, I felt some of my fight enter my spirit. "I always knew them Carter people would be trouble. He my son. I got some say in this."

"Then you should get up and go see them, Annie. Tell them what you feeling."

But that would involve me leaving this bed.

I sank back.

I didn't trust my legs to carry me around, to hold me up, to keep walking. Somehow, they seemed to know that I had no purpose anymore.

Sallie leaned in to me. "You got to see him one time before they put him in the ground."

I whirled on her. "No, I don't. Who said I have to do that? Who said?"

Ruth came in the room carrying a tray with food. I waved her away but Sallie took the tray from her and carried it to me. Nasty noodle soup in a bowl with crackers.

"You need to eat something, Annie. You got to keep up your strength."

"I don't want to."

"Mama." Ruth eased forward. "Come on. Just a little."

I stared into the pretty face of Ruth. "I'm not hungry. I don't care."

She came around the other side of my bed, where the window was, and sat down. "Don't you care about the dresses? The upcoming deb balls? The weddings in the spring?"

Listening to her list these considerations was like hearing someone ask if I still cared about Lee Cone anymore. A little twinge of hurt, but it didn't last. It dissolved. It went away. Like old gum, all of the flavor was gone out of it.

I turned to face her. "I just . . ." I lifted my hands. "I don't have it in me anymore. Not another stitch."

Ruth dipped the spoon into the soup, scooping out a noodle and a piece of carrot. She lifted the spoon to my face and I opened my mouth, taking in the hot liquid like a baby bird. The only reason it was worth eating was that it was hot and my bed was cold 'cause it was next to the window.

Sallie slipped away.

"Mama. All of those rich white folks will wonder where their dresses are. Aunt Sallie, she contacted all your appointments this week, but do you really think Arthur would want this?"

My eyes would have filled with tears, but I had no water in my body to make any more. If I ate more of the salty soup, it would just come out as more tears. "Want what?"

"For you to give up. He loved and respected what you did more than anyone in the world. He believed in you, Mama." She fed me more soup.

"I believed in him."

"He would not want you to shrivel up and disappoint your clients." She shook her head and her black bob moved softly in disapproval.

Ruth dipped the spoon again. "Remember when he was a delivery boy?" The memory brought to mind Arthur, miserable in that old apron he would have to wear. Another spoonful of soup, this time with some shredded chicken on it. I took it in.

"He didn't like that job."

"No, he did not. He worked it to feed Cora and Audrey, but he wanted to give you money to get the shop going again, remember? Remember when he told you it was safe for you to leave Sonja and to work on your own? Oh, Mama, he did so much to help you."

Maybe eating the salty soup was helping the tears flow. "That's why he ain't here no more. 'Cause he was coming to work. If he did some other job, he'd be here."

"No, Mama. He was happy. He loved taking care of you and the shop, even if Cora didn't, well . . ." She shook her head.

I waved away another spoonful. "Where's Cora?"

"At her mama's house."

Of course.

"I want to see her."

"You do?" Ruth pulled the bowl back.

"Yes, I do." I would bathe and dress, and put on perfume for her. Now that Arthur wasn't here anymore, I had to ask her something. A question about Arthur. That was my purpose now.

I took in a bit more of the soup, but just a bit. Ruth selected one of my best black silk dresses. She ran a bath for me and I soaked in there a good long time, until I felt my skin shrivel from the exposure to the cold water. Then I dressed as I usually did for work. A black dress, whole slip, brassiere, stockings, and a brooch at my shoulder.

"Cora's here." Sallie leaned her head into my room. I know she wanted to know how I was doing. I stood up from the small couch I kept in my room for whenever I wanted to sketch.

"She can come in."

I smoothed down the skirt of my dress and waited. The figure of my daughter-in-law appeared in the doorway. She too was dressed in black, in a new-looking dress made of some cheap looking blend fabric, but it didn't fit very well. Sallie could make that right, but Cora didn't like any wardrobe help from us. That's what Arthur told me.

"Miss Lowe?"

"Come here, child. Sit next to me."

Her steps were halting and hesitant. "Next to you?"

It was a small couch. Since I was little, there was room, but we would be sitting quite close together. "Yes."

She sat down, holding her body as distant as she could from me, pressing herself into the other side of the couch. "You wanted something?"

"You never wanted Arthur to work in my shop, did you?"

"Ma'am?"

"This is no time to play ignorant now, Cora. I asked you something."

"I just felt he could make more money someplace else." Cora fluttered her hands around. She never knew how to keep them still.

"More money? Was that what you wanted?"

"Who doesn't?"

"Is that what Arthur was doing with his life? Trying to make you more money? For what, Cora? You don't ever look like anything. So what did you need more money for?"

She drew back as if I had slapped her. Maybe I had.

"I got tired, that's all."

"Tired? If Arthur didn't get you what you wanted, then your mother and father would. What did you need my son for?"

She glared at me and I could see in her brown eyes how Cora really felt about me. For all of these years. And seeing the way the hatred shone in her eyes, I knew.

She had done it.

"Arthur was . . . he was the only person in this world who believed in me. Who thought I could do anything. That I was beautiful."

"He wasn't perfect." I glared at her.

"Leave it to you to say that about him. He was perfect for me. But I never had him one hundred percent because you had to have him. You had to have him, body and soul."

"He was my son. You're a mother. You have Audrey. Arthur

and I grew up together. He was not just my son, he was my best friend. And now, because you needed more money, he's gone."

Cora stood. "May I remind you, Miss Lowe, he was going to work for you. He was on his way to your store, not to our home. He could never do enough for you, to give up his life for your store, to balance the books, to manage the money, to take all of those dresses up to Newport." She turned from me and walked across the room. "That time was our anniversary. Yet he had to go run for you because it was the Kennedy wedding."

I fixed her with my closest look. "He was only gone for one day, Cora. Were you going to stop it?"

She played with her handkerchief. "What do you mean, Miss Lowe?"

"You know what I mean, Cora Cone."

"He was my everything."

"He was *my* everything. And you sought to stop me by destroying the biggest commission of my life."

We sat there.

The radiator hissed in the corner of my room.

Neither one of us took our eyes off the other.

Tears started to slide down her dark-brown cheeks and I could see her quiver from the corner of my eye.

I knew it.

"You thought to hurt me." I shook my head. "You foolish child. Do you know what I've been through to get here? To get to be where I am? And you thought a bunch of sewage water was going to stop me?"

"If the shop closed, then I would get my husband back. That's all I wanted."

"And now neither one of us has him. He's in the arms of Jesus."

I looked away from her. I couldn't stand the sight of her anymore. I wanted to vomit but the four spoons of chicken noodle
soup that I had consumed an hour ago wasn't enough to throw up.

I felt a woosh in the air and before I knew it, there she was, so
much closer to me than she was before, our arms touching, my
black silk sleeves up against her cheap polyester material.

"I tried. I tried so hard over the years to get you to love me,
for you to see how good I was for him, but you never, ever did.
You only saw him. And Audrey, sometimes. But even she wasn't
enough for you."

I turned to her. "I love my granddaughter. She's precious to me.
I hope you aren't doing something to stop her from her dreams."

She grasped my hands. "I'm sorry. Please forgive me. I didn't
mean to hurt you. I just thought . . . I was wrong. I was so wrong."

Her head was in my lap before I knew it, and she sobbed big,
huge tears all into my lap to the point where I could feel the salt
of them crusting on my thighs.

I embraced her, and more tears came to me too, until we were
all cried out.

Together.

"I guess we both loved him as fiercely and as equally as we
could."

"We did." Cora wiped at her white-tracked face with her
hanky. "Listen. Miss Lowe, I need to tell you. I know it hurts
me, but I need to say it."

"What child?"

"He would never want you to give up. That's the worst possible
thing you could do. He believed in your talent. He would say . . ."
She took in a shivering gulp. "He would say, 'She creates Art.'"

"He did?"

"Yes, Miss Lowe. It was like our little joke together. That you created art with all your dresses and his name was Arthur and I called him Art."

The pang of realization that his beautiful mind was gone from this world shook me again. What would I do without him?

"'She creates Art.' I never liked to call him that, but I can see how he thought about it that way. Oh God, I'm going to miss my boy so much."

The pang deep inside of me transformed into a shiver that took over my body, and Cora held me tightly. I held on to her tightly.

That was how we went to see him, laid out like an angel in his casket, and that was how we buried him in the graveyard in Queens.

Together.

Chapter Thirty-Six

I would have never expected that over the next two years, I would grow closer to Cora than I ever thought possible. She'd had Arthur, and I wanted to hold on to that for as long as possible.

However, I also knew that Cora was still a young woman. Young women have needs. Well, so do older women, but I could tell that Cora missed Arthur in a way I understood. Those needs had driven me into the big, broad arms of Caleb West.

When she spoke of seeing a man in our church who had also been widowed, I did what any mother would do: I told her I knew Arthur would have wanted her to be happy, so she should go to dinner with the man.

The year 1961 brought so many changes. Audrey wanted to get married, as did her mother, and Ruth was going to have her first baby.

And, just as his father told me, back in 1953, Jack Kennedy was elected president of the United States. Of course, Mrs. Kennedy soon held a press conference, where one of the society reporters asked her who had designed her wedding dress. Her response was written up in *Ladies' Home Journal* that I was just a colored woman dressmaker. Once more I had no name.

"She said what about Mama?" Cora was not at all happy.

Cora liked to come to the shop after she got off work, partly because she didn't like to go home to an empty apartment. She put the afternoon newspaper, which she had just brought in, down on a table. It was a day when we were all in the back room, where the seamstresses were at work, but we had no appointments for consultations or new commissions that afternoon. From the looks of the appointment book, there weren't going to be any for a while either. Ruth, who was not working while she was awaiting her happy event, had picked up the newspaper from where Cora left it, and put it back down with a sigh.

Sallie shook her head. "She's never been one for being in public. She just had a baby boy and must be under a lot of pressure in this new national spotlight."

"She's had a lot of time getting used to the national spotlight, I think. That did nothing for Mama. Nothing at all." Cora picked up the magazine and read the sentence written in the article:

"The bride's gown and that of her friends were designed by a colored woman dressmaker, not the *haute couture*."

I took in a deep breath. "I wasn't looking for anything from her." I would send her a note, to address the situation.

Cora leveled a look at me. "Mama."

"Okay. I did send her a note to ask her about her inaugural gown, but I didn't hear back. She's moved on to Oleg Cassini."

"He doesn't even sound American," Cora said, exasperated.

"Well, Ambassador Kennedy would not allow her to uplift anything other than American designers. He must be." I moved away from the hateful old magazine to my desk, ready to do some paperwork, something I was not very good at but had to handle since Arthur was gone. His shoes were so difficult to fill. For all of us.

Sallie nodded. "She just had that baby so recently. I can't imagine how hard it must be to have to do all of this talking to people and having parties and such when she just had him. Heard things were touch and go for a bit with the baby."

"She hasn't had the easiest time having babies either. She lost that first one. A stillbirth. Some miscarriages." I put down my pen.

Cora shook her head. "I would say that has to be hard. Those other Kennedy women pop out babies like popcorn. But still, she should have said your name when she had the chance, Mama. That's all I'm saying."

I spread my arm to indicate the ladies with us in the back room. "Well, these seamstresses are all busy in here because the society reporters all know who I am. They all know I've been with the Auchinclosses for a while—well, not in the past few years, but I was for a long while there. So we are doing as well as we need."

But we really weren't. Arthur's absence in our lives told on us in many ways. For one, he had kept the shop's books. Once he was gone, that was left to me. Sallie and I had never been to high school and we didn't do too well with math figures. Math was something for a man back in Clayton, Alabama. Figures weren't a strength of Cora's or Audrey's either.

I should have hired someone, but I just got too busy. And whenever I thought about how Lee Bouvier was so willing to go on to Pauline Trigère for her wedding dress, I would knock another fifty dollars off a dress to prevent the client from going elsewhere.

I was not even sure what was red or what was black when it came to the books. I had so many great relationships with people in the Garment District, relationships that went all the way back to the 1920s. I paid them what I could, when I could. They knew that. They trusted me. When money came in, I would pay out. I didn't have time to write things down. Someone always wanted something—my employees, the purveyors of the fabrics, trim, and such. And I would only select the best. I would not let my clients be dressed in low-cost items.

"You could do cheaper dresses for other women, like Hattie Carnegie does."

"No, indeed. My brand is exclusive and I'm going to stay that way. The Lord will provide. Just trust in Him."

My all-female crew in my life didn't know that I was trusting in the Lord for one more thing.

I went to the doctor at the beginning of the week of John Kennedy's inauguration. I went by myself, because I didn't want Sallie to fuss. I knew the news was not going to be good, and I needed to hear what the doctor said first.

Before I told anyone else.

"Your glaucoma is progressing."

The doctor reached into a drawer and handed me a bottle. "If you keep consistent in using these drops, and rest your eyesight, you might save it for a bit."

"What do you mean, rest my eyesight?"

"No close work, no reading. Things like that."

Close work was all I did! This doctor was asking me to give up my work. I could never do that. Arthur would never want that.

So I worked on.

Ruth was the one who opened my mail at the shop and one day, she let me know that I was going to get an award.

"Who wants to give me an award?"

"New York Fashion Society! Mama, they've named you Couturier of the Year!" She embraced me and I embraced her back.

"I have no idea why they would want to honor me so, but I suppose that's nice."

"It's wonderful. Wait until I tell Tommy."

Tommy was her husband, who was wonderfully supportive of her. I was happy that she had found that kind of love, but it brought to mind how Caleb West had escaped me with a younger, smaller model of an Annie who would do just what he wanted.

Thank the Lord I had my freedom. So necessary, but it did come with a price to pay.

"What will you wear, Mama?"

I waved an arm at her, picking up my sketch pad. "What I always do, child. It's never acceptable for me to draw attention to myself. I'm not a model. I'm someone who creates dresses for my clients."

"No. You're Couturier of the Year!" She squeezed my hands.

"I wish the award came with money," I said jokingly, but I was serious.

"Maybe people will see it and you'll get more commissions."

I tapped my sketch pad with my pencil. Yes, more work was always the answer.

We looked forward to watching the Kennedy inauguration highlights on the news that night when we got home, especially so we could see Jacqueline's day wear. And she looked lovely in her pillbox and fur, standing by her husband's side. I caught glimpses of Mrs. Auchincloss and Mrs. Canfield as well. I prayed they were watching out for Mrs. Kennedy's health. I still worried for her, being out in all of that cold so soon after having a baby. I guess she couldn't have said no, but I really hoped she was limiting her activities.

Later that night, we watched her stepping out into the beautifully snowy night with the handsome Mr. Kennedy, who held his top hat, lest he mess up his beautiful hair. I chuckled. I never saw a man as fascinated with his own hair as Mr.—oh, excuse me—President Kennedy.

Jacqueline, dressed head to toe in white, looked like a snow queen. The line of her outfit was very futuristic and, more importantly, fashion forward. We were silent, watching her move through the snow to the car, taking careful note. Her dress, like other inaugural dresses, would be bound to impact gown design, and I wanted to be ready.

My head was full of ideas when Sallie and I arrived at work the next day, ready to get to work on the debutante, wedding, and evening gowns for the spring. Sonja called me that morning, and I was pleased to hear from her.

"You sound wonderful, my friend!"

"As do you, Sonja. It's been great to hear from you."

"There were two men here who were looking for you. I wanted to let you know they were coming to your shop."

My heart started to beat. Fast. Ever since Arthur died, I knew that my method of robbing Peter to pay Paul might catch up with me.

"I appreciate that, my dear friend. Be blessed."

I put the phone handset back into the cradle, my hands a little slick.

Well, if it came to it, I could beg. I could plead for more time.

Keep me blessed, God and Arthur. Son, please intercede for me. What we need here is more business, not less.

A client came in for her evening gown appointment and I was busy past the afternoon. Then, two nondescript white men in porkpie hats came into the shop.

Sallie greeted them. "What may we help you with, gentlemen?"

"We represent an event committee in Omaha, Nebraska. We are looking for a designer for our annual ball that takes place in the spring. It's called the Aksarben Ball."

I tried to repeat the strange word. The shorter man leaned forward. "It's 'Nebraska' spelled backward, of course."

That made it easier to say. "Of course," I said.

"We would like to hire you to be our designer, Miss Lowe."

I drew back, shocked. An opportunity. "How have you heard of me?"

"Well, you are society's best-kept secret, right? You're listed in the new edition of the *Social Register*. And thank goodness."

I nodded my head. That made sense. "We'll need thirty-three dresses by the middle of April. Do you think you can fill such an order?"

I did not hesitate for even one second. "Yes, I do. What would the ladies like?"

I sat down with the two of them and sketched off five quick designs that pleased them a great deal.

It pleased me too when they handed me a check for three thousand dollars and the promise of more to come.

Sketching out all of those beautiful gowns for the Aksarben Ball brought me back to the days of the Gasparilla, only with designs updated for the new Kennedy era.

For the first time since I lost my Arthur, I had hope in my life again. It was a beautiful time, even though it only lasted a little while.

Chapter Thirty-Seven

Why does a dress have to cost anything at all? I would make dresses because I love the work. It's because of other factors, other things, other people that I have to charge for what I do. And I often don't really know what to charge, because it feels as if I'm stealing from the customer to expect payment when I love designing and making dresses so much.

A new dress is a way of presenting a woman to the world.

So many, so very many, women counted on me to secure themselves and their futures with my dresses. Because if you don't have a skill, or know how to make something like I do, you have to find a man who will take care of you.

And getting a man is a seriously slippery business.

The dress, the right dress, the dress that will shape and form your body, is all a part of that business.

So matching the right dress to the right woman, to me, was less science and more magic.

That's why it hurt my feelings when Lee Canfield, née Bouvier, left my appointment, insistent that she could have her wedding dress made cheaper somewhere else. She soon found out the hard way that my prices were already bargain-basement cheap.

Making that magic for ladies was my business, my dream, my path in life. The practical was not. Unfortunately, I never made an association between my art and those painful times I was in school, struggling to learn math. That was one reason why I believed that God sent Arthur to me. He stood between my art and the awful, sad memories of having my math mistakes being pointed out to everyone in the most humiliating ways. The day I set down my math slate and never picked it up again was one of the happiest of my life.

One morning in February 1962, five years after Arthur was taken from me, nother pair of nondescript white men came into my shop as we were sewing. The Aksarben commission had helped me get requests from wealthy families in the Midwest, so business had picked up even more.

When the bell jangled as these men entered, my heart lifted in hope, but by the stern looks on their faces, I could tell this was not another opportunity like Aksarben.

"How may I help you, gentlemen?"

"Are you Ann Cole Lowe?"

"I am."

The man handed me a stack of slick papers. "I'm John Morgan of the IRS. We are seizing this shop and the contents of this shop for back taxes. You must leave right now."

The papers were a stack of mint green in front of my eyes, all fuzzed together, even through my very thick glasses. "Excuse me? What are you saying? Leave? I have commissions."

Sallie came and stood next to me, protective as always. "What is all of this?"

The other gentleman spoke. "You must leave this space. You owe too many back taxes to stay here."

"There must be some mistake." Sallie picked up the papers and peered at them through her own, more efficient, glasses.

"No, ma'am," John Morgan said.

I'll never forget that name.

"When are we supposed to leave?" Sallie asked after she put the papers down.

"Now," they both said together. Then John Morgan said, "We are taking possession of this shop right now."

By this point, word had spread to the seamstresses, and some came out to see what was going on, forming a group behind me.

"Everyone out!" John Morgan yelled.

"You cannot do that. You just . . . you cannot do that." I waved my arms in front of him.

"Oh I can. You have to go. Right now."

"What about the dresses that I'm working on?"

"All of that is part of the seizure. Drop whatever it is you are doing and leave. Now." Four or five other men had come in and were standing around my bright shop, adding spots of darkness in what had been a happy atmosphere.

I turned to the seamstresses. "I'm so, so sorry. Come back tomorrow and I will straighten all of this out. Please."

They started to dissipate and I looked at Sallie. "Don't we have anything?" she said.

I spread my hands. "No. I'm waiting on delivery in a few days. It won't be enough to pay five thousand dollars."

John Morgan and his accomplice thief went to the back, I guess to see if there was anyone else in the shop to send home.

"I can't believe this."

Sallie put a hand on my arm. "We'll figure this out at home. Come on."

"Sallie, I cannot. I can't just leave like this. What about my orders?"

She shook her head. "He said they have to take it all."

Sallie followed me as I went to the back, where the IRS men were telling the rest of my workers to go home. "What if I have money? Will you leave?"

"Ma'am, you have to settle this through the court."

"But I have clients who will be here to pick up dresses at the end of the week."

John Morgan turned. "That's what I have to tell you, ma'am. You should go to the court and see if you can pick out items from the seizure."

He pointed to the front of the shop. "The door is that way."

As if I didn't know.

Sallie and I wandered into the main showroom, where the other men were standing by, with thick chains and locks in their hands. What did they need all of that for?

"Come on, Annie. Let's put our coats on."

Sallie dressed me first, then we slid on our rubber boots against the cold and wet. Finally, she put on her coat.

"This . . . just isn't right. Something is not right."

We walked out through the front door and stood on the sidewalk. "This feels wrong." My voice grew louder and louder.

"Why are those men in my shop? What are they doing in there?" I reached over and opened the door, looking at them putting their big man hands on my couches, stacking them up. "Stop doing that."

John Morgan came to the doorway. "Miss Lowe, please leave. You are causing a scene for yourself."

"I just cannot believe that you are doing this. Stop at once!"

Sallie had her arm around my waist but I would not be moved.

"Leave my shop! This is mine! My son, Arthur—he made sure

I had this shop. He got it for me after I had worked and worked and worked for others. He was killed a few years ago, and he would never want anyone to take me from it."

My hands, well used to roughness from sewing, wrapped around the door frames and a desire to physically hold on to what was mine came over me. Both John Morgan and Sallie were trying to dislodge my hands, but I would not let go.

One of the other men walked toward us with a crowbar in his hands.

"We will take any and all measures to seize this property." John Morgan's voice was low against my screaming.

"Annie! Please. They'll hurt you. It's not worth it." Sallie's voice, usually low and gentle, loudly filled my ears and I startled, not used to hearing Sallie speak in this way.

I let go of the door and they closed it once more. "Get out! Get out now!" I beat my fists against the door.

"Annie, please! Stop it. Your hands. You need them."

Sallie's voice, still loud and clear, again shattered my focus. All of a sudden, her warm arms wrapped around me and I sobbed against her chest. My usual place of home.

A small crowd had gathered and she protected me from them. Again.

"What are you all staring at? Leave us alone!"

Sallie walked me down the street slowly and some of the seamstresses surrounded us, telling us stories about why they needed to be paid their wages right now. Sallie spoke to all of them.

Then I heard a clink, and I tore myself from Sallie's arms, running back through the slush and the snow to see John Morgan and his thieves threading one of those thick chains through and around my door, and papering up the window with official-looking notices from the government.

"Nooooooooooooo!!!" I screamed, grasping the chain. I struggled so hard with that chain, I tore holes in my pantyhose, but I did not care.

They walked away from us, their jobs done.

I do not know what happened after that. Sallie got me home somehow, on the second worst day of my life. Why was I having so many of them?

It wasn't the same as losing Arthur, but my shop, my livelihood reflected my art and who I was. What would all of my rich clients say when they knew that I had lost my shop? The *Society Register* was a small world and once word got out about what had happened, my customers would abandon me.

I woke up the next day when Sallie came into my room with a plate of dry toast and a cup of black coffee, my usual breakfast, but which I normally ate in the kitchen. It was kind of her to bring it to me.

It was just the two of us in the apartment now that Ruth was married to her husband, Tommy, and our time together lately reminded me of the days before she ran off to marry that goofy boy—minus, of course, Mama and Grandma Georgia and the General.

I sipped at the hot coffee. "I wish I was better at all of this."

"Oh, Annie. It's not your fault. You have such a joy for what you do, you forget about every day stuff like money."

"I just don't know what I'm going to do. How can this happen to me?"

Sallie patted my free hand as I set down my cup. "God will see us through. He always has."

I nodded. "He has. I've sewn out of my house before. Many years ago, but I've done it."

"We live in Harlem, though, unfortunately. Your clients won't want to come here, sister."

She was right about that. White folks did come to Harlem, but it was usually under the cover of night and in secret.

Think.

Think.

Think.

I sipped the coffee as though the answer to my troubles was in the cup.

"Maybe take up a collection among your clients?" Sallie pointed out.

"It's bad enough. I can't go begging through the *Register*."

"Not all of them. Just certain ones. Like Mrs. Post? She rich enough to help."

I shook my head, my blood rising to my fingertips.

"What about the president?"

"Oh no. I can't do that."

"You've done enough for them over the years to ask."

"May I remind you Lee Canfield tried to lowball me on her wedding dress? No."

I put the empty cup down and waved my hand. No toast for me.

The door opened. The only ones who had a key were Ruth and Cora, and Cora would be working right now.

Ruth came into the room, her young face alight. "Mama, it's going to be all right."

"You got money?" Sallie asked.

"No. Not that much. I went to Saks. The Adam Room wants to see you today. They want to talk to you about opening up your own boutique in the store—just like Sonja used to have."

"A Saks Fifth Avenue boutique?"

She held my hands. "A collaboration between you and the Adam Room."

"Would I have my own label or work for the Adam Room under their label?"

"You need to go find out, Mama. I went by there this morning and they had heard what happened to you. They told me to come over here right away to let you know. They want to snap you up before someone else does."

My mind raced. "Maybe they would help me get the dresses out of the store for my clients."

Ruth nodded.

I flipped the covers off my legs. "I got to get ready, Sallie."

She had already gone into the bathroom to run a bath for me.

What would I ever do without my sister?

Chapter Thirty-Eight

*B*ecause of my reputation, the transfer to the Adam Room at Saks was seamless. I was welcomed with open arms there and the label had my name in big, bold script, with *Adam Room* in small print. The split we came up with suited me well and I was only out of business for a few days. None of my customers were made aware of my situation, and Ruth and Sallie were able to track down all of the commissions that had been seized. Some customers were sent their finished dresses once I remade them at home and others were told to report to Saks for fittings. Most were happy to do so because they shopped at Saks anyway. So any thoughts I had about the problem with my taxes being a humiliation were unwarranted. However, I did have to approach the government to make an arrangement to pay my taxes over the next few years.

As those problems were resolved, I soon faced a different but familiar one. I went to the eye doctor for a follow-up appointment, and he was not pleased at all after examining me.

"What have you been doing?"

"Working?"

He frowned. "You might lose your right eye if you don't take better care."

I placed my hand on my cheek, just below my eye. "Lose it?"

"Yes. You'll have to wear a patch on it for the rest of your life."

I gulped, and a numb feeling surrounded me like the white silk cape Mrs. Kennedy wore to the inauguration ball.

I made my way home slowly, wondering how to tell Sallie this, when I decided all of a sudden that I didn't need to tell her anything. What I did with my eyes was my business. I would rather design dresses more than do anything else in the world. I would take on more work so I could pay the tax bill off and that was that.

At home, the mail had been delivered to our apartment box and I retrieved a thick envelope that seemed like a wedding invitation.

That was a strange thing because my clients didn't know where I lived. It wasn't that I was ashamed to live in Harlem—most of them just didn't have that information. Also, when I went to a wedding, I was usually there to assist with the dress, so I didn't often receive an actual invitation. The exception was for my granddaughter Audrey, whose wedding was coming up at Christmas. And maybe even Cora, who I suspected would be married the next year.

I carried it upstairs to Sallie, got involved in some other task, and almost forgot about the envelope until Sallie lifted it from the corner table and waved it in front of my face.

"What is this, sister?"

"Oh my. I brought that up there and forgot about it. Can you open it?"

This was not an unusual request to Sallie. Still, I didn't want to explain that the winter twilight had descended on the day, making it harder to read, even in the strong light we kept in the dining room, where I liked to work at the table.

Sitting herself down, Sallie slit open the creamy envelope and removed what was inside: a piece of writing paper instead of an embossed invitation.

She opened the letter and her light eyes grew wide.

"It's from the White House. It's Jackie Kennedy writing to you."

"Jacqueline." I always corrected folk who called her Jackie. She didn't like that name at all.

Sallie bowed her head, adjusting her own glasses. "She wants you to come and see her."

"Me?" I shook my head. "That can't be right. Read it."

"'Dear Miss Lowe, I understand that it is the busy season for debutante balls and weddings, but I would like to see you for an appointment of a short duration when you can spare the time. Please call my social secretary at the following number and she will set up the particulars. Thank you so much and I hope to hear from you soon. Jacqueline Kennedy.'"

"Do you think she wants you to design for her?"

Joy leaped up like a leprechaun within my chest at the thought, but common good sense struck it back down again. "She said an appointment of a short duration. That's not a consultation."

"Still, she wants you to go all the way to Washington, D.C. To the White House."

"Well, Sallie. We've been in the governor's mansion in Alabama. Other fancy houses in Florida and here in New York. The White House is just one step up." I smoothed down my dress.

Still, it was quite something when I took time to think about it. Grandma Georgia had been held in bondage and here I was, her granddaughter, going to see the first lady in the White House.

"When should you go?"

"Oh, Sallie. I can't travel all that way by myself. You've got to come with me."

"Me?"

"Yes, you ninny. You're my sister."

"Well, I just thought Ruth would go."

"She doesn't want to leave her husband. Besides, I think she's expecting another baby."

Sallie nodded. "She's got that look in her eyes."

I agreed. We both knew. It was so obvious. The eyes always gave a woman away—like she had her mind on the future—her future.

Sallie wasn't looking at me. Like something was in *her* eyes. "You don't want to go?" I asked.

"I just . . . I don't have anything to wear."

"Sallie. You're my sister. We'll get you something appropriate."

"Oh my. I need to write the boys and tell them."

I opened my mouth to say I wanted to tell my boy, but then the pain, that anvil-shaped pain came and smashed me in my brain. Every single time.

I had no boy. I would tell Ruth. Still, I knew Arthur would be proud of me.

And I still had to wonder: What could Mrs. Kennedy possibly want?

THE VERY NEXT day, Sallie called the social secretary but handed me the phone. I felt a small irritation. "Hello?"

"Miss Lowe? This is Tucky. I met you at the wedding so many years ago."

I recalled a thin blond woman who had introduced herself as Jacqueline's Miss Porter's classmate, Nancy Tuckerman, who they liked to call Tucky. She had been a bridesmaid. "Yes, I recall. How are you?"

"Fine. I would like to get this set up relatively soon. How about next Friday? She knows how valuable your time is, so if you take the train down here in the morning, you can probably get here at about 10:30 A.M., come to the White House by 11:00 A.M., and go home the same day. We can send a car to the train station to bring you here."

"Um, I have a problem."

Tucky's cheerful voice came across the telephone line as concerned. "Oh, come now. This is an appointment to see the first lady. What is the problem?"

"I couldn't possibly travel by myself."

"Would you like to bring your husband?"

"I'm not married. I mean my sister."

"Oh, that's fine. She may not attend the appointment, but I'll send two train tickets."

"Yes, that will do. Thank you."

I hung up the phone and Sallie laid a hand on her chest. "I don't have a thing to wear to the White House."

In that moment, I realized that I had never made my sister something formal to wear. She always bought her simple dresses off the rack, insisting that she didn't want me to waste my precious time and energy on her.

I went to her, tucking my arm in hers. "I'll be proud to sew you something, Sallie. Never worry."

She whipped out her hanky from her sleeve and dabbed at her eyes. This gesture made my heart swell.

"What use is my capability if I can't make my sister a dress to wear?"

"I'm going to look so fine by the time you get done with me, Annie. Thank you."

I squeezed her hand. "I'm sorry I didn't think of it sooner."

And I was. Who had I been sewing for all of this time to make Sallie think I couldn't make her one dress?

All of the arrangements were made, and over the next week, I sewed Sallie a navy-blue lace dress that hovered close to her curves. I loaned her one of my costume jewelry brooches to wear on the dress. I wore my usual wide-brim hat on the train, and she wore something that had a little net veil on it. Before we knew it, there we were, two older ladies from Alabama going to Washington, D.C., to the White House to see the first lady.

I'd had train journeys that were not nearly as pleasant as that one, where they served us black coffee and Danish. It was almost as if they knew we were going somewhere important.

When we arrived at Union Station, we went into the large foyer, where a Black man in a chauffeur's uniform of black pants and jacket with a white shirt stood holding a large card that had my name on it.

He guided us to the car, and Sallie and I slipped into the back seat. When the driver heard we had never been to D.C. before, he took the scenic route to the White House, showing us the U. S. Capitol, the Supreme Court Building, and the Lincoln Memorial. It was all so beautiful.

Finally, though, he drove us to the White House and we both marveled at the size and beauty of it as he pulled up to the gates. I showed the pass that Tucky had sent us and we were driven through.

An assistant met us as soon as we got out of the car and guided us along the carpeted hallways of the East Wing, the part of the White House where Jacqueline kept her office.

When we got there, Tucky opened the door and I remembered her merry blue eyes at once. "So good to see you again, Miss Lowe."

"Thank you so much."

"I'll make your sister comfortable while you meet with Mrs. Kennedy. It shouldn't take long. She's expecting you."

She guided me through the door. I took small, mincing steps into a room that, in spite of it being March, was filled with everything light and bright, and so my eyes, as bad as they were, lit on Jacqueline, who sat in a perfect ladylike pose on one of the davenports.

"Ah, Miss Lowe. So good to see you again." Her voice was pitched low and carried a breathless quality, as if she had just finished exercise. The room, which looked out of the back of the White House, carried the faintest smell of cigarette smoke.

"It's wonderful to see you, Mrs. Kennedy."

"My mother asked to be remembered to you."

"Of course. I hope Mrs. Auchincloss is well."

She smiled. "She is."

"Wonderful."

"I was grateful to receive your layette gifts over the years. Thank you so much. They reflected your beautiful work."

"Of course."

She spread her hands. "I'm glad you could come. I don't want to keep you from your work. But I just had to say . . . I heard of your recent, well, difficulty."

I blinked, somewhat embarrassed at being revealed in front of a client. "My difficulty."

"The shop. Your shop. That you lost it."

"Yes. I did. But I do have to say that landing this new position at Saks was a blessing, Mrs. Kennedy. A minor setback."

She shook her head and her famous bouffant, the one women the world over were copying, moved ever so slightly. "I'm glad to hear it. Still, there is the matter of, well, the balance. I've thought about it and well, I feel responsible."

"You do?" I frowned. "I don't see how."

"When people asked me about my wedding gown, I, well, I

didn't speak up as I should have. And I got your letter. When *Ladies' Home Journal* printed what they did, and given some of the design choices I am making now, I understand, in a way that I didn't when this first happened, how important it is to say specific names. I can't help but feel that if I had spoken up sooner, you might have had an easier time meeting your obligations."

Would I have gotten more dress commissions if she had said *Ann Lowe,* instead of *colored seamstress*? I did experience an increase in business after my commissions for Jacqueline's family, but only because society people were whispering my name among themselves and knew where to look for me.

I rearranged my purse on my lap. "Well, Mrs. Kennedy, we'll never know."

She held up a hand. "It's all I can do to make sure that your obligation is met, so you can return to your shop. Consider it done. You won't be bothered by the IRS any longer."

It wasn't money given to me directly but without the burden of having to pay the tax obligation, I could save up my money for a new shop even faster. "I want to thank you for this, Mrs. Kennedy. So very much."

She nodded. "It's the least I can do. And, Miss Lowe? One small favor?"

"Of course, Mrs. Kennedy." I leaned forward.

She leaned forward too. "Please take care of your health. Other young girls and women need your artistic talents in the coming years for their deb balls and weddings. Like my sister Janet Jr. She's growing up fast." She folded her hands and smiled.

I smiled at the thought of Mrs. Auchincloss's youngest child, named Janet Auchincloss after herself, and how her family loved to call her Janet Jr. "I'll do my best."

She stood.

Then I stood. "Please take care of your beautiful babies."

Her face shined like an additional sunbeam had entered the room. "I will. Thank you for asking about them."

She showed me from the room, and like that, the meeting was over in ten minutes.

Tucky showed us back to the car and our driver, a true gentleman, took us to see more sights in Washington, D.C. He dropped us off at a cafeteria to eat lunch, where I told Sallie everything as we sat down to eat.

"That was so generous and kind of her," Sallie marveled.

I nodded. "It was. It almost makes up for the humiliation of it all."

"God never gives you more of a burden than you can carry."

No, he doesn't. I did my best to eat my chicken breast and vegetables. I had more of an appetite just then than I'd had in more than a year.

Chapter Thirty-Nine

$\mathcal{A}$s wonderful as Mrs. Kennedy's blessing was, it still wasn't enough to get me out of financial trouble. I owed something like ten thousand dollars to fabric purveyors and other salespeople, my old friends from the Garment District. They knew that even though I owed them money, I would pay it back eventually, and they understood that my designs were worthy of their fabrics.

So I stayed with Saks for a while to save up money, and for additional work, I contracted with other department stores around the country. I kept myself exclusive, of course, but with what those stores charged for one of my unique dresses, I started to dig my way out of the ten-thousand-dollar hole I was in. Still, I had to declare bankruptcy so that I could start anew.

In 1963, I became a great-grandmother when Audrey had a baby girl. I was so proud of her. When I held that baby, in a layette I had made for her, I could see the tie backward to slavery through my grandma Georgia and into the future through this beautiful child named Clara.

I felt blessed to see her before I lost the sight in my right eye.

"It has to go," Dr. Purell said at my appointment when Clara was two months old.

"What can I do with one eye?"

"I don't know, Miss Lowe." His voice grew softer. "But I warned you of this consequence last year."

I didn't want no one taking my eye. "I don't have the money to pay you."

He shook his head. "Did I say anything at all about your money?" He patted my hand. "This is about your health, Miss Lowe. It won't do any good for you to have an infected eye in your body."

So in August, I went to the hospital to have my right eye taken out. Gone, for the rest of my life. Afterward, my left eye had to do a lot more work, but one of my seamstresses had gotten very good at creating sketches from my descriptions, so I could keep working at Saks once I recovered.

Sallie and I were at home after our light dinner of rice, plantain, and chicken when the newsman came on the television and said Mrs. Kennedy had given birth to a baby boy.

Sallie shook her head. "Oh my. That baby wasn't due until October."

I clutched my chest, worrying for poor Jacqueline once more. "My Lord, won't that poor girl ever get a break in this world?"

I prayed for her baby boy.

Even as I did, though, a familiar feeling shot through me and I remembered those pink gladioli at St. Mary's.

He's not going to make it.

"Dear God, please help Mr. and Mrs. Kennedy. Help their baby son live," Sallie and I prayed out loud right in our living room.

But he didn't. Little Patrick died not two days later. Jacqueline was still recovering from the birth so the president had to do all of the funeral and open, public grieving for their lost boy. Think-

ing of their loss made me think of Arthur, and I cried right along
with the people in the crowd.

God always knows what is best. He was making a way for
President Kennedy to go to heaven. Not four months later, some
hateful little man shot him and made my Jacqueline a widow with
two young children, all alone in the world.

What if Patrick had lived?

Then she would have had those two children plus a newborn
baby.

We never know what is in His mind.

I closed the shop, of course. It was almost time for the Thanks-
giving holiday anyway, and Sallie and I kept ourselves close to the
television, crying and holding hands. My young sketcher, who I
employed to make sketches for me these days, came over for some
parts of the funeral service, since she didn't have a television yet,
and I could still dictate designs to her as we all sat together, grieving for the president and his young family.

What a terrible year it had been.

The only good thing to happen during this time was that
someone wanted to help me financially by putting on my first
fashion show while other houses were showing their new designs
for the season in New York for Fashion Week.

I confided to the mother of one of my clients: "Thirty-six
years. I've been in this town for thirty-six years and I've never
been able to have a show during New York Fashion Week."

"Then it is high time, Miss Lowe. Everyone loves your beautiful work."

"Thank you, dear. I just don't know how I'm going to get
models."

"I'll model for you," said the young woman I was fitting, the
daughter of a vice president at IBM.

"You would?"

"Of course. Make it young women, clients, like me. You won't have to pay us and we'll be happy to model for you."

It was a clever idea that led to a very classy kind of show. I couldn't afford to throw an extravagant party in the evening as other designers did. I could, instead, set up a champagne brunch and have society girls do the modeling for free.

My first fashion show turned out to be a lovely event and even better, I was able to sell every single last one of the dresses, with plans to create more on deck. My young sketcher and I went right back to work.

And still, more disaster loomed.

Not only could poor Jacqueline not get a break, it seemed I couldn't either. My other eye started to act a fool as well in the new year of 1964.

"Well, that's all, Miss Lowe. You can't expect your one eye, your last eye, to carry the burden of the work that you do. You don't want me to remove it, do you?"

"No. I don't." I shivered in his cold office.

"You need to retire. This act of stubbornness isn't doing you one bit of good."

He shook his head—I could tell by the way his shadows moved. He then gestured to Sallie to come and get me so we could go home.

I told Sallie what he had said. She patted my hand. "Annie, you've done so much. This year, so many have seen you and what you can do. They know you aren't just a seamstress. You're a designer. You've been in *The Saturday Evening Post,* on TV with Mike Douglas, your gowns in high-end department stores in Dallas and Philadelphia and Kansas City. It's been amazing."

"I'm only sixty-six, Sallie. It doesn't seem fair."

The thought that my designing life could be over threatened to send me into a spasm of tears not unlike how I cried when those horrible IRS men made me leave my shop and bolted the doors.

He's not the only one.

When I was eating dinner, the words went through my mind again.

He's not the only one.

When I was trying to fall asleep, a time when I usually thought of dresses in my mind's eye, where everything was still safe and healthy, it came to me again.

He's not the only one.

I sat up, stretching my arms out into the darkness.

God, what are you trying to tell me?

He's not the only one.

I pulled my arms back.

Then it hit me.

I could go to another doctor. Dr. Purnell might not like it, but this was New York City, one of the biggest cities in the world. I could even take the subway to a doctor in another borough.

My body sagged in my bed and I went into a sound, deep sleep, the first one I had in a long, long time.

I would forever be grateful to Dr. Purnell for taking out my right eye for free, but I had to find out if this operation was necessary from another doctor.

I made some inquiries with my *Social Register* friends and learned of a doctor by the Battery who would see me. It was a long ride away on the subway, but Sallie and I went there two days later.

This doctor, Dr. Ross, was about the same age as Dr. Purnell and had gentle fingers. I was glad that he attended to us as if he were a courtly Southern gentleman. I had missed that kind of treatment in the nearly forty years I had lived in New York.

"The eye is not unsalvageable. The cataract is deep, and the shape has been impacted by your glaucoma, but if you use your drops as you should, I may be able to help you."

My heart beat fast. "I promise I will."

He had a front-combed hairstyle as if he were a young Elvis Presley, a boy that I knew had respected and loved his mother, and I took that to be a good sign.

He smiled as he left us, and we made an appointment for surgery for the next week.

Sallie and I, as well as Cora and her husband, Ruth and her husband, Audrey and her husband and my little great-grandchild, all made a special effort to attend St. Mark's Episcopal that Sunday to ask for a special prayer over my operation.

Everything I did for the rest of the week until Wednesday, when my surgery would take place at 7:00 A.M. at Morningside Hospital, took on extra meaning. I felt as if I were on borrowed time.

What can I do? What can I do to show God my gratitude if he were to save my sight?

It had to be something. All I could give was my talent, my art, my designs. That's all I knew. My designs were who I was.

As I lay in my hospital bed, I thought back over the previous night when I was at home with Sallie and we watched the Academy Awards on television. Sidney Poitier won the Best Actor award. To witness a Negro man win one of those pretty trophies was something else, even though I knew and understood that if Dr. Ross did wrong, it would be among the last images I would ever see.

And when I thought about that, I knew what God would want me to do. I prayed about it and went to sleep.

Dr. Ross was right there when I woke up out of the anesthesia. "The operation went well, Miss Lowe. I think I got most of it."

Groggy, I said, "We gone pay you. We gone pay you real good."
It was as if Mama and Grandma Georgia were with me all over
again and when I saw them at the foot of my bed, they knew what
I was going to do, and they approved.

He nodded. "Don't worry about that now. Just rest, Miss
Lowe. I'll send your daughter in now."

Ruth came in, her face wrinkled with worry. "How do you
feel, Mama?"

"Like I was back in Alabama again, sewing old-timey things
for Mrs. O'Neal and the other ladies of the Alabama Legislature."

She clenched my hand. "It's okay, Mama. You're safe."

"Where's Sallie?"

Her face was still scrunched up. "Aunt Sallie has been wearing herself out over this. I thought it best she stay at home and
rest too."

"You sure? She okay?"

"Mama, you know she's older than you. Both of you do too
much gallivanting around New York City for two old ladies."

I waved my hand. "We'll be all right."

"Well, I told her I was taking over and that was fine by her."

A prickly thread of something went through my fingers. I
wanted to sew, already, so I felt pretty good. I'll never forget the
day when Dr. Ross removed the bandages from my eye and when
I looked out at him, his Elvis pompadour appeared with nice
sharp lines.

Praise God, I could see him and he sure was pretty.

Thank you, God.

The rest of my time with my sight, for as long as I could have
it, I would sew ball gowns and wedding gowns for those of my
race. I would share my talents. It was past time to make sure that
lovely women with brown skin got to wear Ann Lowe gowns.

I was thrilled to be able to make good on my promise the next week, for a young Negro concert pianist who attended Juilliard and was looking for a concert gown. I charged her less than what the gown cost to make. The money didn't matter.

This is what I needed to do.

Chapter Forty

$\mathcal{I}$t was God's blessing to return my sight. I opened Ann Lowe's Originals in 1965, in a bigger and better location down the street from my old shop. Nearly everyone returned, even my sketcher, because they believed in what I was doing. It was truly inspirational. And I made good on my vow.

The country was changing. Audrey came into my shop one day with her hair cut into an Afro and I barely recognized her. However, the rounded look, coupled with some dangling earrings, suited her face. She was beautiful in a way I never thought possible. God help me, I was jealous that she was able to pull off the look. One needed hair thick enough for an Afro and mine had never been that lush.

One commission came to me most unexpectedly. Officials from the Evyan Perfume company wrote, asking me to work on a special project they had been planning. When the small committee visited my store, they explained that they wanted me to duplicate the very popular exhibit at the Smithsonian of first ladies dresses. The copied gowns, at one-third of the size of the originals, would be exhibited on mannequins throughout the country to attract attention to and boost sales of the company's White Shoulders perfume.

There was nothing new to design—I just had to fabricate smaller versions of the already existing gowns. I would have to travel again to Washington, D.C., to view the gowns in their natural circumstances. I did not ask for, nor did I expect to be allowed, a close-up showing of the dresses, which included the gown Lady Bird Johnson wore to the most recent inaugural ball, in 1965. I could do it just by looking at them and translating details to a sketcher. It would be fun, like making clothes for Miss Nell's dolls.

This time I did not take Sallie, but instead brought a young designer, Donna Dean, who was learning the ropes with me while she attended the Fashion Institute of Technology. She was a lovely young lady and I was happy to bring along someone from the younger generation who was also of my race.

Donna accompanied me to help me throughout the journey. Sallie was getting less able to do such things. I worried over her and when I insisted that she stay home and not come to D.C. with me, she readily accepted.

I put aside my worries about Sallie and instead focused on the fun of the project before me. Donna had family in Washington so we stayed at their house in the Anacostia neighborhood. Her aunt and uncle welcomed me as if I were a queen and took care of me as good as Sallie did. When it was time to go to the museum, Donna's uncle drove us there and picked us up so we didn't have to take public transportation.

At the *First Ladies* exhibit, I showed Donna that the tide of American fashion ebbed and flowed. The early gowns of the republic were nipped in, and light, just like the present day's fashions.

Donna laughed. "You remember those eighty-five we did for the season last year, Miss Lowe? People must have thought you lost your mind."

I shook my head. "Nope. They just didn't know that a nearly

blind lady couldn't see the times coming. People have forgotten the scarcity of material. They want their bodies to show. So here we are again."

The exhibit started with the most present-day dress, Lady Bird's yellow satin sheath with the long butter-colored coat with fur pieces at the neck and cuffs.

"Compare that to what Mamie Eisenhower wore. Is it any wonder she chose a dress like this? Pink, with full fabric studded with rhinestones. She was the wife of a general and remembered just how it was during World War II, a time when you were barely born."

Donna's capacity to sketch was unparalleled and I was grateful again for her appearance in my life. "What do you think of Bess Truman's dress?" she asked me.

"Very prudent. Not showy, not extravagant. The design of this gown shows she also remembers difficult times. The color too." I nodded my head. "She was not a woman who liked the spotlight. She preferred to fade away and the dress shows that."

"That one won't be any fun."

"But we will do it just the same and do a good job on it, as we will for this lovely mint green of Mrs. Eleanor Roosevelt."

"I do like that."

"Not a lot of fabric. It was the Depression, it wouldn't be suitable."

"These gowns from the 1920s—Mrs. Hoover and Mrs. Coolidge—look like ones we could wear today."

"Yes, you could. I have fond memories of a lot of my work from the 1920s and the Gasparilla days. The flirty red dress of Grace Coolidge. Her husband was no fun to be sure, but they say he liked her to look nice and she did. They say she was a descendant of Pocahontas and had that kind of princess look to her."

"Mrs. Harding and both Mrs. Wilsons represent another time as well. Mrs. Taft too. Hers was the first one in the collection." I grasped my purse and closed my eyes, laughing as I remembered. "It was as if the world turned upside down when those hems started going higher and higher. I know some of the older people liked it because the higher hemlines meant less fabric and a cheaper dress."

"I can see that." Donna's hand made swift movements over the page.

"But now, as you can see, the dresses of Mrs. Roosevelt and Mrs. McKinley, that's a different era. This is the kind of work that my mother and grandmother did. And in revisiting their dresses, it's going to be like visiting with them again."

"Or like working with them again, Miss Lowe." Donna smiled.

"Yes indeed, child. It was at their feet that I learned everything that I know now. Look at that lacework on Mrs. McKinley's dress. Just beautiful. There are times when I miss those touches. No one wants that now. But it will be back. I'm not sure I'll be around when those looks come back around, but you will be."

"But right now, you're doing the dresses with the low backs."

"Stop teasing me, Donna." I chuckled.

"You love to cause so much controversy, Miss Lowe."

"That could be. But I don't want the dirty hands of those dates getting my dresses soiled while they are out there dancing."

Donna nodded, putting her notepad down. We went to a little cafeteria in downtown D.C., with no worries of having to seat ourselves or go to a Black restaurant. Unlike the last time I came just a few years ago, Washington, D.C., was fully integrated and we could eat where we chose.

A new day indeed.

TWO DAYS LATER, back at home with my Sallie, I noticed she was tired. And bored. Of course, in her usual way, she loved to listen to me talk about the dresses and the commission that I had before me. We didn't even turn on the television and when it was time to go to bed we lay awake, talking away like we never got to do when we were young women because Sallie had almost always lived at her house with her husband.

"It's too bad I can't help. My legs are so bad these days."

Sallie had the sugar and it was all she could do to get to the bathroom these days. I was afraid of what might happen one day if she didn't get there in time. I was one-third her size. How could I take care of her?

I didn't know, but what I did know was I could occupy her time.

"These being small, Sallie, I can have Donna bring over one of the models and you can create the fit of the dresses with muslin."

She turned in the bed a little. "I can do that?"

"Of course you can. It would be a big help if you did."

"Okay. I'm happy to help."

"It'll be better, since you can fit like nobody's business. Then my seamstresses can focus on the actual dresses."

I turned over and slept more soundly than I had in a while.

Donna was a big help. She brought the mannequins to the apartment for Sallie and by the time I came home from the shop, Sallie would have five patterns down, just from the sketches and photos that she was provided. She did excellent work.

So did my seamstresses. Working on the smaller dresses, which would probably fit a six-year-old child, was a pleasure even if they weren't my designs. I took special pride working on the Jacqueline dress, feeling in some way that I did get to make her inauguration dress after all.

One day, one of my seamstresses read out loud to me a newspaper article saying that LBJ's younger daughter, Luci, was getting married, bless her: "The groom, unlike several White House grooms, is an untried and unestablished military man and the bride will leave her nursing school program for marriage."

"Well, they sound as if they are on the Supreme Court about it all." I shook my head.

"He's mighty cute. I don't blame her," a younger seamstresses said.

The seamstress who read the paper folded it up. "Cuteness ain't everything. She's only nineteen years old and giving up her nursing career to get married. Not very smart. Especially since the article said he what . . . he's in the military? What's he going to do to support her?"

"It's a very different time now than it was then," I interrupted as I worked on a lace edging for the Ida McKinley dress. It was my favorite.

"Yes," Donna agreed. "A woman has to be able to support herself apart from a man. I don't think she's considering all of the alternatives."

I looked up from the lace edging that I was whipping together by hand. "She wants him. Only way to get him is by marrying him."

Several of the seamstresses laughed a little nervously. So did Donna. "Back in my time, nineteen was plenty old enough. Miss Sallie was sixteen and shoot, I was twelve," I told them.

The room went absolutely silent. As I knew it would. Now, in the Space Age of the 1960s, a child-bride marriage looked positively archaic.

"Miss Annie? You said you were twelve when you got married?"

"Yes. For the first time. Second time I was twenty-two."

I handed over the edging to Donna and picked up another dress to work on.

"What was that like?" Donna handed me a newly threaded needle. I couldn't do that anymore by myself.

"I was a child. I didn't know how to be anyone's wife. But that was part of my appeal to old Lee Cone."

"Why did you do it?"

Yes, why did I do it?

That child, that hideously foolish child who wanted to get on with life with a quickness, knew so little. Now here I was, and I knew so much more. "I was trying to grow up fast. Everyone around me were women. I wanted to be one too. My mother wouldn't let me sew on the dresses. Thought if I got married, she would see I was grown up and let me leave school to sew on dresses like she did."

"Did she?"

"Ultimately, but it was a long time. Wasn't no need to rush. But tell that to a woman who wants a man. She's not listening to reason right now. Probably that's why it's a good idea to write her a letter and ask if she's looking for a dress designer."

The seamstresses, a little downhearted after hearing my sad story, perked up. "Yes. You should! Write to her and let her know. We would love to make her dress!"

I wrote my letter with Donna's assistance and mailed it that very evening. I didn't get a reply and a few weeks later, it was announced that a designer in Boston was going to make Luci's dress. A month later, my letter was returned to the shop, with stamps all over it, like it had been on a trip around the world. The short of it was that the contact that I wrote to at the White House wasn't the right one.

This chance, just like life, had passed me by.

Chapter Forty-One

The next year, 1967, provided another opportunity for another wedding dress design, for the president's older daughter, Lynda Bird, the one who looked like her mother was engaged. Lynda was going to have a winter wedding, actually at the White House, and it would be a great commission. I sent a letter offering my services to the right person this time, but I received a polite refusal from the first lady.

I still had a good amount of business lined up. The White Shoulders' first ladies minidresses created a lot of enjoyment as they traveled around the county. One of the White Shoulders ladies who had been appointed to take care of the traveling exhibit remarked to me, when she picked them up for the tour, "But there's so much work in there that you can't even see. You went to so much trouble."

I shook my head. "The eye knows as soon as it sees the dress. It makes all the difference in the world."

"You're more than a designer, Miss Lowe! You're an artist."

I didn't know what to say in response to that, but I just smiled at the kind words.

Later that day at our plain dinner of chicken and rice, I told Sallie about what the White Shoulders lady had said, and I shook my head. "It's so funny. These dresses remind me of Nell Lee."

"I think you told me about her."

"Yes. She was just a child when I went to stay with the Lees in Tampa, Florida. I sewed doll clothes for her just like this. That's who I thought of when I had them make the mannequins and the dresses."

"That's why they show great workmanship." Sallie nodded.

"Yes. And Miss Nell, bless her, had more and better sense to wait for the right man and to marry a good one."

"She's still married?"

"Oh my yes. She's a grandmother by now."

"Time flies."

Those were the last words my sister said to me.

Something, I still can't say what, nudged me in my spirit at 4:13 A.M. that October morning.

It was quiet in our room. Too quiet. I couldn't hear Sallie breathing.

I got up and went over to her, and I could tell from the way her eyes had rolled back in her head that she was gone.

I called Ruth and she came right away with Cora. They instantly took over everything and made all of the necessary calls to Sallie's sons, who, tall, strong, and handsome and old enough to be grandfathers themselves, came to claim their mother's body and take her back down to Alabama to be buried.

That's what Sallie would have wanted.

I found it hard to cry. I didn't want to. Sallie had been in some pain for a while and this was her release. For the first time, I understood what the phrase *gone to their great reward* really meant.

My nephews chose to have Sallie be buried in the navy-blue dress that I had made for her, the only one I had made for my big sister. That was an honor for me.

I could see that it was in God's plan to not have me design Lynda Bird's dress, because for the rest of that fall, I felt lost, and as if I were my actual age. I would be closing in on seventy the next year, even older than Grandma Georgia when she had passed on, and she seemed ever so old to me when I was growing up.

Now I was alone among them all.

Now I had outlasted them all.

And I couldn't be happy about that.

When I was in the shop one day, closing in on Christmas, I knew I should not be sad. I would spend the holidays with Ruth and her family. Cora and her husband and Audrey and her daughters would be there. I had many people around me. But this present time—this strange 1960s when so many people didn't want cloth on their legs anymore, women didn't want to wear support undergarments anymore, people didn't want to get married anymore—was starting to feel like too much different. The Johnson girls resembled some curious relic of the past in their overly white, overly long wedding dresses. There seemed to be so little left for me to do.

One day late in 1967, the tinkling of my doorbell brought an older lady into my shop. I had no appointments, but I turned to her and those eyes of hers, warm and sparkling brown, comforted me. I knew them. Well.

I opened my mouth, gaping like a fish off the hook and out of the water.

"Miss Annie. It's me. Nell Greening. Well, Nell Lee."

I grasped her arms. "Well, praise God. It's so good to see you, honey."

I hugged her and she hugged me. Just like that, a reminder that I had a past, someone who had cared for me all those years ago, was back in my life. I felt anchored again. She turned to the young girl next to her.

"This is my daughter."

"Does she need a wedding gown?"

Nell and the young woman laughed. "No one is getting married, Miss Annie. We're here in New York to do some Christmas shopping. And I wanted to look you up to come and ask you something."

I gestured to them to sit down on one of my couches. "It is so good to see Tampa folk again."

I leaned toward Nell's lovely daughter. "I knew your mama from when she was a small fry. I made her dolls clothes and then her trousseaux when she married."

"And my wedding dress, and my dress for when I was queen of the Gasparilla," Nell put in.

"I sure did. You were the best queen ever, Nell."

"That's why we are here. Ye Old Krewe." She paused to swallow.

"Take your time, honey. I'm here all day."

"I'm fine, ma'am. Ye Old Krewe and the Junior League want to honor you. Can you believe it was forty years ago when you last designed for us?"

"So hard to believe." I shook my head. The years had just flown by.

"Yes. That's why, we think"—she squeezed my hands—"it's long past time that you were honored."

I shook my head again. "I'm still not understanding you, honey."

Her daughter leaned in, her bright young face shining under

the glare of my shop's lighting. "As part of the Gasparilla, the Junior League wants to hold a dinner dance in your honor. We want you to come to Tampa for it."

"A dance. For me?" Something about the ludicrous nature of the words made me laugh a little. "So long, all these years, I would hear talk about the Ann Lowe dresses that went to dances. How the Ann Lowe dresses went to dinners. How they would go out in the world and see things and do things that I, a small Negro woman, could never see and do."

Nell's daughter nodded as if she understood. But how could she?

"One time, one of them came back to the shop. That was a first. The dresses never came back, but this one did. The girl said her date had cut one of the roses off—he thought it looked so real. So I made a new one to replace it. And back out it went." My arms shot out in front of me.

I brought them back in again, this time hugging myself, bringing the warmth back to me.

"You know. I wonder if that is what I was doing."

Nell nodded, peering into my face, not at all shaken by the fact that I had only one eye nowadays.

"What do you mean?"

"All the dresses I made, were they extensions of me, getting to go out into the world and see things and do things? When I was little, younger even than when I first met you, Miss Nell, I told my mother and grandmother that I would get to go to those big fancy balls they were always making the gowns for. I told them even as a six-year-old that I would be there. My sister, Sallie, was there. She even laughed at me. All of them did. It's nearly the first thing I remember because I wondered if I had said or did something wrong. I remember my mother, she bent down, leaned in real close to me, saying, *People like you don't get to go to those balls. It's all we can do to make the dresses so they can go.*"

My mind was so wrapped up in the memory of Sallie being young again, talking to me gently like the great big sister that she was, of her not wanting to tell me, but having to tell me, having to shape for me, having to show me the outlines of my life. I heard my little voice. And remembered the entire thing this time.

"But why?" I had asked.

"Because," Mama said from behind her sewing machine, stopping for once. "You're colored. You can never go. You can never be at a ball. They aren't for us. They are for white people."

"I'm colored?" I said in my little voice. Like a question.

"Yes, honey." Grandma Georgia had sensed the moment and the tension in the room and stopped her sewing. But she didn't come over to me. "You're colored. A Negro."

Now that was a word I had heard before. "Negroes don't go to balls?"

I looked to Sallie. "Well, yes and no, Annie. They can go to serve the drinks. They can go to drive the white people to the balls. They might even make the food they serve there."

"Yes, that's right." Mama nodded. "But Negroes don't dance at the ball. They don't go to the ball for the dance. But you, if you keep on learning, you keep on sewing, you keep on growing, you can sew dresses that will be at the ball. That's what we are doing right now. We're important because the white ladies wouldn't have a thing to wear if it weren't for us."

Sallie's pretty face relaxed and it was the same look she had later when she said "time flies" to me. Back then and now. Connected.

"SO, THAT'S WHY I wanted to grow up fast. To always be the one whose dresses went to the ball. And now, you are saying I can go? Me? Short Ann Lowe with the short name?"

Nell grasped my hands again. "Oh, Miss Annie. We love you in Tampa. If I had known, I mean, if we had known, it might have been different."

I shook my head. "No. Don't apologize, Miss Nell. Or say things like that. We both know that so much time, so many things had to happen and change for anyone at the Gasparilla krewe to even think about having a ball for me so I could attend. I mean, have any other Negroes been at a Junior League ball?"

The way they looked away from me told me everything I knew to be true. "See? There was so much that had to happen. Rosa Parks, down there in Montgomery. Martin Luther King Jr. preaching. Me at the S. T. Taylor Design School, taking classes from the next room. Getting named Gasparilla designer for three years straight. Making the dress for Mrs. Kennedy two times. World War II. Korea. Vietnam. So much war. So many people had to die so we could see each other, I mean, really see each other. Before your Junior League could see that maybe little Annie Lowe can come to the ball and not just the dress."

Tears streamed down Nell's face and I handed her a paper hanky.

"No crying, Nell. Please. 'Cause to be honest, it took all those years of things to happen and all those years of things to happen to me to even come to the realization that I could go to the ball in a dress."

"Just like Cinderella," her daughter whispered.

I shook my head. "No, honey. Just like Cinderella's designer."

And to be called that was my fairy tale come true.

Chapter Forty-Two

Ruth became my right hand. I thanked God for her every day. Even if she was not interested in the shop or sewing in particular, she still willingly performed many administrative tasks, including taking over the books from me. Whenever I still had dreams about that horrible moment when Arthur was killed, those fleeting thoughts I had about Ruth . . .

All of that was in the past, thank goodness, and I was grateful for her.

The Junior League ball to honor Mrs. Ann Lowe was scheduled for the last Saturday in March of 1968. Nell made all of our arrangements, including booking flights for us to Tampa. Even though I had flown to Paris and so wasn't a stranger to flying, I would have much rather taken the train to Tampa. But this was 1968 and I should experience what flying was like now, more than twenty years after my first air travel.

The flight, as it was, was uneventful since I slept the whole way. As soon as we arrived, a driver was waiting for us and took us around Tampa. We attempted to see my old apartment and my old shop, but that was all gone for another series of apartment houses.

Nell had us stay with her in her home in Tampa. The Lee home on the lake was still there but was the property of her brother, LaMarcus, and his wife, who we would see at the ball. I recalled Nell's sister-in-law well. I had designed her wedding dress too.

Ruth and the seamstresses, once they realized what was going to happen, made a big fuss over what I would wear. I would design it myself. Even though it was a springtime event, Florida in March would be hot, so instead of wearing my usual black to blend in as a designer and observer of form, I chose a lighter, soft lavender color. I kept the sheath simple, in a chiffon material that moved, with an additional cape, and a neckline and edging on the dress made up of roses.

However, to be at my neckline but not be heavy on my neck, they had to be baby rosebuds. I held off both Donna and my best seamstresses from trying to take over the task of making the rosebud flowers for my own dress. I didn't need to see to accomplish the task, and I put my foot down. "I have been doing this my entire life. I can do it."

To take the cool lavender chiffon into my hands, to cut it, fold it, and shape it into thirty baby rosebuds for me, for a dress that I would wear to a ball, was like a dream. Donna marveled at each one as it emerged from my fingers.

The soft fabric flowed around my ankles and I could see how wonderful it would be to get dressed for an event. Arthur used to take me to certain dances, but never one where I was to be honored. I think he would be proud of me.

Ruth wore a pink satin sheath with pink roses twining on the sides and along the neck.

I never expected that my return to Tampa would raise such interest. A reporter came to Miss Nell's house to talk to me, and a television crew from the local news station would even do a story. It all reflected the fact that Tampa had come a long, long way from the slow, small town that it had been when I left it forty years ago in 1928.

We drove to the hotel where the dinner dance would be held. The old hotel where Caleb had worked had a different purpose now and something twisted in my stomach as we passed the old Tampa Bay Hotel and drove to the Tampa Bay Hilton instead. Still, the modern architecture of angular metal combined with light colored bricks did not reassure me. Would I be allowed to go to my own Junior League dinner dance at a brand-new hotel in the South? When the car pulled up, I held up a hand and spoke to Nell Greening.

"This is where it is?"

"Yes, ma'am. This hotel."

"Are you sure?"

Nell nodded. I didn't want to embarrass her or Mr. Greening, her husband, but neither did I want to be embarrassed by not being allowed to attend my own dinner dance.

When we all got out of the car, I took Ruth's arm and pointed, seeing the side entrance some distance away. "We'll go on in over there."

Miss Nell turned from giving instructions to the driver. "Oh no, Miss Lowe. You come right this way." She hooked her arm through my other arm and I looked over at Mr. Greening. He just smiled at me.

And sure enough, with Ruth on one side of me and Miss Nell on the other, they walked me right through the front door of that hotel, where the air was cool inside and it smelled as if someone had baked bread.

They guided me to a large ballroom, where the tables were set with beautiful silverware and the candles were lit. A band played a fanfare of some kind as we scraped along to the front of the room.

"I'm sorry I can't move any faster."

"You're fine, Miss Lowe. This is your day."

I looked left and right as we walked through the tables. So many warm and friendly faces surrounded us that I was so astonished. They sat me and Ruth at a table at the very front of the room. Nell and her husband sat on my other side and even Paulina was there in a lovely peach dress. I waved to her and she blew me a kiss. I guess my sewing lessons worked out for her in the end after all.

Miss Nell went up to the front podium. "Welcome, all. We are so pleased to have all of you at this important reception to honor one of Tampa's own, Mrs. Ann Lowe, designer extraordinaire."

People stood up and applauded, roaring and cheering.

"Should I stand up?" I asked Ruth over the din.

She shook her head. "Just wave to them, Mama. And enjoy." Her eyes sparkled. Did she know something of what was going on?

"We'll eat our delicious dinner first and then we'll have a pre-sentation before our dear honoree comes to the stage for some words."

Words? From me? I guess I could think of something to say.

They served us plates of the kind of food I liked: chicken, salad, rice, plantain. Some had fish, I could see, but I was fine with the chicken, which was nice and tender. There was a big cake over in the corner, like I was some kind of bride!

When a waiter tried to bring me a slice, I held up a hand. "I would like some Jell-O please."

The waiter looked a little startled. Ruth took the plate of cake he offered. Nell gestured to him. "I'm sure you have some Jell-O back there somewhere, don't you?"

He snapped to attention and soon returned with a bowl of orange cubes with orange slices. Now that was what I liked.

After we ate, Nell slipped from her chair and went to the front podium again. "Many of you know the history of how Miss Annie came here, with her small baby in her arms, to start a new life for herself in Tampa. My dearly departed mother saw her in a Dothan department store and was just amazed by her clothing. She instantly invited her to come to Tampa, and we were blessed from the moment she came."

Tears threatened at the corners of my eyes, but I wouldn't cry. It just made me happy that I had decided to leave old Lee Cone that day. The best decision of my life.

"She was our designer for the Gasparilla Ye Old Krewe for a few years and here she did exceptional work. Without further delay, we're going to have a fashion show of some of her work from when she was here, work that shows how an Ann Lowe creation will stand the test of time."

I rubbed my hands together and sat up, marveling at seeing my old dresses walk by on those young, young girls. They wore lots of the dresses I had designed for Mrs. Lee. Some little girls wore the outfits I had made for Nell and several of them carried baby dolls with the clothes on them I had sewed for Nell's dolls. The final figure in a fashion show is, of course, a bride, and who was it but Nell herself in her own wedding gown! She looked marvelous and it still fit her after more than forty years.

Even I stood and applauded at that feat. Once the applause calmed down, Nell gestured down to our table. "And now, our esteemed honoree, Mrs. Ann Lowe."

The entire room stood and applauded. Ruth's face was bathed in a sea of tears, so I took the arm of that handsome Mr. Greening and made my way up to the stage as slow as an old lady should. When I got there, someone had installed a microphone and adjusted it for my petite height. I was glad to have it there because I knew my voice was not made for speaking loudly, but rather softly, to customers, to cloth vendors, and to seamstresses.

"I'd like to thank each and every one of you for coming tonight. I'm truly honored and proud to call Tampa my home."

The audience sat down and just looked over at me, expecting me to say wonderful things that they could take away with them in their hearts, some special knowledge that an old lady like me should be able to impart. What could I say?

Then I knew.

"It took one person, one lady with a good heart, to see who I was and what I could do in this world. To see what I could do with my needle and my eyes and to give me a chance. That was Mrs. Josephine Lee, my benefactress, who helped me, a young woman in a bad marriage with a baby, to get out of Dothan, Alabama. And I knew, from that moment when she gave me a twenty-dollar bill to buy a train ticket to get from Alabama to Tampa, that the way she had seen me and treated me was the way we should all see and treat one another.

"For, to be able to see someone, to see them as a human being, to see them for what they can contribute in this world, to be a light, to be a force or an influence in someone else's life, is all that we need. For all of my life, ever since I was a little girl, I thought that what I wanted was to be at one of these lovely dinner dances. Well, now that I'm here, it's been marvelous, but I know that the main thing about this is not the dinner. And it's not the fashion show. It's that I know that you see me. You see what I've tried to do all of these years. And I may only have one eye now, but I see you too. And let me tell you, I appreciate that. It has been the honor of my life to be here among you and I thank you so very much."

The room erupted into applause.

Nell handed me a bouquet of real red roses, and I held the lovely blooms in my arms, smelling their scent, knowing, believing, embracing the one true moment of love and appreciation that I had ever had in my life.

And it was, for me, enough.

Acknowledgments

Just as Ann Lowe had support from many to achieve her dream career as a fashion designer, I have also had people who have supported me in this, my first published historical fiction novel. Thank you to Tessa Woodard, my editor at William Morrow who sent out the tweet about Ann Lowe that captured my attention and made me believe that a story about her was possible. Thank you as always to my supportive agent, Emily Sylvan Kim of Prospect Agency. A big thank-you to the librarians at George Washington University who gave me access to Margaret Powell's seminal thesis.

A special thank-you for this one goes out to El and Heather Harris, my sister and brother-in-law. They provided me a space that allowed me to finish *By Her Own Design*. During the very difficult time my sister was undergoing two brain surgeries, I distracted El with the story of Ann Lowe's life, and his early enthusiasm encouraged me. During the copyedit stage, my computer began to act a fool, and El let me borrow his, so thanks much to the Harris family!

About the author

About the book

Insights,
Interviews
& More . . .

Meet Piper Huguley

@ LoveByrd Photo

PIPER HUGULEY is the author of
the Home to Milford College and
the Migrations of the Heart series.
She is a multiple-time Golden Heart
finalist. Piper blogs about the history
behind her novels at piperhuguley.com.
She lives in Atlanta, Georgia, with her
husband and son. ∾

Author's Note

There is a lot we don't know about Ann Lowe's life because she was born a Black woman in the deepest South, in a time and place that did not value Black women or their contributions.

One of the ongoing controversies about her life is when she was born. Her obits consistently state that she was eighty-two when she died in 1981, which puts her birth date as December 12, 1898. Then the 1910 census has her living with Andrew Lee Cohen in a house by herself at the time of that census. You do the math. It doesn't come up right. If the 1898 birth date is right, she was twelve years old, or even younger if you consider that the census is usually taken earlier in the year, but it's hard to go there. The record on the census says that she was twenty-one. Was she?

People tend to accept census records as gospel. However, as I've learned from genealogists, I've found that people tell lies and census takers write down lies. How else to explain that in the very first census record taken about my almost-two-year-old grandmother in 1920, she and her entire family are recorded as being white—which was not at all true.

So who lied? Was it Lee Cohen (in most Ann sources it is spelled this way, but in my book I spelled it as it would ▶

Author's Note (*continued*)

have been said: "Cone" in one syllable)? Was he regretful about having married a child? Trying to evade the law? Or was it the census taker who did so?

I believe it was Lee. Given everything that we have learned about him and how he kept Ann from doing what she loved the most, he would have had no compunction about lying to a white man who had come to his door asking for information that he would have felt was his own business.

Once she reached New York and greater heights of success, Ann Lowe reinvented herself (as well as her name) and concealed her first marriage, even though she couldn't conceal her son, Arthur. She seemed to come to the understanding that marrying so young was nothing to brag about. It is true that she never had another child. It only made sense to me that Arthur's birth must have created some sort of secondary infertility. Arthur Cohen was real and he was married and had a daughter and maybe even a son, but I fictionalized the tense relationship between Ann and her daughter-in-law. There was never an explanation given for the burst pipe that ruined Ann's shop in 1953; one newspaper article said someone left a tub running too long.

Black women in the South, prior to the civil rights movement of the mid-twentieth century, were rarely addressed as Mrs. (whatever their married last name happened to be). They were called by their first names, or Auntie, not with titles of respect, a pattern of onomastics used to reflect the caste society that existed back then. So in seeking to take back her own name, her real name, Ann seemed to make it clear that her creations needed to be under her name and not anyone else's.

Ann's first marriage was apparently, according to Margaret Powell, something that she spoke about on her appearance on *The Mike Douglas Show* in December 1964. The fact that she escaped what was in all likelihood an abusive situation to re-create herself into a fashion designer of extraordinary capability, just gives heft to the term *Black Girl Magic*.

To be sure, many people took advantage of a talent who enjoyed her creations and couldn't believe that people were paying her money to make dresses. However, once the civil rights movement started, she seemed to understand the value of her creations and charged more money, enough so that she was able to avoid any more encounters with the IRS.

I've collapsed the number of shops that Ann Lowe owned to three in total and eliminated some of the partnerships that she engaged in for a clearer story line. What is clear is that financial struggle, particularly after Arthur's death, was ever present for her.

Her last shop, Ann Lowe Originals, closed in 1972 and she was retired for the remaining eight years of her life. Ann died on February 25, 1981, one day after the announcement of Prince Charles and Lady Diana's engagement. Did she know that a new day would dawn in wedding dress design? Did she bemoan the fact that at eighty-two years old (or ninety-one if you believe the census record) she likely wouldn't get to see another famous dress design? We'll never know, but I thought the irony of the date of her death was too good to pass up.

Another question that lingers is whether Jackie purposefully reduced and erased Ann Lowe, a woman who had known her for years, to just a "colored woman dressmaker." Well, in the original *Ladies' Home Journal* article of April 1961, the author Mary Van Rensselaer Thayer writes, "The bride's gown and that of her friends were designed by a colored woman dressmaker, not the haute couture." This all-important sentence is written as exposition and is not represented as a direct quote from Jacqueline Kennedy. We don't have Thayer's notes to understand how Thayer found out this information. Still, she unfortunately chose to put it forward in a way that erased Ann Lowe and removed her from the high-society fashion world, where she had been society's best-kept secret for decades.

I invented the meeting at the White House between Ann Lowe and First Lady Jacqueline Kennedy, but what matters about that scene is that Lowe's IRS debt was taken care of by someone who remained anonymous. She believed that the First Lady had taken care of it, and since the president of the United States oversees the IRS, I think that is what happened. I created the dialogue for Jacqueline Kennedy, not to make a savior of her, but so the connection between what she did not say and what might have happened for Lowe could be made clear. ▶

About the book

What remains is the dress, an exquisite and incredible feat of design that Ann Lowe had to pull off not once, but twice. All we know is that the dress Ann Lowe made for Jacqueline Bouvier contained all of the love for and spirit of her Southern heritage.

It's too bad that it wasn't the dress that Jackie wanted.

Here are some sources I used to create my story about this remarkable woman:

"Celebrating Ann Lowe—Honoring the Legacy of Black Fashion Designers." College of Education and Human Ecology. YouTube video. https://youtu.be/XJV9OT5ARZg.

Mulvaney, Jay. *Kennedy Weddings: A Family Album*. New York: St. Martin's Press, 1999.

Pottker, Jan. *Janet and Jackie: The Story of a Mother and Her Daughter, Jacqueline Kennedy Onassis*. New York: St. Martin's Press, 2001.

Powell, Margaret. "The Life and Times of Society's Best-Kept Secret Fashion Designer." Unpublished thesis, George Washington University.

Reed Miller, Rosemary E. *Threads of Time, the Fabric of History: Profiles of African American Dressmakers and Designers, 1850 to the Present*. Washington, DC: Toast & Strawberries, 2002.

Smith, Julia Faye. *Something to Prove*. Self-published, CreateSpace, 2016.

Way, Elizabeth. "Elizabeth Keckly and Ann Lowe: Recovering an African American Fashion Legacy That Clothed the American Elite." *Fashion Theory: The Journal of Dress, Body & Culture* 9, no. 1 (February 2015): 115–141.

Reading Group Guide

1. How did the circumstances of Ann's young years allow her to dream big?

2. Did her missing father contribute to the decisions she made in her life?

3. Mrs. Josephine Lee was a real woman. Why do you think she was so good to Ann Lowe?

4. Who do you think helped Ann the most in her climb to be a Negro fashion designer?

5. Why do you think the high-society clientele that Ann designed for always sought to lower her prices?

6. Were you surprised by Ann's decision to design for only white clients?

7. Should Ann have stayed to obtain her education at S.T. Taylor Design School?

8. The conversations between Ann and Jackie on Jackie's wedding day were fictionalized. I had to find some way to explain why Ann never got another commission from Jackie. Do you think Ann overstepped her boundaries in telling Jackie she should be glad to have the father she had?

9. Did Ann go too far in reaching for her dream to be considered a Negro fashion designer?

10. Did Ann Lowe have a happy life in your opinion? ❧